Having worked in the law, journalism and numismatics, K. J. Parker now writes and makes things out of wood and metal (including prototypes for most of the hardware described in this book).

Parker is married to a solicitor and lives in southern England.

By K. J. Parker

THE FENCER TRILOGY

Colours in the Steel
The Belly of the Bow
The Proof House

COLOURS IN THE STEEL

VOLUME ONE OF THE FENCER TRILOGY

K. J. PARKER

An *Orbit* Book

First published in Great Britain by Orbit 1998
This edition published by Orbit 1999
Reprinted 2000 (three times)

A CIP catalogue record for this book
is available from the British Library.

ISBN 1 85723 610 6

Typeset by Solidus Ltd, Bristol
Printed and bound in Great Britain by Clays Ltd, St Ives plc

Orbit
A Division of
Little, Brown and Company (UK)
Brettenham House
Lancaster Place
London WC2E 7EN

For my father,
who made me want to make things.

CHAPTER ONE

It was just a run-of-the-mill shipping dispute, nothing more; a disagreement over the interpretation of a poorly worded contract, some minor discrepancies in various bills of lading, coinciding with a notorious grey area in the mercantile statutes. Properly handled, it could have been settled out of court with no hard feelings. Not the sort of cause you'd choose to die for, if you could possibly help it.

Everyone rose as the judge, a short man resplendent and faintly ridiculous in his black and gold robes of office, made his way across the wide floor of the court. He stopped once or twice, pawing at the ground with the toe of his black slipper to check that the surface was even and true, and Loredan noticed with approval that he was wearing proper fencer's pumps, not the fancy pointed toes favoured by clerks and deskmen. Not all the judges in the Commercial and Maritime Division were ex-fencers – there simply weren't enough to go round – and Loredan never felt comfortable with a lay judge. It was hard to have confidence in a man whose experience of the law stopped on the edge of the courtroom floor.

The clerk – elderly, short-sighted Teofano, who'd been here long before any of the current advocates had been born – declared the court in session and read out the names of the parties. The judge nodded to the participants, the participants nodded back and everyone sat down. There were the usual comfortable settling-down noises from the spectators' benches, the shuffling of buttocks on the stone seats, the rustle of straw as bottles were opened and snacks put handy where they could be reached without having to take one's eyes off the proceedings for even a split second. The judge peered at the documents in front of him and asked who appeared for the Mocenigo brothers.

Loredan looked up. On the opposite side of the court a huge blond boy was rising to his feet, his head instinctively ducking from a lifetime of low ceilings. He gave his name as Teofil Hedin, stated his qualifications and bowed. There was an appreciative buzz from the spectators, and money started changing hands among those inclined to speculation.

'Very well,' said the judge. 'Who appears for the defendants—' he hesitated and glanced down at the papers, '—the Dromosil family?'

As usual, Loredan felt a twinge in his stomach as he stood up; not fear so much as acute self-consciousness and a great desire to be somewhere else. 'I do, my lord,' he said, a bit too softly. He raised his voice a little as he gave his name; Bardas Loredan, fencer-at-law, of the College of Bowyers and Fletchers, ten years' call. The judge told him to speak up. He said it all again, detecting a slight hoarseness in his own voice. He knew it was the last stage of a mild cold, but the spectators drew their own conclusions and coins chinked softly on the stone.

The judge began to read the depositions. It was a stage in the proceedings that Loredan particularly disliked; it served no useful purpose and always left him tense and fidgety. The other man, whatever-his-name-was Hedin, was standing gracefully at ease with his hands behind his back, looking for all the world as if he was actually listening to what the judge was saying. Some men, particularly the older ones, had some little ritual worked out to fill this gap; a prayer of exactly the right length, mental checklists, even a song or a children's rhyme. Loredan, as usual, stood awkwardly and shuffled his feet, waiting for the droning voice to fall silent.

Which, at long last, it did; the cue for Loredan's hands to start sweating. At his side, Athli was fumbling with knots and buckles; if she's forgotten the ash for my hands, Loredan promised himself, this time I'll wring her neck.

Without looking up, the judge called for any last submissions, assumed (correctly) that there were none, and gave notice to the advocates. Loredan took a deep breath and turned to his clerk.

'The Guelan,' he muttered.

Athli frowned. 'Are you sure?'

'Of course I'm sure. You have brought it, haven't you?'

Athli didn't bother to reply; whatever her faults, she was reliable when it came to equipment. He also knew that whichever one he'd chosen – the Boscemar perhaps, or the Spe Bref – she'd have said, *Are you sure?* in exactly the same tone of voice, one which never failed to irritate him. She put her hand into the kitbag and produced the bundle of soft grey velvet, tied at the neck with blue cord. He took it from her and flicked open the knot. Perhaps the Boscemar, after all? No. It was his rule never to change his mind once he'd chosen.

The Guelan. He let the cover fall away – he'd never dream of telling anybody, but it always made him think of a bride's dress falling to the ground – and wrapped his hand round the plain grip, feeling for the slight grooves that marked the place for his thumb and little finger. Of his three swords it was the longest and the lightest, not to mention the most expensive, well over a hundred years old. Once there had been a design of vine leaves etched on the blade, but you had to hold it just right against the light to make them out now. It had seen him through thirty-seven lawsuits, nine of them in the Supreme Court and one before the Chancellor himself. Five nicks spoilt the edge (there had been others, but small enough to be taken out with a stone) and the blade was slightly bent a hand's span from the tip, the fault of some previous owner. The Boscemar took a keener edge and the Spe Bref was supposedly better balanced, but in a lawsuit what matters most is trust. After a century of hard work in these courts, it ought by now to know what to do. *Just as well one of us does.*

The usher gave the order to clear the floor. Athli handed him the dagger – at least he only had one of those, which meant one less thing to agonise over – and he slid it into the sheath behind his back, promising himself as he did so to fit a new spring to it, first thing tomorrow.

Yes. Well.

The judge raised his hand, savouring the drama of the moment, and called on the advocates to approach the bench. As he took his place under the raised platform, Loredan felt his leg brush against the other man's knee. He winced. It would be particularly unfortunate to die in a shipping case, at the hands of a tall blond bastard. All the more reason, therefore, not to.

As the other man handed his sword up to the judge for inspection, Loredan couldn't help noticing the flash of light on gilded inlay just above the hilt. A Tarmont, only a year or so old, scarcely used by the looks of it. There were hardly any stone marks to mar the deep polish of the blade; sharpened four, five times at most from new. Oddly enough, the sight raised his spirits a little. An expensive sword, crafted by one of the five best living makers, but new and untried. It suggested overconfidence, a tendency to assume that things will be as they should be. Ten years' call had taught him that assumptions like that can kill a man, if correctly exploited.

Having handed his own sword over and received it back after a perfunctory glance which he found mildly offensive, he made his usual neck-bob of a bow and walked to his place in the middle of the floor. Under his feet the flagstones felt firm, with just the right amount of sawdust and sand for the best purchase. He was wearing his oldest pair of pumps, long since moulded to his feet, the fairly new soles lightly scuffed with a rasp. Athli took his gown from his shoulders, and he shivered slightly in the chill. One close shave long ago had taught him to fence in nothing but a linen shirt, loose across the shoulders and arms, tightly laced at the sleeves, and a comfortable pair of breeches with no buckles to snag or catch at the wrong moment. He'd watched men die a sword's length from his face because they'd put on a heavy woollen shirt against the autumn chill. Ten years' call, and you learn that *everything* matters.

When the order came he was ready, and just as well. The other man was quick and obviously strong; the trick would be to stay alive for the first half-minute, and then for the three minutes after that. The first thrust came high, and wasn't at all what he'd been expecting. He was forced to parry high, and the weight behind the other man's sword was almost too much for him to deflect with only the strength of his arm and wrist. He managed it somehow, but he had to step one back and two right, opening his chest; no chance of a counterthrust. The next attack, predictably, was low, but none the less awkward for being what he'd expected. Two quick steps right got him out of the way, but his guard was still too high, and a cut to his unprotected right knee would have settled the matter.

Fortunately, his opponent went for another high thrust. Two steps back gave Loredan the room to parry forehand, his bodyweight behind the blade to push the other man's sword wide right; then he dropped his wrist for a short jab, more of a heavy push with the wrist turned over, straight for the stomach. The other man stepped back, but not quickly enough; the point of the sword went in maybe half an inch before Loredan snatched it out and, taking the risk of a cut across his right shoulder, threw himself down and forward for a sprawling lunge. His knee and left hand hit the ground together and he felt a twinge of pain as a ligament protested. The other man parried wildly, deflecting the thrust but not far enough, so that the first nine inches of the blade sliced into his right hip. Good work so far; but probably not good enough. Not yet, at least.

Loredan, kneeling on the ground, pushed hard with his left hand and leg to regain his feet; but his left knee didn't seem to work – cramp, of all the wretched ways to die! But the other man was too preoccupied with the sight of his own blood to notice Loredan's difficulties, and he somehow managed to force himself vertical on his right leg and fall back into a ragged imitation of a guard. Not a good time to try moving his feet; he'd fall over as sure as day. Everything depended on the other man, and how well he was able to handle being hurt. Waiting for him to move, Loredan cursed all shipping cases, all actions based on the laws of contract and all tall blond fencers ten years his junior. A lot of cursing to get through in less than a heartbeat, but speed is something that comes with long practice.

Mercifully, the other man seemed to have lost his nerve. Instead of lunging, as Loredan would have done in his position, he rocked back and went for a sideways slash at elbow level; as effective a way of killing yourself, Loredan reflected as he turned the blow neatly aside and leant into the inevitable lunge, as jumping off a high tower. He felt the point of the blade encounter bone, saw it bend—

—and snap, clean as the stem of a wine glass, ten inches or so from the point. Disgusted, he turned the thrust into a short-arm cut, wrist power alone, that slit the other man's throat as neatly as a sheet of parchment. There was a clatter as his sword fell – that extravagant, ill-fated Tarmont; never could see the point in buying new – and a soft wheeze as the other man tried to draw breath down a throat that wasn't there any more. And lots of blood, of course, and the usual heavy thump as he hit the ground.

Damn all shipping cases.

The judge rapped with his little hammer and gave judgement, rather superfluously, for the defendant. A round of applause from the spectators – somewhat muted, it had been a very short fight with no really memorable strokeplay – followed by the shuffling of feet, the resumption of interrupted conversations, some laughter, a sneeze at the back. The other man's clerk gathered up his papers, tucked them under his arm, in no hurry to reach his clients at the back of the gallery. Athli had picked up the Tarmont – Loredan's property now, by ancient custom; worth ten times his fee but its value wouldn't buy another Guelan, even if he could find one. An unsatisfactory day, except that he was still alive.

'What happened to you?' Athli asked. 'I thought you'd had it there for a moment.'

'Cramp,' Loredan replied. He wanted to retrieve the front end of his blade, but he wasn't keen to get that close to the body. There'd be blood everywhere as soon as he pulled it free, and he wasn't in the mood. 'Look at that,' he muttered, staring at the broken sword in his hand. 'Looks like I've just acquired one very expensive carving knife.'

'I told you that thing had had its day,' Athli said. 'If you'd sold it, like I said—'

She held out the velvet bag, and he dropped the hilt-end in. She tied the cord and stowed it in the kitbag. 'How's the knee?'

'Better, but it'll need resting for a week or so. When's our next one?'

'Four weeks,' said Athli, 'and it's a divorce, so it ought to be all right. I'll let them know, though, just in case they want to instruct someone else.'

Loredan nodded. Divorce, being an ecclesiastical jurisdiction, wasn't supposed to be to the death, although death didn't invalidate the judgement if it turned out that way. Nevertheless, it was only fair to warn the client if you were carrying an injury, particularly in a case where substantial marriage settlements were riding on the issue.

'I could always cut it down, I suppose,' Loredan mused. He was aware that he was hobbling, and the distance to the courtroom door seemed much longer than usual. 'Short blades are quite fashionable in some courts at the moment.'

'Not that short,' Athli said. 'Have it ground down for a second dagger. You could do with a spare.'

'Sacrilege.' A couple of porters were carrying the other man away, a sack thrown over him so as not to distress the public. 'Talking of which, since when have I been doing divorce work?'

'Since you started having trouble with your knee.' Athli looked up at him, frowning slightly. 'No offence,' she said, 'but have you given any thought to when you're going to retire?'

'As soon as I can afford to,' Loredan replied, feeling something bitter in his throat. 'Or when they make me a judge.'

'I thought you'd say that,' Athli said.

Punctual as the mailcoach, the shakes came after the second bottle, just as he was about to open the third. Without saying anything, he handed it to his clerk.

'You ought to go easy on this stuff,' she observed, filling his cup. 'For one thing, it's expensive.'

Loredan scowled at the distorted image of himself reflected in the cup's polished side. 'Tradition,' he replied. 'It's a mark of respect.' He remembered something. 'Did we buy his clerk a drink?' he asked. Athli nodded.

There were quite a few spectators from the court in the taproom, and several of them were nudging each other and pointing. Loredan didn't like that much; on the other hand, there was always a chance of picking up work in the tavern immediately after a hearing. He'd got the Khevren brothers that way, and the cinnamon-merchants' cartel. Several of the leading families sent men to all the hearings on the lookout for good advocates, usually bright lads talented enough to survive but still young enough to be cheap. Ten-year men were well enough known to potential clients, but there was the risk of pricing yourself out of the market; and lowering the fee was as good as admitting you were past it. The same went for taking divorce work; for a ten-year man, tantamount to a confession of decrepitude, loss of nerve or both. It'd be different, Loredan reflected, if I was getting better as I get older. But I'm not.

'Well,' Athli was saying, 'you've done the easy part. Now I've got to get the Dromosil boys to pay up.'

Loredan grunted. 'Tell 'em we'll sue,' he said. Athli sniggered; professional debts, for example advocates' fees, were a personal action, fought between the litigants themselves with no legal assistance allowed. In practice, however, advocates with a reputation of suing for their fees tended to find work hard to come by. 'You'll manage,' he went on. 'Not a bad day for you, with the sword money.'

Athli shrugged. Her ten per cent would be a tidy sum, but she'd never admit to being pleased. 'And every penny of it hard-earned,' she said. 'Drink up. We're meeting the charcoal people in an hour.'

Loredan groaned. 'Have I got to?' he said. 'Can't you say I'm still recovering or something?'

'That'd sound good. I've had to sweat blood persuading them you're not a doddering old ruin who needs help going to the privy. And for pity's sake don't limp. You look about a hundred and six as it is.'

Defiantly, Loredan refilled his cup. 'Where am I going to get another Guelan from?' he asked gloomily. 'Of all the bastard things to happen.'

Athli frowned at him. 'Next thing you know you'll be getting superstitious,' she said. 'Which is a dangerous hobby for a man in your line of work.'

Loredan growled. 'Proper tools for a proper job,' he replied. 'Nothing superstitious about that. And I think it's about time tools and equipment came off the gross. Other clerks do it,' he added defensively, before Athli had a chance to speak. 'They accept that it's an essential expense of the business.'

'No chance.'

'Athli, it's my *life*…' He stopped, painfully aware that he'd broken the rules. Between advocate and clerk, the possibility of death was never recognised. He slumped forwards a little, ashamed of himself. 'When did you say we're meeting the charcoal people?'

Athli was looking at him. She'd been doing it a lot recently. Another unbreakable rule was that clerks didn't worry about advocates. They found them work, the best quality they could get; the fact that too high a class of work could get a man killed quicker than a lightning strike was strictly outside the terms of the relationship. 'It's all right,' she said. 'I'll say you had to go on to a victory party.'

'With the Dromosil brothers? Do me a favour.' He

finished his drink and turned the cup over. 'I'd better come with you,' he sighed. 'Can't really trust you to handle difficult clients on your own. And *then*,' he added ferociously, 'we'll go out and get drunk. Agreed?'

'After an hour with the charcoal people,' Athli replied gravely, 'agreed.'

'This Principle,' said the Patriarch gravely, 'which of course we do not name, provides the power that makes these things possible. Never forget how limited it is, or how little it can actually do.'

He paused and looked round the hall at the packed benches. Five hundred eager young students, every one of whom had no doubt sworn a childhood oath to be a magician when he grew up. Alexius was a cynical man by nature, and achieving the Patriarchate had ground away what little idealism he had left, but even he admitted that he had one serious – even sacred – responsibility to each year's intake of novices. He must make them understand, as soon as possible, that they were *not* going to be taught how to be wizards.

'Fundamentally,' he continued, 'the Principle can be used as a shield; and, to a much lesser extent, as a sword. That is all; defence and offence. Its virtues cannot heal the sick or raise the dead, change lead into gold, make a man invisible or attractive to women. It cannot make anything, or change anything already made. It can deflect curses, and it can curse; and even these things are largely incidental to the true purpose for which the Principle exists. The power is a by-product, as leather, bonemeal and glue are by-products of pig-breeding.'

As he'd intended, the homely image caused a mild ripple of disgust among the members of his high-minded young audience. This wasn't the way they expected the Patriarch to talk. They had come here to be let in on a magnificent secret, the best and most profitable guild mystery of them all. With any luck, there would be twenty or so fewer ardent young faces gazing up at him by this time tomorrow, as the younger sons who wanted to learn how to turn their brothers into frogs, and the merchants' sons who'd been sent to learn how to raise favourable winds and summon genies for the purpose of bulk-freight carriage, packed their bags and went home again. If he did his job properly, he'd be rid of half of these young fools before the term ended.

'Tomorrow,' he said, 'I will explain to you the four great assumptions on which the Principle is founded. Once you have grasped these – if you manage to grasp them, which is by no means guaranteed – you will be in a position to decide which of the six aspects of the Principle to study, and we will then be able to allocate you to appropriate classes and tutors. May I also remind those of you who still have fees to pay that you cannot be allocated until all sums due have been received. You are dismissed.'

So much for the education of the young. Back in his own cell, a square stone box with a plank bed, a massive oak book box and the most dazzling mosaic ceiling in the city, he shrugged off his robes of office and his ridiculous purple boots, sat on the edge of the bed and patiently struggled with flint and tinder until his lamp reluctantly gave him some light.

Directly below his cell they were setting up the evening meal in the refectory. Fairly soon, the hall steward would knock on his door, asking permission to untie the knot that anchored the great chandelier that hung over the high table, so that it could be lowered and filled with the evening's candles. The Patriarch couldn't help resenting the intrusion, even though it was part of the daily ritual; the noise of the evening meal disturbed his reading, and scarcely a day passed when he didn't stub his toe on the damned anchor-post as he pottered about in the gloom of his cell.

He had insisted on a room with no windows; lamplight, reflected in the thousands of gilded tesserae that made up the legendary mosaics, was good enough for a man to read by, provided that he leant close to the flame and held the page a few inches from his nose. Alexius knew that he was fatally prone to distraction. If he had a window, he'd look out of it instead of reading his book. If there were tapestry hangings or frescos, he'd sit gazing at them instead of applying his mind to the dense arguments of the Fathers. And if he went down to dinner in the refectory, instead of making do with a loaf of coarse bread, a jug of water and an apple, he'd do no further work that day, or the morning of the next.

In consequence, he was held to be a great ascetic and given honour accordingly. He was - a good joke, this - probably the most deeply respected Patriarch the city had known in a hundred years. Not bad for a man who moved his lips when he read, and made no effort to conceal the fact. And if it took him twice as long as his colleagues to master each new development and hypothesis in the orthodoxy, at least he did master them. Lazier, more gifted men who didn't bother to read the actual text, relying instead on someone else's summary, made mistakes and could be confounded by a painfully learnt quotation.

Some of them even liked him. He had no idea why.

The source of tribulation he had set himself to read this evening was a new discourse on the nature of belief; a short monograph apparently flung together in an idle moment by the young Archimandrite of one of the city colleges, a man who had more intuitive understanding of the Principle in his toenail clippings than the Patriarch had in his whole body, but who devoted most of his waking hours and a considerable proportion of the income of his House to the trotting races. In his treatise, the dashing young sportsman proposed that belief acted as a focus for the Principle in the way that a prism of crystal or glass can concentrate the light of the sun. The Principle, he argued, was as universal as light and as diffuse. Only when filtered through the willing mind could it become strong enough to illuminate subterranean darkness or burn a hole.

The Patriarch scowled. It was a succinct and accurate way of saying what he'd always felt about the Principle but had never been able to clarify properly in his own mind;

clearly the boy had an exceptional gift, and this was only the first chapter of the text, the part usually reserved for stating the blindingly obvious premises of one's argument. The startlingly new hypothesis that had been recommended to his attention lay in the seventy-eight chapters that followed. It was going to be a long night.

He was just starting to develop a headache (it didn't help that his copy was vilely written on thrice-used parchment) when he heard the knock at the door he'd been expecting this past half-hour. He grunted, and a blade of light appeared in the doorway.

'Sorry to trouble you, Father.'

He grunted again, trying not to look up from the book. For some reason it wasn't the hall steward tonight; he hadn't recognised the voice, but it was young and female, one of the housekeeper's girls presumably, and if he was to stand any chance of wrapping his slow brains around this confounded hypothesis—

'Sorry to trouble you,' the voice repeated. 'But if you could spare me a few minutes—'

Damnation, it was a *student*. 'I'm reading,' he growled, bringing the page up against his nose. 'Go away.'

'It won't take long, I promise. Please.'

Alexius sighed. 'Patriarch Nicephorus the Fifth,' he said severely, 'on being interrupted while reading the scripture *All Things Shall Cease*, let fly such a curse that the unfortunate fool who had disturbed him was at once struck by lightning. Only with great difficulty was the victim later identified as Nicephorus' own daughter, who had come to warn her father that the house was on fire. I suggest you see me after the lecture tomorrow.'

It is well to avoid distractions; but if distractions refuse to be avoided, far quicker to let them have their way. He picked a rush off the floor and laid it in the book to mark his place, then looked up.

Maybe this wasn't going to be such a serious distraction after all. She was long and bony, with a thin face and pale blue eyes; fifteen, maybe sixteen years old, wearing her body like an elder sister's coat she'd be sure to grow into eventually. It's always the scrawny ones who get pushed off into a trade. He had been just as stringy himself at that age. He relented a little.

'Hurry it up, then,' he said. 'What can I do for you?'

The girl knelt on the ground; not obeisance, just the instinctive habit of someone who came from a house where they had no chairs. 'I'd like a curse, please.'

Alexius closed his eyes. It was starting early this year. He was about to say someting fierce and dismissive, but somehow didn't. There was something appealingly – what was it? – *businesslike* about the child that almost tempted him to do what she asked.

'What for?' he asked.

This seemed to strike her as a silly question. 'I want to curse someone,' she said. 'Could you teach me the right words, please?'

I could explain, Alexius thought. I could start with the four assumptions, work on through the theoretical basis of the Principle, briefly summarise the role of belief (which might be said to resemble a glass used to concentrate the rays of the sun …), explain the reciprocal effect of action and reaction and the futility of unfounded use of the powers, and so make her understand exactly how silly her request has been. Or I could just say no.

'That depends on who you want to curse and why,' he replied instead. 'You see, if a curse is going to do any good – sorry, I didn't mean it that way – if it's going to work, it has to have a firm foundation in something the victim's done. The old saying *No one can curse an innocent man*, though not strictly speaking true, isn't so far from the mark—'

'Oh, he's not innocent,' the girl interrupted confidently. 'He killed my uncle.'

Alexius nodded. 'That's a good start,' he said. 'At least we've got an action on which a curse can be founded. Better if the killing wasn't justified, but even a man who is in the right can be successfully cursed so long as the act itself is violent or causes damage. Hence my caveat to the maxim

I quoted just now about cursing an innocent man.'

The girl thought for a moment. 'It was legal,' she said. 'But not justified. How can you justify killing someone? You can't, that's all.'

The Patriarch decided not to pursue that one. 'When you say legal—' he began.

'My uncle's an advocate. Was.' The girl smiled. 'Not a very good one. *He* never killed anybody in his life. All wills and divorces, you see.'

Alexius suppressed a smile, thinking of the famous statue in the suburb where he'd been born—

DEDICATED TO THE MEMORY OF
NICETAS THE BOXER
OF WHOM IT MAY TRULY BE SAID
HE NEVER HARMED ANY MAN.

'Perhaps he was in the wrong line of work,' he said. 'Presumably it was another advocate—'

'His name's Bardas Loredan,' the girl said promptly. 'I think he's quite famous. Can you tell me the words now, please?'

Alexius sighed. 'It really isn't as simple as that,' he said. 'For a start, there aren't any special words; in fact, you can curse someone perfectly well without saying anything. What you really need is a picture—'

'I've got one,' said the girl, reaching into her sleeve.

'In your mind,' Alexius continued. 'A strong mental image of the act that makes you want to lay the curse.' He gritted his teeth; better in the long run to explain it now, it'd be bound to save time. 'The way it works is that a qualifying act - something violent or hurtful - causes a disturbance in the forces we refer to as the Principle.' That, he knew, was putting it very badly, but he couldn't be bothered. The girl seemed to understand. 'It's like when you drop a stone into water. For a split second, the water is pushed away and there's a sort of gap where the water used to be. Then the water comes back into it, but the ripples carry on spreading.

What we can do – sometimes – is catch hold of that gap and put into it something of our own. That's what we call a curse.'

'I think I see,' the girl said. 'So what happens to the water? The water that should have gone back into the gap, I mean?'

Alexius smiled, impressed. 'That's a good question,' he said. 'By interfering where there's already been an interference, you see, we always make things worse – no, that's a bad way of putting it. We increase the level of the disturbance, and inevitably there's a reaction. More to the point, the reaction tends to be much more intensive than the curse itself.'

'It hits you harder than you hit the victim?'

Alexius nodded gratefully. 'You've got it,' he said. 'Which is why, before you learn cursing, you have to learn how to deflect curses. Otherwise you might succeed in making your enemy break a leg, but you'll break your own neck.'

The girl shrugged. 'I'm not bothered about that,' she said. 'Will you tell me how to go about it?'

Alexius drummed his fingers on his knee. One thing the adepts of the Principle did *not* do was to hire themselves out as metaphysical assassins, cursing perfect strangers to order. Quite apart from the social implications, there was the danger. The reaction to a curse in your own mind's eye was bad enough; warding off the reaction when you were inside somebody else's head was next to impossible unless you knew exactly what you were doing. And the Patriarch was perfectly willing to admit that he wasn't sure about that.

'No,' he said. 'It's out of the question. All I could do is try and lay the curse for you, but—'

'Would you?'

The carefully phrased explanation he'd prepared faded away inside his mind. 'It's very difficult,' he said. 'And it probably wouldn't work. You see, I'd have to try and look at what's inside your mind.'

'Can you do that?'

The Patriarch tugged at his beard. It would be easy to say no, it's impossible; because it *was*, or at least it was a simple matter to prove it wasn't possible. In three weeks' time, he'd do just that in the lecture hall. One thing you had to learn, however – the so-called fourth assumption – was that just because a thing's impossible doesn't mean to say you can't do it if you really try. But to try, you have to want to.

'Sort of,' he replied.

'How does that work?'

Alexius grinned rather feebly. 'I'm not sure that it does,' he replied. 'It happens sometimes, but that's not quite the same as something working. A clock works if you wind it. Sometimes a clock that's wound down happens to tell the right time.'

The girl looked at him. 'What's a clock?' she asked.

Alexius made a vague gesture. 'I'll try if you like,' he said. 'But I'm not promising anything.'

'Thank you.'

'You're welcome. Now then, I've got to try and visualise exactly what happened; I've got to see that stone hitting the water. And not just any stone; that particular one and no other. Do you understand?'

'I think so.' The girl pressed her chin with her hands, her brow furrowed. 'You want me to tell you what happened.'

The Patriarch shook his head. 'No,' he said. 'I want you to tell me what you remember, there's a difference. When you think of it, or when something reminds you, isn't there a picture that immediately comes into your mind?'

'Yes. Like a single moment, frozen.'

'Very good.' Alexius took a deep breath. 'Tell me what you can see.'

The girl looked up at him. 'Uncle was trying to hit him – sort of cutting rather than thrusting. He pushed Uncle's sword away and stabbed him, and then his sword broke. I can see the broken-off bit in Uncle's chest. It looks so strange, a big bit of metal like that stuck in a person. Reminds me of a pin cushion, or the knife standing in the butter.'

Alexius nodded. 'And what about the look on his face? Your uncle's, I mean. Can you see that?'

'Oh, yes.' The girl looked down at her folded hands. 'He was cross.'

'Cross?' Alexius repeated.

'That's right. It's like when you do something clumsy, dropping a cup or tearing your sleeve on a nail. He was cross because he'd got his fencing wrong. He was very proud of his fencing. He knew he wasn't *that* good, but he practised for hours. He used to hang a sack full of straw from the apple tree and bash at it with a stick; and he knew the names of all the different strokes, and he'd call them out as he did them. When he made a mistake, he was cross. I think that was all he had time for.'

'I see,' Alexius said, and then added irrelevantly, 'You must have been very fond of him.'

The girl nodded. 'He was eight years older than me. They say twenty-three's a good age for a bad fencer.'

Well, now, the Patriarch thought. Twenty-three. In the western suburbs, it's quite usual for uncles to marry their nieces. Helpful; nothing like love to help you get a grip on a fleeting image. He closed his eyes—

'Are you doing it now?'

'Yes. Don't interrupt.'

'But I haven't told you what I want the curse to be yet.'

Alexius' breath came out in an exasperated gasp. It wasn't enough that he was expected to do a curse once-removed; it had to be a specific curse. This was turning out to be quite a performance.

'Well?'

'I can see him,' the girl said. 'He's in the court, and I'm facing him. We've both got swords, and he stabs at me. And then—'

Alexius waved his hands in alarm. 'Stop,' he said, 'or you'll do it yourself, and then the reaction'll bring the roof down on both of us. Trust me; I think I know what you've got in mind.'

He closed his eyes again; and there, as if painted on the

inside of his eyelids, was the court, with its high domed roof, the rows of stone benches encircling the sandy floor, the judge's platform, the marble boxes where the advocates waited for the command. He could see Loredan's back, and over his shoulder the girl; older now, grown up, extra-ordinarily beautiful in a way that made him uneasy. He could see the red and blue light from the great rose window burning on the blade of her sword, a long, thin strip of straight steel foreshortened by the perspective into an extension of her hand, a single pointing finger. He saw Loredan move forward, his graceful, economical move-ment; and the girl reacts, parrying backhand, high. Now she leans forward, scarcely moving her arm at all except for the roll of the wrist that brings the blade level again. Loredan's shoulder drops as he tries to get his sword in the way, but he's left it too late, the sin of the overconfident man. Because Loredan's back is to him, Alexius can't see the impact or where the blade hits; but the sword falls from his hand, he staggers back and drops, bent at the waist, dead before his head bumps noisily on the flagstones. The girl doesn't move, the blade points directly at him. He realises he never saw the man's face, or asked the girl her name...

Wait for it. Here it comes.

Imagine the fly that buzzes round your head, or the moth that flutters aggravatingly in your study at night as you crouch over the flame of your lamp. You reach out, your huge fist dwarfs the insect as your fingers close to crush it. Either it gets out of the way in time, or it doesn't. If it does, the disturbance in the air as your enormous hand goes past flings the insect aside, and it wobbles helplessly for a moment, out of control. Alexius could feel the enormous hand sweeping down on him from behind, though he couldn't see it; he could feel the displacement of air, buffeting him like a big wave at sea. There was nothing he could do; either the hand would catch him, or it wouldn't.

It didn't; but the slipstream slammed him down, like a door slamming in his face. He tried to make a noise but there was no air left in him. He opened his mouth, and fell off the bed.

'Are you all right?'

'No,' Alexius replied. 'Help me up.'

The girl grabbed his sleeve; she was very strong. 'What happened?' she asked. 'Did it work?'

'I haven't the faintest idea,' the Patriarch grumbled, rubbing the back of his head with rather more vigour than the slight bump warranted. 'In my mind's eye, or our minds' eyes, I killed him. Or you did, rather. Whether or not it'll actually—'

The girl let go of him abruptly. 'But that's wrong,' she said. 'That's not the curse I wanted.'

Alexius glowered at her; the whole thing had stopped being a pain and was getting ludicrous. 'But you must have,' he said. 'It's revenge you're after, isn't it?'

'I told you I don't believe in killing,' she replied, coldly furious. 'What good's killing him going to do? If only you'd let me tell you—'

Alexius let his head fall back onto his one hard pillow. 'Then what did you want, if you didn't want him killed?' he asked wearily. 'Be fair. The two of you, in open court—'

'I wanted to cut off his hand,' she said, as if it was the most obvious thing in the world. 'I was going to cut his hand off and then walk away, leaving him standing there, in front of everybody.' She turned away, her hair falling across her face. 'Getting killed isn't a punishment for him, it's part of his job. I wanted him to *hurt*.'

'Well, tough,' Alexius snapped. 'You'll just have to make do, that's all. Assuming that it works, of course. As I told you, there's a good chance that it won't.'

The girl stood up. 'I don't think so,' she said. She walked towards the door.

Why is it, Alexius asked himself, that young people are simply incapable of saying thank you? She was just about to vanish into the sharp blade of light she'd come in through when he remembered.

'What's your name?' he called out.

'Iseutz.' Her voice, in the dark. 'Iseutz Hedin.'

'See you in class,' he called out as the door closed. He knew he wouldn't. One down, four hundred and ninety-nine to go.

When the hall steward came to lower the chandelier, Alexius threw a book at him.

CHAPTER TWO

Traditionally, the best way to approach the island on which Perimadeia, oldest and most beautiful of cities, is built is from the seaward side. At first, only the lighthouse is visible over the skyline. As the ship comes closer, the towers of the Phylax and the spires of the Phrontisterion poke up above the horizon like green shoots of corn. Shortly after that, the mountain itself rises up out of the water and the foreigner sees the first distant prospect of the Triple City. The summit of the mountain is an unworldly flash of white marble and gilded rooftops, and ignorant offcomers who know no better than to believe in gods at once assume that here is where they live. When they're told that the upper city is the residence of the imperial family, they find it easy enough to make the association in their minds between gods and emperors, a natural-enough reaction which generations of Perimadeian diplomats have exploited to the full. Since nobody ever enters or leaves the upper city, the assumptions of barbarian visitors cannot be refuted; not that the Perimadeian state ever tries too hard.

Below the white and gold crown lies the second city, a breathtaking jumble of palaces, temples, banks, market halls and public buildings of all kinds interspersed with and often indistinguishable from the private residences of the rich and mighty. All great Perimadeians intend their houses to look like glorious and awe-inspiring office buildings, and many a confused envoy or merchant has wandered for an hour among the cloisters and corridors of a second-city edifice only to find out eventually that he's in some private citizen's home.

The lower city can only be seen when the ship is close to land, since it is largely obscured by the colossal sea walls, invulnerable guardians of the city for seven centuries. Once visible, the largest and busiest section of the city looks like any city anywhere, except that it's much larger and more concentrated; as if the great conquering emperors of the past had scooped up the cities acquired on their campaigns, picked out the loot and everything else worth having and dumped the empty buildings at the foot of the mountain like a huge pile of oyster shells.

If the city is approached from either of the two branches of the river in whose fork the island lies, the prospect is slightly less dramatic; the traveller sees the whole mountain at once as he comes through the narrow passes of the surrounding hills, and the land walls don't mask the lower city in the same way as the maritime defences do. From the river approach, Perimadeia appears as a very large city divided into three levels, with freshwater estuaries on two sides and the sea on the third; impregnable, arrogant, infinitely rich, but not necessarily a dwelling-place of gods. Gods would have servants' quarters, but they would be cleaner and not quite so dark and cramped.

Another advantage of approaching from the sea, as a result of the prevailing winds, is that the smell only becomes noticeable once the ship has made landfall in the harbour of the Golden Crescent. Travellers arriving by river get the smell rather earlier; by way of compensation, they have time to get used to it before they arrive at the bridge gates, whereas sea-travellers get it as an unpleasant shock when they walk off their ship.

Only one in a hundred native Perimadeians is even aware of the smell; on the contrary, citizens born and raised in it tend not to notice it and complain about the thin, bland air they find when they go abroad. There is no one single flavour to it; rather, it's a rich and complicated mixture of wood and charcoal smoke, tanneries, refineries, distilleries, glassworks, bakeries, cookshops, perfumeries, brickyards, furnaces, workshops, fish, cattle dung, essence of humanity and rotting seaweed, the like of which is not to be encountered anywhere else in the world.

Temrai's caravan had followed the western branch of the river down from the high plains, and accordingly they entered the city across the Drovers' Bridge and through the Black Gate. Once through the gateway, the road becomes the main thoroughfare of the carpenters' and machine-makers' quarter, and the first thing Temrai saw in the City of the Sword was the famous bone-grinding mill that stood beside the gateway on the left-hand side.

It was an extraordinary sight for a young man newly arrived from the plains. What Temrai saw was a deep pit, out of which rose a huge wooden circle with fins radiating from it like the spokes of a wheel. Someone had cut a hole in the city wall seven feet or so from the bottom of the pit; since this was below the level of the estuary on the outside, water poured through the hole, fell onto the sails and pushed the wooden circle round before being fed back through a smaller hole controlled by some sort of mech-anism which allowed the millstream out without letting the river in. The circle itself turned around an axle formed from the bole of an enormous pine tree. On the other end of the axle was a smaller wheel with pegs driven in all round it, which fitted into similar arrangements of pegs driven into yet another wheel standing at right angles to it. In fact there was a whole family of the things, all biting into each other like a pack of wild dogs, which were in turn connected to the grindstone itself. The miracle was that although the axle turned slowly, the millwheel went round much faster, ensuring that the bones fed into the hopper were crushed to fine powder.

Temrai had never seen so many bones in one place; more even than littered the plain at Skovund, the site of the great battle between the eastern and western clans three generations ago. Two men stood on top of the hopper, shovelling them in from a plank bin. Most of the bones were bits of ox and horse and goat, but mixed in with them were the occasional patently human shin, arm, rib, and skull. The crackly crunching sound as the millwheel rode over them was like horsemen riding over dry twigs and bracken in a forest, but much louder.

'What's it for?' he asked the men with shovels.

They couldn't hear him; or if they could, they couldn't understand his accent. But the man who had the copper-ware stall next to the mill tugged his sleeve and explained; bonemeal, he said, was highly prized by farmers and market gardeners. It made things grow.

'Oh,' Temrai said, 'I see. Thank you.'

'You're a plainsman, aren't you?'

Temrai nodded. He could understand the stallholder perfectly well, although he found the man's sing-song voice rather irritating. He'd been told before he set out that the city people sang rather than spoke; until now, he hadn't seen how that could be possible.

'In that case,' said the stallholder, 'you'll be wanting to buy a genuine Permadeian copper kettle. And it just so happens— '

Explaining that he had no money (fortunately the stallholder believed him) Temrai escaped and led his horse up the hill to where he'd been told the city arsenal was to be found. On the way he passed any number of even more remarkable and fascinating stalls and workshops – a man who was using a bent sapling to turn a spindle, to which was attached a chair-leg which the man was shaping with a chisel as it spun; a crossbow maker chiselling out a latch socket from a bar of iron; two men working the biggest bow-drill Temrai had ever seen, with which they were boring a hole through a cast-iron wheel; carpenters joining the frame of a magnificent beam-operated press, presumably for crushing grapes or olives. Temrai was astonished by what he saw, so much so that he was nearly responsible for several disasters as he narrowly avoided walking into carefully arranged displays of merchandise through not looking where he was going. It was incredible, he told himself, that men's hands had made all these marvellous things. There was clearly more to the business of being human than he'd realised.

And this was the city where he was going to earn a good living as a metalworker. That didn't seem right, somehow; with all this amazing knowledge and all these unbelievable machines and devices, how was it possible that he could know something they didn't?

Had it been up to him, he wouldn't have dared. But of course it wasn't; so he tethered his horse outside the imposing bronze doors of the arsenal, found the rather less imposing side door, and went in.

Unlike most of his race, Temrai had been inside buildings before. He knew what it was like to be between walls and underneath a roof, and although he didn't exactly like the experience, it didn't bother him too much. This, however, was something else entirely. It was dark, like the inside of his father's tent, and what little light there was consisted of a flickering red glow. That and the oppressive heat came from the enormous furnaces, from which bare-skinned sweating men tapped off streams of brilliant white molten iron into long rows of identical gang-moulds that clustered around the base of the furnace like piglets round a sow.

The noise was worse; at home, there was nothing that pleased Temrai more than the sound of the smith's hammer, but these must surely be the hammers of the thunder-genies. When his eyes were a little more accustomed to the light, he was able to identify the source of the noise: a battery of what could only be gigantic mechanical hammers, vast wooden piles shod with iron or copper that were lifted by thick beams until some mechanism tripped them and let them fall. Behind the machine hammers he saw another giant wheel, similar to the one that had driven the bone mill but even larger still. Remarkable; these men made the river do their work for them. The very thought disturbed Temrai; it was like enslaving the gods. Except that, by all accounts, there were no gods in this city. Perhaps, Temrai reflected, with all these machines they didn't need any.

'You.'

He turned round to find a short fat man with two little feathers of white hair in either side of a shiny bald head staring at him. Temrai smiled.

'You,' the bald man repeated. 'What do you want?'

Like all the other men in the building, this one was naked except for a little kilt of grubby white cloth. Understandable, Temrai thought, if you had to work in this heat all day, although with all the sparks flying about from the spitting furnaces, he reckoned he'd rather keep his shirt on and sweat. And this was the place he'd come to find work in. He felt a great urge to run away, but managed not to.

'Please,' he said, 'I want a job.'

The man looked at him as if he'd just asked for a slice of the moon between two pancakes. 'A job,' he repeated.

'Yes, please,' Temrai said. 'I'm from the plains. I'm a blademaker.'

The bald man raised both eyebrows, and nodded. 'Are you indeed?' he said; or rather, sang. If he lived here for the rest of his life, Temrai reflected (and gods forbid!) he'd never get used to that extraordinary way of speaking. It cost him dearly not to giggle.

'Yes,' Temrai replied, not certain what else he was supposed to say. 'And I've brought some solder with me. Would you like to *see*?'

The man nodded; whereupon Temrai reached into his satchel and produced five sticks of the thin silver wire that these remarkable people were said to covet so much. The man took them from him reverently, as if he'd just been handed the soul of his grandmother.

'You know how to use this?' he asked.

Temrai nodded. 'Also the ordinary brass and lead solder,' he said. 'And I can make wire and sheet and weld them for the cores, and forge the hard edges.'

'Quite the young master,' the man replied. 'You don't look old enough to be out of your indentures.'

'Excuse?'

The man shook his head. 'Indentures,' he said. 'Like you're still a 'prentice. Forget it. Come over here.'

The part of the vast room the man led him to was mercifully quite close to one of the tall windows, and for the first time since he'd stepped through the door, Temrai felt as if he could actually see. There were anvils, properly set up on elm logs; racks of hammers, tongs and pincers, hardies, swags, fullers, mandrels and setts; all reassuringly familiar among the strange and wonderful things that crowded out the rest of the room. There was also a neat little brick hearth with a goatskin bellows, in which a sword blade was glowing dull red; and beside it sticks of spelter and lead solder, and an earthenware jar of flux. When he saw these, Temrai understood what was being asked of him and was instantly reassured.

In every part of the world, swords are made in approximately the same way; a soft iron core, around which hundreds of layers of iron wire or ribbon are wrapped before being heated and hammered into a single fused piece; and the separate cutting edges, made from old nails or horseshoes melted down, hammered, tempered, hammered again and baked in an oven with charcoal, dried blood and ground leather to make the iron into steel. By this method a blade can be made to take a true edge that will cut the softer materials from which helmets and armour are made, but which is not so brittle that any sort of hard blow will shatter it like a cup dropped on stony ground. Provided the smith has the basic skill and plenty of time and patience, the separate parts aren't hard to make; the trick lies in joining the edges to the core, using solder and flux.

Temrai selected a pair of tongs, pulled the red blade out of the fire and examined it. The edges were wired to the core, and all down the join were little orange crumbs of glowing flux. He looked round, found the bucket of water and plunged the blade into it.

'Sorry,' he explained. 'Wrong way.'

The bald man was scowling, but Temrai took no notice. When the blade was cool he cut the brittle wires with pincers and tapped the edges free of the core with a small hammer. From his satchel he took his own jar of flux – a ram's horn hollowed out and full of the dusty white powder that constituted the most substantial part of his nation's greatest miracle.

He shook out a few pinches of the powder onto a flat stone, nudged it into a heap and spat into it a few times; then he mixed with the tip of his little finger until he had a smooth, creamy paste. Taking care not to lay it on too thick, he smeared the core and the edges where they were to join, having first scraped off the old, baked flux with his small knife. The bald man handed him a length of wire, and he bound the blade up tight, making sure that the seams were true. Then he put it back into the small furnace and pumped the bellows enthusiastically until he could feel the heat pricking his legs.

'We must get it hot,' he explained, 'or the silver won't run.'

The difference – virtually the whole difference – was that here they used spelter (made from copper and zinc), or (even worse) soft solder made out of lead and tin. On the plains, they knew better. Three parts copper, one part zinc and six parts silver made a solder that flowed like water at a far lower heat and joined steel to iron in a way that spelter and lead never could.

When the blade was bright orange, Temrai took a stick of solder from his satchel, rolled it in what was left of the flux and spat down it for luck. Then he lifted the blade out of the heat and drew the stick along the join. As soon as the stick touched the blade, the solder melted and vanished into the thin crack, leaving only a trace of a white line under a greyish crust. When he'd done both sides, front and back, he returned the blade to the fire, recited the prayers to the swordsmith's god under his breath (not because he expected the god to hear him in this distant place, but because that was how long it took to cook the solder deep into the joint), pulled the blade out and looked round for the pot of oil. There wasn't one.

'No,' the bald man said when he asked. 'There's water. What d'you want oil for?'

'Oil,' Temrai repeated. 'If you have any. Or lard or butter if you don't.'

The man shrugged and walked away, returning a few seconds later with a tall jar full of rancid butter. 'Sure we use it for tempering,' he said. 'But water's for cooling.'

'No,' Temrai replied, as kindly as he could. 'Oil is best, but butter will do. Otherwise the blade cools too quick, and the joint is weak.'

The blade slid into the butter with a hiss and a curl of foul smoke. He left it there for the space of three invocations to the fire-genie, pulled it out and let it rest in the water bucket.

'Done,' he said.

'That's it?'

'Yes.'

'Oh.' The bald man shrugged. 'I thought there was more to it than that. I thought you people did magic and stuff.'

Temrai shook his head. 'No magic,' he replied. 'Silver. And flux. And oil or lard is better than butter, if you could get some.'

He lifted the blade onto the anvil, praying that he'd done it right and that when he knocked the crust off there'd be a beautiful, straight, golden line with no holes or pockets. He wasn't disappointed; it was a good job. He nipped off the wires, took a small file from the rack and wiped away the few little knobs of flash that stood up proud of the blade. Now all that remained was to heat the blade gently until it turned a dark straw colour and quench it in water (not oil, lard or butter, as the man had said; how come they didn't know these things?), then polish it and grind the edges; simple work that anybody can do, a chore the master can safely leave to the boy. Strange, though, that here in the City of the Sword, where everything was decided by swords and good blades were valued above all else, they didn't know the proper way to make things. And yet on the plains, where they had the skill and the knowledge, swords were largely an afterthought, little valued by a nation of archers. If you came close enough to the enemy to be able to use the sword, the chances were that someone had made a serious mistake.

The man looked at the blade, rubbing his chin. He inspected both sides, ran his fingertip up and down the seam a few times, then quite suddenly swung his arm over and brought the blade down with all his might on the beak of the anvil. There was a dreadful clang, the sword cut a gash the thickness of a bowstring in the metal of the anvil, bounced off, twisted out of the bald man's hand and fell on the floor with a clatter.

'You're hired,' the man said. 'Five gold quarters a month. Be here an hour after dawn tomorrow.' He rubbed the palm of his right hand with the thumb of his left. 'I'll get some oil,' he added. 'Olive do you?'

Temrai shrugged. 'I don't know,' he said 'Where I come from we have purified fat. I expect your sort will do just as well.'

Five silver pennies bought him a corner of a room in an inn round the corner; the old, thin woman who ran the place had grumbled about something-or-other foreigners in her nice clean house (except that it wasn't clean, and a man and a woman were making love noisily in the far corner and an old man was apparently dying in the bedspace next to his, and nobody but Temrai seemed to notice) and took pains to make sure he understood about no animals in the room and meals being extra. If the half-eaten messes on the various plates that lay about on the tables in the common room were anything to go by, Temrai reckoned he'd far rather get his own food. As for animals, he sold his horse later that evening and got two gold quarters for it. At home you could buy a string of good horses for two of the Emperor's gold quarters, and have somewhere to ride them into the bargain.

So here he was, he reflected, as he squirmed his way into a comfortable part of the straw and pulled his coat under his head for a pillow. So far he'd done everything right, greatly to his own surprise. He would be able to learn what his father needed to know; where the walls were weak and how the sentries were organised, how many people lived here and who held the keys to the gate; how many arrowheads and spear blades the arsenal could produce in a day; at what times of day the tides were low in the estuary and whether the bridges could be cut in time to prevent an assault party gaining control of them.

If he did his work well, he might make it possible for his father to fulfil his oath and find peace when his time came to ride into the sky; and that would all be well and good. Nevertheless, he couldn't help but wonder exactly why his father wanted this place. To burn it to the ground would be a waste, hateful to the gods. To sack it – but all the wagons of his clan couldn't hold the wealth of this city, and none of it was anything anybody actually *needed*. And to drive the city people out and live here themselves; that was truly unthinkable, an abomination. There had to be some other reason why his father would shed so much of the blood of his archers in order to buy this strange thing; but for the life of him he couldn't work out what it might be.

Which (he reflected, as he fell into a doze) is why I'm still not ready to be a clan chief. So that's all right.

At the last moment, Loredan stepped into the other man's lunge, turning his body sideways, and thrust out his right arm as far as he could. The other man's blade scored a line across his chest an inch above his nipples; his own sword stuck neatly in the other man's eye, killing him before he even had a chance to take the smug grin off his face. The usual dead-weight *flump!* as the body hit the floor; judgement for the plaintiff.

The usher waved languidly to the court surgeon, but Loredan shook his head; contrary to popular belief the official doctors didn't kill quite as many people as the lawyers did, though not for want of trying. It didn't hurt yet, though the blood was coming freely. Gingerly, Loredan picked the sodden cloth of his shirt away from the cut and shivered.

'Come on,' said Athli at his elbow. 'That needs cleaning up. I really thought you'd had it then, you know.'

'So did I,' Loredan replied quietly. 'I *hate* divorce work.'

'You should have quit,' Athli said, leading him by the sleeve. He was still holding his sword, and it was awkward threading a way through the milling crowd of spectators without accidently laying someone's knee open. 'He had you beaten from the start.'

Loredan shook his head. 'Quitting's for losers.'

'That is the general idea, yes. But you're *allowed* to lose in divorce, that's the whole point. Gambling your life on a split-second reflex and winning by a thousandth of an inch – well, in this context it's just plain *silly.*'

'Thank you so much.' Once they were outside, Loredan handed the sword over to Athli, who wiped it and put it away in the case. He felt weak, and sick, and rather as if he was the one who'd been killed but nobody else had noticed. 'Drink?'

'Forget it. Home.'

Loredan decided not to protest. 'Your place or mine?'

'I knew you'd say that to me one of these days. I think yours is nearer.'

Of course, Athli had never been to Loredan's home; no reason to, after all. She knew roughly where it was, and guessed from the address that he lived in one of the 'islands', the tall, jerry-built apartment blocks that had sprung up in the circus district after the great fire a hundred years or so ago. Some of them, she knew, were better than others; some of them had clean water in the courtyard, hypocausts to provide heating in winter, walls that stayed put because of sound engineering rather than force of habit.

The block Loredan lived in was not one of these.

'Seventh floor,' Loredan said, leaning against the door-frame to catch his breath.

'Right,' Athli replied through gritted teeth. The weight of his arm was crushing her shoulder, and he kept treading on her feet.

The stairwell was dark – some 'islands' had lamps

burning on the stairs at all hours of the day and night; not this one – and the stairs were narrow and slippery. It was a long climb.

'Key?'

'There isn't one,' he replied. 'Kick the door, it sticks.'

Loredan's home turned out to be bare, cold and immaculately clean. There was a bed and a table, a finely carved chair with dragons' heads for arms, a once-valuable threadbare tapestry on the far wall; one cup, one pewter plate, one spoon, a large book box with a heavy padlock, a clothes-press, a chopping block with a knife lying across it, the blade worn foil-thin with careful sharpening; a spare pair of shoes and a leather hat hanging from a nail driven into the wall; a pottery lamp; a jar with the monogram of some wine shop embossed in the side; one spare blanket.

'All right,' Athli asked. 'What *do* you spend your money on?'

Loredan groaned and flopped onto the bed. 'There should be some wine in the jug,' he said. 'And bandages in the press.'

Athli watched while he bathed the wound, swabbed it out with wine from the jug and wound himself up in bandages with a skill that clearly came from practice. 'What about something to eat?' she asked.

Loredan turned his head towards the chopping block. 'Apparently not,' he said. 'I'll go down to the bakery a bit later on. Thanks for the help.'

Athli shrugged and said nothing. She had blood all over her clerk's gown. Loredan was making it clear he expected her to leave now. 'Can I get you something?' she asked awkwardly. Loredan shook his head.

'When's the next one?' he asked.

'Three weeks.'

'The charcoal people?'

Athli nodded. 'I'm afraid so.'

'Doesn't matter. Any idea who they've got yet?'

'I haven't heard anything definite,' Athli lied.

'Indefinitely, then.'

She pulled a face. 'Alvise,' she said. 'Perhaps. Like I said, it's not confirmed.'

'Alvise. I see,' Loredan sighed; he looked very, very tired. 'Looks like our boys offended the opposition good and proper, if they're prepared to lay out that sort of money.'

What a dismal epitaph, Athli reflected. What she said was, 'Probably just a rumour, to make our boys settle out of court. He'd cost them twice the sum in issue.'

Loredan shrugged painfully. 'Matter of principle, quite probably. Ah, well, we'll see.'

Athli opened the door. 'If you like, I can drop by later on, make sure you're all right.'

'I'll be fine. Thanks again.'

Athli could feel the blood seeping through her gown onto her skin; cold and clammy, like sweat. 'Be seeing you, then,' she said, and closed the door behind her.

Loredan listened to the clicking of her footsteps on the stairs; then he rolled uncomfortably onto his back and lay staring at the long crack in the ceiling. In three weeks, with this messy cut just starting to knit together properly (if he was lucky and it stayed fresh) he'd have to stand up in court against Ziani Alvise, the Advocate General and Imperial Champion. There was better fencers; four of them, maybe five, none of whom was Bardas Loredan. Strange, he reflected, how calmly I've accepted advance notice of my own death. A nod of the head, a wry face, as if to say, *Well, that's that, then*; two lines of script cut on a plain headstone—

BARDAS LOREDAN
He Gave His Life For The Charcoal People

There were, Loredan knew perfectly well, no gods; and if there were any, they lived far away in less enlightened lands, well out of earshot. Nevertheless, he prayed; *If I get out of this, I'll pack it in for good, retire, set up a school or something*. And if there were gods, he knew they wouldn't believe him, because they'd heard it all before. And here he still was, an advocate of ten years' call, a man who showed promise while still young but failed to live up to it, and then simply failed to live.

Perhaps the charcoal people would settle, after all. Men like Alvise only fight one in ten of the cases they're retained for, because no litigant likes to go into court when there's money at stake knowing for certain he's going to lose. But the charcoal cartel weren't the settling kind; he'd met them, recognised them at once. They were the sort of men who get themselves tangled up in the most desperate messes through their own pig-headed greed, and then react with astonishment and fury when the inevitable disaster follows. He could picture them, striding out of the court with their heavy gowns flapping round their ankles, muttering bitterly about the incompetence of their late advocate and the unfairness of the legal system, and swearing great oaths that they'd rather be skinned alive than pay one penny of the bill for such a badly handled case.

I could always back out, he thought. There is always that possibility. It would make perfectly good sense; I'd be finished in the profession, but so what? I'd still be alive. I could do something else.

He grinned, and rolled over onto his side. Of course, he could never withdraw from a case just because he was afraid, or even because he knew he was going to die. It was one of those things that just don't happen; if it did, the whole system would collapse and then where would everyone be? It was, after all, the solidity of its commercial law that had made Perimadeia the greatest trading city in the world. And besides, you didn't become an advocate in order to live for ever.

He had decided, many years ago, that the last thing he wanted to do was live for ever. Twelve years later, here he was; and if he hadn't done much, he'd done enough. Traditionally, a fencer's coffin is borne by six of his colleagues in the profession, wearing their collegiate robes and with empty scabbards on their belts, while on the coffin lid rides the deceased's second-best sword – his best sword, of course, having reverted to the winner – and a single white rose, symbolic of Justice. In practice it was rather different, of course; the coffin rode on the shoulders of six men who'd had the sense to leave the profession early and take up pallbearing instead, the sword was hired from the under-taker and, somehow, it always seemed to rain. He'd stood beside a lot of muddy graves when he was younger. These days he didn't bother to go.

Just my luck that the Guelan should break right when I need it most.

A thought occurred to him and he leant over, groaning, and groped under the bed until his fingers made contact with a coarse woolen bundle. He pulled it out. It was garlanded with cobwebs and grey with dust, but the knot fell away easily, leaving him holding a battered black scabbard with a plain brown steel hilt projecting out of it. Now here's a thing, he said to himself; I haven't given it a thought in ten years. But why not? It can't make any difference, after all.

Twelve years ago, a young man already old after three years in the foreign wars had joined the fencing school by the Protector's Gate, paying his fees in ready money from a fat purse and bringing with him a cheap, plain sword with no maker's name on the ricasso. Once he'd finished the course, there was enough coin left in the purse to buy a genuine Guelan, and the cheap, plain sword had ˙been consigned to second best, third best, emergency use only and finally a blanket under a bed on the seventh floor of Island Thirty-nine. It wasn't, properly speaking, a lawyer's sword at all; just a military blade from the arsenal ground down to reduce the weight, roughly re-tempered and fitted with a plain turned grip. It had killed a lot of men before it lost weight, but since then it had been used for school work and practice, never once being called upon to carry the weight of a man's life. It was worth a quarter and a half, if that. He'd never liked it much. It didn't owe him anything. It would do.

He closed his eyes and went to sleep. His dreams were not pleasant.

* * *

Temrai looked down into his cup and saw that it was still almost half-full of the stuff. He wished it wasn't. He was tempted to pour it away while nobody was looking; but his new friends had bought it for him and to pour away a gift would be an insult as well as waste. Even so; it tasted horrible and it was making him feel ill.

'And is it true,' one of them was asking, 'that when you get old they take you out into the desert and leave you there to die? Only I heard somewhere ...'

They had stopped by his bench earlier that evening; four broad-shouldered middle-aged men who worked on the furnaces, cheerful, loud-voiced and sociable. When he'd seen them bearing down on him, Temrai had felt a little apprehensive. It'd only be natural if they resented a foreigner (and a plainsman, at that) walking into the arsenal and taking a job that would normally have gone to one of their own. From what he'd overheard, many of the more skilled workers in the arsenal belonged to some sort of secret clan reserved for masters in the craft; perhaps these men belonged to it and had come to chase him away. It was something of a relief to find out that all they wanted was to invite him to drink with them.

'No,' he replied, shaking his head (and for some reason that was enough to make him feel dizzy). 'That's not right at all. We have great respect for old people, who are so wise and know so much. They make all our decisions and tell us how things ought to be done. My father ...'

He caught himself just in time, and covered the mistake by pretending to choke on his drink. The men thought that was highly entertaining and pounded him on the back with their enormous hands. Strange, that; he had a vague impression that they were sharing some hidden joke, almost as if someone had tied a rat to another man's pigtail without him noticing.

'What you're probably thinking of,' he went on, 'is when a man grows very sick, so that he knows he's going to die. When that happens, quite often he'll go off into the plains on his own, so as to spare his clan the distress of watching him die. And it saves on rations too, of course. Among my people, waste is a terrible thing.'

He noticed that he was slurring his words a little, like a man with bad toothache whose jaw becomes inflamed. That and the dizziness made him want to go back to his sleeping place and lie down. He would have assumed it was something to do with the drink, except that the men had drunk far more than him, and if anything they were even livelier than usual.

'Drink up,' said one of them, whose name was Milas. 'Don't they have wine where you come from, then?'

Temrai replied that in his country they drank milk. The men nodded sagely and their eyes sparkled. 'Wine's better than milk,' said another one, Divren. 'Good for you. Full of sweetness, makes you strong.'

Milas tilted the jug and Temrai found his cup was full again. He took a long pull at it, to get it over with. They were really very kind, hospitable people, but the stuff was disgusting.

'We heard,' said the oldest of the men, Zulas, 'that in your country the men all have a hundred wives each. Is that true?'

'Oh, no,' Temrai assured him. 'Never more than six, and that's only great lords, like my— Most people just have one or two. It's because there's more women than men.'

'Are there? Why's that?'

'Because a lot of the men get killed,' Temrai replied. He burped, but nobody seemed offended. 'Fighting, or lost on the plains, or else they just go away for a few years. And then their wives marry someone else. Although,' he added, frowning, 'I don't think marriage means the same here as it does at home.'

Zulas winked at the others. 'Doesn't it?' he asked. 'What's the difference, then?'

Temrai thought hard. 'Well,' he said, 'where I come from the men are out on the plains most of the time seeing to the horses and the sheep, while the women stay back at the wagons, so they don't tend to spend a lot of time together. But here, they live with each other all the time. I think it's amazing. Men and women weren't meant to be together like that. They're different. They get on each other's nerves.'

'True,' said Milas, nodding gravely. 'Here, have some more.'

'Puts hairs on your chest,' Divren agreed.

'But then,' Temrai went on, 'there's so many things that are different here. Like buying and selling, for instance. In this place, everything's bought and sold; what you eat, what you drink, clothes, where you live. So you have a whole lot of people who do nothing but make shirts, and another lot who do nothing but buy food from one load of people and sell it to another load.' He waved indiscriminately at his surroundings. 'And there's people who earn their living owning a house that other people live in. That's strange. Or take you, I mean, us; it's all different back home. All you do, or rather *we* do, is make swords all day. At home the smiths do smithing one day in ten, and the rest of the time they're running their stock or fixing up their wagons or curing hides or whatever, just like everyone else. Even my – even the great lords ride out to the flocks when they haven't got clan business to deal with. So we hardly buy and sell anything. It's odd,' Temrai went on, 'because our way seems to work pretty well, and so does yours. They're just as good as each other, but different.'

'Wise words,' said the fourth man, Skudas. 'Wisdom in wine, isn't that what they say? Have another.'

'Thanks,' Temrai said, holding out his cup. It got better the more you had. 'And another thing,' he said. 'Here you've got people whose only job is fighting, and when they're not fighting they're practising fighting. All my people fight when there's fighting to be done, but the rest of the time we don't fight at all. Well, hardly at all. Mind you, we do fight quite a lot of the time, clan against clan and nation against nation. But it's always over in a day, while you people go on fighting the same war for years on end. Where's the point in that? Surely the whole point of fighting's to see who's the strongest, not who's got the cleverest lords who can spin the war out even though the enemy's got heaps more men. Doesn't make sense to me.'

Zulas waved his hand for another jug, then said, 'So you don't like it here, then?'

'I didn't say that,' Temrai replied, shaking his head vigorously. 'Didn't say that at all. I think it's absolutely wonderful here, all these incredible things you've got, and the way you all live heaped on top of each other and hardly ever lose your tempers. If my people had to live here cooped up like horses in a corral, they'd be at each other's throats in a day or so. But it's hard to have feuds and quarrels when you're all doing things together, like getting the caravan across a river or bringing the horses in to be broken.' He stopped to drink more wine, and then continued, 'I think the clan's much more like a family than your city is. Everybody's a man on his own here, and you all live in your own houses and shut the doors at night and lots of you don't even know the people who live half an hour's walk away. That's strange.'

Another strange thing, Temrai noticed, was the way the room was going round. He'd only ever felt this way before when they'd banked up the fire for a dance for the gods and the old women had burnt herbs and holy leaves. It was all right to feel dizzy and strange then, because the gods came down and joined in the dances, and the presence of gods has a peculiar effect on mortals. Could it be that there were gods in the inn tonight? He'd heard stories of gods going round in disguise to keep an eye on mortals, and if the gods were travelling, it was only logical they'd put up at an inn for the night rather than sleep out in the open. Surreptitiously he glanced round, trying to spot anybody who might be a god. He couldn't see any obvious candidates, but that didn't mean anything. But wasn't it the case that there weren't supposed to be any gods in the City of the Sword? Well, maybe there were, and perhaps that's why they're in disguise. In which case, best to pretend he hadn't noticed anything.

'And another thing,' he said.

He carried on talking for a while; but now he couldn't clearly make out what he was saying. It was like trying to listen to a conversation in the next tent. He could hear a voice, but the words were all bent and worn away, like on a coin picked out of a river. If he'd been right about gods, then the chances were there were quite a few of them in the inn tonight. Also, he didn't feel terribly well.

The next thing he was aware of was the landlord shaking him by the arm and speaking to him in a weary, disagreeable voice. Temrai tried to explain about the gods, and that appeared to annoy the landlord, because soon after that he found himself out in the street, lying in a puddle of something that didn't seem to be water and feeling very sick. He looked around for Zulas and Milas and the others but they'd gone. He was terribly afraid he'd offended them by acting strangely; he was, after all, a foreigner, and a plainsman into the bargain. It had been very kind of them to buy him all that wine. He'd have to make a point of thanking them the next day, and saying he was sorry.

Eventually a soldier with a lantern came along and kicked him until he got up. After that he wandered around for a while trying to find where he lived, gave up and went to sleep under a wagon. His last thought before his mind slipped away was that the city was a very strange place indeed, but some of the people were very kind and good-hearted; good old Zulas and Minas and Skudas and Divren. He would have to remember to make a point of asking his father to spare their lives, once the city had been taken.

Twelve years ago, a party of horsemen rode in through the Dawn Gate. They looked ragged and tired; their clothes were patched and threadbare, their mailshirts mostly held together with wire. Many of them were as hideous as the ogres in children's stories; badly set fractures left limbs out of shape, scar tissue had formed over wounds that had been inadequately dressed or septic. Men and horses alike were almost comically thin, their hands and feet seeming out of all proportion to their bodies.

They were, or course, heroes, though nobody came out to meet them, and a few people threw things at them because they'd lost. They were all that was left of the army.

Maxen's Pitchfork had been, for as long as anyone could remember, the city's one and only defence against the vague and constant threat posed by the nomadic clans of the western plains. Because they did their job so well, the citizens took them for granted, giving them honour, respect and twenty-five quarters a month all found; accordingly they never thought to ask themselves how a thousand heavy cavalry could possibly be expected to hold back the virtually limitless manpower of the clans. After all, it worked, and they did manage it; and whenever a citizen woke up in the middle of the night out of a nightmare of shrieking savages and clouds of arrows, he would remember General Maxen, Lord Count of the Exterior, turn over and go back to sleep.

But Maxen, who had spent thirty-eight of his sixty years in the field fighting the clans, suddenly did the inconceivable thing and died – of gangrene, following a fall from his horse during a routine punitive expedition. As soon as news of his death spread among the clans, there came the inevitable explosion. For the clansmen, Maxen had been quite simply the most terrifying thing in the world, a demonic force that appeared in the middle of the night, surrounded by blazing torches and slashing swords, killing every living thing in a whole caravan and then melting away into some crack in the earth, invisible in the vast emptiness of the plains. Maxen's death was like the death of fear itself; so, when his second-in-command, Alsen, met the assembled clans beside the Crow River, they threw themselves against the Pitchfork as if charging straw dummies in a training exercise. Alsen, who had been on the plains twenty-five years since joining the regiment as an ordinary trooper, was a brilliant soldier, the kind whose campaigns might under other circumstances have been studied in military academies. As it was, he faced odds of twenty-five to one and inflicted such devastating losses on the enemy that an assault on the city was rendered impossible for many years to come. But he fell, and eight hundred and eighty of his men died with him. The husk of his army hurried back to Perimadeia under the command of Maxen's nephew, a lad of twenty-three who had only been on the plains for seven years; one Bardas Loredan.

CHAPTER THREE

'To say that the Principle enables one to tell the future,' said the Patriarch, his mind elsewhere, 'is tantamount to saying that the main function of the sea is the delivery of driftwood. It would be more accurate, though still basically erroneous, to state that one who closely observes the Principle can make certain assumptions about the effects it is likely to have on the material world. Anything further than that would be misleading.'

The young woman whose name he couldn't remember wasn't a member of the class any more. She had got what she came for, or something approximating to it, and left. Alexius had the troublesome feeling that he was in the position of an innkeeper's daughter who has spent an amusing night with a handsome stranger and is beginning to feel sick in the mornings. The after-effects of the curse were getting to him; he needed to see the girl again if he was to have any hope of putting things right.

'Consider a road,' he continued, as the students bent their heads over their writing tablets, diligently committing his wisdom to marks in wax. 'A man rides along a steep-sided valley, in a region notoriously infested with robbers. From where he is he cannot see them waiting for him around the next bend of the road, although he suspects they may be there. An observer high up on the hillside can see him and the robbers as well. There is no magic in this; simply a high vantage point. It follows also that you cannot see the ambush if you are riding the road; only the impartial observer, watching the affairs of others, can perceive the imminent danger.'

It was, Alexius knew, a hopelessly flawed comparison; but it would do for freshmen. Later, when they knew better, they could have the pleasure of gloating over its obvious faults, which would be good for their confidence.

'Or consider,' he went on, 'a cup of water standing on a table. The cup cannot move or spill the water of its own accord; but if there should chance to be an earthquake, or even a train of heavy wagons passing in the street below, the cup will appear to tremble of its own accord. The man who detects the first signs of the earthquake, before it is perceptible to the untrained eye, or who sees the wagons entering the street, will know that the cup will move. He can predict; he can interfere by picking up the cup, preventing it from being shaken off the table and breaking. If he is unscrupulous, he can claim that by his tremendous powers he can cause the cup to shake and the water to spill, and then appear to make good his boast.'

Putting ideas into their heads? None that weren't there already an hour after they were born. Alexius detested fortune-tellers even more than those who pretended to heal the sick or lay curses for money. The sad fact was that such prophecies had a tendency to come true, mostly of course because the customer expected them to and acted accordingly.

'We who study the Principle,' he resumed, 'can stand back and see the lurking robbers or the approaching wagons. Sometimes, our observations make it possible for us to intervene; in which case we expose ourselves to all the dangers we warn others about; we run down into the pass to warn the traveller, or hurry to where the earthquake is to be in the hope of saving someone. To assert that we can avert bandits or spill water from a cup without touching it, however, is not only dishonest but terribly dangerous. The bandits will leave the traveller alone and attack us. We, rather than the person we have come to warn, will spill the water. There are those who say that when we see a disaster approaching and do nothing, we are acting reprehensibly; think of it rather as preferring that the robbers will have only one victim instead of two. That concludes the lecture; by tomorrow, read the first twenty chapters of Mycondas' *Syllogisms* and be prepared to answer questions.'

He stopped speaking and, as far as the students were concerned, ceased to exist. Some of them, he knew, would quite simply not believe him. They would far rather assume that he and his fellow masters were trying to keep the best tricks back for themselves. Let them; too ignorant as yet to harm anybody but themselves.

As the last few of them trooped out, chattering to each other about everything except what they'd just been told, Alexius let his mind slip back to the question of the young woman and the curse, which was still hurting him like a grain of sand trapped under an eyelid. Where was she? Perhaps one of the other students might know; except that she'd been here such a short time that it was highly unlikely that she'd confided in any of them. Besides, in comparison they were all hopelessly young and immature. Who would entrust secrets to a mere child? If she told them why she was leaving and explained about the curse, doubtless there would be a few fools who attempted to do the curse for themselves. Well; if they were lucky, they might escape with nothing worse than the failure of a trick.

The Patriarch of Perimadeia, hunting high and low after a girl student who had left the course on its second day; a girl who had spent a considerable part of the evening of the first day in the Patriarch's cell. He could imagine what his junior colleagues would make of that if they got the opportunity. Which, he decided, they would not. He would have to find some other way to cure himself of this malady.

He was aware of someone behind him, walking quickly to catch up. Without looking round, he slowed down.

'Fascinating.' He recognised the voice; Gannadius, the Archimandrite of the City Academy. Too late now, however, to quicken his pace. 'Every year five hundred new faces, and yet within a week or two they look and sound exactly the same as their predecessors. Do we do that to them, I wonder, or are all young people basically interchangeable?'

'Both, I suspect,' Alexius replied. 'Whatever individuality they may still have when they arrive here is soon ground away by the necessity of being indistinguishable from their peers in appearance, tastes and opinions. The best thing anyone can say for youth is that eventually we all grow out of it.'

The customary exchange of epigrams having taken place, Alexius hoped that his colleague would now go away. No such luck; today, Gannadius had something to say. When he would eventually get around to saying it was anybody's guess.

'It distresses me to think that I was once that young,' Gannadius sighed. 'I assume that I was, although for the life of me I can't remember it. As far as I'm concerned I've always been the same age. My friends, however, have grown old around me.'

Wonder why? Alexius asked himself. 'I read once,' he replied, 'that each man has a certain age that is appropriate to him; once he reaches it, he stays there, although his body continues to wear out.'

'In my case, it would have to be forty-three.'

In spite of himself, Alexius was interested. 'Really? Why forty-three?'

'I was that age when I first read the *Analects*,' Gannadius said simply. 'What about you?'

'I don't think I've reached it yet,' Alexius confessed. 'I can distinctly remember being three, and wondering what being three meant. And I was seventeen for a very long time, but I'm not any more. I think I stopped being seventeen when I realised I was no longer afraid of my immediate superiors.'

'And that was when?'

'When I became Patriarch,' Alexius replied. 'Now I'm afraid of my immediate inferiors, but that's scarcely the same thing.'

Gannadius nodded wisely. 'To change the subject completely,' he said, 'are you feeling well?'

Alexius stopped walking and rubbed his chin to cover his surprise. 'Is it that obvious?' he asked.

'My dear friend, you've been walking around like a man with his foot in a trap. Would it be impertinent for me to speculate that you have, so to speak, trodden on a hidden rake among the proceedings of the Principle and been struck a sharp blow on the nose in consequence?'

Alexius smiled. 'No,' he replied. 'Because I knew exactly what I was letting myself in for. I did a curse, and I'm afraid it didn't agree with me.'

'Oh. Anyone we know?'

Alexius hesitated. Gannadius was frequently inopportune, often tedious, always pompous; but as far as Alexius knew he had no dark ulterior motives or savage ambitions, and his writings revealed a surprisingly perceptive and practical mind and a sharp intellect. And Alexius needed help if he was ever to get rid of this wretched affliction.

'A fencer,' he said, 'by the name of Bardas Loredan. With whom, I might add, I have no personal quarrel whatsoever. The curse was on behalf of someone else, which is probably why I've taken it so badly.'

Gannadius bit his lower lip, suppressing a grin. 'In which case,' he said, 'I really must congratulate you on the quality of your work. I must remember to be extremely polite to you at all times.'

Alexius raised an eyebrow. 'What's happened?' he asked.

'Ah, you wouldn't know, would you? It so happens that I have a small sum of money invested with a cartel that produces and sells charcoal. They're in dispute with a rival concern, and the matter goes to court shortly. Our opponents have briefed one Bardas Loredan to represent them.'

'I see. And?'

'And we've retained Ziani Alvise,' Gannadius replied. 'You've heard of him, no doubt?'

Alexius frowned. 'I think so. I don't follow the courts at all, but the name rings a bell. Is he good?'

'You might say that. I understand that among the sporting fraternity, Loredan is being offered at a hundred and twenty to one and finding no takers.'

'I see.' Alexius nodded slowly. 'In which case,' he said, 'I'd strongly recommend that you put your last quarter on Loredan. In fact, while you're at it you could put fifty quarters on him for me.'

Gannadius looked puzzled. 'My dear friend,' he said, 'modesty is an admirable quality, but don't you think you're taking it a little too far? I would argue that the mere fact of the fight suggests that your curse is working very well indeed.'

'You don't understand. In my curse he's committed to die at someone else's hands. One person in particular. Not Ziani Alvise.'

'Ah.' Gannadius looked thoughtful. 'That's rather tiresome, since I've already backed Alvise quite heavily. Still, I suppose I can find a few more quarters to cover the bet. Thank you; you may well have rescued a poor man from abject poverty. In return …'

Alexius acknowledged the offer with a slight tilt of his head. 'I must admit,' he said, 'I could do with some help. This curse is proving confoundedly sticky. I think I must have done a rather better job than I thought.'

'In cursing, as in cooking with garlic, it is best to resist the temptation to add just a pinch more for luck. Will you come to the Academy or shall I call on you here this evening?'

Alexius considered. On balance, it would be better if the proceedings didn't take place under the noses of his brothers in the Principle. 'After dinner,' he said, 'at the Academy. All your people ought to be in Chapter by then.'

'And I with them,' Gannadius pointed out. 'Still, a personal request from the Patriarch—'

'I'd rather you said it was urgent affairs of the Order,' Alexius replied. 'Which isn't that far from the truth. Ever since, I've had no end of difficulty in concentrating on anything. The paperwork is starting to get out of hand, to say nothing of my reading.'

'This evening, then, after dinner. If you call at the side gate, I'll make sure I open the door personally.'

'Thank you.'

Gannadius trotted away, the soles of his fashionable slippers clacking on the flagstones. A curious man, Alexius reflected. He had been Archimandrite of the City Academy for seven years, a record tenure for an office that was generally regarded as a tedious preliminary formality on the highly structured road to the Patriarchate; yet in all that time he had never displayed any inclination to accept promotion, let alone scheme and contrive for it. He could have had the Patriarchate of the Canea for the asking three years ago, but preferred to allow his own archdeacon, whom he particularly loathed and despised, to advance on the vacant post like an invading army and virtually take it by direct frontal assault. And yet to all appearances he was the very model of the archetypal career man; younger son of a powerful city family, owning substantial estates and investments inherited from his mother's family and assiduously courted by the small weevil-like men who spend their lives under the flat stones of district politics. Alexius shook his head; perhaps the cold winds and the sea frets of the Canea hadn't appealed to him. Or perhaps he was an honest man at heart. Curiously enough, Alexius was inclined to believe the latter.

Accordingly, Alexius slipped out while the evening meal was still raging below his cell, and made his way cautiously through the streets of the middle city to the northern stair. The gate was locked for the night but the porters knew him well enough; since the inhabitants of the upper city were never seen, the Patriarch was the closest thing the city had to a visible civic figurehead. For a man doing his best to cross the middle city incognito, this was a serious drawback; nevertheless, Alexius eventually managed to reach the City Academy without being either recognised or robbed, and rapped on the side gate with the pommel of his walking-sword.

'Ah, there you are,' said Gannadius through the sliding panel in the door. 'I was beginning to wonder if you were coming.'

The Archimandrite's lodging was about five times the size of Alexius' own cell. There were valuable tapestries on the walls, five extremely fine carved and gilded chairs, a curtained bed on a low dais, several quite beautiful chests and coffers of well-figured walnut, a high desk inlaid with hunting scenes in mother of pearl, a footstool of highly polished whalebone and a handsome silver-gilt wine service; all quite new and smelling strongly of camphor and beeswax. Alexius had no doubt that his colleague would have been able to give an accurate up-to-date valuation, sale price or replacement cost, for each individual item or the whole as a job lot.

'You disapprove,' Gannadius said equably.

Alexius shook his head. 'Not in the least,' he replied. 'You live in the style appropriate to a great temporal lord, which of course you are. Myself, I'd find it all too distracting, but only a savage disapproves of beauty *per se*. And I'm sure you appreciate it all far more than the dried-fruit merchants and anchovy barons who need to fill their houses with such things simply to prove to themselves that they're now men of stature.'

'You disapprove, nonetheless. Personally, I'd gladly trade all of this clutter for the mosaics on your ceiling. But I doubt whether they're for sale.'

Alexius smiled. 'One day you may well be sleeping under them as a matter of course,' he replied. 'Or do you still maintain that you have no ambitions in that direction?'

Gannadius shrugged. 'It's more a question of whether I'm fitted to do the job,' he replied. 'And the fact is that I'm not. Not yet, at any rate.'

'That's a very honest reply to a rather snide remark. Mind you, I'm not saying for a moment that I believe you.'

'Just because a remark is honest doesn't necessarily

mean it's sincere,' Gannadius replied with a grin. 'Shall we stop fencing round each other and get to business?'

'That would be best,' Alexius said, and he told Gannadius what had happened, leaving nothing out. When he'd finished, the Archimandrite sat for a while in his rather magnificent chair, rubbing the bridge of his small, blunt nose with the forefinger of his left hand.

'I think I see what's happened,' he said. 'In the event, the curse you laid was not the right one.'

'It wasn't the curse the girl intended. Since it was her curse, and I was just the instrument by which she laid it, it could well be significant that I got it wrong. The result will have been an error in the Principle.'

'Quite.' Gannadius nodded. 'In essence, you've taken a gap in nature and put into it something that doesn't fit. You are now having to contend with the effects of the disruption.'

Alexius nodded slowly. 'It makes sense, I agree. What I'm not sure about is how to put it right.'

'Oh, but that's simple,' his colleague interrupted. 'You must return to the moment and put it right. If you take off the wrong curse and replace it with the right one—'

Alexius held up his hand. 'Naturally, I've tried that,' he said. 'The only problem is that I can't. After all, it's not my curse, so I can't lift it. All I can do is put a shield around the confounded man to prevent the curse working; and even that's proving difficult. Every time I've tried, I've found it gone again by the next day. I really don't relish the prospect of having to raise new shields around this fellow every day for the rest of my life.'

'It's a difficult problem,' Gannadius said. 'All I can suggest is that we try it together. And before you say anything, I quite agree that there's no evidence for assuming that our joint efforts will be any more successful than your solitary attempts. What we really need, of course, is the girl.'

Alexius sighed. 'I'm inclined to agree with you there,' he said. 'Still, if you're willing to join me, I think it must be worth trying – provided you're prepared to take the risk. I can't recommend the state you're likely to be left in if it backfires.'

'Ah, well.' Gannadius shrugged. 'There's no gain without risk. You forget, I haven't named my price yet.'

'A permanent view of my mosaics, presumably,' Alexius replied. 'I'm not sure I can make that promise; and besides, you're about the same age as I am. There's no guarantee whatsoever that you'll live to collect your fee.' He smiled. 'I'm assuming you're not planning on taking steps to collect it early.'

Gannadius looked genuinely offended. 'Actually, no,' he said. 'If I'd wanted the Patriarchate, be sure I'd have taken it by now; or at the very least I'd be coughing and blowing my nose in the Canea. My price is far more esoteric than that. I want you to tell me the seventh aspect of the Principle.'

In spite of himself, Alexius was shocked. Knowledge of the seventh aspect was a secret shared only by the Patriarch of Perimadeia, the Primate of the Holy Pirates and the Abbot of the Academy of the Silver Spear; in effect, it was what defined high office in the Order. It was also the one secret that had always been kept, no matter how grave the circumstances or how venial the office-holder. 'Why?' he said quietly.

Gannadius frowned. 'Because I want to know,' he replied. 'Is that so remarkable? Whether you believe it or not, I joined the Order to learn how to understand the Principle, or what little of it there is that can be understood. Logically, I need to know all seven aspects if I'm even to begin my studies.'

'I think I believe you,' Alexius said. 'That doesn't make your request any less offensive.'

'I've named my price. It goes without saying that the secret would be safe with me. After all, a man doesn't steal a fortune in gold only to throw it out of his window in handfuls to the crowds below.'

Alexius thought for a moment. 'All I can suggest,' he said, 'is that in due course – it won't be long now anyway, the poor man's over eighty – you will succeed Teofrasto as Primate. Then you'll at least be authorised to have the knowledge, and the practical effect will be the same.'

'Must I? I really have no desire to leave this comfortable place and go and live on a rocky island in the middle of the sea with nothing but thieves and murderers for company.'

'It's a job men have killed and stolen for,' Alexius replied, slightly nonplussed. 'I'd have thought you'd be pleased.'

'Certainly not. True, they have a good library there, but nothing to compare with what I have available to me in the city. Still,' he went on, 'once I know the seventh aspect, there won't be very much left that books can teach me. Oh, very well then. You have my word, if that's good enough for you.'

Alexius allowed himself the luxury of a wry smile. 'I suppose it'll teach me to do favours for young girls,' he said. 'Payment in arrears, naturally; and nothing unless it actually works.'

'Naturally. Shall we begin?'

A thin, cruel blade of light forced its way between the shutters.

'Wake up, it's a lovely morning.'

His hand already closed on the hilt of the Boscemar, Loredan countermanded his instinctive reaction and opened his eyes.

'What the hell,' he croaked, 'do you think you're doing?'

'Making you get up,' Athli replied, throwing the shutters open. 'Come on, rise and shine.'

Loredan drew the blanket up under his chin. 'What possible reason could I have for getting out of bed at this loathsome hour of the morning? Go away.'

Athli half-filled a cup from the wine jug and topped it up with water. 'You should have been up two hours ago,' she said briskly, 'instead of lounging there like a pig.'

'Why?'

'Training. Drink this and get some clothes on. I think we'll start you off with ten laps of the city cloister before we head off for the Schools. Oh, come *on*, for pity's sake. I've seen livelier-looking faces with apples in their mouths.'

'Oh, for …' Loredan closed his eyes, but all the sleep had gone. 'Go away while I get dressed,' he commanded.

'All right. Don't dawdle.'

It had been a long time since he'd deliberately run any distance, and ten laps of the cloister left him with weak knees and a sharp pain in his chest, which he offered as reasonable grounds for going home. Athli was not impressed.

'You sound like my grandfather dozing in front of the fire,' she said. 'A morning in the Schools will do you a world of good.'

By the time they'd climbed the long stair to the middle city, Loredan was feeling quite ill. He diagnosed the trouble as either a heart attack or a minor stroke.

'Don't be silly. And don't dawdle.'

The Schools were housed in a long, narrow single-storey building between the old circus and the rainwater tanks. Inside, the main floor was crowded with the usual clutter of fashionable young men and women in expensively impractical fencing suits, leaning on their sword-cases and watching the handful of professionals going through their practice routines. Attendants scurried to and fro with straw targets and buckets of wet clay, trainers shouted, the inevitable vendors wandered about on the edge of the crowd with their trays of wine and sausages, the sword dealers did quiet business between the pillars of the rear colonnade. 'Did we have to come here?' Loredan asked miserably. 'I can't stand this place.'

'Practise,' Athli replied.

First, Loredan set up a mark. He decided to be realistic; show-offs and the truly skilful liked to use a silver halfpenny, but he'd never been that good, even in his prime. Instead he marked up a knot-hole on a target frame, which would do just as well for all practical purposes.

'Seven out of ten?' he suggested.

'Make it nine.'

'I don't have to do what you say,' he replied, 'because I'm an advocate and you're only a damn clerk.' He measured off three paces back and drew the Boscemar out of its case.

'Nine out of ten,' Athli repeated. 'Ready?'

Loredan nodded. The object of the exercise was to lunge full stretch off two paces, transfixing the mark each time. The trick was to straighten the thrust as late as possible by turning the wrist. He made the mark seven times out of ten.

'Now do it again,' Athli said. 'Only better.'

Out of the next ten he registered six hits; six again from the next ten. On his fourth try, he connected with all ten thrusts.

'You see?' Athli said smugly. 'Practice makes perfect.'

'Oh, shut up,' he replied, leaning against the target frame to catch his breath. 'Now I suppose I've got to do the numbers.'

The target itself was a woven straw boss about an arm's length across. Dotted about it at random were numbers from one to twelve, the figures being about a thumb's length high. The drill was for the trainer to shout out a number, which the fencer would then impale with his sword-point off one pace. Fifteen out of twenty was a good score.

'Ready?'

'Sixteen, all right?'

'Eighteen.'

In the event he made eighteen at his first attempt. The second stage of the drill was the same but twice as fast. At this speed, ten out of twenty was tantamount to showing off. Loredan made all twenty.

'All right, clever,' Athli said. 'Now we'll do it with the plumb line.'

The plumb line was a lead weight on a string, arranged to hang where the point of an opponent's sword would be if he was standing with his back to the target face. The fencer had to knock the weight out of the way, make his lunge, withdraw and parry the weight again on the way back. A missed parry meant instant disqualification. Fourteen out of twenty at normal speed or half that at double speed was good enough going for anyone. Cutting the string didn't count.

'Not bad,' Athli observed, when Loredan had scored nineteen hits at standard speed. 'Now let's do it the hard way.'

A clear round at double speed; so Athli insisted that he do it again, and then one more time at triple speed. They'd got as far as fourteen out of fourteen when Loredan cut the lead bob in half with a sharp flick of his wrist, and refused to push his luck any further.

'So you can do lunges,' Athli said. 'Now let's try something you're not so good at.'

The quintain was designed to practise recovery from a parried cut. It consisted of four wooden spokes set at right angles to each other in a hub which rotated around an upright axle at about chin height. The fencer had to hit one spoke, then parry the next one as the hub turned. The faster and harder he hit, the quicker he had to be to parry the next spoke. The refinement on the standard course of play was to use only the second and fourth spokes, which meant having to lift the sword blade out of the way between strokes, as opposed to simply rolling the wrist back and forth.

'My arm hurts,' Loredan complained after four clear rounds of both courses. 'It isn't going to help matters if I go into court with a whole bunch of pulled muscles.'

'You're just lazy,' Athli replied. 'Right, let's do some footwork.'

This time Loredan's complaints were eloquent and sustained, albeit fruitless in the long run. The footwork course consisted of a series of silhouette footprints painted on the floor, each one designated with a number. In the orthodox course, the fencer had to move his feet to cover the numbered footprints as the trainer called them out, starting slowly and working up to a high-speed frenzied dance. The advanced course was the same, but blindfold.

'Now can I have a rest?' Loredan panted. 'I keep telling you I hate practice, but you never listen.'

'Do that last set again. You missed number twenty-six.'

He had to have three tries at the blindfold course before he managed to do it perfectly. Thirty-one out of forty was held to be a top-class performance.

'Satisfied?'

'That wasn't too bad,' Athli conceded. 'Now you'd better have a go with the ring.'

'Athli …'

'The ring.'

From a crossbeam in the roof hung a steel ring about the width of an apple. Underneath it was a circle five paces in diameter. For this exercise, the fencer had to work his way round the circle, first forwards and then backwards, half-lunging so as to pass his blade through the ring each time. As a refinement, he had to parry a plumb line suspended from a hoop, which rotated as it was struck so as to follow the fencer round the circle. Of all the exercises in the Schools, this was probably the one Loredan hated most.

'I'm quite pleased with that,' he said, raising his voice slightly for the benefit of the crowd of onlookers that had gathered while he made his second perfect circuit against the plumb line. It wasn't every day that a man scored a clear round on the ring. To manage it twice in a row was rather an exceptional feat.

'Come on,' Athli said, 'while we can still get your head out through the door.'

'Does that mean I can go home now?'

'After you've done the sack and the sheaves.'

The sack was a leather bag full of wet clay, which made a fair approximation of the consistency of a human body for practising running through. The sack had an understandable but nevertheless alarming tendency to split open after a while, and in winter the School used condemned pigs' carcasses from the butchers' market instead. In the heat of summer, however, the fencers had to make do with wet clay. The sheaves were coils of plaited straw wound tightly into a rope about the thickness of a man's neck. A good fencer with a sharp sword could usually cut through them in two strokes.

'I'm going to get all muddy,' Loredan protested as an attendant filled a sack and hung it up from a frame.

'So?'

'I'm just saying, that's all. Mud all over me, head to foot. How many shirts do you think I own?'

He had made about a dozen good thrusts at the sack when the blade of the Boscemar hit something hard – a stone in the clay, or some particularly resilient stitching in the sack – whereupon it bent like a drawn bow and snapped about a foot down from the point. Loredan scowled at the hilt in his hand and swore fluently. For her part, Athli had the common sense not to say anything.

'That's that, then,' Loredan said, dropping the hilt on the floor. 'Ten days before the fight, and I break my best sword. As messages go, that one's not too hard to understand.'

He left the hilt where it was and headed for the front door. There was a dense crowd gathered around the popinjay cage. He recognised the man in the cage and stopped to watch.

Inside a high, narrow birdcage stood the celebrated advocate Ziani Alvise, his opponent in the forthcoming suit. All around him on the ground were the bodies of dead hummingbirds, and the attendant was about to put in another boxful. Usually the targets in the popinjay cage were ordinary sparrows; hummingbirds are far harder to hit than sparrows.

As the attendant closed the cage, a fly drifted in through the bars past Alvise's right shoulder. Without turning his head, he flicked his sword sharply upwards, cut the fly precisely in two and brought the sword back to guard in time to decapitate the first of the new batch of hummingbirds.

Loredan spent the afternoon getting very drunk.

Perimadeia, the Triple City, the bride of the sea and the mistress of the civilised world, was in decline. True, she had been sick before, but never as badly as this. Barely seventy-five years ago, her land empire had stretched from Zimisca in the high plains to Tendria, whose twin mountains bracketed the mouth of the middle sea. Now, the site of Zimisca was discernible only by patterns in the high couch-grass and a few outcrops of fallen masonry, while the two great castles of Tendria were garrisoned by rival warlords, each styling himself the True Emperor and ruling a few rocky islands and a swollen fleet of pirate warships. Canea, the last of the empire's island possessions, was in practice an autonomous state, and the ships that brought the nominal annual tribute plundered a hundred times as much from Perimadeian merchantmen in what had once been sacrosanct imperial waters. For all her splendour, the bride of the sea owned nothing except what she stood up in, and the Emperor's empire was bounded by the sea and the freshwater estuaries that lapped the feet of the land and sea walls.

Not that anybody cared. Every citizen knew that the walls were completely impregnable. Five hundred men could hold the city against all the nations of the world, as the Emperor Teogeno had done two and a half centuries ago. That was how it had always been. The external power of Perimadeia ebbed and flowed like the tides; one century saw the empire's boundaries stretching right across the known world, the next saw the city penned inside its walls like a caged bird, while three generations later there would be Perimadeian governors back in the islands and the great mainland cities. It never seemed to matter. Trade, not land or castles, was all that mattered in Perimadeia, and the city had never been busier, more crowded or more prosperous. That seemed to be the pattern, and there was a sort of logic to it. Conquest and occupation cost money and manpower. With no empire to protect, there were no war levies to pay and no draft commissions to interrupt the business of the markets and factories. Likewise, there was no promise of loot and adventure to lure men away from the glassworks, the foundries, the potteries, tanneries, shipyards, mills, kilns,

studios and workshops from which poured an unquan-
tifiably vast stream of goods of every quality and kind. For
a thousand years the city had boasted that one in three of
all manufactured articles in the world was made in the noise
and bad air of the lower city. Now, for the first time, it was
quite possibly true.

Having no gods to distort their values and distract their
attention, the Perimadeians understood and valued
material objects like no other nation. The citizens of the
Triple City saw their lives as a brief but enticing opportunity
to make and do as much as possible in the short interval
between birth and death. And if, from time to time, they saw
the need to own land and build castles, the way rich traders
have always done, it was probably because there was
precious little else to spend their money on, since
everything a man could really want they already had.

Provided, of course, that the walls stood; but that was a
safe enough assumption. As for pirates; well, they were a
nuisance, but nothing more. All it meant was that instead of
taking their goods out to the customers on Perimadeian
ships, they stayed at home and let the customers take the
risk of coming to them. Sooner or later some strong foreign
prince would get tired of losing good money on his
mercantile interests and sweep the vermin from the sea. No
need for the city to waste one gold quarter or one
Perimadeian life doing what someone else would be glad to
do for them. The same would undoubtedly hold true of
enemies to the landward side, if any managed to get close
enough to confront the frustrating barrier of the land walls.
All it would take would be a few fast galleys dispatched to
the islands and the coastal cities, and the sea would be
jammed solid with troopships hurrying to protect the one
true source of universal prosperity. There was even talk of
mothballing the fleet and disbanding what remained of the
city guard; why waste money on something that would
never be needed, even in the worst conceivable
emergency?

In consequence, there was no hysterical panic or rioting

in the streets when news reached the city that the Anax valley, the spacious and fertile region that separated the city from the plains and supplied two-thirds of the city's food, had been overrun by an alliance of the White Bear and Fire Dragon clans under a chief whose unpronounceable name sounded something like Sasurai. So what? the citizens said; their prices were getting too high anyway. Plenty more where that came from. And if the plainsmen living in the city had expected lynch mobs and tar barrels, they had sadly misjudged their cosmopolitan hosts, who were above that sort of thing and always had been. For example, the day after the news broke, young Temrai was greeted with the same friendly nods as he sat down to work at his bench, and the subject was never mentioned. Whether this would have been the case if his colleagues had known he was Sasurai's son, it is of course impossible to judge.

Alexius the Patriarch and Gannadius the city Archi-mandrite stood on the floor of the courthouse, watching a man and a girl taking guard.

They had been a day and two nights getting here, and they were exhausted. Ironically, it was their exhaustion that had finally made it possible, for both men lay fast asleep in their chairs in the Archimandrite's lodgings, and the courthouse was nothing more than the backdrop of their mutual dream.

'Can you hear me?' Alexius whispered.

'Yes, but it seems they can't,' Gannadius replied. 'I arrived a couple of minutes before you did, and I've been making a few preliminary experiments. As far as I can see, we aren't really here.'

Alexius shuddered. 'Good,' he replied. 'I'd hate to think I was standing in front of the whole city in my shirt.'

'It would appear to be a remarkably good house,' Gannadius said, glancing round at the packed benches. 'I wish there was some way of telling how far we are into the future.'

'The girl is older than when I saw her last,' Alexius said. 'Unfortunately, with our rather limited experience of women, I don't suppose we can accurately judge how much older. She's definitely improved with age, but that's all I can safely say on the matter.'

'What happens now?'

Before Alexius could answer, the judge gave the sign, the courthouse was immediately silent and the two advocates began their performance. Once again, Loredan had his back to the Patriarch; this time, however, Alexius noticed that he was holding a broken sword. He mentioned this to his colleague, who nodded.

'That's sure to be significant,' Gannadius said. 'I only wish I knew what it meant.'

'Pay attention. It happens quite early in the fight.'

This time, however, it didn't. Although he was on the defensive right from the start, Loredan fought with the desperate energy of a man who truly appreciates precisely how much trouble he's in. Lunges and cuts that should have been the death of him were somehow nudged away at the very last moment, and although his counterattacks met a defence as invincible as the land and sea walls, they bought him the time and space he needed to carry on defending. All in all, it was a breathtaking display of virtuosity by both parties, almost worth waiting up forty-eight hours for.

'This is all seriously wrong,' Alexius muttered. 'When I think that for weeks now I've been on the receiving end of this level of mess, it makes my blood run cold.'

'Serves you right,' Gannadius replied, his eyes fixed on the contest. He was something of a connoisseur of the art of litigation, and this was very much a collector's item.

The girl lunged left, and Loredan swerved out of the way; but the lunge had been a feint, and the blade was directly on line for his throat. A last frantic reflex allowed him to get his hand in the way. He deflected the blow, but the girl's blade hit him squarely in the palm. From where he stood, Alexius could see an inch of the blade sticking out through the back of Loredan's hand.

Now's his chance, he told himself, and as Loredan lunged forward at the girl's unprotected body, Alexius stepped between them and tried to catch the moment.

He felt nothing as Loredan's sword ran him through – how could he, he wasn't actually there? – but as he looked down and saw the blade vanishing into his own chest, he knew at once that he had made the worst mistake of his life. A moment later, the girl stepped round him and cut Loredan down where he stood; he collapsed, face down, leaving his sword stuck in the Patriarch's body. Alexius was just wondering how this was possible when Loredan had been using a broken sword with no point when he woke up.

It was the pain in his chest and arms that had woken him; a heart attack, no question at all about that. Gannadius was still fast asleep, and Alexius couldn't move or speak to rouse him. It was quite possible, he realised, that he was about to die. More than anything else, he found the idea thoroughly unfair.

Gannadius lifted his head. 'It's all right,' he said, 'don't worry. You'll live.'

The pain stopped.

'Keep still,' Gannadius went on. 'And calm down. Try and breathe normally.' He stood up, stiff and awkward after his cramped sleep, and poured half a cupful of strong black wine. 'This'll help,' he said. 'Go on, drink it. If you were going to die, you'd be dead by now.'

Alexius made a face as the wine burnt his insides. 'What happened?' he asked. 'Was that a heart attack or was I stabbed?'

'Both. My fault, I'm afraid. Give me the cup, I'll get you another.'

'*Your* fault?'

Gannadius nodded. 'I had to do something to stop him killing the girl. Shoving you in the way was all I could think of. It's just as well you weren't really there, or it could have been very dangerous.'

'Of all—' Alexius waved the cup aside feebly. 'You do realise what you've done,' he said. 'Now I'm under a curse of my very own. And the girl still killed him, so it was all for nothing.'

Gannadius shook his head. 'Think,' he said sternly. 'You were under that curse already; that's what's been wrong with you these past weeks. All I've done is bring matters to a head, so to speak. No,' he continued, 'if it hadn't been for me things would have been much worse. Loredan would have killed the girl, and then where would we all be?'

'You're not the one who's going to get run through,' Alexius pointed out. 'At the very best, we're back exactly where we started.'

'Oh, no,' Gannadius objected, 'not at all. For one thing, we've done some extremely valuable practical research into an area of the Principle about which deplorably little was hitherto known. I shall write a paper about this.'

The Patriarch closed his eyes and took a deep breath. 'That aside,' he said.

'That aside, I do believe we've made some worthwhile progress. Instead of having a vague idea that you were suffering from an adverse reaction but not knowing what form it's taken, we now know exactly what you can expect. Likewise, we were in time to prevent the potentially disastrous consequences of this second intervention, no small achievement in itself. Add to that the fact that none of the reaction appears to have attached itself to me, and I believe we can congratulate ourselves on a job well done.' Gannadius smiled. 'And now I suggest that you try and sleep for a while. I'll have a guest room made up for you. Heart trouble isn't something to be taken lightly, you know.'

Alexius groaned. 'What really depresses me,' he said, 'is that you and I are the world's leading exponents of this particular skill. If this is the best we can do, perhaps we ought to leave well alone. For pity's sake, we're supposed to be able to do this sort of thing for a living.'

Gannadius looked at him for a long time. 'A living,' he said. 'Perhaps you may care to rephrase that.'

*   *   *

The chief trainer was vexed.

'True,' he conceded, 'there have been female advocates before. Some of them lived to be nearly twenty-five. But that was mostly because nobody wanted to hire them, so they scarcely ever got any work. You don't want to join this profession. Go away.'

The girl said nothing; instead she held out a squat leather purse on the flat of her hand. The trainer couldn't help noticing how full it looked.

'We aren't really equipped to take female students,' he said. 'We'd need separate changing rooms, and we simply haven't got the space. Not to mention chaperones,' he added, suddenly inspired. 'And before you say you don't need chaperoning, you try telling that to the Public Morals Office. That's just the sort of thing that could get me closed down, just like that. And what about the costume?' he went on, wondering why none of this seemed to be having any effect at all. 'You couldn't be expected to fight in trousers, and there just isn't an accepted form of solemn-procedure dress for women in the courts. You'd be a laughing stock.'

The girl said nothing. The purse sat there on her palm. A sense of bewildering frustration swept over the trainer; why couldn't he get through to this pig-headed girl? Over the years he'd talked literally hundreds of stupid young kids out of joining a profession in which they stood no chance of survival. He was a conscientious man and besides, he had his trainer's licence to think of. He could just imagine himself trying to explain to a frantic mother and father and a stony faced Public Safety Office official why he allowed a slip of a girl to join up and get herself killed in her first fight. It was a fat purse, but not fat enough to compensate him for the loss of a business he'd been nurturing for nine hard years.

'Please?' he said. 'If you won't listen to sense, then at least go away and make life miserable for one of my competitors. I can give you a list of places to try.'

'You're the best,' the girl said. 'I want to learn here.'

Behind them, the long exercise hall echoed to the clatter

of blades and the shouts of short-tempered instructors. The floor shook as thirty feet came down hard in unison in the first, second, third steps of the Orthodox guard, the back foot riposte, the fleche, the defensive lunge, the Southern parry, the fencer's turn, the *mandritta*. Every day brought a fresh crop of bright, keen, idiotic young faces, of distraught fathers whose only sons had run away from home and family businesses to follow the wild dream of becoming a lawyer. Every week there were funerals to attend, new names to inscribe on the roll of ex-pupils who had given their lives for the profession. One way or another, the chief trainer saw an awful lot of young people with an urge to die, but never one as persistent as this. Mostly, he reckoned, it was the way she wasn't pleading or cajoling or begging that was getting to him. It was as if she was demanding an inalienable right which he was trying to cheat her of on the flimsiest of pretexts. It'd serve her right, he told himself, if he did let her join.

'All right,' he said, 'here's the deal. You tell me why it's so all-fire important to you to be an advocate, and then maybe I might be persuaded.'

Silence. For the first time, the trainer could sense a slight trace of reluctance; a questionable motive, perhaps, some-thing on which he could quite reasonably base a refusal. He decided to press the advantage.

'The point being,' he said, 'that there's only one valid reason for wanting to join this profession. Anything else, and you're disqualified instantly. And I've got an idea it's not the reason that's motivating you.'

The girl said nothing, but her cheeks were beginning to glow red. Professional that he was, the trainer could sense a fault in her guard that would repay pressure. He moved onto the offensive.

'The only reason for fighting people for a living,' he said, 'is money. Not love of justice, or honour, or adventure, or prowess, or the desire to be the best. Certainly not the pleasure of killing; most definitely not because secretly you want to find a way you can die before your time without it being your fault. It has to be the money, or nothing. And if you're about to tell me that it's all right, you don't actually intend to practise once you finish the course, you're just here for the education, then I suggest you get out of my establishment before I have you thrown out into the street. Of all the dirty, disgusting words I know, the very worst of all is *amateur*. And that's what you are, isn't it?'

He was winning; because when the girl replied her voice was unsettled, worried. 'How would you know?' she said sullenly.

'Because,' he said, 'you turn up with payment in full in advance, all ready, not even a pretence of haggling or offering to pay in instalments or asking me to wait till you've started earning. That's what professionals do. Obviously, therefore, you're not a professional.'

Victory. The girl's hand closed around the purse and dropped to her side. 'The hell with you, then,' she said. 'I'll just have to go elsewhere.'

'Best of luck,' the trainer replied, relieved that the fight was over. Even so, now that he'd won, he couldn't help feeling a burning curiosity. After all, she hadn't answered his question. He asked it again.

'None of your business.'

'If you tell me,' he said, 'I might be able to point you in the right direction.'

The girl shrugged; the matter was no longer important. The mere gesture seemed to devalue his victory. 'Revenge,' she said. 'That's all.'

'Ah,' the trainer replied, 'I might have guessed. If there's one thing I despise almost as much as amateurs, it's melodrama.'

The girl gave him an unpleasant stare. 'My uncle was killed by an advocate called Bardas Loredan. The only way I can legally punish him is to become an advocate myself. So that's what I'm going to do.'

In spite of himself, the trainer couldn't help being intrigued. 'What's so significant about being legal?' he asked. 'If it's so terribly important to you, why not just hire a couple of bright lads to cut his throat in an alley some-where? I could definitely give you a few recommendations there; quite a few of our ex-students diversify into that area of the profession after a couple of years.'

The girl shook her head. 'That would be murder,' she said. 'I don't believe in murder, it's wrong. This has to be done right.'

Several replies occurred to the trainer, but he voiced none of them. 'All right,' he said. 'Start a lawsuit against one of his regular clients, and hire a better fencer. He'll be killed and it'll be completely legal.'

'That would still be murder,' the girl replied. 'It's not as if Loredan's done anything wrong, after all. He was just doing his job, so he hasn't committed any crime that would put him outside the law. But he killed my uncle and so he's got to be punished.'

Before the trainer could say anything, she had turned and walked away; out of the hall and out of his life. Most of him was only too glad to be rid of her; but there was one small dangerous part of him that regretted losing so unusual a subject for observation. The trainer had seen all kinds of strange people – the sad, the sick, the disturbed, the crazy and the plain old-fashioned stupid – but never one like this. Probably, he reminded himself, just as well. Bad trouble on two legs is always best avoided.

It wasn't until quite late in the afternoon that Loredan woke up. He was hung over, depressed and angry with himself for not coping better. He decided to go out for a drink.

If a man wants to get thoroughly drunk in the lower city of Perimadeia, there are any number of places he can go, between them covering all the nuances of the mood, from boisterous jollity to utter self-loathing and all the fine gradations in between. From the fashionable inns where respectable people talked business over good wine to the unlicenced drinking-clubs behind a curtain in the back room of someone's house, there was an abundance of choice that was sometimes offputting. There were taverns that advertised their presence with enormous mosaic signs, and others which did their best to be invisible. There were taverns that were government offices, taverns that were theatres, taverns that were academies of music or pure mathematics; there were temples to forbidden gods, corn exchanges and futures markets, dancing floors and mechanics' institutes, places that allowed women and places that provided them, places to go if you wanted to watch a fight, places to go if you wanted to start one. There were even taverns where you went to argue over which tavern you were going to go to. And there were places you could go and sit on your own until you were too drunk to move. In fact, there were a lot of those.

The one Loredan chose didn't have a name or even many customers; it was basically the back room of a wheelright's shop, with four plain tables, eight oil lamps and a hatch you banged on when you wanted more to drink. Nobody spoke much, though occasionally someone sang for half a minute or so. There was a channel under the back wall to piss in if you were feeling refined. If you happened to die where you sat, nobody would hold it against you. The wine was no worse for you than a dose of malaria.

Loredan was halfway through a small jug of the stuff when someone walked up and sat down opposite him.

'Bardas,' he said.

Loredan raised his head. 'Teoclito,' he replied. 'Aren't you dead?'

'Not yet.' Teoclito put down his jug and filled both cups. 'Mind you, I'm not trying as hard as you. How's life in the legal profession?'

'Depressing.'

'Good money, so I hear.'

Loredan shrugged. 'Better than the army, and you get to wear your own clothes. What about you?'

Teoclito looked about seventy; in fact, he was only five or so years older than Loredan. The last time the two of them had sat together over a jug of wine had been in a tent pitched among the ruins of a town they had reached three

days too late. The next day, there had been a bit of a
scrimmage with the clans; Teoclito was one of the wounded
who was past helping. They'd gone back to put him out of
harm's way, but he hadn't been where they'd left him. It
followed that the clans had him. It helped not to think too
hard about such things.

'Been back three years now,' Teoclito said. 'I work in the
dancing school, sweeping up after the young ladies. It's a
living.'

Loredan refilled the other man's cup. 'And before that?'
he asked.

'Not much fun. You don't really want to know.' Teoclito
smiled; he had five teeth. 'They have surprisingly good
doctors, but a wicked sense of humour. Eventually they
turned me loose.'

'Just like that?'

'No room for passengers in the caravan, and they're a
superstitious bunch. Terrible bad luck to kill a cripple.'

'And after that?'

Teoclito sighed wearily. 'Oh, I walked to the coast, got
there, found I'd been going in the wrong direction. After that I
didn't feel much like walking any more, so I stayed put.'

'Where was that?'

'Solamen.' Loredan raised an eyebrow; Solamen was up
on the north coast, two months' walk from the place where
they'd parted. Among other things, it was a flourishing slave
market. 'I got a job, of sorts. Unpaid. Sort of like voluntary
work.'

'Ah.'

'Finally I ended up helping row a big boat,' Teoclito
continued. 'And when this boat got sunk off Canea, I swam
ashore, and now here I am. I'd like to say how nice it is to
be back, but I have a basic respect for the truth that
prevents me.'

'You've been busy, then.'

Teoclito shrugged, awkwardly. 'Like you said, it beats
being in the army. Anyway, enough about that. You see any
of the old crowd nowadays?'

Loredan shook his head. 'Not many of us made it back,' he said, 'and we don't have reunions. You didn't miss much, at the end.' He yawned. 'Saying that, I did run into Cherson the other day, down by the city wharf. He's running a brass foundry, doing quite well. Employs a lot of people.'

'Never could stand the man myself.'

'Nor me. Funny, isn't it, the way bastards live for ever.'

Before his presumed death, Teoclito had been Loredan's Company Commander. Every inch the hero, in a society that discouraged the type; first man into the engagement and last out. He seemed much shorter than Loredan remembered. He was almost completely bald, and there were scars across his crown. Loredan had taken over his command; to the best of his knowledge, they were the only two men alive out of that company.

Teoclito was looking at him intensely. Mostly, Loredan recognised, it was contempt.

'Yes,' he said. 'They do, don't they?'

They filled their cups again and sat quietly for a while. Loredan couldn't think of anything to say.

'Anyway,' Teoclito said at last, finishing his drink and standing up. 'Can't be too late, got to work tomorrow. Be seeing you.'

'Clito.' Loredan wished he hadn't spoken; he was afraid that what he was about to say would be the wrong thing.

'Yes?'

'You … Are you all right for money? I mean—'

That look again. 'I told you,' he said, 'I got a job. Go carefully, Bardas.'

'You too.'

'Oh; one more thing.' Teoclito leant against the table, favouring his right leg.

'Yes?'

'I'm sure you had a good reason,' he said, 'for leaving me and not coming back. Just don't ever try and tell me what it was.'

'Take care, Clito.'

'I always do.' He walked away, his right foot dragging. His

whole body had been twisted like a length of wire. It must have seemed a very long way from the high plains to Solamen, walking like that.

The lengths some people'll go to just to stay alive.

Loredan left the rest of his wine and went back to his 'island'. He was virtually sober, but that was all right. No more drinking, he told himself, as he lay down to sleep. Regular meals, exercise, practice in the Schools, perhaps even a new sword, and maybe he'd be in shape to beat Ziani Alvise. After all, it was just another fight, something he was supposed to be good at. It wasn't as if he was being asked to do anything difficult, like walking home.

CHAPTER FOUR

'What are you staring at?' demanded the engineer.

Temrai stepped backwards. 'I'm sorry,' he said. 'I was just looking.'

The engineer scowled, and spat into the sawdust. 'Haven't you got any work to do?'

'I finished it. I'm waiting for the next batch of blanks. So I thought I'd just look around.'

The engineer muttered something and went back to what he was doing. He was working on the frame of a small trebuchet, the kind that threw a hundredweight stone. Using a chisel and a beech mallet, he was cutting dovetails in a thick twelve-foot-long plank; earlier, he and another man had sawn it out of a massive billet of seasoned ash, using a ten-foot saw.

'Is that for the main frame?' Temrai asked. The engineer looked up, surprised.

'Left-hand A-frame,' he replied. 'Already done the right one. How come you know so much about engines?'

'I'm interested,' Temrai said. 'I've been watching.'

The engineer, a man of about sixty-five with shaggy white hair on his chest and arms like a bear, nodded. 'I know you,' he said. 'You're the offcomer kid, the plainsman.' His mouth twitched into a small grin. 'Bet you ain't seen anything like this up on the plains.'

'Oh, no,' Temrai said. 'I think it's fascinating, seeing all the different machines.'

This time the engineer actually laughed. 'There ain't

much to these buggers,' he said. 'Trebuchet's a very basic design; you just got a bloody great big heavy weight on one end and a sling to put the stone in on the other, and it pivots around a pin supported on two A-frames. So you hoist up the weight with a winch, load your stone and let go. The weight goes crashing down again, and the stone gets slung out. Piece of cake. Compared to some of the machines we make here, there's nothing to it.'

'Oh,' Temrai said. 'I thought they were quite good.'

The engineer shrugged. 'Oh, they work all right. We got trebuchets'll throw a four hundredweight stone three hundred an' fifty yards, straight as a die. This here's just a baby; got the same range but only takes a quarter of the load.'

Temrai nodded appreciatively, and the engineer was secretly pleased to see the light of enthusiasm in his eyes. All true engineers are enthusiasts; they value admiration and respect every bit as much as painters and sculptors do, and they know they deserve it even more. All a sculpture need do is look a certain way. A machine has to work.

'How do you know how big to make it?' Temrai asked.

The engineer laughed again, not unkindly. 'That, my son, is a bloody good question. Some of it you can work out by figuring; there's what we call formulas. The rest just comes by trial and error. You make one, you see if it works; if it doesn't you make it again a different way, and you keep on over and over till you got one that does work. That's what we call prototypes.'

'Ah,' Temrai said.

'F'rinstance,' the engineer went on, carefully marking out the rectangle he was about to cut with light taps of the chisel, 'the Secretary of Ordnance comes to me and he says he wants ten light trebs to cover the angle of the sea wall just along from the Chain, where they've just put in them five new bastions. So he tells me what he wants these trebs to do and I go away and I have a think. Now, I know that we built a treb once that had a beam thirty-three foot long, with a counterweight of a hundred hundredweight, and we found it could chuck half a hundredweight a couple of hundred yards. Now that ain't much for a treb, more like a kiddie's toy, but it gives me somewhere to start. So I reckon, if I can sling fifty pounds two hundred yards with a hundred hundredweight off thirty-three, maybe if I want to sling a hundred pounds three hundred and fifty yards, I could start with maybe a forty-foot beam and fifteen hundred hundredweight. And then I think, hang on, a fifty-foot beam and two and a half hundred hundredweight'll chuck three hundredweight two hundred an' seventy-five yards, 'cos I made one that did. So I try a hundred hundredweight off forty foot of beam, and if that busts the beam, I know forty's too long with a hundred, so next time I try thirty-six. But I've made the beam shorter now, so I gotta up the weight on the other end; so we up the counterweight to a hundred an' seventy. Now if it breaks, I gotta make the beam stronger, and that throws out all the other measurements.' He paused for breath. 'Not a quick job,' he said, 'making engines.'

'It sounds really complicated,' Temrai said. He sounded so downcast that the engineer smiled at him.

'It is complicated,' he said, 'making things that work. Any bloody fool can make things that don't work. No offence, son, but that's what you foreigners do. You see a machine and you think, that's a good idea, we'll make one of them; but you never stop to think about how long it ought to be or what it ought to be made out of, and then it don't work and you say the hell with that, alas, the gods are angry, and you pack it in. That's the difference, see,' he added, tapping his forehead. 'Up here.'

'I can see that,' Temrai replied. 'That's what makes you all so very wise.' He surveyed the various finished and half-finished parts of the engine standing against the wall in order or cradled on specially built jigs, and his lips moved as if he was counting under his breath. 'And I suppose it's not just the arm and the weight,' he went on. 'I suppose it's important to get the frame the right size, too.'

'You're getting the idea. We might make an engineer of you yet.' He patted the timber in front of him, which was secured by broad iron cramps to a substantial trestle. 'I been thinking, and I reckon if I make the frame twelve by eight by twelve, I won't be too far out; it's not like I was trying to mount a sixty-foot beam with clearance for three an' a half hundred. The more weight, see, the more clearance you need, so the taller the A-frame's gotta be. But the more acute you make the angle, the likelier they are to bust under the strain, so you gotta beef them up, and then some prat from Ordnance comes along and tells you to lose twenty hundredweight off it or it'll be too heavy for the tower they want it on.' The engineer rolled his eyes dramatically. 'See what I mean?' he said.

'I think so. What else do you make besides trebuchets?'

'You name it,' the engineer said proudly. 'This year so far I've made catapults, oistoboles, onagers, scorpions, mangonels, all that sort of bloody stuff. Doing a nice simple treb's a pleasant change, I can tell you.'

As he sat at his bench, carefully wiring hardened edges to a soft steel core, Temrai couldn't help thinking of his uncle Tesarai; how once, many years ago, he'd managed to capture a Perimadeian artilleryman, and set about torturing him with tremendous ingenuity and enthusiasm in an attempt to wring from him the secrets of building war engines. The harder Tezarai tried the less he achieved, until the time came when the prisoner died with his secrets intact, leaving the clansmen with a deep sense of baffled respect. At this point Tezarai declared that it was plainly impossible for the city ever to be taken, since its people were prepared to face the ugliest forms of death rather than betray it. Whereupon Temrai, who was twelve at the time and only just old enough to be allowed to attend councils, tentatively suggested that they'd gone about it in the wrong way. Trying to extort information out of these people was obviously futile; wouldn't it have been a good idea simply to have asked nicely? To which he'd added quickly (for fear of being sent straight to bed) that these people who were so puffed up with pride in their city that they preferred to die rather than let it down might very easily tell an enquirer everything he wanted to know, so long as he asked the questions in a way that allowed the Perimadeians an opportunity of showing off in front of ignorant savages.

And now, five years later, here he was; and it was proving even easier than he'd imagined. He now knew the dimensions and construction details of the siege tower, the long ladder, the scorpion, the gravity-operated ram and the trebuchet. He'd learnt the art of sapping and undermining walls simply by going to the library and reading a book. He'd been given a tour of the walls and watchtowers by a member of the guard he'd met in a tavern, and had sat drinking with him while he timed the intervals of the watch and counted the number of men on duty. His job in the arsenal meant that he knew more about the city's stocks and production capacity of arrows than the guard commanders. There was even a book, which the librarian had promised to find for him, that described ten perfectly feasible ways of breaching the defences and storming the city; it had been a prescribed text at the military academy twenty years ago, and since then had been largely forgotten about. It was wonderful; like everything about the city, wonderful, unsettling and deeply sad.

He finished wiring up and put the assembly into the fire to heat up for brazing. He'd make a good job of it, never fear; the least he could do, in the circumstances, was make sure that they had a few decent swords to defend themselves with when the moment came.

Among the large crowd who paid their copper quarter and stood in line to see the Alvise-Loredan case were a tall, thin young man and an equally tall, rather more rounded girl. They were wearing matching cloaks of an unfashionable colour and cut—

('How was I supposed to know? The last time I was here was five years ago.'

'And it didn't occur to you that fashions might have changed?'

'To be honest, no.'

'Men!')

—and when they whispered together, their dialect, although more quaint than barbarous, was enough to make the people behind them in the queue nudge each other and wink. Islanders, they muttered to each other, and made a show of checking that their purses were still there.

'I'm not sure I want to see this,' the girl muttered as the ticket clerk took from her the little bone counter she'd been handed at the door. 'Where on earth's the fun in seeing two grown men killing each other?'

Her twin brother shook his head. 'They probably won't do that,' he said. 'Extremely difficult, for one thing. Much more likely that one'll kill the other and that'll be that.'

'Don't be obtuse,' his sister replied. 'You know perfectly well what I mean. And I think it's barbaric.'

Her brother shrugged. 'I'm not defending it,' he said, 'it's just something you ought to see if you ever hope to understand these *pazze*.'

'Shh! They'll hear you.'

'Ah, but they don't know what *pazze* means. Look, you want to join the firm and do business here, one thing you've got to get your head round is their *paz*' legal system. Which is,' he added, 'the finest in the world if anyone asks you, all right?'

The girl nodded. 'All right,' she said. 'But I still don't see—'

'Shut up. Here's the judge. Stand up when I do.'

'Barbaric,' the girl sniffed.

Three days in the Triple City had cut a huge swathe through the fine romantic notions that had filled her head when the white crown of Perimadeia had poked up above the sealine. The smell still bothered her, and she definitely didn't hold with the streets. It was one of the crazy contradictions that made up this place; every market stall seemed to offer ever more astoundingly lovely clothes and fabrics, with colours and textures beyond the dreams of the Island, but if you wore them in the street they'd be ruined inside five minutes. The buildings, even in the lower city, were as tall and majestic as the Prince's own lodgings back home, but the streets outside were squelchy with mud and muck, the roadways rutted and crowded with carts and wagons that splashed the passers-by with foul water and tried to run them down even if they stayed inside the gutter-lines. Everyone she saw in the streets looked prosperous and well-dressed, but she noticed that her brother wore his sword openly on his belt all the time and avoided doorways and dark alleys. It was a fine place to visit, she'd decided, but you wouldn't want to live here.

'There's the advocates, look,' her brother hissed, jabbing with the knuckle of one finger—

(And that was another thing; at home it was rude to point; but here, everyone did it. She'd spent the first day and a half with her face permanently red with embarrassment.)

'That's the plaintiff's man, and that's the defence,' her brother continued. 'I think the famous one's the plaintiff.'

'I shan't look. You'll have to tell me when it's over.'

'Please yourself.' He leant back, trying to find a comfortable place on the stone bench, and looked around to see if he could spot anybody he recognised.

It hadn't been his idea bringing Vetriz on this trip; but now she was here and had proved not too much of a liability, he had changed his mind. True, it made the evenings rather dull; but in consequence he was saving money hand over fist, in spite of having Vetriz's expenses to pay, so that was all right. It was also undeniable that she was good for business. Back home a pretty face got you precisely nowhere, but for all their vaunted canniness the Perimadeians could be snared by a smile and a flash of ankle as easily as hungry pigeons with grain in winter. Not a tactic he'd ever consider using at home; there was a word for men who didn't immediately cut the throats of strangers who ogled their sisters, and it wasn't very polite. Different here, of course; and fairly harmless too, provided Vetriz didn't find herself getting used to it …

At this rate, he'd be all done here in record time. Four-fifths of the wine and oil had already gone, and for good money. The flax, timber and spices had made nearly half as much again as he'd expected (which more than made up for his embarrassing mistake with the two thousand oil lamps in the shape of hedgehogs; might as well dump those in the harbour and make space for more return cargo). As for buying, he had pretty well everything he'd wanted, and the prices hadn't gone up too much. The only commodities he still needed were padlocks and threaded bolts; just his luck to make the trip at a time when there was a freak shortage of both …

'What's happening?'

'Hm? Oh. Sorry, miles away. This bit's called the pleadings, it's where the—'

'Ssssh!'

He cringed, turned his head and apologised. 'This bit,' he went on in a low whisper, 'is where they go through the facts of the case. It's usually a bit technical—'

'Why?'

'Sorry?'

'Why bother? I mean, if it's going to be decided on the basis of who can bash whose brains out first, how can going through the facts help?'

Venart shrugged. 'I don't know, it's not my legal system. Look, I'm not asking you to approve of it, just to know how it works. You want to be in business, you've got to know at least the basics of commercial litigation.'

Vetriz sniffed. 'Well,' she said, '*I* think it's silly.'

'Ssssh!'

Eventually the pleadings ground to a halt and Vetriz, who would probably have fallen asleep if the stone seat had been slightly less uncomfortable, yawned and squinted down at the two men in white shirts who were now tentatively dancing round each other in the centre of the courtroom floor. The tall blond one was, apparently, the favourite; accordingly, she decided she wanted the other one to win.

He'd be short if he was an Islander, she decided; about average for these people. From what she could see this far back, he was older than the other man, shorter and slighter;

but she still couldn't understand why everybody thought he was going to lose. As far as she could judge, it was the other way about. Not, she reassured herself, that she knew the first thing about all the technical stuff – Venart had tried to explain some of it; she'd put up with a few minutes of fleches and mandrittas and Zweyhenders and the like before announcing that it all sounded rather like hockey, only sillier and slightly more dangerous. No; if she was going to place a bet it'd be on the shorter man. She asked herself why, and finally decided that it was because the other man looked brash and arrogant, which meant he was more likely to get careless.

I hope the short man wins, she said to herself. *Because*.

Then it all started to get rather violent; they stopped dancing round and began lunging at each other, and in the excitement Vetriz forgot for a while how silly it all was and leant forward in her small seat. She wanted to shout encouragement, as if it was a horse race; but everyone else was sitting absolutely still and quiet. A strange lot, these; where's the fun in going to a show and not being allowed to yell?

'Won't be long now,' Venart whispered, with the calm assurance of an old hand. (He'd been to precisely three of these performances, as she well knew, but that was Venart for you; probably what made him such a good merchant.) 'He's getting tired, look.'

Vetriz looked, and briefly wondered if they were watching the same fight. Not that she knew or cared to know the first thing about it; but she guessed that what her brother took for exhaustion was actually the short man cleverly moving into the centre of the floor, making the other fool do all the moving about. That, she reckoned, was experience over arrogance. The tall man was also starting to slash with the edge rather than lunge with the point, which she took for desperation. Yes, she agreed; probably won't be long now.

The tall man aimed a terrific blow at his opponent's head, which the other man blocked neatly and with a graceful economy of movement. Vetriz decided that she approved of the man; in a silly situation he was trying to be sensible. Now, wouldn't it serve the other idiot right if, next time he tried one of those melodramatic slashes, his sword were to snap in two?

Loredan felt his chest tighten, and knew it could only be a matter of time. He sensed that Alvise had already won the fight in his mind; his intellect had lost interest in the matter, and he was no longer bothering to fence, relying on his superior speed, reach and strength and using the edge rather than the point. Quite safe; he knew as well as Loredan did that his opponent was too tired to do much by way of a convincing counterattack. It had all been over from the moment Loredan had allowed himself to be forced into the centre of the floor.

He wasn't even reading the cuts any more, he realised; instead of anticipating them and trying to work out where the blow was going to fall, all he had time for was the instinctive parry, too much of a reflex after so many years to fail him completely, but merely prolonging a fight that could only have one outcome. Sooner or later Alvise would deceive him with a feint, and that would be that.

Alvise feinted high left, drawing Loredan into a backhand parry off the back foot. As he moved into position, he knew he'd got it wrong; the true blow would be directed at his knee and he didn't have the time to do anything about it. Damn, he thought calmly, observing Alvise's sword move as if he was watching from up in the gallery and not down here on the floor. A despairing reflex jerked him round, his left shoulder going forward as his right leg scraped back. The sword missed his knee by the thickness of a shoe-sole; and ten years in the business made him realise that Alvise was now out of position and vulnerable. He couldn't spare the time to look where he was hitting; he cut at where he remembered Alvise's neck to have been, and hoped he wasn't making an even bigger mistake himself.

He hit something.

First, get out of danger – footwork, body movement,

distance between him and the other man, sword back into guard, and then spare the time to see if the other man's still got his head on.

Yes; but there was a fat bubble of blood swelling out of the side of his jaw, and he was stepping back, making time and distance. Immediately, Loredan lunged; a defensive move, more a prod than anything else, just to push him back a little further. Alvise turned the blow, but clumsily. *He doesn't like the pain*, Loredan realised. *Fancy that.* He lunged again, this time rather less half-heartedly. The reply was somewhat more proficient, but still defensive. Alvise was now in the middle of the floor.

Quite suddenly, Loredan saw how it might be done. He lunged a third time, deliberately opening his left side by leaning his left shoulder over. He lunged low, so that Alvise would counterthrust high, and when the other man's lunge came, Loredan quickly crossed his back foot behind his front and swayed right, dropping his sword under Alvise's and hoping he'd done enough to get out of the way. He felt something touch his flank, ignored it and swung his arm for a short cut.

And realised he'd been tricked.

Alvise had circled too, and here was his blade coming straight down, with nothing between it and Loredan's skull except the possibility of getting the basket of the hilt in the way; pointless, because the next cut ...

Never came.

There was a crack, not a loud one, and the topmost eighteen inches of Alvise's sword flew past Loredan's cheek. As he followed through, probably only half-aware that his sword had broken, Loredan turned his wrist and poked a short, weak thrust at Alvise's face. A rather feckless and silly stroke, if Alvise had had a sword to parry it with. Since he hadn't, the point of Loredan's sword hit him in the eye, killing him instantly.

'Do we applaud, or what?' Vetriz hissed.

'No.'

'Oh.'

It hadn't happened the way she'd expected; the other man's sword breaking like that made it look like pure luck, which she was sure it wasn't. No doubt all that meant was that he'd forced the other man to do something which was bound to break his sword, or else he'd have killed him anyway with the next thrust. She relaxed, and reached into her pocket for an apple.

The sight of a man being killed before her eyes hadn't disturbed her, she realised; probably because she was too far away to see facial expressions or blood. From up here it was a game, and the dead man might just as easily not be dead at all, only shamming or acting. It had been exciting, she had to admit, and it was good that she'd spotted the winner from the very start. Nevertheless; she'd seen a Perimadeian lawsuit now, which meant that with any luck she wouldn't have to see another one. As a means of settling a dispute over the late delivery of four tons of charcoal, it seemed excessive and in poor taste.

'Can we go now?'

'We should wait for the verdict.'

'Verdict? But he's ...'

'Well?'

Athli's face, staring up at him out of a bloated dream of horror and incongruous detail. She looked as white as snow.

He didn't reply. As he handed her the sword, he realised that he hadn't wiped it. So what?

'*Well?*' she repeated.

'Well what?'

Athli swallowed hard. 'What *happened*?' she demanded. 'I thought—'

'So did I,' Loredan replied, collapsing into his seat. 'Do you mind if we don't talk about it? And for pity's sake keep those bastards away from me. If they come over here, I swear I'll kill them.'

Athli gave him a horrified look, and hurried away to fend

off the charcoal people. Probably come to complain about the stress of watching him nearly get killed; good reason for docking twenty per cent off the bill.

He thought about Alvise's sword breaking. Just my luck, he reflected; two-thirds of the takings were now just so much scrap metal, just as their owner was so much meat. Who'd have thought the hilt of an old army broadsword could snap the blade of a top-quality law-sword? It only went to show something he couldn't currently be bothered with.

Interesting, though; a tiny flaw in the steel, a bubble or a speck of grit or crap that had somehow been missed by the smith's hammer, can reverse the outcome and over- turn justice. He could feel that there had been something there that shouldn't have been; something small and not accounted for, something somehow *unfair*.

Probably, he decided, I cheated.

'I got rid of them,' Athli said, flopping down beside him. 'They said—'

'I don't want to know.'

Athli nodded. 'Quite right. Large drink?'

Loredan shook his head. 'I think I'd like to go somewhere and lie down,' he replied. 'And then I'm quitting the business. Permanently.'

'Large drink.'

'Oh, all right then, large drink. And *then* I'm quitting the business.'

'You know,' Athli said, pouring wine out of the pewter jug, 'for a moment there I really thought you meant it.'

'I did,' Loredan replied. 'And I do.' He shifted his hand on the pad of wool he was pressing against his side. The bleeding had stopped long since, thanks to a smear of brandy and a few winds of cobweb from the rafters of the tavern, but for some reason he didn't want to stop the pressure on the cut, as if he felt it ought to be far worse than it was. 'Too old and not enough natural ability. I think it's high time I did something else.'

Athli looked at him over the rim of her cup. 'Such as what?'

'I'm not sure.' Loredan carefully nipped a small fly out of his wine. 'The obvious thing would be to start up a school.'

'You could do that, certainly,' Athli replied. 'Mind you, there's a difference between knowing the moves and being able to teach them to other people.'

'Well, it's that or setting up as a clerk. Would I make a good clerk, do you think?'

Athli shook her head. 'You'd be hopeless at it,' she said. 'You'd insult all the clients, for one thing. Also, you don't realise how much hard work's involved. Take me, for instance. I was up an hour before dawn, dictated twelve letters before breakfast, then out to meetings till it was time to come and collect you. And this afternoon I've got more letters to write, accounts to do, pleadings to draft—'

'All right, you've convinced me. All that reading and writing'd drive me mad, not to mention the getting up early in the morning. If I'd wanted to get up early in the morning, I'd never have left the—'

He broke off, clearly embarrassed. Athli was intrigued.

'Go on,' she said. 'If you'd wanted to get up early you'd never have left the farm. Am I right?'

Loredan grimaced and nodded. 'Yes,' he said. 'Horrible life, glad to be rid of it. So—'

'Well, well,' Athli purred, amused. 'So you're a farm boy really, are you? Honestly, I'd never have thought it. I'd have been prepared to bet money you'd never been outside the walls in your life.'

Loredan kept his face completely blank. 'Once or twice,' he said. 'My father had a small manor in the Mesoge. He was only a tenant, of course. Do you mind if we change the subject?'

Athli shrugged, slightly offended. 'If you like,' she said. 'I was just interested, that's all.'

Deliberately, Loredan refilled his cup and drained it, letting a few red tears trickle down his chin. 'Anyway,' he said, 'that's enough about that. So if you reckon I couldn't

make a living as a clerk, it looks like it'll have to be teaching.'
He sighed. 'It'd have been nice to have had an option or two
which weren't something to do with this loathsome
profession,' he said. 'Trouble is, I can't do anything else.'

'Open a tavern?'

'Too much like hard work.' He smiled. 'Plus I don't
actually know how you go about innkeeping. Isn't that
what old time-served soldiers are supposed to do when
they retire from the wars?'

'In theory, yes, though generally it's their wives and
daughters that do the work.' Athli grinned. 'My uncle ran an
inn for a while after he retired from the sea. He did very
well, got bored, sold the place at a profit and bought
another ship.'

'Is that a hint? I'll have you know I can't swim.'

'Neither could my uncle. The general idea is to avoid
putting yourself in a position where you have to.'

Loredan shook his head. 'Too dangerous,' he said. 'You'd
have to be out of your mind to spend your life entirely
surrounded by water.'

Athli wasn't listening, being too busy eavesdropping on
the conversation at the table behind them. Loredan
scowled, then tried to listen too.

'Don't be so obvious,' Athli hissed at him. 'It's embarrassing.'

'Look who's talking. Go on, then, what're they talking
about that's so interesting?'

'You, actually. They've just come from the court.'

'Oh.'

'Foreigners.'

'Ah. That would explain it.'

Loredan craned his neck and took a closer look. He saw
a long, skinny man with a thin face and high cheekbones,
and a girl who was almost certainly his twin sister. On her,
the shared features looked rather better.

'Don't be silly,' the man was saying. 'If his sword hadn't
snapped like that he'd have carved your man up like a roast
hare. Never seen a bigger fluke in all my born days.'

'Venart—'

'Not to mention a miscarriage of justice,' the man continued. 'He was totally outclassed in every department. The other man was just playing with him, could've finished it long before if he'd wanted to. Serves him right for taking pity on the old buffer, I suppose.'

'Venart—'

'Amazing, really, that he's still fighting at his age. I mean, it's supposed to be a highly competitive business, only the best survive and all that. Dammit, I could've made a better job of it than he did with one hand tied behind my—'

'Venart, he's sitting behind you.'

The man froze as if he'd just put his foot in a trap. Loredan found that he was looking the girl straight in the eyes. He turned away.

'Shit, Vetriz, why the devil didn't you *say*—'

'I tried to, idiot. You'd better apologise quick.'

'He can't have heard me.'

'Of course he did. You were braying like a donkey.'

'I do not bray like—'

'Well, if *you* won't, I suppose I'll have to.'

'Vetriz! For pity's sake, what d'you think you're—'

The girl stood up and walked over to Loredan's table. Athli put her face in her hands, trying desperately not to giggle, while Loredan suddenly found the toes of his boots irresistibly fascinating.

'Excuse me.'

Loredan looked up. 'Yes?' he said.

The girl smiled sweetly and Loredan, who up till then had found the whole business mildly amusing, started to feel irritated, as he always did in the presence of deliberate charm. 'I'd just like to apologise for my brother,' she said. 'You see, we're strangers here, and—'

'Forget it,' Loredan said. 'Besides, he was quite right.' He made a show of turning away and pouring more wine, and effect that was spoilt by the jug being empty. But the girl didn't seem to have noticed. Foreigners, he thought, and shot a rescue-me glance at Athli, who ignored it.

'He had no idea he was being so tactless,' the girl went on. 'Honestly, I'm ashamed of him sometimes. He's always doing things like that.'

Loredan gave her an unfriendly smile. Her accent was beginning to grate on him. 'Really,' he said, 'it doesn't matter. Athli, what time did you say that appointment was?'

'What appointment?'

'You know, the appointment on the other side of town.'

Athli made a faint snorting noise and shook her head. 'News to me,' she managed to say.

'The least he can do is buy you a drink,' the girl said, and waved to her brother, who was doing his best to be completely invisible behind an empty cider jug. 'Venart,' she called out, 'buy these people a drink.'

Venart got slowly to his feet, privately swearing his best commercial oath that this was the last time he took his sister anywhere. She'd never dream of behaving like this at home; the sooner they got back to the Island the better. He shuffled away, ordered a large jug of wine and reluctantly joined his sister.

'That's very kind of you,' Athli was saying. 'Do please join us.'

Loredan glowered at her and tried to kick her under the table, but she moved her feet out of the way. 'Yes, sit down, please,' he grinned in as hostile a tone as he could manage at short notice. 'My name's Loredan and this is my clerk, Athli.'

The girl looked slightly surprised. 'Your clerk?' she repeated.

'That's right. I'm an advocate and she's my clerk.' He realised that the girl had assumed Athli was his wife. He wished both of them would go away.

'I see,' the girl said, settling herself down opposite him. 'My name's Vetriz and my brother's Venart. We're from the Island.'

'Here on business?'

Vetriz nodded. 'Venart's showing me the ropes,' she said.

'It's my first time abroad. Our father left the ship and the stock to both of us equally, and I said I thought it was time I started pulling my weight.'

'Really.' Loredan did his best to sound bored. He did it very well. 'I suppose you've been doing the rounds of all the sights while you've been here.'

'Oh, yes,' the girl replied cheerfully. 'That's why we were in the court today. Venart said I couldn't think of coming to Perimadeia and not seeing the courts.'

'I hope you enjoyed the show,' Loredan said grimly. The girl's ability to miss undertones was obviously outstanding, because she nodded enthusiastically.

'Very much indeed,' she said. 'Quite thrilling. Actually, that's what we were arguing about just now. Venart thinks he knows all about everything, you see, and I was telling him I knew you were going to win from the very start.'

'You were wrong,' Loredan said. 'Like he said, it was a fluke.'

'Really?' The girl looked surprised. 'I'm sure you're just being modest.'

'I have a great deal to be modest about.'

Vetriz thought about that for a moment, then laughed. 'You do surprise me,' she said. 'I thought you made it all look very easy, though I don't suppose it is really.' She hesitated for a moment, then went on. 'So the other man's sword breaking like that was pure chance, then?'

Loredan caught Athli's eyes; she wasn't giggling any more. He decided to make her suffer a little by carrying on with the conversation.

'Pure chance,' he said. 'Although it's something that does happen from time to time with the swords we use in court. The blades are much thinner than ordinary swords – sorry, I'm being technical, but it's all to do with how the core is tempered and joined to the edges. If the core gets cooked up too much in the brazing, you can get brittle spots. Hit one of those and the blade just snaps off.'

'I see,' Vetriz replied. 'I only asked because just a second or so before it broke I had the strangest sort of feeling that something like that would happen. Odd, don't you think?'

Loredan shook his head. 'Like I said, it happens now and again. It's something you have to learn to expect. Like death,' he added melodramatically. Athli gave him a come-off-it look, of which he took no notice.

Vetriz's eyes widened. 'Are all these duels to the death, then?' she asked.

'All except wills and divorce. Strictly speaking they come under a different jurisdiction, though in practice they're heard in the same court in front of the same judge. Goes back to the time when the priests had their own courts, and probate and family actions were heard there.'

'I thought you didn't have any gods,' Vetriz objected.

'We don't. But we used to.'

'I see. Did you get rid of them, or did people just stop believing?'

Loredan shrugged. 'A bit of both, I think,' he said. 'Religion gradually started being less popular, and that allowed the emperors to step in and confiscate ecclesiastical property when they needed money. And even when they didn't, as I understand it. Anyway, once they'd lost all their gold and silver and land, there wasn't much point in being priests any more, so the whole thing just ground to a halt.'

Venart, who had been sitting still and quiet, thought of a way to end the ordeal. 'Excuse me,' he said, 'but didn't you get hit during the fight?'

Loredan nodded. 'Nothing much,' he said. 'As you pointed out, I was very lucky.'

'Shouldn't you get it seen to?' Venart asked earnestly.

As he spoke, Loredan realised the cut was bleeding again. He looked up sharply, then nodded. 'You may be right,' he said. 'If you'll excuse us ...'

The girl looked disappointed. 'Well,' she said, 'it was lovely meeting you. When I get home I shall tell everyone we had a drink with a real Perimadeian fencer.'

Loredan smiled through his cringe. 'You do that,' he said. 'Have a safe journey.'

When Loredan and Athli had gone, Venart took a deep breath. Vetriz forestalled him.

'It was your fault,' she said. 'I tried to warn you, but you wouldn't listen.'

'I might have known it was all my fault,' her brother sighed. 'Let's get safely back to the inn before you can do any more damage. And don't you ever—'

'It's strange,' Vetriz interrupted. 'I did know he was going to win, honestly. He was quite an ordinary man once we started talking to him.'

'I don't know,' Venart replied. 'I heard him get at least three words in edgeways. By my reckoning that makes him some kind of hero.'

Vetriz ignored that. 'Right,' she said. 'Let's go down to the cutlery market, and you can teach me how to buy copperware. I thought you said we had a lot to get through today.'

Alexius looked up from his book. 'Well?' he said.

'He won.'

The Patriarch nodded briefly, closed the book and laid it endways on the lectern shelf. 'That's all right, then,' he said. 'Come in and have a cup of cider.'

At the word *cider*, Gannadius' lip curled slightly. 'Not for me,' he replied. 'It was a strange business,' he went on, sitting down on the cell's one plain chair. 'Sheer luck, at the finish. Alvise had him at his mercy, and then his sword just snapped.'

'We made a good defence,' the Patriarch replied. 'I just hope we weren't too obvious about it.'

Gannadius shook his head. 'That's the point,' he said. 'I don't think it was us. Or at least,' he added, stroking his short beard, 'not just us. I'll swear I could feel another signature—'

'Oh, come now,' Alexius interrupted. 'You know what I think about that sort of thing.'

His colleague furrowed his brow. 'It's a matter of opinion,' he conceded. 'For myself, I'm morally certain I could detect something else there apart from our defences. And before you lecture me about gratuitous mysticism and the doctrine of economy of effect, I'm basing this purely on observation. I think our defences were working on him alone, and as a result he was able to keep hopping about warding off good strokes with bad ones. Alvise's sword breaking was something quite other.'

Alexius nodded. 'Well, of course. It affected Alvise, presumably quite drastically.' He considered for a moment. 'Somebody else's curse on Alvise, perhaps?' he suggested.

'It's possible. But maybe curse is putting it too strongly. My sense of it was that it was just a little touch; not because it was a little power, more that it was a trivial application of it. A gentle nudge rather than a sharp blow, if you follow me.'

Alexius leant back against the wall and stared at the mosaics on the ceiling. Without realising, he began to count the stars. 'That would be a highly unusual phenomenon,' he said. 'If this power was as great as you're suggesting, the reaction must be terrible. Who would risk that for the sake of a gentle nudge, as you put it? If I was letting myself in for a high-level reaction, I think I'd want to slam down on the victim like a sledgehammer.'

'That occurred to me too. But what if it's a natural?'

Alexius' eyes narrowed. 'An unconscious action,' he said thoughtfully. 'It's possible, I suppose, though the phenomenon is mercifully rare. My ex-student, perhaps.'

Gannadius shook his head. 'You'd have noticed it in her, surely. You'd never have overlooked a power like that.'

'It could be very deeply rooted,' Alexius ventured, rubbing his shin to clear the pins and needles. The bed in his cell was uncomfortable enough when used for its ordained purpose. Using it as a chair was a foolhardy act. 'But no, I think I'd have noticed. And besides,' he added as a thought struck him, 'if she'd had any real power of her own, she'd have stopped me before I got the curse wrong. And there'd have been little telltale traces of her malice already present when I got there. I think we can rule her out. But the idea of a natural at the court today is a sound one. I can just imagine someone in the crowd rooting for the underdog, visualising the sword breaking, the underdog saved and exalted; it would be purely instinctive—'

'Quite.' Gannadius stood up, walked a few paces in a circle, and sat down again. 'In which case,' he went on, 'doesn't it complicate things even more? If we have to go back into your visualisation again, who knows what we'll find when we get there?'

Alexius lay back on the bed and closed his eyes, trying to clear his mind. *Above all, keep a sense of proportion.* 'The consequences,' he said. 'Let's think it through, shall we, before we lose our sense of proportion. The worst that can happen—'

'Is that the curse will come back directly on you,' Gannadius interrupted peevishly, 'with dire consequences for you and, by implication, your colleagues. The Patriarch of Perimadeia, killed by one of his own curses—'

'How would anyone know that?' Alexius objected.

'My dear fellow, perfectly healthy, well-fed men don't just curl up and die for no reason.'

'Tell them I'd been ill for some time. Natural causes. A merciful release, in fact.' He opened his eyes. 'You really think it might come to that?'

'My dear fellow—'

Alexius sat up and swung his legs to the floor. 'I think it's time I was perfectly frank with you, Gannadius. I don't understand this.'

'Alexius, you're the Patriarch of—'

'Yes, I am. By definition I know more about the operation of the Principle than any man living. And I don't understand how the wretched thing *works*. And neither do you,' he added, before Gannadius could speak. 'The sum of our knowledge – our combined knowledge, mind you – is that it does work. It's taken us our joint lifetimes studying the work of thousands of philosophers and scholars over hundreds of years, but we know that it works. That's it, the extent of our knowledge. Controlling it's another matter entirely.'

'Yes, but—'

'And now,' Alexius went on, 'there seems to be evidence that there's a natural in the city who *can* control it. Probably,' he added bitterly, 'quite instinctively and possibly without even realising what he's doing. In addition, just to add a little human interest, there's a curse of my making charging around the city out of control and apparently hell-bent on attaching itself to *me*.' He bit his knuckles savagely. 'Do you know, if only we'd confined our studies to mathematics and ethical speculation, which is after all what we're *supposed* to be doing—'

'Yes, but we didn't. Or at least, *you* didn't.'

'You were only too pleased to get involved.'

'All right.' Gannadius rubbed his face with his hands. 'This isn't helping. If we can't control this problem, do we know anybody who can?'

Alexius sighed. 'As you yourself pointed out just now, I'm the Patriarch of Perimadeia. And you're the Archimandrite of the City Academy. Asking for help's a luxury we gave up when we accepted the promotion.'

'The natural,' Gannadius said suddenly. 'Maybe *he* could put it right.'

'But didn't we just agree he probably doesn't even know he's doing it? Even if we could convince him that he's got the power, there's no reason to believe he can do it on demand.'

'We don't appear to have any other options.'

'True.' Alexius slumped, his chin on his chest. 'But how do we find this natural of yours? We can't very well wander through the city until we find a miracle.'

Gannadius thought for a long time. 'Actually,' he said, 'I don't see what else we *can* do.'

'But that could take years. And I haven't got …'

'I know,' Gannadius said. 'And there's more, if you think about it. You're assuming the natural's a citizen; what if he isn't? What if he's a foreigner, here on business and due to leave in a day or so? Or perhaps he's already left.'

'There's no reason to think that.'

'Isn't there? Ask yourself: if he's a citizen, someone who lives here permanently, why haven't we come across his work before? The odds must be against this being the first manifestation of his power.'

'It could be.'

'Yes, but the odds are against that. A power so strong that it gives effect to a hardly conscious wish—'

'That was only theorising.'

'And my observation too, remember. I was there, in the court.'

'That's true.' Alexius groaned. 'Go on, then, you suggest something.'

Gannadius shrugged his shoulders. 'Apart from combing the streets, I can't think of anything. And of course there's no guarantee whatsoever—'

'A trap,' Alexius said suddenly. 'No, not a trap as such. A lure. Something likely to provoke him into using the power, or make the power happen without him doing anything consciously. Flush it out into the open.'

'Splendid idea. How do you propose going about it?'

Alexius sniffed, then blew his nose. 'I don't know,' he confessed.

Gannadius leant forwards, his chin cupped in his hands. 'There must be someone we can ask,' he said.

'How many times have I got to tell you—?'

'It's a speciality,' Gannadius replied. 'We need a specialist. How many students of the Principle are there in this city? Thousands. There must be one of them who's made a study of this little corner of the subject. Everyone has to study *something*.'

'So we hold a conclave, tell all our people we're in desperate trouble, and ask if anyone happens to know the answer. Please, Gannadius.'

'Obviously we'd have to be circumspect about it. We could issue a paper full of mistakes and wait to see who takes issue with it.'

'Fine. Have you any idea how long that'd take? And suppose the natural's a foreigner, as you suggested, and all set to leave the city. We simply don't have time to do this properly.'

'Guess, you mean?'

'Educated guess. A trap to catch a natural.' Alexius gazed over his steepled hands at the chandelier moorings in the middle of the floor. 'Anything's better than sitting here bickering with each other.' He smiled painfully. 'Remarkable, isn't it? We're supposed to be *good* at this.'

'We are,' Gannadius replied gloomily. 'That's what worries me.'

CHAPTER FIVE

Loredan woke up with blood on his shirt. He examined the cut, bound it up with fresh wool and damp moss, and put on another shirt.

No bread in the apartment; so he struggled painfully into his coat (his side was stiff, and putting his arm in the sleeve wasn't pleasant), trudged down the stairs and through the maze of narrow streets to the south of the 'island' and a bakery he knew well. They were used to him there, and were no longer offended when he came in asking for mouldy bread.

'Saved some for you,' the baker's son replied. 'It's the blue kind you like, isn't it?'

He'd given up trying to explain long ago, and smiled instead as he handed over a copper quarter. The boy waved the money away. 'On the house,' he said magnificently. 'We don't get many famous people in here.'

'In that case I'll have a fresh loaf as well. What d'you mean, famous?'

The boy chuckled. 'The great Bardas Loredan, they're calling you. Made a lot of friends round here yesterday.'

'Did I? How did I manage that?'

'Bet on you, didn't we?'

Loredan raised an eyebrow. 'Neighbourly loyalty?'

'Bloody good odds, more like. Hell, if I'd known you were going to win, I'd have laid more'n a copper half. Still, at two hundred to one—'

Loredan picked up his bread. 'Sounds like you made more out of the case than I did,' he said irritably. 'Why didn't anyone tell me they were offering two hundred to one? I could have done with some of that.'

Back home, up the interminable stairs. Other fencers kept in shape by running or fooling about in the gymnasium at the Schools; all he had to do was get from the street to his front door. The loaf the baker had kept for him was admirably suited for his purpose; covered in horrible-looking blue and white spots all over one side. Carefully he scraped the best of the blue bits into the palm of his left hand with the point of his dagger, and poured them onto a fresh sheet of parchment. Then he unwound the bandage, patted the mould gingerly onto the raw cut, and tied the harness back up again. He had no idea whether this particular ritual did any good or not; he hadn't had a badly infected wound since he'd started doing it, but law-swords were usually kept clean and rust-free anyway, so perhaps it was simply coincidence. He cut a slice of the new loaf and tipped out the last half-cupful of yesterday's wine.

The business with the bread mould was something he'd learnt on the plains, a long time ago. When he'd first heard about it, he'd assumed it was just another leg-pull for the benefit of a raw recruit, a joke in the same category as mules' eggs and the legendary left-handed arrows every kid soldier gets sent to fetch from the quartermaster. In time he realised it wasn't a joke, though he shrank from using the treatment himself. The old story was that a group of wounded men who had nothing to stop their wounds with except the stale bread in a saddlebag had all healed up in record time. A likely story, Loredan felt. His own theory was that it had something to do with the similar-looking mould the plainsmen deliberately put into their evil-tasting goats' milk cheese. After all, they did have a way with unlikely sounding cures and medicines. There was one highly suspect recipe involving willow bark boiled in water that really did work against headaches, to his certain knowledge.

The plainsmen; it was the second time he'd thought about them since the fight. It was the snapping of yet another good sword that brought them to mind, and the explanation he'd given the tiresome girl at the tavern. Because they brazed the edges of their swords to the cores with some sort of solder that melted at a much lower heat, they were far less likely to muck up the temper of their blades and in consequence their swords tended not to snap. True, the plains sword was a curved single-edged affair, totally unsuitable for legal work; but the technique was presumably valid for any design. He wondered if anyone in the city knew how to use the plains method, and if so how he could find out who it was without letting anyone else know what he had in mind.

Then he remembered. Through with all that now; quitting the profession, going to do something else. He scowled, and cut another slice of bread.

He'd considered it many times before; after practically every fight these last six years. Thinking about it and actually doing it were different matters entirely. Always his excuse had been that there was nothing else he could do, no other way of making a living, too late to learn a new skill and so forth. Until yesterday, he'd managed to force himself to believe it, although he'd known for a long time it wasn't true.

The truth was that for the last ten years or so he'd been walking around with a terrible sense of being left over from the war, needing to be used up like scraps of meat or offcuts of leather. It was a stupid attitude, not to mention a dangerous one, and he despised himself for it. But he had never quite managed to face up to it, with the result that he'd carried on, a fight at a time, collecting scars on his body and cutting a thick swathe through a whole generation of advocates.

It was time to admit that it didn't work. If it was going to work, it should have done so yesterday.

Even so. Starting a school or running a tavern. All the wonders of the world are at your fingertips; all you have to do is stay alive long enough.

He put his coat back on (even more painful this time) and

toiled up the hill to the Schools. It was the last place he felt like going the day after a big case. There would be other advocates, clerks, the unsavoury hangers-on, the profession in all its glory, and he'd rather not have to make conversation and put up with a succession of left-handed congratulations. He pulled his collar up round his neck and crept in through the side door.

The number of trainers working in the Schools tended to vary, depending on a large number of factors ranging from the health of the economy to the time of year. There were six long-established and savagely expensive schools which had appropriated sections of the building and installed their own fixtures and fittings; a constantly changing pool of old men and nerve-cases who hung about the colonnades offering to make you invincible in a day, money back if you get killed within a year; and ten or twelve establishments between the two extremes providing some sort of training in arms for a vaguely realistic fee. The latter group, mostly comprising the proprietor, perhaps one assistant and a combination clerk, registrar and bursar, used the main hall and the communal fixtures, and paid a modest rent to the governors for the privilege. To start up a new school, you paid a month's rent in advance and put up a wooden board on the wall with your name under it, beneath which students could assemble at the start of each day.

On his way to the governors' office, Loredan saw someone he recognised. There wasn't time to turn round or duck behind a column.

'Congratulations.'

'Thank you,' he replied.

The man's name was Garidas. He had been an advocate for six years before losing an eye in a banking dispute; now he worked as an assistant with the second-best of the grand schools, as well as helping out with the book-keeping. His father had been in the cavalry, and Loredan had watched him die of an arrow wound one cold morning in a ruined sentry post on the plains. His last words had been a desperate plea to look after his boy, and Loredan had happened to be the nearest. He was fairly certain the dying man had thought he was talking to someone else.

'I'm not sure where that puts you in the ratings,' Garidas said. 'Alvise was somewhere around sixth, so you must be up in the top twelve.'

'Not any longer. I've retired.'

'Oh.' Garidas seemed taken aback. 'Since yesterday?'

'Since and because of. I may be stupid, but I can take a hint.'

Garidas nodded. 'It was certainly that, from what I've heard. Oddly enough, we were all set to take a party along to watch, but somehow we didn't.'

'Wouldn't have been a good example to the students,' Loredan replied. 'Classic case of the best man not winning; very offputting.'

'On the contrary. Salutary warning of the dangers of carelessness and underestimating your opponent. So what've you got planned? A life of ease and luxury?'

'As if,' Loredan said, frowning. 'No, I'm going to have a go at your racket. On my way to see the governors now, in fact.'

'Really?' Garidas grinned. 'I could put a word in for you at our place if you like.'

'No thanks. Never did fancy the idea of working for anybody else. Having to have clients was bad enough, but at least I was my own master in theory. I'll put up a board like everyone else and see what happens.'

'Best of luck.' Garidas smiled. 'I always said we never saw enough of you down here. I'll bear you in mind for any we turn down.'

Loredan nodded. Garidas probably would, at that; he'd always been very friendly, although there was no way he could have known that his fees at the expensive school he'd attended (the one he now taught at) and his living costs while he was there had all come out of Loredan's army pay and prize money. Add to that several lucrative clients Loredan had turned down to avoid having to fight him in the court, and one way or another Garidas had cost him a lot of money over the years. It would be agreeable if he could start paying some of it back after all this time by recommending a few students.

Later that morning he set off to the signwriters' district to have a board painted. Traditionally the board carried a portrait of the trainer, seated wearing his court clothes and armed with the classes of weapon he professed to teach, with his name and a tariff of charges at the bottom; lately, however, there had been a tendency to depict ex-fencers in the act of winning their most famous case, with the man himself shown rather larger than his cringing and mortally wounded opponent. Some trainers even commissioned laudatory verses, to be inscribed in gold letters all round the edge. Loredan decided he'd have to be firm about that sort of thing.

'Bardas Loredan,' he said accordingly, 'three eighths a day, standard and two-handed sword and dagger, no fancy dress.'

'Just the portrait and the fight scene?'

'No fight scene.'

'You sure?' The painter was disappointed. 'No extra for the fight scene.'

'No fight scene.'

'I do good fight scenes. They're good advertising.'

'No.'

The painter thought for a moment. 'I can do you in a radiate crown representing the protective influence of the Principle,' he said.

'Not if you expect to get paid.'

'Sit in the chair,' the painter said huffily. 'Be with you in a minute.'

He turned around and started fiddling with bottles and jars at the back of the booth. Loredan sat back and tried to relax. It was an unseasonably hot day, and the shade offered by the booth's canvas awning was pleasant. From where he was sitting he had a good view of the square that formed the main trading area of the signwriters' district. Like so many of the small specialists' enclaves of Perimadeia, it consisted of a square with a fountain in the middle, loomed over by an old and neglected statue. Round the fountain was a clutter of tents and booths, obscuring the grander frontages of the ground-floor shops. At regular intervals there were stairs up to the galleries onto which the first-floor shops opened, and thence up to the houses and workshops on the second floor. At the four corners of the square arched gateways led off to the neighbouring districts; needless to say there were shops built over the arches, so that the sides of the square presented a solid wall of commerce. In every shop on the sunlit side, a signwriter sat in the doorway, making the most of the light; because the buildings were so high, the occupants of each side could only work by daylight for a quarter of the day.

A constant procession of carts, wagons and trolleys rumbled through what clear space there was between the booths and the central fountain; except when the traffic came to a standstill and backed up, with an accompanying chorus of bad temper and traditional carters' oaths. Unlike most of the city, the signwriters' district had no one distinctive smell peculiar to its own particular trade; only the residual background smell that nobody noticed. So many people, Loredan mused, so many trades, so many different ways of making a good living or scraping a poor one, and for every useful and profitable trade a separate and suitable district, where everything necessary for production of the particular commodity could conveniently be obtained. So much order and settled existence, with every man in his proper place fulfilling his part in the whole.

In the next square lay the shops and stalls of the colourmen, who soaked seashells and walnuts, ground rust, lapis and lead to get the colours that, mixed with egg white or limewater, made the paint used in the next square over. The most skilful and aristocratic of the colourmen made the universally famous Perimadeian gold paint, grinding up oxides, mercury and tin on a marble slab, adding triple-strength vinegar and dusted lead, crushing the mess together and drawing off the result into tiny stone bottles.

In a corner of the colourmen's square were the brush-makers, a speciality within a speciality, who spent their day guillotining bristles to size and serving them to the handles, boiling up pots of glue and hammering down the ferrules. They had to walk twelve squares to get to the glue-makers' district, a part of the city people walked through as quickly as possible, their collars up around their noses against the stench of rawhide macerating in limewater. The gluemakers, on the other hand, had only to walk round the corner and over a bridge to reach the lime kilns in one direction and the tanners' and knackers' yards in the other. On their way they passed through the sawyers' quarter, where they would probably pass signwriters collecting newly sawn and planed boards from the sawmills that huddled beside what had once been a waterfall before the city people harnessed it to turn a hundred clever wheels.

All these people, all these things; and everything a part of the whole, all useless and unable to function without a score of other trades and tradesmen, all of them similarly dependent on the union and fusion of many parts. As he sat and watched, Loredan had an uncomfortable feeling of being the only thing in this city that wasn't a component, a dedicated part of something else. Yesterday, of course, it had been different; then, he had been very much a part of the business of Perimadeia, albeit the most specialised of specialists perched at the extreme edge of the process, where agreements some-times slipped their gears and the smooth running of the machine occasionally needed to be lubricated with a little blood. Foolish speculation, he knew; because as soon as he had his board and his piece of parchment from the governors allocating him a pitch, he'd have a place once again, a part to play, a function to perform in the process. It would make more sense to relish this brief interval rather than agonise over it; few men in Perimadeia ever had the chance to stand aside and spend an hour or so not participating.

'All done,' said the painter. 'You want to look before I put the varnish on?'

Loredan nodded and stood up. It turned out to be a perfectly adequate piece of commercial art, with no fight scene and no radiate crown whatsoever. He was relieved.

'Do my ears really stick out like that?'

'Yes.' The painter dipped his brush in solvent and wiped it on a scrap of rag. 'Tell you what,' he said, 'just so happens I've got this really nice set of laudatory verses, five stanzas of elegaics, cancelled order, dirt cheap. Just go nicely round the edges, look. Two quarters.'

'No.'

'Trouble with some people is, they fail to recognise the vital importance of positive marketing.'

'Tragic.'

The painter sighed and cut the beeswax round the neck of a jar of varnish. 'How about a set of five identical miniatures to hang up in places where the rich and fashionable love to congregate? Gesture of goodwill, call it three quarters?'

'You can call it what you like so long as you don't expect me to pay for it.'

'The miniatures *and* the laudatory verses for seven eighths, and I'll throw in half a yard of picture cord.'

(—From the ropewalks, three squares over to the west, where they stretch the skeins right across the square on sliding wooden pins; another trade, another hundred or so men whose lives extend just so far and no further.)

'Thanks, but no. Finished yet?'

'Give me a chance, will you?' the painter groaned. 'If you're not careful it smears for a pastime.'

And of course, Loredan reflected as the painter daubed on the varnish, there's far more to it than that. On each of these busy tradesmen depends another complex system; wives and families to feed and clothe, children needing to be taught their proper skills, have husbands or apprenticeships found for them; rent to be paid, guild fees and licences and taxes to be met, parents and parents-in-law to be supported in their declining years, burial clubs and friendly societies to be given their dues. By these subsystems each component is locked into the whole so fast that he dare not stir out of his place, so that every part of the machine needs to run smoothly for fear of destroying everything. Curious to think that in other parts of the world, people somehow managed to live without all of this. They were, of course, savages, little better than beasts, creatures who never in all their lives had their portrait painted or took a case to the courts of law; which was why they had to be kept back where they belonged, out of sight of the walls and gates of the Triple City, just in case a busy man on his way to work in the morning might chance to see them and wonder just why in hell he bothered.

'Finished,' the painter announced. 'Still be wet for an hour or so, mind. You can take it now if you like, but you'll get dust in the varnish, sure as eggs.'

'I see,' Loredan replied, nodding. 'How'd it be if I left it here for a couple of hours and then came back?'

'Fine,' said the painter, wiping his hands on a hank of flax. 'That'll be five quarters, please.'

Two hours with nothing to do. Ordinarily, he'd find a tavern (when you have time to kill, it makes sense to take it to a purpose-built abattoir), but he remembered that he didn't do that sort of thing any more. No money to waste on wine, no drinking in the middle of the day and sleeping it off in the afternoon. Well, then; he could walk back to the Schools, ask if his piece of parchment had been drawn up, be told to come back in an hour or so and still have time to get back to the signwriters' district before the varnish was dry. Instead, he strolled lazily out in the direction of the Drovers' Bridge, a part of the city he didn't often visit. Hectically successful trainers don't have time to go sightseeing during working hours, so he might as well make the most of it while he could.

''Scuse me.'

He looked round, then down. A small child, female,

slightly grubby, was pulling his trouser leg. He sighed and felt in his belt pouch for a coin.

''Scuse me,' the child said, 'but you're Bardas Loredan.'

Don't blame yourself, kid, it isn't your fault. 'That's right,' he said. 'How do you know who I am?'

'You're an advocate, aren't you?' The child said the long word like a chicken laying a hexagonal egg: slowly, carefully and with a triumphant flourish at the end. 'You're the best in the world, my dad says.'

'Was,' Loredan replied, frowning. 'What's your dad do, then? Is he an advocate?'

The girl shook her head. 'He makes barrels,' she said. 'But he likes watching law. He takes me to see law, sometimes.'

'Does he? How ... That's nice.'

The girl nodded. 'He took me to see you yesterday when you killed that man.' She beamed. 'I like going to see law, because my dad always buys me a cake to eat when I'm watching.'

'You like cakes, then?'

'Cakes are my favourite.'

He fished a copper half out of his pouch. 'Then why don't you go and buy yourself a nice cake right now? You'd like that.'

The girl shook her head vigorously. 'My dad says I shouldn't take cakes from strange men.'

Loredan sighed. 'Your dad is quite right,' he said. 'But I don't think it applies to being given money and sent to buy your own. Go on, shoo.'

The girl thought for a moment. 'I could go to my dad's shop and ask him if it's all right,' she said. 'You wait here.'

'Tell you what,' Loredan suggested. 'You go and find your dad, and take the money with you to show him. How'd that be?'

The girl hesitated, then nodded. 'All right,' she said.

As soon as she was safely out of sight, Loredan hurried across the street and dived into the nearest large building, which happened to be the city arsenal. With any luck, she wouldn't follow him in there.

Over ten years since he'd last been in the arsenal. He winced – first meeting Garidas, now this; the damned army was following him around today like a hungry dog. It didn't appear to have changed much since he'd come here with his uncle to collect twenty barrels of arrows, frequently promised and never delivered and finally having to be fetched personally. (Why was it they'd had to tussle with the Ordnance Department for every last hobnail, bow cover and biscuit?) Still a hot, dark, noisy place, with sweaty backs gleaming in the forgelight, sparks flying unexpectedly and sizzling on bare skin, huge billets of metal in transit to be sidestepped, incomprehensible shouts from men high up on scaffolding towers, the clanging of dropped tools, the thump of mechanical hammers seeping up through the paved floor. Boiling glue, burning fat, smoke, sawdust and the distinctive smell of freshly cut metal, the squeal of badly lubricated drills and lathe tools, the scudding rhythm of treadles and the scouring sound of hard-driven grindstones, the clatter of ball-peen hammers beating out sheet metal over wooden forms, the fizz of tempering. In another mood, he'd find it an exciting place; there was no lack of vitality in the midst of all this creation.

'You.'

'Me?' He glanced round but couldn't see where the voice was coming from.

'Yes, you. What d'you want?'

Loredan grinned sheepishly. 'Sorry,' he said, 'just looking around. I didn't mean to—'

'Then bloody well go and look around somewhere else. This isn't a park.'

Still he couldn't see who was talking to him; not that he particularly wanted to carry on the conversation. 'Sorry,' he repeated and headed for the door, to find his way blocked by a cart full of charcoal. He walked round it and found himself eye to eye with a short, slight young man who was holding a billet of red-hot iron in a pair of tongs about six inches from his face.

'Ah,' he said. 'Sorry.'

The young man quickly moved the iron out of the way. 'My fault,' he said in a familiar accent. 'I didn't see you with the cart in the way.'

Plainsman; all he needed. Haven't seen a plainsman in a *very* long time. Never particularly wanted to see one again. The flaming sword waggling about a few inches from his nose didn't improve matters, either. He smiled bleakly and edged his way past, not stopping until he was out in the fresh air again.

He wandered for a while until he came to the city gate; if he was going to spend the day rubbing his own nose in his inglorious past, he might as well make a complete job of it. He climbed up onto the wall and stood for a long while, thinking in general terms about a great many things, all of them now past mending. Then he found a tavern.

Strange man, Temrai thought. Quite a few of them in this city, mind; certainly more than at home. Chances are, they have better odds of surviving here. At home there wasn't much use for the weird, the feckless and the inadequate, and they tended not to live very long.

He stood beside the forge watching the colours change in a once-heated steel blade as the warmth soaked into it; from grey to yellow, yellow to dull red, to purple and finally blue, the right colour for the second quenching. Having checked that the brine bath was just nicely tepid (too cold a quench would crack the steel), he pulled the blade out of the heat and plunged it under the surface of the water. A round ball of steam lifted off the brine, the hissing reached its peak and died away, like the squeaking of a drowning puppy. Curious, the way a hot flame and lukewarm water can turn a soft, malleable piece of steel into a hard cutting edge. Not for the first time, he wondered why it worked.

They had known the answer back home. Steel is like the human heart, they said. To make a man hard enough to be useful, first you must heat him up with the fires of anger and cool him immediately in the quenching bath of fear and the awareness of his own weakness; for metal quench in brine, for men, in tears. This is only the first stage; this makes a man hard but also brittle, and as such no use as a tool, or a weapon. Now he must be heated again in the slow, careful fire of deliberate hatred, and quenched a second time in salt water; it's the second process that makes him useful, able to cut and inflict wounds but unlikely to shatter. Only men of a good temper are useful to the gods of the clan.

Having cleaned off the colour with a file, he tapped the blade sharply a couple of times against the beak of the anvil, just to make sure that the tempering hadn't upset the brazed join between blade and core, then took a pot of pumice paste and went over to the buffing wheel to start the long, tedious job of polishing. By rights this was a cutler's work, the sort of chore a bladesmith shouldn't be bothered with; but the cutler assigned to him was at home with his sick wife, and Temrai had willingly offered to cover for him. Another curiosity of the city, this. At home if a man's wife or child fell ill, it went without saying that others would do his work and bring him his share of the milk and cheese. Here, a man was lucky to lose only his day's wages if he stayed at home to look after his own. Presumably it was that way for a reason, although nobody seemed to know what it was.

Yesterday he had watched them erecting the great torsion engine that had been a month in the making; a fine machine, reckoned to be able to hurl a two hundredweight stone over three hundred and fifty yards. Most of the workers in the building had been called in to help, pulling on ropes or leaning on levers while the wooden frames were positioned and locked in place with dowels, pegs and nails. Once the frame was together and had been pronounced sound, they had wound in the rope skeins that, when twisted, gave the engine its power. Another parable? It was an easy game to play; to say that the ropes stood for the men of his clan, who having lain slack and peaceful for so long were now twisted and racked and ready to strike ... Portents and omens are all very well, but it's too easy a game to be worthwhile. Observing an eagle with a fawn in its claws flying over your enemy's army is really only nature study; now, if you saw a fawn with an eagle in its velvet-covered hooves soaring and wheeling above their standards in the early dawn, that *would* be a portent.

Still; the great engine, officially named by the Department of Ordnance *mangonel, large, stationary, number thirty-six* and known to its creators as the Hardened Drinker (it takes a long time to get it to chuck up, but when it chucks it chucks *hard . .)*, was now in place on the third mile-tower of the land wall, wet with pitch against the damp east wind and covering the last undefended blind spot; or, at least, the last blind spot apparent to the unimaginative officials from the Department. The city, in its own estimation, was now ready for anything. *Anything* would need to be fairly obtuse not to recognise so obvious a cue.

Two hours beside the buffing wheel and the blade was polished; not to the clear mirror surface he'd have liked, but good enough for government work, as his colleagues put it. It joined the rest of the week's output in a rack on the wall, ready to be hilted, assayed and placed in store; which meant being smeared with grease and packed in oily straw in a barrel along with twenty identical swords, humped into a cellar in a guard tower, and left. Temrai washed his hands, returned to his place and started again.

He made three complete blades that day and started on a fourth. 'What's the hurry?' his colleagues demanded, annoyed that he turned out half as much work again as they did. 'You know something we don't?' He didn't answer that.

After work he swept up, oiled his tools with camellia oil and tidied them away, put on his coat and walked back to the hostel. It was the cool part of the evening, the little respite between the fresh heat of the sun and the stored heat of the night, radiating out of the stone like warmth from a firebrick. An attractive time in the city; friendly light leaking out through the doors of shops and taverns, cheerful voices and the sound of music played well or badly. Wherever you went, you could see men and women walking together, in no particular direction and no apparent hurry, husbands familiarly with wives, boys tentatively with sweethearts, drunks erratically with tavern girls. At home, generally speaking, you rode or you sat down; more sensible but not so picturesque.

At the door of the hostel he saw a man in a long leather coat leaning in the shadow of the doorway. So, he thought. It was an omen, after all.

'Jurrai,' he said softly. 'Has he …?'

The man nodded. 'Peacefully,' he replied – so strange, to hear his own language again. He felt longing, regret and mild distaste, all at the same time. 'The fever, a week ago.' It occurred to the man that he'd forgotten something. 'I'm sorry,' he said. 'He was a great chieftain.'

Temrai shrugged, knowing the praise to be false. Not a great chieftain; a good one, perhaps, just as he'd been a reasonably good father, an adequate teacher. He hadn't been the sort of man the gods could make use of; put into the fire too late, cooked up too hot, likely to prove too brittle. His son, now, there was a different case.

'I suppose I'd better come home,' he said. 'Where did you leave them?'

'At the Korcul ford,' Jurrai replied. 'The flood was heavy this year – it won't be fit to cross for another week, they reckon. If we hurry, we can catch them there.'

'They won't be hard to find, even if we don't,' Temrai replied absently. He couldn't help thinking that he had work to finish here; but he hadn't. He had learnt everything he'd come to learn, more in fact. And he had worked hard, earned his wages, done some good while he was a guest in the city. A man should always try and do good wherever he goes, leave any place better than it was when he found it.

'They'll probably wait,' Jurrai said. 'There's plenty of timber there, and you'd said you'd be needing …'

'True.' He frowned. 'I suppose I'd better get ready. Did you bring a horse for me? I sold mine.'

'One each and a change,' Jurrai replied. 'We don't want to hang about.'

'Good. Right. I won't be long.'

He left Jurrai there and walked into the hostel. Strange; it felt very much like home, this huge stone wagon without wheels that never went anywhere, where you had to pay money just for the privilege of being in it. He could smell the evening bread in the oven, and the women were laying the table. A group of men, his friends, looked up from a game of dice and nodded. Under the circumstances, he hoped he'd never see them again.

The hostel keeper was stirring a large pot of soup, occasionally sipping a sample off the end of a long wooden spoon, adding a pinch or so of some herb or other with a faintly ridiculous air of precision. She smiled when she saw him, and promised it wouldn't be long.

'Actually,' he said, 'I'm not stopping. I'd like to settle up, please.'

'You're leaving?' She seemed disappointed. 'Oh. Nothing wrong, is there?'

'My father's died.'

'I'm sorry. Had he been ill?'

Temrai nodded. 'I'd better be going as soon as I can.'

The hostel keeper laid down the spoon. 'I expect your mother will be glad to see you,' she said.

'She died,' Temrai replied. 'When I was young.'

'That's sad. So you'll be the head of the family now, I suppose.'

'That's right.'

'Large family?'

'Quite large. Sorry, but I really must be going. How much do I owe you?'

The woman shook her head. 'That's all right,' she said. 'It's only two days since last rent, have that on me. Would you like me to put you up something to eat for the journey?'

Temrai refused politely; she insisted; eventually, just to be able to get away, Temrai accepted half a loaf, a sausage and two apples. 'It's been nice having you here,' she said, handing him a basket covered with a piece of clean sacking. 'Make sure you come and see me if you're ever in town again.'

'I might be coming back,' Temrai said. 'Fairly soon.'

'I'll look forward to that. Have a safe trip.'

'I will. Thanks for everything.'

'You're very welcome.'

Feeling like a murderer, Temrai gathered up his few bits and pieces in a bundle and managed to get out without talking to anybody else. *Please,* he prayed silently, *be among the first to leave, when the dust clouds appear in the east and everyone starts to panic. I mean you no harm, really. It's just—*

'Ready?' Jurrai asked, handing him the reins of a tall, neat horse.

'Ready,' he replied.

'I nearly forgot. You get what you came for?'

'Yes.'

Jurrai chuckled. 'That's good,' he said. 'Next time you see this lot, it'll all be rather different.'

Temrai gritted his teeth. 'Let's hope so,' he said.

They mounted up (strange, the sensation of sitting on a horse again, after all this time) and rode slowly through the streets, fearful for their horses' legs among the ruts and cobbles. It was a rare sight to see mounted men in the city, and the evening promenaders were in no hurry to get out of the way and let them through. Temrai felt foolish and conspicuous, towering over his fellow citizens (no, no more of that) like some great nobleman taking part in a procession, his tall, fire-breathing plains stallion pawing and shaking his head with impatience behind a little, fat, bald baker and his circular wife, out for a leisurely stroll. They could have taken all night to reach the gate, except that the baker and his wife stopped to buy pancakes and let them through.

They were in sight of the gate when a man came out of a tavern, not looking where he was going, and walked directly in front of Temrai's horse. He yanked the reins hard back and to the right, slewing the horse round; it was enough to save the fool drunkard from serious injury, but the toecap of Temrai's boot (iron-capped, necessary precaution for workers in a place where there were all manner of heavy things waiting to fall and crush unshielded toes) slammed into the side of the man's head, knocking him to the ground. Temrai cried out in alarm and slipped off the horse, throwing the reins to Jurrai.

'Are you all right?'

The man rubbed his head. 'No thanks to you,' he grunted. 'Why don't you look where you're damned well going?'

His voice was slurred, the edges rounded by a few too many drinks; just the condition, Temrai knew, that led to most of the fights in this city. He apologised, therefore, and helped the man to his feet, brushing mud and street muck off his coat and picking up the flat bundle the man had been holding. Unfortunately, the horse had trodden on it.

'You clown,' the man exclaimed, 'look what you've done to my sign! Go on, just look at it!'

The light streaming from the tavern doorway revealed a smart new portrait, very impressive except for the horseshoe-sized hole where the man's face should have been. Temrai noticed the man's hand drop to his belt, where a sword would hang. Fortunately, there wasn't one.

'That's terrible,' Tamrai muttered. 'I'm so sorry. Please, you must let me pay for the damage.'

'Too bloody right I will,' the man snarled back. 'Not to mention loss of earnings, pain and suffering and careless handling of a horse on a public thoroughfare.'

That, Temrai felt, was a little excessive coming from a drunk who'd tried to walk under his horse; but the significance of the sign, the legal terminology, the instinctive hand to the belt, weren't lost on him. Drunk or sober, right or wrong, he didn't particularly want to find himself trading knife thrusts with a professional advocate. 'Of course,' he said hurriedly. 'How much does that come to?'

The drunk was looking at him curiously, his sodden brain doing its best to interpret the promptings of some half-forgotten memory.

'You,' he said. 'You're the plains boy from the arsenal.'

'That's right,' Temrai replied; and then his own memory found the right place. 'I saw you there this afternoon. You came in and went out again.'

The man nodded, and with relief Temrai sensed that the moment of danger was over. A drunk might stab an offensive stranger in an outburst of drunken fury, but not an acquaintance. The man's face relaxed into a sort of grin.

'You've ruined my sign,' he said. 'Took me all day to get that bloody thing done. If you only knew how *boring* it is having yourself painted ...'

'I can imagine.'

The man shrugged. 'Never mind,' he said. 'Look, I'll tell you what. I'll forget about the sign and all that stuff, if you'll do me a favour. Agreed?'

Temrai hesitated. He was in no position to promise favours now that he was leaving the city; on the other hand, to refuse would undoubtedly infuriate the drunk and land Temrai in a worse mess than he'd been in before. 'Um,' he said.

'Swordsmith, aren't you?'

'That's right.'

'Thought so.' The man nodded slowly. 'Swordsmith from the plains. You'll know all about brazing edges to cores so they won't snap, then.'

'Yes,' Temrai said. 'How do—?'

'Friend,' the drunk said solemnly, 'you could just be the man to save my life. See, I'm an advocate. Fencer-at-law. Or was, till today; giving it all up, going to be a trainer. Good life, training, 'cept for the getting up in the mornings. Anyway, still going to need a good sword that won't bust on me in the middle of a fight. Two perfectly good swords I've had bust on me lately,' he added bitterly, 'and seen another go the same way, close to my face as you are.' It was true that he was leaning up close; even with his limited experience, Temrai could identify two of the cheaper popular vintages on his breath. 'And then I thought, those buggers out on the plains, they know how to make swords that don't bust, or they did a dozen years back. So that's what I want you to do for me, and we'll say no more 'bout the busted sign. Deal?'

Temrai's face was completely void of any expression, as was his voice when he replied, 'Deal.' The drunk didn't seem to have noticed.

'Good stuff,' the drunk said, smiling, and he slapped Temrai mightily on the back. 'Loredan's my name, Bardas Loredan. Find me at the Schools any time. You ever want to learn fencing, do you a special deal.'

'Thank you,' said Temrai quietly. 'Crossing swords with you would be a pleasure.'

The drunk was now full of good humour; he held Temrai's stirrup for him as he mounted, and waved him cheerfully on his way before dumping the ruined sign in the gutter, turning round a couple of times as if uncertain of where he was going, and finally heading back into the tavern. Temrai rode on in stony silence until they were past the gatekeeper and on the bridge.

'What was all that about?' Jurrai asked.

'That man,' Temrai answered, 'wanted me to make him a sword.'

Jurrai shrugged. 'More fool him.'

Temrai turned round in his saddle, and Jurrai saw by the torchlight reflected on the water that there were tears running down Temrai's face. 'Jurrai, do you realise who he was?'

'A drunk. Oh, yes, an advocate, whatever that means. I got the impression he's some sort of hired fighter.'

'That's what he is now. Think, Jurrai; a man who knows about silver soldering, says he learnt about it twelve years ago. Work it out, Jurrai.'

A moment's thought; then Jurrai swore under his breath. 'Maxen's raiders,' he muttered. 'You think he was one of them?'

'Twelve years, Jurrai. Someone who learnt about silver soldering on the plains. And he was no merchant, believe me.'

'Dear gods. If I'd been you I'd have killed him where he stood.'

Temrai shook his head and smiled. 'He'll keep. Actually, he did me a good turn. Do you know, I've been here so long I'd nearly forgotten what I came for.'

Jurrai clicked his tongue. 'I doubt that's possible,' he said.

'I did say nearly,' Temrai replied. (Forget Maxen? No, he was a stain that couldn't be shifted, no matter how often you washed or how hard you rubbed with the pumice. Twelve years and he was still there, sunk into the fibres, along with the smell of burning bone and hair, like the lingering scent of cedar in a clothes-press.) 'Everyone else in the arsenal takes their shirt off to work, because of the heat. Not me.' He half-wriggled out of his coat and pulled his shirt down over one shoulder, to reveal the edge of a shiny white scar. 'I didn't fancy explaining where that came from, not when we were all getting along so well.' He slipped his shirt and coat back on – Jurrai noticed his slight clumsiness; been out of the saddle too long – and pulled his collar tight around his neck, then turned round to look at the lamps burning on either side of the gateway. 'I'm going to bar those gates from the outside when I burn the city, Jurrai, it's the least I can do. It's a pity,' he added, in the tone of voice of someone throwing out a still-wearable pair of trousers, 'I quite like them, really. But it's got to be done, and on balance I'd rather it was me that did it than some stranger.'

Jurrai looked at him, a little apprehensively. 'It's what your father would have wanted,' he said awkwardly.

'I dare say,' Temrai replied wearily. 'He was bloodthirsty when he was young, weak when he first became the chief, and pretty well bunged up with frustration and hate the rest of his life. *He* could never have burnt Perimadeia. But I will.'

His companion regarded him steadily. 'You reckon?' he said.

'Oh, yes. Now they've been kind enough to show me how.'

CHAPTER SIX

        Trawl the streets of the city, Gannadius had said. Walk down every thoroughfare and through every square till you feel that tug on the reins that means you've found the natural. It's the only way.

Quite possibly true, Alexius muttered to himself, sitting on the steps of a fountain with his left boot in his hand, but my feet hurt. And what they'll say if ever they find out I've spent the last three days walking the streets…

Was it possible, he wondered, that he'd got the whole thing completely out of proportion? True, he was still getting the sudden attacks – blinding headaches, sweating fevers, sharp pains in his chest and legs, vomiting and diarrhoea – but they were becoming less severe and less frequent, and he was at last beginning to sleep again, now that the dreams were fading. Triple-reinforced wards and protective fields were probably helping, though the strain of keeping them up was possibly worse for him than the attacks themselves, and even then he had the feeling they wouldn't have done any significant good without Gannadius working virtually full-time on them as well. It was more likely, he felt, that the curse itself was slowly starting to decay, helped no doubt by Loredan's miraculous survival of the fight with Alvise and the fact that he'd apparently quit the profession. As he became steadily less vulnerable to the curse, so it declined for lack of something to feed on. Indeed, Alexius was toying with the idea of trying to break it up altogether; feasible, he felt certain, although of course it had never been done before.

No, he reflected, pulling the boot slowly over his heat-swollen foot, that's not the way. The only real hope lay in finding this dratted natural, and that was proving harder even than he'd expected. Maybe he had left the city, as Gannadius was sure he had. Alexius devoutly hoped he hadn't; having to put up with all this for the rest of his life wasn't an especially cheerful thought.

Wouldn't it be nice, he said to himself, if I could really do magic? I'd have a locomotion spell to carry me about, for one thing, and the hell with all this walking. Or, better still, I'd scry the pest out from the comfort of my cell and drop a thunderbolt on him. Of course, if I could do magic, I wouldn't need to be doing any of this; I'd just take the curse to bits and get rid of it, and everyone'd be happy then. Except that loathsome and elusive girl who got me into this in the first place; and her happiness no longer concerns me all that much. Should've listened to what my mother told me about talking to strange women.

In the workshop across the street, two men were building a mechanical saw, to be installed in the sawmills down by the flood stream. The blade was held vertically, linked to a waterwheel at the bottom by a crankshaft and suspended at the top from a thick stave of yew, cut like a bowstave so as to have sapwood on top and heartwood underneath; this acted as a spring, drawing the blade up to make its cut through a log fed horizontally against it along a platform of rollers. Each turn of the waterwheel drew the sawblade down again, and then assisted the cut as the crank drove it upwards on the return stroke, giving the cut the same measured force that two men would achieve on either end of a long handsaw. The two carpenters were finishing off the final stage, fitting two slanting struts to hold up the gallows on which the yew spring was mounted.

No engineer himself, Alexius could still appreciate the design, the like of which he hadn't come across before. Another new machine, then, marking an improvement, most likely leading to increased productivity and cheaper, better-sawn planks. For a brief moment he felt incredibly

jealous; why couldn't he spend his life in a craft where
things could be improved, made better by a little intelligent
thought and practical application? All over the city, men
were working on projects like this; you could see them in
every square, marking out designs in the dirt with a stick or
scratching them on the back of a board with a nail, forever
seeking a better way, more economical, more graceful,
more pleasing to the eye. But the Patriarch of Perimadeia
spent his life explaining that magic didn't work, the
Principle was largely incomprehensible, and even the
effects that could reliably be made to perform had no real
practical use. And here he was in silk and linen, while the
busy carpenters wore coarse wool and went barefoot.

Call themselves wizards? Frauds. Yah! Run the lot of 'em
out of town on a handcart.

The two craftsmen finished driving in the last few dowels,
and the older man sent his assistant to hand-crank the
wheel for a test run. Hard work, it looked like, turning the
handle; so much more sensible to make falling water do
the job. Now here, if you liked, was an example of the
Principle truly being put to good, productive use. The
young man grunted, the wood groaned under the stress,
and the wheel turned.

With an alarming crack, the yew spring snapped neatly
in two. The saw-blade, no longer supported at the top,
slowly toppled and fell sideways, ripping the crankshaft
away from the wheel and sending the younger man diving
frantically out of the way. He just made it; an inch or so
more, and it'd have landed across his shoulders. At once the
older man started swearing, and the young man swore
back, shook his fist at his master, and gave the wooden
frame a savage kick, which hurt his foot rather more than
it did the machine. They were still yelling and cursing as
Alexius, feeling rather more at peace with himself than he
had been a minute or so ago, stood up and set off on his
quest.

He was passing a locksmith's shop in the next square
over when he felt the tug. It was nothing like what he'd

expected, but it was unmistakable; an urgent pressure on his mind, like the feeling in the air when a thunderstorm is long overdue, except that it was massively concentrated in the proportion of say, cider to applejack. The sides of his head began to ache.

He stopped at once, certain that the source of the feeling was inside the shop. A glance through the doorway revealed the locksmith, an elderly man Alexius had once bought a padlock from (not him, then) and a man and a woman who were obviously foreigners. Interesting; so Gannadius' theory seemed to be correct after all.

The man was tall and thin, with high cheekbones and a friendly, slightly comical face. The woman, obviously his twin sister – he remembered something he'd read about twins and naturals a long time ago, an attractive theory about two minds with an inherent, spontaneous empathy somehow attracting the Principle, in the same way copper attracts lightning – was strikingly similar, yet at the same time beautiful where her brother was, at best, odd-looking. When Alexius glanced at her, the sides of his head throbbed painfully. So.

It would have been helpful, he realised, to have anticipated this moment and to have worked out in advance what he was going to say. There was, however, a reasonable chance that the locksmith would recognise him and greet him in a manner that would make it plain to a foreign visitor that they were in the presence of one of the local sights. He stuck his hand in his pocket, checked that he had some money with him and went into the shop.

It began well. The locksmith and the male foreigner had been engaged in some sort of complicated negotiation, and a distraction was apparently to the locksmith's tactical advantage, for he immediately broke off and made a show of welcoming his distinguished visitor, pointedly asking Alexius if the padlock he'd bought from him had been satisfactory. The words *By Appointment to the Patriarch of Perimadeia* seemed to hang in the air like sea mist in the early morning.

The foreigners exchanged glances. It was working.

'Don't let me interrupt,' Alexius said. 'I'm in no particular hurry.'

After a moment's hesitation, the foreigner and the locksmith resumed their duel, which seemed to be about a special rate for four dozen padlocks with keys and fixings. Alexius was just wondering how to start up a conversation with the female when he found it wasn't going to be necessary.

'Excuse me,' she said, 'but I was wondering. I've heard ever so much about you, and what you do. Is it really true you can do magic?'

It would have been better if his head wasn't hurting so much, but he managed to tune out the discomfort. He smiled.

'Not really,' he said. 'It's true that the philosophical and scientific researches we engage in offer us some rather abstruse insights into principles of nature that, generally speaking, the layman cannot observe for himself; in consequence, and purely incidentally to what we actually set out to do, we can perform certain, well, let's call them effects, which lay observers confuse with magic. But we can't change lead into gold or men into frogs, or fly through the air or hurl lightning.'

It took her a while to translate all that; then she looked a little disappointed. 'Oh,' she said. 'I've always wanted to meet a real magician. Oh, I'm sorry. That sounded awfully rude.'

Alexius' cue to smile avuncularly. 'Not at all,' he said. 'I've always wanted to meet one too. But the nearest I'm ever likely to get to a real magician is what we call a natural.'

'Oh? What's that?'

Out of the corner of his eye, Alexius observed the state of the negotiation; if anything, it was getting more entrenched. His head was splitting—

She's doing this. She wants to talk to me without being interrupted, so she's making the deal get complicated. How—?

'Ah,' he said. 'I wish I knew. You see, naturals are very rare, and the chances of actually encountering one are very small, at least here, in the city. We just don't seem to produce them locally.'

'I see. Where do they come from, then?'

Alexius raised an eyebrow. 'Oddly enough,' he improvised, 'a surprising number of the documented instances appear to have originated on the Island. Am I right in assuming that you—?'

The girl beamed. 'That's right,' she said, 'that's where we're from. Oh, I suppose it must be obvious,' she added, 'from our accents and clothes and such. It's odd, though, because I've never heard of any of our people being able to do magic.'

'That word again,' Alexius said. 'The point is that you could live in the same town as a natural for fifty years and never even guess. The most that a natural can do is make things happen - perfectly ordinary, everyday things, nothing anybody would notice; a slate sliding off a roof, two men falling out over the price of milk - but he would *make* them happen. Quite possibly,' he added, involuntarily massaging his temples, 'without even knowing it.'

'Fancy,' the girl said. 'So I could be one myself and never even know?'

The pain was no longer an irritation; it was downright intolerable, and it was as much as Alexius could do to keep it from showing. Even so, he couldn't help feeling that this was all too easy.

'It's possible,' he said. 'Extraordinarily unlikely, of course, simply because there are so few—'

'That you know about,' the girl interrupted. 'What I mean is, if what they do is just ordinary things, as opposed to raising storms and turning people into frogs, how would you know? Or could someone like you recognise one if you met one?'

Perhaps, Alexius wondered, the pain is a sort of diversionary tactic, to keep me so preoccupied that I won't realise I'm being led by the nose. But why would she want to?

'Never having met one, I wouldn't know. That's the point, you see; the phenomenon is so rare that next to nothing is known about it. For all I know,' he added, all too aware that potentially he was walking into the most desperate ambush – but all he wanted was for this to be over so that he could take his head away and stop it hurting – 'For all I know, every one in six Islanders, or one in twelve, or any proportion you like; perhaps all Islanders have the ability to a greater or lesser extent. It's *possible*, but of course nobody's researched the point yet. It would be an interesting study,' he added, with as much conviction as he could muster.

'Would it?' The girl looked interested, pleased. 'Then how'd it be if – No, please forget I spoke. I'm sure you're very busy.'

As he replied to the effect that if she was volunteering herself and her brother as specimens for study, he and his colleague would be only too delighted, Alexius could almost feel the hook catch in his lip. It was too late now, of course, and this damned headache—

'Assuming,' he added, 'that your brother could spare the time—'

'Oh, we hadn't got anything planned for this afternoon. Venart,' she added, nudging him in the ribs, 'we aren't busy this afternoon, are we?'

'What? Oh, no. At least, weren't we going to have a look round the second city? I thought you wanted to see the Academy and—'

'In that case,' Alexius said, and he could almost feel strings pulling him, like a wooden puppet in a children's show, 'please allow me to be your guide. There are a number of features of interest not open to the general public—'

'Oh, how wonderful!' The girl's eyes were shining, and the pain in his head— 'Oh, Venart, do let's! It'd be such fun.'

Not long afterwards, Alexius escorted his two new companions through the second-level gate. Every time he took a step, it was like jarring a broken bone. One small consolation: fairly soon, Gannadius was going to have a bad headache as well. On balance, he felt it would serve him right.

After a day's ride, Temrai was stiff and sore, although he dared not admit it. He was, after all, the chief of a nation of horsemen.

'We'll stop here,' he announced, when the pain at the base of his spine became more than he could bear. 'There's water, and we can camp under the trees.'

Jurrai shrugged. 'There's an hour more of daylight,' he replied. 'I was thinking we could make Okba ford before dark if we pressed on.'

'We'll stop here.'

'All right.' Jurrai reined in and slid off the back of his horse, landing easily on his toes. *I could do that once,* Temrai reflected in awe. *Only a few months ago, I could do that.* Instead, he waited until his companion's back was turned before levering himself off the horse and alighting awkwardly on the side of his left foot.

Interesting, he reflected; *I've known Jurrai since I was a kid and he was my father's First Rider. Gods, how I looked up to him then; and now here he is, doing what I tell him to.*

He decided to experiment.

'Jurrai,' he said, as casually as he could manage. 'Run and fill my water bottle, would you?' He held the bottle out, fully expecting a clip round the ear. Instead, Jurrai took it without a word and ran – yes, *ran*, after a hard day's ride – down to the stream. *Amazing,* Temrai thought; *I can order him about, almost as if I was my father…*

Yes. Well, just because I can doesn't mean I have to. 'It's all right,' he called out, as Jurrai set about picking up sticks for the fire. 'I'll do that. You see to the horses.'

There was a grin on Jurrai's face as he tied the hobbles and took off the bridles; *of course, he knows me as well as I know myself, should do after all these years. Except he doesn't know what happened while I was in the city. Not that there's all that much to know.*

'Well, then,' he said, once the fire was glowing (at least I can still light a fire; thank the gods for that) and they'd built the low wall of dry thorns that no traveller on the plains would think of neglecting when sleeping away from the caravan. 'You'd better fill me in on what's been happening.'

'Apart from the main thing, not much,' Jurrai replied, and at once embarked on a succinct but nonetheless interminable report that covered the state of the herd (including losses from wolves, disease, straying and beasts swept away in river crossings), old horses lost, new geldings broken in, milk yields, cheese production, the number of hides cured, tanned and in store; sundry quarrels, fights, conspiracies, adulteries, betrothals; the results of horse races, polo matches, chess games, archery tournaments and musical contests; a brief itinerary, with reports on the state of important roads, fords and mountain passes; old folk dead, children born, a few fatal accidents, injuries serious and trivial, illnesses lingering and likely to prove terminal; one man blinded for hamstringing his enemy's horse; two tents blown away by a freak wind, all losses and damage made up by special dispensation of the chief from clan reserves; an abortive raid by bandits forestalled by an observant herd-boy (duly commended for his actions and rewarded with a horse from the chief's own herd), a few arrows loosed, no stock lost or men hurt on either side.

'And that's about it,' he concluded, taking a sip of water from his bottle. 'How about you? I get the impression you got everything you went for.'

Temrai nodded. 'If I say it's going to be easy,' he said, 'the gods'll hear and it won't. Let's say I've got a reasonable idea of what's got to be done.'

'And the city?' Jurrai went on, avoiding his eye. 'What about it? What's it really like?'

'Ah.' Temrai shook his head. 'Jurrai, you just won't believe what it's really like. It's …' He hesitated. 'It's different,' he said.

'Just different?'

'*Really* different.' Temrai gestured despairingly. 'In small ways mostly, except for the really big differences, of course.'

'Lord Temrai,' Jurrai interrupted, his voice low and faintly sarcastic, 'I find it hard to believe that a mere three months among the enemy have made you forget completely how to file a coherent report.'

Temrai looked up; angry at first, then ashamed of his anger. The voice had been his father's, the soft, sardonic tone that cut more deeply than a hazel switch. He nodded abruptly.

'You're right,' he said. 'Very well, then. It'll be good practice for when we get back.' He paused, and concentrated for a moment. 'The walls of the City of the Sword on the sides that face the confluence of the two rivers are approximately forty-two feet high, eighteen feet thick at the base and fifteen at the top, so that two carts can pass each other on the walkway. There are watchtowers every hundred and fifty yards, each tower rising a further twenty-four feet above the line of the ramparts and capable of providing full cover for a dozen archers, a siege engine and a full crew of engineers. Each tower carries a store of fifteen hundred arrows and fifty projectiles for the engine, and guards the stairway connecting the rampart walkway with the ground.

'The four gates on the landward side are each flanked with bastions, capable of accommodating two hundred archers, five of the ordinary siege engines and one of the heavier sort for use against siege towers and rams. The bridges that cross the rivers end in drawbridges, and the water is something in the order of twenty feet deep, although the bottom is reasonably firm. The walls and towers are in good repair, the drawbridge mechanisms are well-maintained and adequately shielded, and the engines are frequently examined and used for target practice by permanently assigned crews ...'

Jurrai nodded. 'Carry on,' he said.

'Once inside the walls,' Temrai continued, 'an invading force would be faced with severe difficulty in making an orderly advance in the event that the lower city is diligently defended. The streets are narrow enough to be readily blocked, and the arrangement of side streets and alleys would make it a relatively simple matter for an insurgent force to be outflanked and surrounded with very little warning. Setting fire to the lower city would probably result in the insurgents being trapped and unable to escape.

'The defences are designed to be held by a relatively small number of men, and any number significantly above the optimum would most likely prove a hindrance rather than a help. I would put the optimum at roughly five thousand archers and three thousand men-at-arms, which more or less agrees with the numbers of trained men on standby at any given time. This force can be mobilised and in position within twenty minutes of the alarm being raised; there are also reserves of some ten thousand able-bodied men with the relevant training and equipment. As for military stores of all kinds, I wasn't able to get any definite information, probably because none exists; they've been stockpiling for many years, and for all practical purposes the stores can be regarded as infinite, leaving aside the daily production capacity of the city arsenal.'

'All right,' Jurrai grunted. 'But will they fight?'

Temrai nodded. 'Oh, yes,' he said. 'No question of that. They are not an overtly warlike people, but their history is full of sieges and attempted assaults both by land and sea. They are brought up from childhood to expect attacks – the most recent attempt was thirty years ago, when an armada of significant size and quality was dispatched by a coalition of states from the western cities, which was effectively destroyed by the long-range siege engines installed on the sea walls before the ships were able to come within bowshot. They claim to have sunk over two hundred vessels in the course of one day, and the claim is credible if you've seen the engines.'

'So,' Jurrai said, 'suppose you've managed to force the lower city. What then?'

Temrai nodded. 'The wall dividing the lower city from the second city is not as tall or as thick as the land wall, but the gradient on which it stands and the crowded nature of the buildings at its foot make it, if anything, a more daunting proposition. The watchtowers are of a similar pattern, and are placed at intervals of a hundred yards; they hold only a token garrison, but are fully supplied with arrows and other stores. The main granaries are all in the second city, as are the principal cisterns from which the lower city draws its water. In an emergency, there would be enough room for the entire population to withdraw to the second city should it prove necessary to evacuate, and plans for this contingency have been in existence for many years and are well-known to the citizens, although there hasn't been a full evacuation drill for some years. About the upper city I have no information, as only a few high-ranking officials are allowed to go there; there are rumoured to be large rainwater tanks and separate granaries up there, and a permanent garrison of élite troops who form the Emperor's personal guard.'

'I see,' Jurrai said, poking the fire with a long stick. 'And you reckon you've worked out a way of prising this strongbox open?'

'Not me,' Temrai replied with a grin. 'They did it themselves, years ago. Then they forgot they'd done it.' He sighed, and lay back on his saddle. 'That's the Perimadeians for you. Too clever for their own good.'

'So? Are you going to let me in on the secret, or have I got to wait till the council?'

'You'll wait rather longer than that,' Temrai replied with a yawn. 'You'll know soon enough, believe me. Actually, it's all pretty simple.'

Jurrai grunted, and broke off a handful of bread. 'Beats me how they can live on this stuff,' he said. 'It bloats you out and then you feel hungry again soon after.'

'You get used to it,' Temrai said drowsily. 'Only the rich can afford meat more than once or twice a month, and even then it's salted and spiced to buggery. You can have all the cheese you can eat for two coppers, but it doesn't taste of anything. Oh, and they eat fish.'

'So I've heard,' Jurrai replied, frowning. 'I had fish once.

Won't forget that in a hurry. They're welcome to it.'

'Theirs comes from the sea,' Temrai murmured, his eyes closed. 'Mostly it's dried and salted, or else they smoke it. You get used to that, too. It's cheap.'

'What about the drink? Wine and cider, isn't it?'

'You want to be careful of that stuff. It's evil.'

'And the women?'

Temrai snored.

'Right,' said Bardas Loredan, masking his true feelings, 'let's have a look at you.'

It wasn't an inspiring sight. A long, straggly lad of about eighteen, with a jealously tended wisp of beard on what there was of his chin; another, similar, but without notional beard; an enormous sullen boy of maybe sixteen in an obviously new and slightly-too-small set of what the prosperous farmers of Lussa thought the city was wearing this season; a small, wiry kid with a baby face who might possibly have made the grade if he was six inches taller and forty pounds heavier; a girl who stared at him; a plump young man of good family, too old at twenty-four and plainly not really interested. Great.

He took a deep breath. 'First things first,' he said. 'Names.'

In fact, he knew most of their names without asking. The huge peasant was called Ducas Valier; throw a handful of pebbles at a hiring fair in any of the market towns of Lussa, and be sure you'd hit at least three Valiers, one of them called Ducas. The lad with the beard was Menas Crestom – a city name, pottery or brickyards district, younger son of a second-generation affluent family with a depressingly misguided idea of what constituted giving a kid a good start in life. His beardless shadow was the same basic stock; Corrers were as thick on the ground in the foundries as piles of fluxed skimmings or splashes of waste metal, and a quarter of the kids his age in the city were Folas, after Folas Manhurin, champion boxer five years in a row a quarter of a century back. The wiry boy had the good eastern suburbs

name of Stas Teudel and the rich kid was inevitably a
Teo-something, though the variation was a new one to
Loredan – Teoblept Iuven. When he heard the boy's family
name, Loredan cringed. A century back, the Iuvens had
owned fifty of the best merchant ships in the bay; these days
they still lived in one of the most prestigious houses in the
second city, but their tailors insisted on something on
account before they set shears to cloth. As for the girl, she
was something nondescript that went in one ear and out
the other; with any luck, she'd answer to 'You' and a nod in
her direction.

'Next,' he said. 'Money.'

Out came the purses, from under coats, off belts or out
from where they hung round sweaty necks. Master Iuven
offered a gold five-piece, apologising smugly for not having
anything smaller. Loredan forgave him and kept the
balance on account.

'Good,' Loredan said. 'Now we can get down to business.
Who's got their own sword? Anybody?'

All except the girl, unfortunately; as offbeat a collection
of ironmongery as you'd ever expect to meet outside a
scrapyard. The peasant boy held up a two-hundred-
year-old broadsword that would have been big medicine
back in the days when men lumbered into battle under sixty
pounds of steel scales and boiled leather. A collector would
probably offer him good money for it, despite the heavy
pitting and the missing point. The three city lads proudly
offered for inspection the latest in cheap and shiny fashion
accessories – young master Teudel looked deeply offended
when Loredan took his pride and joy and bent it almost
double over his knee without apparent effort. The sprig of
the nobility had a genuine Fascanum, which Loredan
immediately told him to put away and not look at again for
six months, remembering a lean patch a while back when
he'd lived for the best part of eight months on the sale
proceeds of one of those. He could just picture the
expression on Daddy's face when the family heirloom came
home after the first day's parrying practice, with five

notches in each edge and the exquisitely chiselled lion missing off one end of the quillon.

'Fortunately,' he said, 'I took the precaution of bringing a few practice swords, which I'll issue you with when you're fit to be trusted with them. For the time being, we'll use wooden foils; with which,' he added sternly, 'it's perfectly possible, not to mention fatally easy, to put someone's eye out if you're careless.' He handed out the foils; two and a half feet of arrowshaft set in a simple wooden hilt, with a big button on the business end just in case anybody did happen to land a blow on his sparring partner. Luckily he'd managed to get a case of the things cheap; sure as anything, at least one of these idiots would contrive to break one in the course of the first day. On cold mornings he could still feel the cuff round the ear he'd had from Master Gramin for just such an offence.

It turned out to be a long day; but, by the time the Schools closed Loredan had taught his unlikely pupils the elements of both kinds of guard, the advance step and the retreat step, the crouched shuffle forwards and backwards along a straight line of the City fence, the straight-backed circular movement of the Old fence, until in spite of their natural ineptitude and individual deficiencies they bore a passing resemblance to fencers. The high-class schools, he knew very well, didn't even touch on the Old fence until the end of the first week, and even then most of their scholars tended to move like old women taken short in the middle of the night.

Of his six, he reflected, as he slumped into a chair in the nearest affordable tavern (the new rule was No Taverns, but just this once wouldn't hurt), the two tall, skinny lads did more or less what they were told and seemed desperately eager to learn. He knew their type; he'd killed enough of them over the last ten years. The peasant wasn't as clumsy or as stupid as he looked, and with his obvious strength might make a good Zweyhender fighter, but Loredan was fairly certain he'd drop out after a week or so. The wiry boy from the suburbs had turned out to be a lost cause; he'd learnt the drills well enough by rote, but showed no indication at all of being able to think. It would be cold-blooded murder ever to allow him to practise law in Perimadeia. Master Iuven had proved irritatingly competent once he'd at last consented to pay attention, but Loredan already knew he'd never make a fencer, call it cowardice or call it enough sense to avoid a fight. Which left whatsername. The girl.

Nearly every one of the abominably numerous courtroom romances, churned out in such profusion by the hack professional poets and any number of talentless amateurs, had as the heroine the lovely swordmaiden, slender as a wand but quick and deadly, capable of skewering the mighty advocate or cutting a bloody path through any number of bandits, pirates or barbarian warriors. Once upon a time, Loredan had bothered to explain to lay acquaintances exactly why this poetic fancy was impossible; that without weight and reach and a strong enough wrist to turn the other man's blade, all the speed and athleticism in the world wouldn't save you from an early death. He'd told them how quickly the arms and knees tire, how a full-blooded slash from a fifteen-stone man would knock a sweet young thing off her feet even if her parry was textbook perfect; how, in short, the courtroom floor was no place for a woman, or any decent human being, come to that. He still believed it; nevertheless, the girl had talent.

Of course, she was no willow wand. She carried no superfluous weight, but she was strong and sure on her feet – clearly used to working, though not farm work, to judge by her hands. The only child of a craftsman, Loredan guessed; a daughter who did a son's work because it had to be done and there was no one else to do it. (In which case, what the hell was she doing here?)

Mostly, though, she was determined. It wasn't the boyish eagerness of the tall, thin twins; no sense of a childhood ambition being realised, no *fun*. It was almost as if this was something she had to do successfully, whether she liked it or not, as if her life depended on it. Thinking about her,

Loredan shook his head and took a long pull at his cider. The ticklish feeling she gave him was more than his dislike of female fencers. It was—

—Personal.

He yawned, suddenly aware of how tired he was. Next day he'd have to teach these tiresome children the grip, more elementary footwork and the basic elements of the defence. The next day he'd have to drill them in the lunge and go back over everything they'd done so far and make them learn it all over again. That was assuming his voice held up and he didn't get accidentally spitted or lose his temper and murder one of them. If he was really lucky, he'd educate this lot, get rid of them and start all over from scratch with another bunch of inadequates.

Really fallen on my feet this time.

Yes. Well, at least nobody was deliberately trying to kill him.

He really wanted another jug of cider. Instead he stood, gathered up his various props and kitbags and trudged home, across the city and up the stairs. There was someone waiting in the doorway.

He saw whoever it was before he/she saw him, and flattened himself against the wall just outside the meagre circle of light thrown by the sconce. Once he'd calmed himself down, it occurred to him that if the muffled and cloaked figure was an assassin he was a pretty incompetent one; besides, who could possibly be bothered to have him killed? A robber wouldn't waste good darkness lurking outside a door in a fairly poor area on the off chance that the householder might come home and be worth robbing; in the unlikely event of there being anything worth stealing, he'd have pushed open the unlocked door, helped himself and gone away.

Nevertheless. Carefully and by feel, Loredan teased out the knot at the top of his sword case and let the canvas slip fall away. Then, as quietly as he could manage after climbing all those stairs, he edged up the last few steps and grabbed the torch.

'Athli!' he groaned. 'You scared the living daylights out of me.'

'Sorry,' Athli said. Damn! It hadn't even occurred to her. 'I was just passing, and ...'

'Really?' He knew that wasn't true. 'Well, you'd better come in. The door's not locked.'

She was looking at the sword in his hand. He felt foolish. 'You startled me,' he said, replacing the torch in the sconce. 'Been here long?'

'No,' she said.

He closed the door after them and fiddled with his tinderbox to get the lamp lit. The tinder was damp; like everything in this rat-trap.

'Why do you live in a place like this?' she said, sitting down on the edge of the bed. 'You make good money.'

'Used to,' he replied, lifting the wine jug and finding it empty, as usual. 'I've retired, remember. Now I'm nothing but a humble trainer, with precisely six pupils.'

'At a silver quarter a day each, makes six quarters,' she replied. 'Most of the people in this place are lucky if they see that much in a month. What is it with you? You can't have drunk it all – you'd be dead.'

Loredan grinned. He wouldn't say anything about the gold five in his pocket; for which, incidentally, he'd had change. 'My business,' he replied. 'Maybe I like it here. I mean, it's such a picturesque district that people go out of their way just to stand in doorways.'

'I—' She was looking at the toes of her boots. 'I was wondering how you were getting on, that's all. Six pupils; is that good or bad?'

'Pretty fair average, actually,' he replied. 'And, as you say, if I can keep it up it's a fair living. Hard work, though.'

'Are you any good at it?'

He shrugged. 'Give me a chance,' he said, 'it's my first day.' He kicked off his boots and flexed his cramped toes. 'I've been afflicted with five idiots and a Valkyrie, and I've taught them how to shuffle in a straight line without falling over. I reckon they had their money's worth.' He leant back in the chair and closed his eyes. 'So what are you really doing here?'

Good question, at that. Of course, there was one reason why a young girl should fabricate an excuse to come and visit a man she hadn't seen in three whole days – Athli *was* a young girl, after all, although it was something he'd not allowed himself to notice more than a handful of times in the three years they'd known each other. In fact, it was the only reason he could think of. Which could be – embarrassing.

'You don't think, do you?' she replied petulantly. 'Bardas, how many fencers do you think I clerk for? Have you ever stopped to wonder?'

He frowned. 'You're right, I haven't. You're good at it, no reason why you shouldn't have a pretty good practice.'

'One,' she replied. 'Until just recently. And then the selfish pig went and retired on me, leaving me out of a job.'

'Oh.' He opened his eyes. 'Why didn't you say?'

'Well, of course, I should have said something. I should have said, Oh, no, you can't retire, I need you to carry on risking your life at regular intervals so I can keep getting my ten per cent. Don't be so …'

'All right, point taken. In which case, if you'll forgive me being ruthlessly logical, why mention it now?'

She gave him a nasty look. 'Because I need to earn a living,' she said. The nasty look evaporated, and was replaced by embarrassment. 'So I was wondering. Trainers have clerks, don't they? Have you got one yet?'

He shook his head. 'Figured I could do that myself. But why would you want to give up the job you know just because I've retired? You've got regular clients who produce good work. There's plenty of fencers who'd give anything for a client base like that.'

'Oh, yes,' she replied, looking at him steadily now. 'Including their lives. Use your imagination, Bardas. Why d'you think I only clerked for you?'

He frowned. 'I don't know,' he admitted.

'Because you never looked like getting yourself killed,'

she said quietly. 'Bardas, I don't want to send young men to their deaths. I don't think that'd be a very nice way to live. I only stuck it out with you because…'

'Because?'

'Because I trusted you,' she replied sharply. 'Oh, I knew that the odds were that one day you'd – lose. But not *needlessly*. Not…'

'Not until I absolutely had to?' He smiled. 'I'm flattered.'

'Anyway,' she said briskly, 'I asked you a question. Do you need a clerk?'

He thought for a moment, or at least made a show of doing so. Apparently he'd been wrong about the reason, which made sense. He didn't really need a clerk, and he couldn't pay her less than twenty-five per cent. It'd cut into his earnings and still be a meagre living compared with what she'd been used to, even if he had been her only fencer. (And what about that? Think about it later …) On the other hand—

'Yes,' he replied. 'Provided you can pull in extra pupils and earn your keep that way. Based on my vast twenty-four hours' experience of the training profession, I reckon I could train twelve as easily as six. What d'you reckon?'

'How about a month's trial?' she suggested. 'I've been in the training profession a whole day less than you, remember. I might not like it.'

Loredan grinned. 'Oh, I think you'll take to it all right,' he said. 'Because, when all's said and done, it's basically sending young men to their deaths. It'll be like old times.'

'Now then,' Alexius said, 'close your eyes, and then I want you to tell me what you see.'

The twins shut their eyes obediently; the male, Venart, with his face screwed up into that inevitable embarrassed-but-determined scowl a man always wears when he suspects he's being made a fool of but daren't give mortal offence by refusing; the female, Vetriz, with a rapt expression of pure bliss, as befits a nice girl having a wonderful adventure. Alexius shot a glance at his colleague; he looked scared half to death, and grey with pain. The Patriarch smiled thinly at him; he knew exactly how he felt.

'Anything?' he asked.

Venart said, 'Um,' obviously unable to decide what was expected of him. The girl shook her head.

'Very well.' That, of course, had just been mummery, to see if they were faking. Satisfied that they weren't, Alexius took a deep breath, tried vainly to relax the steel clamps that were slowly squeezing his brain out through his ears, and—

The courtroom. This time, for some reason, the public benches were empty; no judge, ushers or clerks. Nobody there except the man he now knew to be Loredan, with his back towards Alexius, his feet nearly together and his right arm extended straight from his shoulder, holding out his sword in the guard of the Old fence; and the girl he'd done the curse for, all that time ago as it seemed; and—

'Hello,' Vetriz said. She had materialised quite suddenly in the small area of floor that separated the two motionless fencers. She walked round them as if they were statues in a square, admiring them.

'I recognise him,' she said at last. 'He's the advocate we saw the other day. Is the other one a lawyer too? I didn't realise women did this as well as men.'

Alexius nodded. No sign of Gannadius either; but here at least his head didn't hurt. 'I don't see your brother,' he said.

Vetriz looked round. 'He can't have made it through, then. What about your assistant?'

Oh, what a pity he isn't here to hear that! I'd never let him forget it. 'Apparently not,' Alexius replied, trying to conceal his apprehension. 'You know, this is very interesting. Do you know how you got here?'

Vetriz shrugged. 'No idea. Same way I've got no idea how I make my arms and legs work. They just do.' She looked around again. 'Are we *really* here, or is this just a dream or something?'

'I don't know,' Alexius confessed. 'Usually it's not like this, that's the strangest part of it. Usually – I say usually, makes it sound like I do this sort of thing every day, and of course I don't – usually you come in just before some crucial piece of action, either in the future or the past depending on why you've come. As far as I can tell, this isn't either. For all I know, it could just be a dream after all. Or, if you really are a natural, perhaps you do these things in a totally different way.'

Loredan, he observed, was definitely breathing; so was the girl. But their arms weren't wobbling as they held the guard, and *nobody*, no matter how many thousands of hours they'd spent practising the manoeuvre, can stand with his sword-arm outstretched for more than a minute or so without moving at all ...

That was it. That was what they were doing; not fighting but *training* ... And this wasn't the courts, it was the big exhibition arena in the Schools, deliberately modelled on the courts so that when students took their final examinations here, they'd be in the most realistic setting possible.

The girl's sword-tip wiggled, just the tiniest amount.

Extraordinary, Alexius muttered to himself; she's plucked the picture from my mind and taken it back – or forward? No idea – entirely of her own accord. I have absolutely no idea how you'd set about doing that.

The girl made a little grunting noise, which Alexius recognised as pure agony, and her sword-tip wobbled again. It was of course one of the most fundamental – and arduous – of the fencer's training exercises, the holding of a position for a specified time. From what he'd gathered, it taught you all sorts of useful skills and toned up the muscles like nothing else. Alexius, who knew perfectly well he couldn't do anything of the sort for more than a few seconds, winced at the thought.

A wider, more uncontrolled twitch this time; and then Loredan lunged at her, moving much faster than Alexius' eyes could follow. She parried almost as quickly and they fenced two or three returns of strokes until he knocked the sword out of her hand with a short, apparently effortless flick of the wrist. That done, he bent almost double, hugging his forearm and swearing under his breath.

The girl looked furious with herself, and said nothing.

'If it's any consolation,' Loredan gasped, 'that was really quite impressive. You're getting the hang of it just fine.'

'I failed,' the girl grunted back. 'I let you beat me.'

Loredan looked at her oddly. 'Be fair,' he said. 'I'm supposed to be your instructor.'

'Being good isn't enough,' the girl said. 'You can be very good and still die, if the other man's better.' There was an edge to her voice that Alexius definitely didn't like; neither did Loredan, by the look of it.

'You know,' Loredan said, 'I'm so glad I retired when I did. If there's one thing I could never stand, it's perfectionists.'

The girl just looked at him, resentfully. *Definitely a menace, that one. Whatever possessed me to get involved with graveyard bait like that in the first place?*

'This is tremendous fun,' Vetriz interrupted, 'but shouldn't we be *doing* something?'

Alexius looked up, startled. 'What?' he said.

Vetriz frowned. 'When you were explaining all this stuff,' she said, 'you told me that when you go barging in on people like this—'

Alexius was about to say something, but didn't. All in all, *barging in on people* was a very apt way of describing it.

'—Isn't the idea that you do something? You know, interfere. Right wrongs, set things straight. Or didn't I understand it properly?'

'Well, ordinarily—' Somehow, Alexius couldn't find the right words to explain. 'You see, we aren't here for anything like that. This is just an experiment, remember.'

'Oh. Right. Only I thought, since I'd actually seen this man fencing, and here he is obviously in some sort of trouble with that truly ferocious creature over there—'

Once again, Alexius had the strangest feeling, as if he was being lifted up and frogmarched along a row of squares on a chessboard. 'To interfere just for the sake of interfering would be terribly dangerous,' he said gravely. 'Not to mention, well, just plain wrong. We have no idea what the background to all this is.'

Liar, he told himself. And this is definitely getting out of control. Now it seems that dreadful girl's enlisted in his fencing school; presumably she's getting him to teach her how to kill him. If this turns out to be all my fault ...

'I see,' said Vetriz. 'So what would you like to do now?'

'I suppose,' Alexius said slowly, 'we should be getting back.'

'All right.'

—And he opened his eyes and found he was looking straight at Gannadius, who was almost comical in his terror. He scowled at his colleague to make him pull himself together, and glanced at Vetriz.

She still had her eyes shut.

'Excuse me,' Venart said diffidently, his eyes still screwed shut and his face still ludicrous, 'but how much longer are we going to be?'

She still had her eyes shut. If she stayed behind, did something there after he'd left – oh, in hell's name, what *is* going on?

'Gosh,' Vetriz exclaimed, opening her eyes and smiling. 'That was *amazing*.' She beamed at Alexius, her cheeks glowing. 'You *are* clever,' she added. 'I knew you could do magic really.'

Alexius' head was hurting more than ever.

CHAPTER SEVEN

—————————

The outriders must have seen them before they entered the Drescein pass, because there was a full escort waiting for them at the other end.

'You'd better be careful how you handle this,' Jurrai whispered, as they emerged into the sunlight once more. 'It's the first time they've seen you as their chief, remember. First impressions count.'

'It's all right,' Temrai replied softly. 'I know what to do.'

He couldn't help feeling, even so, that it was all rather silly; after all, the five riders who were waiting for them in advance of the main party were men he'd known for as long as he could remember. There was Basbai, holding the eagle standard and looking desperately solemn; Temrai could remember Basbai Mar chasing him all round the camp with a cattleprod (and catching him, worse luck) on the ill-fated occasion when he and Basbai's youngest daughter had been about to embark on a little tentative research into the great mystery of adolescence. Ceuscai, now – tall, magnificent Ceuscai, five years older than himself and his champion and defender against the casual brutality of the playground; it wasn't all that long ago that he'd finally managed to find the courage to presume to speak to Ceuscai as an equal. And what Uncle An thought he was doing in that crazy skins-and-feathers outfit – except that Anakai Mar had been the clan's high priest for fifty-two years, and was rumoured to play chess once a year with the gods themselves.

He squeezed his heels against his horse's flanks and left

Jurrai to catch him up as best he could. The occasion called
for a little pantomime; something he was just going to have
to get used to.

When he was within a few yards of the five outriders he
pulled his horse round, still at a slow gallop, and rode across
the front of their line. As he passed Basbai, he reached out,
grabbed the standard from his hand and raised it in the air,
somehow managing not to fluff the pass or drop it. The
hundred or so riders behind the advance party broke into a
cheer – fair enough, it was a pretty piece of horsemanship,
particularly since he was badly out of practice. He wheeled,
raised the standard again, handed it to Basbai as he passed
him, wheeled again and drew up in front of Uncle An, who
winked at him out of an otherwise monolithic face.

'Hail, Temrai Tai-me-Mar,' Uncle An growled in his business voice. 'May our Father Temrai live for ever.' Then, in his
normal voice, too soft to be heard by the ranks behind, he
added, 'You've put on weight, our Temrai. At least they've
been feeding you properly.'

'Don't make me laugh, Uncle An, or I'll fall off my horse.'
Temrai raised his right hand in a grand salute, and held it
there while the five great and good men of the clan slid off
their horses and knelt before him on the hard ground.
They're doing this because they mean it, Temrai realised,
and for a moment he felt uncomfortable. But not longer
than a moment. What it meant was that they wanted him
to get it right, they were trying to help. The least he could
do was try too. He took a deep breath and hoped his voice
wouldn't wobble.

'I am Temrai ker-Sasurai Tai-me-Mar,' he heard himself
saying. 'Rise, my children.'

Gods, what a performance! He tried to call to mind the
way his father usually coped with this sort of thing; but that
wasn't much help, really. After all, his father was the chief,
and you tended to assume the chief knew what he was
doing …

Then it occurred to him that his father was dead. And
that he was the chief now. And, what was worst of all, his

father was dead but Temrai couldn't cry or even refer to it ever again, even to his family or closest friends, because of course the chief lives for ever ...

I want to go home, he thought.

I am home.

He started to feel better again once the camp was in sight; then he felt a whole lot worse. What he really wanted to do was jump off his horse, run to the tents, cuddle the dogs, give everyone their presents, run off and see Pegtai and Sorutai and Felten and Codruen quickly, just to say hello before his father got back—

He slowed down and rode along the main avenue between the rows of tents, head up, back straight, the way he'd been taught. People were coming out to see him, but nobody waved or shouted; even the dogs hung back, their tails wagging uncertainly as if they were afraid he'd be angry. He'd never known the camp this quiet before.

This is silly. No, it isn't. This is how the clan should behave in the presence of its chief.

Had his father ... had Sasurai Tai-me-Mar felt this way, he wondered, the first time he rode into his camp as Father of the Clan, protector of his people, nephew of the gods? No, probably not; remember your family history, Temrai, you can't afford to be careless about this sort of thing any more. Sasurai Tai-me-Mar had already been middle-aged and the established junior partner in the chiefdom when Jaldai Tai-me-Mar was cut down by Maxen's Pitchfork on the Sela plains. Sasurai would have ridden back at the head of a defeated army, and the people staring from the tent flaps wouldn't have been looking at him, they'd have been trying to catch sight of their fathers, husbands, sons, brothers among the riders at his back, trying not to scream and sob when they realised they weren't there ... It was probably safe to say that Sasurai had enjoyed this moment even less than he was, and probably made a far better job of it, too.

I must do this properly. From now on I must do everything properly.

'The next exercise,' Loredan said, 'is one you're going to hate for the rest of your lives. It hurts, it's boring, and if you make a mess of it I'm going to make you do it all over again. Ready?'

As his group of disciples glowered at him with combined fear and hatred, Loredan put his heels together at right angles, straightened his back and stretched his sword-arm out in the guard of the Old fence. A minute later (in this context, a long time) he said, 'You should all have got the idea by now. You do it.'

The result was fairly predictable, so he made them do it again; and again, and again after that, and again ... One of these days, he muttered to himself as he patrolled the line of foil-points waiting for the first one to twitch and wobble, I'm going to find out exactly what this torture is supposed to achieve. Must be some reason for it, or why the hell have twenty generations of fencers been made to practise it, three times a day, every day?

This time, Iuven the rich boy was the first to break down. Loredan knocked the kid's foil first sideways then down with the back of his hand, growled, 'And again,' and walked on down the line. As soon as one of them failed, the others would inevitably follow suit. It was only the fear of being the first one to lose it that kept the rest of them going.

When he couldn't bear to watch any longer he snapped, 'All right, that's enough,' and knocked all six foil-points down in turn. 'I'd just like to remind you,' he added, 'these practice foils you're using are much shorter and lighter than real swords. And in future, we're going to do four minutes, not two. Right, now you're going to learn the backhand retreating parry of the City fence. Start with the front foot on the line, both knees well-bent, like you're sitting on a chair that isn't there. Master Teudel, you look just like a constipated spider.'

The female, now; she was no less awkward and cack-handed than the other five, but there was something almost frightening about her determination. It was as if –

well, would-be advocates learn fencing with the objective of earning a living without getting killed. This one wanted to learn how to kill. Ten years in the racket, and he'd never come across one like this before. He wasn't sure he liked the idea.

'That one,' he confided to Athli as the class clumped and swished through its newly learnt manoeuvre, 'is going to be a menace.'

'Good,' Athli replied. 'Best sort of publicity, a successful graduate.' She was sitting on a folding chair with her nose in a pile of wax tablets; lists of names, as far as he could tell by reading them upside down. 'You know what these are?' she added.

'No idea.'

'They're the names of all the students who enrolled this term, with the schools they've joined, where known. There's over thirty who don't seem to have found places yet. Once I've finished this I can go out and start recruiting.'

'Keen, aren't you? But I've already got a class.'

'Ah.' Athli smiled. 'But what if you were to take two classes at once? Several trainers do it,' she went on as Loredan's face contracted into a frown. 'It's no big deal. Take now, for example. While they're practising what you've just shown them, you could be teaching another class. We could double our turnover.'

Loredan shook his head. 'It's running me ragged just looking after this lot,' he said. 'Two classes at the same time'd kill me.'

'Ah, but you haven't got into the swing of it yet. Once you've had a chance to work out the most efficient way of teaching—'

'Nice idea, but no thanks. I could cope with one class of twelve, but two lots of six'd be too much. Besides, we're aiming at a reputation for quality through individual tuition. Means I've got to watch 'em all the time if I want to spot their mistakes. Couldn't do that if I was giving my full attention to another class for half of the time.' He glanced down at the carefully written tablets and thought of all the wasted effort she'd put into them. 'You should have checked with me before you started doing all that.'

Athli frowned at him. 'All right, then,' she said, 'what should I be doing? I finished all the stuff you told me to do hours ago.'

'I don't know, do I?' Loredan replied. 'Oh, no, will you just look at that clown Valier. If he'd only listen occasionally to what he's told—'

He bustled back to work, while Athli sighed and dropped the stylus she'd been writing with into the satchel at her feet. She had made a point of watching nearly all the other trainers in the Schools and, looked at objectively, Loredan was more or less completely average. True, he shouted less and explained more than some, but between his six charges and all the others doing practically the same thing all through the building there was no appreciable difference.

She let her attention wander. One of the grand schools had its pitch nearby, and the trainer was drilling the advanced class in the use of the Zweyhender. Rather an esoteric skill; the heavy two-handed sword was virtually obsolete, being used only in such outlandish jurisdictions as libel and witchraft – it survived there only because cases were so infrequent that nobody had yet bothered to repeal the laws. In her time in the courts, Athli had never seen it used. She knew Loredan had a Zweyhender put away somewhere, though she hadn't seen it at his apartment (and something that size would be hard to miss), but she had no idea how it was actually used. She watched.

The instructor started off by showing his class how the sword was held. He produced one; it was over six feet long from point to pommel, nearly a quarter of its length being the handle. The quillons of the crossguard were each almost a foot long, and in front of them, about six inches up the blade, was another smaller guard comprised of two wing-like projections from the blade itself. Athli watched as the instructor took a silk handkerchief and wrapped it round the blade between the two handguards; he gripped this with his right hand and positioned his left halfway

down the handle proper. Then he demonstrated the basic
moves.

Athli, who had imagined great haymaking sweeps
and cuts, was disappointed to discover that in practice
the Zweyhender was used more as a long-bladed poleaxe
or halberd than as a sword. Employed in this way, with
its nicely calculated weight and balance, it could be used
for fast, accurate lunges, wicked little prods and intricate
parries, all executed with a minimum of movement.
Far from being a heroic weapon, she realised, such as a
dragonslayer or mighty man of valour might wield, it was
the tool of the man who plays the percentages, providing
a solid and foolproof defence as first priority while
allowing its user to go on the offensive quickly and with
an acceptable minimum of risk when it was reasonably
prudent to do so. At least with the slim, sharp law-
sword there was a degree of grace and style, a residual
trace of flamboyance in the ebb and flow of the fight.
The Zweyhendermen trundled forward into a minimum-
exposure scenario and negotiated rather than fought,
tracing a series of formal measures which made it hard
to lose and equally hard to win. It was sensible; it was
businesslike and extremely practical. It was no fun. She
couldn't imagine why it wasn't in wider use.

Four or five students sparred against the instructor for
varying lengths of time – one surviving a whole two
minutes, others being checkmated within a few passages. It
was fairly easy stuff to follow; a flurry of neat little prods
and pecks, the advantage established, the loser being forced
to huddle behind his impregnable guard and tacitly
conceding the exchange. The ease with which a complete
novice could hold off the trainer explained why the weapon
was no longer used; where the fight had to be to the death,
each case could go on all day without a result, and the
no-hoper could keep the moral victor four feet away from
him even though he had no chance at all of winning. That
wouldn't serve the interests of justice, which demanded a
short contest and an outright winner, unambiguously

identifiable as being the one left standing.

The sixth student was taking a little longer. He was a short, stocky youth, not particularly well-dressed and patently out of breath after the first thirty seconds. Athli didn't know the techniques and so couldn't say for certain, but she had a fair idea that he was staying in the game by virtue of some recklessly imaginative improvisation, which was beginning to get on the teacher's nerves. The class seemed to think he was being extremely clever; they weren't cheering him on, of course. Cheering during a real fight counted as contempt of court, for which offenders got a week in the cells underneath the courtroom. It was obvious, though, where their sympathies lay, and as the trainer's movements became stiffer and his blows struck with more force, Athli could see his fear of losing face and respect if this farce went on much longer.

The trainer upped his game, moving faster, throwing in some tricks he hadn't included in his demonstration. The student's reply made an enthralling spectacle – the boy was a natural, no doubt about that – but he was simply making things harder for himself; and besides, the whole thing was pointless, not to mention counterproductive, since the reason he was there was not to defeat his trainer in a duel but to learn orthodox swordmanship. Athli began to feel annoyed; he'd proved his point, it was time to concede gracefully and accept the applause of his peers.

But he didn't. He fenced on, and Athli saw a gently pushed cut to go home, drawing a red line across the thick part of the boy's forearm. The rest of the class gasped and muttered and the trainer took a step back, assuming that that would be an end of it. It wasn't; the boy shifted his right hand back onto the main handle and swirled the massive blade round his head, aiming a blow at the trainer which would have split his skull like a pine log if it had connected. As it was, the trainer sidestepped and blocked, taking the blow awkwardly just above the lower handguard. The force of the strike pushed him back and his right foot slithered six inches or so before he regained a solid footing, during which time the boy had swung again – a devastating blow delivered from bent knees and an arched back, cutting from the side rather than downwards with the blade addressing his opponent at neck level. The trainer rocked back on tiptoe, just making enough height to get the forte of his blade in the way of the stroke before it sliced him in two. As it was, he lost his balance completely and staggered; and in that moment of real danger, instinct must have taken control of his mind, because he counterattacked with a full-blooded low thrust into the gap between the boy's arms and sword blade, direct and uninterrupted passage to the heart—

Someone screamed. The boy's sword dropped from his fingers and crashed noisily to the floor, and a moment later his whole dead weight fell on the trainer's blade, pulling the handle out of his hands, the hilt of the sword, projecting out of his ribcage, cracking sharply on the flagstones. He was dead before he hit the ground.

The trainer stood like a statue (*what's the matter, haven't you ever killed anyone before? And you call yourself a professional*) while the class slowly backed away and people in the rest of the hall turned round to stare. Loredan, suddenly looking round, got a slap from a foil-point across his cheek but didn't seem to notice. Someone shouted; people began to run. One of the trainer's pupils grabbed him by the arm, but he didn't move. Several voices now were yelling for help, or a doctor, or some other external but ineffectual agency to come and intervene. They were crouching round the dead boy now, gingerly poking at him, trying to find a pulse where there was never one to begin with. Athli could feel her knees weakening, a tightness in her stomach that suggested she was about to be sick.

'Gentlemen.' It was Loredan speaking, his tone mildly annoyed, as if he was about to rebuke a child for talking in class. 'If you find this sort of thing disturbs you, might I suggest you're training for the wrong profession? Nothing to do with us. Now then, where were we?'

* * *

Because Temrai had been away at the time, the clan had postponed Sasurai's funeral games. The winners would have felt cheated if they didn't receive the prizes from the hand of their new chief, and the prizegiving was traditionally the occasion for the new chief to make a formal address, setting out his aims and objectives for the first few years of his reign.

They'd used the time to make more than usually elaborate preparations; marking out the course for the horse race with stone cairns, putting up wooden goalposts for the polo match, digging proper butts for the archery and so forth, and the main contenders had had the luxury of several clear days' match practice. The compressed-felt archery targets were already well-pocked, with a few tell-tale holes and splinters in their wooden frames demonstrating how badly needed the practice had been. There had even been time to catch a live eagle for the popinjay shoot, instead of the stuffed dummy that usually had to suffice. Best of all, the stewards had cajoled the clan into digging a long, low bank to serve as a grandstand, which meant that for once people who weren't in the front row would stand some sort of chance of seeing something more entertaining than the neck of the man in front.

For Temrai there was a proper wooden throne, with carpet for him to walk on and a table to one side to display the prizes on. Traditionally, of course, the prizes consisted of special treasures from the dead chief's personal possessions, and Temrai had to make an effort not to glance wistfully at various select components of what he'd hoped would be his inheritance, laid out splendidly as tokens of his semi-divine munificence. There, for instance, were Sasurai's golden spurs, his personal drinking horn, a pair of his finest and most richly embroidered slippers and a quiver of first-class flight arrows with purple fletchings to identify them as the chief's own.

Damn, said Temrai to himself. Oh, well, never mind.

It was, to all intents and purposes, obligatory for him to enter at least one event, and the height of bad form for him to win – a graceful fourth place was the ideal, enough to demonstrate prowess but well clear of the prizes – so he'd announced he'd take part in the close -range archery match and the popinjay shoot; he was a good enough archer to be able to throw the short-range match if need be without being too obvious about it, and if he shot near the bottom of the order in the popinjay event, someone else would be bound to have skewered the eagle before his turn, therefore relieving him of the obligation of taking part. As befitted the prestige of the discipline, the archery came at the end, which allowed Temrai to sit back and watch the riding events in comfort.

The horse races – five, ten and fifteen circuits of the course with and without hurdles – went smoothly and with a bare minimum of cheating. There were no surprises in the results. Tobolai Mar and his six sons shared all the prizes in four of the six races and were well-represented in the others, with Remtai Mar and Piridai winning the short and medium hurdles by a clear margin.

The polo matches were the usual joyful mess. Bestren cheated blatantly throughout the women's game, but there would have been a riot if he'd sent her off before the young men had had a good long look at her in her riding costume, and since she stopped short of actually killing anybody, there was no harm done. In the event her team lost by seven goals to ten, so everyone was happy; especially Temrai, who was thus spared the embarrassment of having to give her the prize. She'd been after him in a painfully obvious way since she'd been old enough to choose a husband, and for all that she was unquestionably decorative, the most he'd ever been able to feel for her was a sort of fascinated loathing. It was far more agreeable to be able to hand over the golden belt and brooch to Sargen-pel-Tazrai, a sensible girl with a pleasing sense of humour, whose engagement to Limdai's eldest son had apparently evaporated while Temrai had been away. He managed to keep his congratulatory smile from turning into a leer, and had held onto the belt just a fraction of a second longer than necessary when handing it over. All in all, it tended to improve his opinion of polo matches.

After the horseback events came the foot races. These had never been popular with the spectators, and were really only there to provide an interval between the riding and the archery. It was during the buzz of revived interest that followed the last foot race that Temrai stood up and made his surprise announcement. It turned out to be a felicitous piece of timing.

There would be, he announced, one additional event; not a new event, because there were references to it in some of the clan's oldest songs, but one which hadn't been staged in living memory. A team event, he went on, because team games serve to foster a spirit of co-operation and mutual support – and so on, until he got bored listening to himself. Then he announced the log race.

It wasn't a complete surpise, of course; he'd chosen the team captains the day before, and the crews who'd found and cut the logs were obviously in on the secret as well. Nevertheless there was a gratifying air of excitement as the two enormous tree trunks were unloaded from the long wagon and dragged into the middle of the lists by two teams of horses. There was certainly no shortage of young men wanting to take part; fortunately he'd anticipated that and the two captains were properly briefed on who to select out of the crowd of eager volunteers.

The object of the race, he explained, was to carry the log from the start to the finish without dropping it or allowing the other team to get there first. The prize would be a Perimadeian gold piece for each man and a red and purple hat for the team captain. As soon as the teams were in position he stood up, raised his cap in the air and let if fall.

It soon became evident that the competitors' skill fell rather short of their enthusiasm. They weaved in and out like drunks, trod on each other's heels and ended up running more sideways than straight, ultimately colliding with rather than crossing the rope. As far as Temrai was concerned, this was no bad thing. It demonstrated the need for practice as far as this particular skill was concerned, something he could stress when he made his closing speech. In the event, it was such a close-run thing that the decision had to be made by the referees he'd wisely positioned on the finishing line. Quite properly, Ceuscai's team won in the end, which was just as well since it was his measurements Temrai had given to the feltcutters for the prize hat.

In common with most of the clan he allowed his attention to wander slightly during the athletic events; instead, he permitted himself the luxury of observing his people. It wasn't something he'd ever done before, understandably enough. He was, after all, one of them, and had been all his life. Now, however, he felt an undefinable but definitely perceptible barrier between them and himself; partly because he was now the chief, but mostly because he'd been to the city and seen something different – something, he was forced to admit, that was in many ways better, or at least more advanced. After the stone and brick houses, the paved streets, the abundant water instantly available in every square, the tents of the clan seemed primitive, and he was no longer able to be content with primitive surroundings. The clan couldn't be blamed for not having invented for itself the wonderful things they took for granted in the city; there's nothing wrong or wicked about not being as clever as someone who's cleverer than yourself, because some people are cleverer than others just as some are taller. But to know that better things were possible and not to want to have them; now surely that *was* stupid, possibly even wicked—

(Zandai Mar clearing the high jump by the thickness of a hair; too old to take part, but prestige demanded it. Ostren tripping over a loose divot and falling nose-first into the water jump. Only four men competing in the arrow-throwing, and none of them managing to get the arrow in the circle …)

—Unless, of course, the price demanded for these wonderful things was more than they were worth; there, he suspected, was the answer he was looking for. It wasn't a new idea. Quite the opposite – it had been the complaint of generations of self-justifying travellers returning from the city. He considered it.

The Perimadeians have gained all manner of wonders, but they have lost the best part of themselves; so said the travellers, smugly sipping mead and milk beside the fire under the bright, cold stars. They have become hard and selfish, despising lesser races and thinking themselves justified in plundering them in order to maintain their own reprehensible taste for unnatural luxury.

Yes, Temrai thought, well. Travellers tell many other stories, including encounters with enormous flying lizards and creatures with the bodies of men and the heads of animals, and some of us believe them and some don't. I have seen the people of the city and they're not very different from us, once you cut through the bark and the sapwood to the core. There were some differences, it's true; they accepted strangers, even strangers from nations that were traditionally their direst enemies, without suspicion or hostility. If they said anything, it was more likely to be an interested enquiry about the truth of some wild rumour they'd heard (is it true you people all have seven wives? Is it true that where you come from men and women do, well, you know what, in the saddle and at the gallop? Do you really make your enemies' skulls into drinking cups and cut off the scalps of men you kill in battle? And what's it *really* like …?)

Another difference: in the city there was a whole neighbourhood occupied by doctors, whose business it was to try and keep alive people the clansmen wouldn't bother with, because even if they got well they'd be too old or frail to be any use. The clan looked after its people, sure enough, but only up to the point where doing so was in the clan's interest. In the city, keeping people alive was an end in itself. It went further than that, too. Here, apart from one or two people who had skills the rest didn't, everyone did the same work and owned more or less the same amount of property, and no-one thought any more about it. In the city, it was different. More than that he couldn't really say, because it was complicated; but since the poorest people there seemed to have more than most of us here in the plains, where was the harm in it? A man could stay where he was in the city's infinitely complex hierarchy, or he could work hard and maybe raise himself three or four degrees in the perpetual order. Temrai couldn't make up his mind about that, but at least he could recognise that there was a difference.

And now here he was, back again, looking at his people. The first thing that struck him was how many there were of them. It was nobody's business to know exactly how many, and he certainly didn't. At the start of a major war, it was the custom for the fighting men to file past the chief's tent, each man putting an arrow in a basket as he passed. The baskets were then loaded onto packhorses, and used as a reserve supply for the main war-party. The last time this was done, some twelve or thirteen years ago, there had been over a hundred horses in the arrow train, but it was too long ago for him to remember how many baskets each horse carried, or the average number of arrows in each basket.

There were other ways in which he could work out the numbers, more or less – how long it took the clan to ford a particular river, how long the line of march was over a known stretch of straight road, how many hides went to the tanners each month (which would tell him how many steers were slaughtered, and thus how many mouths had to be fed), but he had to admit that he wasn't interested enough to bother, and besides, it wasn't his legitimate concern. Numbering his people would feel too much like counting his herds. It would imply that he owned them, which of course he didn't. He'd heard it said that once upon a time in the city, men owned other men in the same way they owned livestock and tools, but he didn't believe it, any more than he believed in the two-headed lions or the talking trees that were also supposed to have existed long ago when the world was young.

And now he found himself actually *looking* at his people, as if he was a man from the city come to spy on the clans. He saw men between five feet four and five feet nine inches tall, women a head or half a head shorter, who wore wool and felt and leather, ate dried meat, cheese, millet when there was any to be had, apples and olives in season provided they timed the itinerary right; people who lived in tents of felt and hide, smeared lard on their skins in the depth of winter to keep out the wind and the wet, wasted nothing, owned no more than a wagon and two packhorses could carry.

Here were people who had found a use for every part of a horse or a steer: milk, meat and blood for food; tallow for light, cooking and waterproofing; hide for clothing, tents, harness, hats and armour; hair for felt, rope and bowstrings; bones and teeth for buttons, needles, bow cores and nocks, buckles, tool handles, chesspieces, jewellery, flutes and glue; sinews for bow-backings; and dung for fuel for the fire. They were people who had no leisure and who never hurried, who had little and wanted nothing more, who wrote no books but knew the names of their ancestors for a hundred generations, who had no machines but knew about silver solder and could read the colours in the steel. Looking at them for the first time, he recognised how strange they were, how different.

This is what we are. The people who live in the plains. A hundred and one things to make with a dead cow.

Someone nudged his arm; it was time to present the prizes for the running about and jumping over things. Having done that (and wondered, in passing, how come he'd allowed Sasurai's second-best saddle and a brand-new pair of hawking gloves to be given away to men whose only remarkable talent was their ability to launch themselves over a frame of sticks on the end of a long pole), he picked up his bow and quiver and walked down into the arena for the archery.

At least, he thanked the gods, nobody'd tried to make him give away Sasurai's bow. By rights it ought to have gone to Forever with him, and Temrai honoured in grateful silence the kind friends who'd managed to overlook it at the time. He had bows of his own, expertly made by himself and others, but this was the bow he'd learnt to shoot with. He knew this bow, and it knew him. If there was a better bow in the world, he didn't want to know.

As he stepped inside it to fit the string, it was like coming home. A new string since he'd seen it last, but a good string nonetheless; the long sinew from a horse's leg served from top to bottom in silk and properly waxed, with neat bone beads around the nocking point and an ivory kisser. Having braced the bow, he fitted the tab to the fingers of his right hand and buckled the guard round his left forearm, adjusted the height of his quiver, checked the fletchings of his arrows, fidgeted, tried to think of something else. Now that he was standing with his left foot beside the line, with an invisible tunnel between himself and his mark, he realised it was going to be hard work trying not to win. About the only thing going for him was the fact that the whole clan was watching him. That ought to be enough to put anybody off their aim.

When the time came for him to shoot, he'd made a fairly good job of talking himself out of what residual ability he had. The line judge gave the command to nock, and his hand shook a little as he fitted the horn notch of the arrow onto the string, cock-feather upmost. On the command 'Draw', he lifted the bow, grunted as he pushed with his left arm, drew with his right until he felt the bow yield and the weight shift from his shoulders to his back. As the socket of the arrowhead slid across the bottom joint of his left thumb, his right thumb brushed his chin and the kisser on the string touched his bottom lip, guaranteeing the alignment of arrow, hand and bow.

He fixed his eyes on the mark, eliminating everything else in the world, and for a second and a half was excused thinking about his father's death, the city of Perimadeia and its defences, the duties and responsibilities of a clan chief and his own unanticipated strangeness among his own kind. There was too much else to think about; the left arm slightly bent, the elbow outwards, the second finger of the right hand more bent than the third to make sure the string lay level in the crease of the top joint of all three fingers holding the string, the impossibility of not thinking about the act of straightening those fingers as he loosed the string – for the perfect loose is simply the transition between the state of holding a string and the state of not holding it; as simple and as impossible as that—

And then the follow-through, and a distant *plump* as the arrow struck the mark, low and to the right, symptom of a sloppy loose. *Ah, well, if it was easy there'd be no point doing it.* He nocked his second arrow and drew. For the time it took him to loose a dozen arrows he had the luxury of being Temrai, the competent but mediocre archer, nothing more or less than the sum of his own strength and skill. At the back of his mind he knew that this was a moment to savour while it lasted, for there was no knowing when he would be allowed to be this Temrai again.

He came fifth in the end, and that was the best he could do. In a way it pleased him more than winning. He'd made a reasonable show, and he had the comfort of knowing that there were at least four archers in his army who were better shots than he was. In the circumstances, it would have been downright depressing if he'd won.

He stayed just behind the line while the remaining distances were shot, unwilling to go back to his place of honour until he absolutely had to. If his presence among them was a little unsettling to the other competitors, that was no bad thing. No doubt the two-hundredweight stones from the trebuchets on the land-wall towers would be more unsettling still, and they'd have to cope with them soon enough. The standard of marksmanship was really rather good. He made a mental note to call for the aggregate once the match was over, and wondered if anybody remembered any comparable scores which would help him work out whether the clan's shooting had improved or declined over the intervening years. A conscientious chief, he reasoned, ought to know such things.

It was time for the popinjay, the grand finale. Precisely why the people of the clan found it so enthralling to see men shooting arrows at a bird tethered by its foot to the top of a fifty-yard-high mast, Temrai had never been quite sure. Perhaps it was because it was faster-paced than the conventional rounds at the marks; one shot from each competitor, and if the first man to shoot hit the target, that was the end of the competition. Maybe the thrill lay in something tangible actually getting hit and falling over – hard to be enthusiastic about hearing the gentle *tock* of distant arrows dropping into felt, when only the people nearest the marks could see where the shots had landed. It couldn't be good old-fashioned bloodlust, because usually the popinjay was a leather bag stuffed with straw, dipped in glue and rolled in feathers. His own personal theory was the frisson of danger from all the arrows that didn't hit the mark and fell erratically back to earth, as often as not landing among the spectators.

This time there was a real bird; a big tawny eagle, tethered by one foot to the masthead and protesting savagely about the indignity of it all. That would account for the more than usual excitement, since every man who'd lost kids and lambs to the mountain eagles could share in the symbolic revenge. For his part, Temrai would just as soon have shot at the bag of straw. He'd spent too many hours with the herd as a boy, vainly trying to keep the loathsome creatures at bay with shouts and stones, to feel sorry for the wretched bird, but this wasn't pest control so much as a public execution. Besides, the straw version didn't jiggle about so much.

One shot. He looked down at his quiver until he saw the one particular arrow he'd been looking for. It had been his favourite ever since he was young, even though it was an inch too long for him. He had no idea where it had come from; it bore the chief's purple fletchings, but it hadn't been made on the plains. The clan made their arrows from one piece of wood, the same diameter for the whole length of the shaft. This arrow had a cedar mainshaft spliced into a cornelwood footing, and it tapered very slightly from a point eight inches below the head down to the nock. The narrow, unusually heavy head was almost square in section, as opposed to the familiar three-sided profile favoured by the clan smiths. He had a feeling that it was very old, and had originally come via the city from Scona, where the finest bowyers and fletchers in the world made equipment for the finest archers. The fletchings were goose rather than eagle or crow, and in need of replacement fairly soon. He held it up to his eye to make sure it hadn't warped or split, then had to jump quickly to one side to avoid a descending arrow that had caught the wind at masthead level and come straight back down again.

He had drawn the seventh shot, so he didn't have long to wait. No real danger of winning this particular event; the specialised skill of shooting straight up in the air wasn't one he'd ever seen any point in mastering, since it wasn't needed in war except when you were right under the walls of a city, and he'd never mastered the knack of shooting birds on the wing. Plenty of people had, however, and five of the clan's best birdhunters had drawn places ahead of him.

Somehow, though, they all contrived to miss, with the result that Temrai found himself standing on the line, craning his neck and staring almost straight into the sun, trying to make out the bird's outline against the painfully bright sky. He drew and took aim in the general direction, relaxed the fingers of his right hand and got ready to let fly.

He was just about to commit to the loose when the sun dipped behind what was virtually the only cloud in the sky, giving him a clear view of the target. He felt the string biting into his fingers through the tab, and his shoulders ached. It was time to get rid of this wretched arrow. He concentrated on the bird and stopped holding the string.

Damn, he thought.

How many times had there been when he'd have given anything to have hit the mark in a popinjay shoot in front of the whole clan? More times than he cared to remember, when he'd spent days driving arrows into a felt boss hung from the side of the wagon, trying to find that last elusive touch of skill that would make the shot go exactly where he wanted it to, instead of somewhere in the general direction. As he watched the arrow strike, the bird fold up, topple and hang like a saddlebag from its tether, he cursed and wondered how such a thing could possibly happen. All he could think of was that the gods had stored up ten years' worth of his prayers for a straight shot and then maliciously chosen to grant them now just to spite him.

There was an awkward silence as the entire clan tried to work out whether they were meant to applaud, or whether they were free to express their disapproval of so wanton a breach of etiquette. The other competitors picked up their arrows and put their bows back in their cases without a word or a glance in his direction. It would have to be the popinjay, the one event where he couldn't magnanimously disqualify himself and let the real contestants carry on. And how in the gods' names was he supposed to go about presenting the prize to himself?

All he could think of to say was, 'Sorry.'

Still, nothing he could do about it now. He cased his bow and walked back to his seat. Now, of course, he had to make his speech.

He'd prepared it, and he knew it was good. First, a succinct and gracefully worded eulogy for his predecessor. Next, a formal declaration of his intention to lead the clan against the enemy, stating his reasons and motivating his people for the struggle that lay ahead. A few words on the clan's manifest destiny, a bit of mysticism for those who expected it, and, to conclude, a nicely phrased summary and a memorable saying that folks could tell their grandchildren. He had it all off pat.

Instead, he cleared his throat and said, 'You don't want to listen to a lot of speeches, so here's what we're going to do. Once we've made it through the Nadsin pass, we're going south out of our way to cut timber. We're then going to float it down the river – we've never tried it before, but I know it's been done, so we can do it – and once we're there, we're going to build siege engines. It's all right, I've learnt how and there's nothing to it, really. The archery's pretty good – too good, in some cases – but we're going to have to practise with the logs if we're to have a hope in hell of bashing in the city gates, so I'll want volunteers for a specialist ram detail; names to the wing leaders in the next three days. There's a lot I haven't thought out yet, but we've got time in hand, and I'll keep you posted as we go along. That's about it, really, so I'll shut up and let you get on with the party. Here's health. Oh, and if you didn't want your eagle shot, you shouldn't have left it there.'

It wasn't much of a joke; but even as he sat down he knew he'd just given a new proverb to the language. A hundred years from now, men who'd let their unbranded cattle get mixed up with someone else's herd, or whose neglected wives started to look elsewhere, would have their protests met with a smirk and, 'Yes, well, if you didn't want your eagle shot—' In the meantime, he'd just spoken to his people like a chief, as opposed to a boy wearing his father's oversized hat. He'd have his volunteers for the ram squads, and his rafts of timber floating down the river; and nobody would mutter behind his back that they reckoned Chief didn't have a plan at all, because he'd just admitted it and that was fair enough. It was probably going to work, and it was because he'd learnt that if a target's there to be shot at, you shoot at it and the hell with the rules.

Sasurai hadn't realised that; Sasurai didn't storm Perimadeia. I do, and I will.

He was still sitting reflecting on this when they came to load up the throne and the carpets. They didn't exactly turf him out onto the ground, but they made it clear that they had work to do and he was in the way. He apologised and left them to it.

CHAPTER EIGHT

The enduring popularity enjoyed by the Patriarchs of Perimadeia with their fellow citizens was an aspect of their high office which they found baffling, endearing or infuriating, depending on how deeply they allowed themselves to think about it. Since the Patriarch was nothing more than the head of an order of philosophers and scientists engaged in research into an abstruse subject of no practical value whatsoever to the layman, there was no reason for him to be loved and admired, and that was baffling. The fact that his fellow citizens carried on loving and admiring him no matter what he did or didn't do was certainly endearing. The discovery that his popularity was due to the universal misconception that he was some kind of official wizard whose job consisted of battling with the forces of darkness on the city's behalf, averting swarms of malicious demons, outbreaks of plague and violent storms that might interfere with profitable commerce on the sea was invariably infuriating. After he'd been through each of these three stages, the Patriarch tended to put the matter out of his mind and think no more of it.

Nevertheless, when news of Patriarch Alexius' serious illness became widespread there were any number of spontaneous demonstrations of public goodwill, no doubt from worried citizens who wanted him up, about and fighting demons again before anything horrible could happen. Flowers, fruit and a wide selection of good-luck charms appeared outside the doors of his lodgings every morning, well-meaning old ladies left gallons of warm, nourishing broth with the porters, and important officials of the Order who had better things to do with their time spent hours receiving delegations of smiling, noisy children bearing garlands of aromatic herbs woven by their own innocent, unskilled hands. Such was the inconvenience caused by all this unsolicited solidarity that as soon as he was well enough to stand up, Alexius was chivvied out onto a balcony and exhibited to cheering crowds in the hope that the well-meaning persecution of the last couple of months would now cease.

'I think it's rather moving,' Gannadius commented as Alexius tottered back to bed, his arm cramped from half an hour of waving. 'All these people you've never even met, standing outside the doors in all weathers, deluging the place with flowers—'

'If someone could possibly explain to me how a cartload of scented weeds is supposed to cure heart disease, I could publish the cure and make a fortune,' Alexius grunted, burrowing back under the blankets in search of any lingering traces of warmth. 'As it is, I think I'd rather be universally loathed and get some sleep.'

'Well, you can't,' Gannadius replied. 'You have a duty to your fellow citizens, who need to love something, can't love the government because nobody ever loves the government, and so have chosen you instead. You might at least have the good manners to be gracious about it.'

Alexius growled into his pillow. 'You know what they're saying?' he retorted. 'They're saying I was locked in magical combat with malevolent unworldly creatures conjured up by our enemies, and that although I ultimately triumphed the struggle left me a gibbering wreck. All the effort I've gone to explaining that we're not magicians—'

Gannadius smiled pleasantly. 'Which of course makes them all the more firmly convinced that you are,' he said. 'Whereas if you strutted round the place in a long blue robe covered with mystic sigils, they'd dismiss you as a rank charlatan and throw eggs at you.' He stood up. 'You'd better get some rest. All this excitement's making you more than usually bad-tempered.'

'I know,' Alexius replied. 'Mostly I think it's the frustration of being cooped up in here when there's so much I should be doing—'

Gannadius frowned. 'Nothing important,' he said firmly. 'Those bright-spark secretaries of yours are dealing with all the routine business – rather better than you used to, I might add – and reading up all the latest developments on the theoretical side so that I can explain them to you in baby language has meant I've nearly caught up myself. As for the other business—' He looked Alexius squarely in the eye. 'It does rather seem to have taken care of itself, now that those two have gone back to where they came from. I think we should just be grateful we're rid of them and forget it ever happened.'

Alexius nodded slowly. The devastating reaction he'd suffered half an hour after the two Islanders had gone away was something he'd never be able to forget, but two months of lying flat on his back staring at those rather over-rated mosaics on his ceiling had helped him put the whole episode into proper perspective. With hindsight, it was fairly clear what had happened; an unfortunate coincidence of his own foolish experiments at remote cursing and the presence in the city of a natural, wielding extraordinary power within the Principle without having the faintest idea what she was doing and therefore by implication completely unable to control the effects of her interference. Once she'd gone, the reactions had stopped (just as well, or he'd unquestionably be dead by now) and it stood to reason that if there were no reactions, everything had somehow sorted itself out. As far as Gannadius' discreet enquiries had revealed, Loredan the fencer was living a blameless and prosperous life as a trainer, the mysterious girl seemed to have vanished completely and so far at least there had been no visitations of plague or freak earthquakes. So that was all right—

(But it wasn't, of course; however firmly he reassured

himself that it was all over he couldn't put out of his mind that terrifying feeling of being manipulated, so easily manipulated, by someone who handled every aspect of the Principle with the dexterity and confidence of Bardas Loredan with his favourite sword. And it wasn't the girl herself, he was sure of that, and it couldn't have been her rather ordinary brother, or anybody who lived in the city, come to that – so who could it have been? And, more disturbing still, why?)

'I'll be going, then,' Gannadius said. 'I'll see you— Ah, here's Delmatius with your letters. No rest for the wicked, after all.'

Alexius smothered a groan as his pushiest, most bustling young secretary entered the room. Gannadius, quite sensibly, fled and left him to cope as best he could on his own.

'Nothing much to bother you with today,' the young man chirruped, dumping a thick wad of parchments on Alexius' lap and balancing the candle precariously beside him. 'Encyclical letters to the archimandrites on the new doctrinal protocols—'

'What new doctrinal protocols? And since when did we have doctrines? We're scientists, not priests—'

Delmatius gave him a patient look, making it clear that Alexius was being suffered gladly. 'I explained it all last week,' he said. 'About the general conclave resolving the synthesis-diathesis debate by simply reducing the agreed number of elemental principles from seven to six. It's all quite ...'

'Marvellous,' Alexius grumbled. 'It's perfectly all right to change the laws of nature provided it's done by a democratic vote. I think it's high time I got out of this bed and put a stop to all this nonsense.'

'Don't you even think of it,' Delmatius replied with ferocious jollity. 'You even set foot to floor and the doctors'll skin you alive. Anyway, that's them,' he went on, separating one thick sheaf of documents and waving another under his nose. 'This lot here's just decretals and your private correspondence.'

While Alexius was sealing the letters and trying to concentrate on not setting his bedding alight with the candle, Delmatius told him the latest news.

'They do say,' he twittered, 'that the clans are up to no good again. If you ask me, it's high time something was done about them.'

Alexius, who had just spilt hot wax on the back of his hand, looked up. 'Really? Such as what?'

'Send an army,' Delmatius replied. 'Clean 'em out once and for all. I mean to say, it just doesn't make sense, having hordes of savages right there on our doorstep.'

Six years ago, Alexius recalled, Delmatius had been on a boat crossing the Middle Sea from the unlovely city-state of Blemmya, along with a couple of hundred other refugees who'd been thrown out for having big noses and the wrong colour hair. To this day he was capable of getting lost between the Carters' Bridge and the City Academy. It was pleasing to think that in six short years he'd recovered so completely from his nasty dose of human intolerance that he could now cheerfully recommend the mindless persecution of others. 'I didn't think we still had an army,' he said mildly. 'I'm sure I'd have noticed if we had.'

'There's the levy,' Delmatius explained, 'and the city guard, of course. More than enough to teach a mob of savages a good lesson. Apparently they're playing some game or other upriver. Hauling great rafts of logs, would you believe. Load of nonsense, it goes without saying. I mean,' he added, with a grin, 'what would a lot of savages want with a riverful of logs?'

Loredan, having been asked roughly the same question, forebore to answer. He was mending one of the practice foils with sailmaker's twine and glue, which gave him an excuse for not having heard.

'Apparently,' Athli went on, 'there's talk of sending out an expeditionary force, under that man – oh, what's his name? It's on the tip of my tongue.'

'Do me a favour and put your finger just there – no,

there, that's it – while I slap some glue on this. Careful, it's sticky.'

'Maxen, that's it. General Maxen. They say his name's a legend out on the plains.'

Loredan frowned and dipped his brush in the glue pot. 'He's dead,' he replied. 'Been dead for twelve years now.'

'Oh.' Athli shrugged. 'So who's in charge of the army, then?'

'Nobody.' The glue was too thin. Loredan clicked his tongue, added another pinch of beads and stirred the pot. 'And there isn't any army either, unless you count the wall decorations they call the city guard. We haven't had an army for twelve years. Good thing too, if you ask me. We should count ourselves lucky we don't need one and leave it at that.'

'Can I move my finger yet?'

'Just bear with me a second till I've got this glue hot. So what are the clans supposed to be up to, according to your reliable sources?'

'I don't know, do I? Someone was saying something about large shipments of timber being floated down the river in this direction, but I thought the clans didn't go in for that sort of thing; boats and sailing and rivers and stuff.'

'They don't. Or at least,' he conceded, 'they used not to. Maybe they do now. Given the rate we use timber in this city, perhaps they're bringing it here to sell it. It'd be worth their while if they did.'

'That's probably it, then. Only I did hear it said that they'd declared war on us or something. Apparently the old chief's died and his son's a bit of a firebrand.'

'Oh, that's just bluster, probably,' Loredan said, his eyes fixed on the join he was glueing. 'When a new chief takes over, it's traditional to make a bit of noise and rattle the bow-cases. Makes everybody feel good about being a mighty warrior. They don't mean anything by it.'

'Ah.' Athli sneezed, the result of being close to the steaming glue. 'You seem to know a lot about the clans,' she said. 'How come?'

'Things I've heard. Soldiers' stories, that sort of thing. You tend to meet a lot of old soldiers in grotty taverns. Right, you can take your finger away, thank you. Pass me the twine and I'll get this served up.'

'It's a worrying thought, though,' Athli went on after a short pause. 'What if they did take it into their heads to attack us? If we've got no army—'

Loredan pulled a face. 'If we had an army,' he replied, 'there'd be someone for them to fight. It's the only possible way we could suffer a defeat; and they're a tough proposition in a pitched battle,' he added, 'or so I've heard. As it is, all they could do if they did come for us is sit on the other side of the river and watch the grain ships sail into the harbour. You may have noticed the big stone things, we call them walls—'

'All right, there's no need to be cocky about it. I still think – well, we're all brought up thinking the walls are guaranteed impregnable, but I don't know the first thing about sieges and the like. How do we know if they're impregnable or not?'

'Well, the fact the city's never fallen to a land assault's a pretty good hint,' he replied, as he patiently wrapped the twine thickly round the shaft. 'Not for want of trying, either. If you were going to bust in here, you'd need the proper equipment; engines, siege towers, rams, bridging gear. That's way beyond the capacity of the clans. No, the only way they'd get in is if someone opened the gate for them, and somehow I don't see that happening.'

'That's all right, then.' Athli stood up, wiping her hands on the piece of rag draped over the back of Loredan's chair. 'I guessed it was just a rumour, or else the Emperor'd be doing something about it.'

'Well, of course. That's what he's for.' He tied a neat, tiny knot and bit through the twine. 'If you want to terrify yourself to sleep with the thought of foreign invasions, you'd be better occupied panicking about the Islanders.'

'But I thought they were our allies,' Athli objected.

'So they are, up to a point. They do a lot of business with

us, but that doesn't mean to say they wouldn't rather take without paying. More to the point, they're the only ones with a fleet that's even remotely strong enough. It'd take some doing, though, getting past the engines and the boom across the straits. I can't honestly see anybody with half a brain trying to attack the city. There's plenty of softer targets to pick off first. Right, that's that done. Only the second one I've had to repair so far. Not bad going, if you ask me.'

He lit a candle and snuffed out the lamp. There was nobody else left in the Schools at this time of night; fortunately, he'd managed to talk the governors into letting him have a key to the side door. 'Let's go and have something to eat,' he said. 'It's been one of those days.'

He had the key in the lock when someone called his name. He turned round and was surprised to see whatsername, the strange girl from his class. 'Hello,' he said. 'What're you doing here at this time of night?'

'You told me I needed to practise the arm's-length hold,' she replied, sounding as if she was offended that he'd needed to ask. She looked tired; her forehead was shiny with sweat and her fringe was spiky. 'If you can spare me the time, I'd like it if you could watch me through it. Is that all right?'

Loredan raised both eyebrows. 'I suppose so,' he said dubiously.

The girl looked at him, then at Athli. 'If there's an extra charge, I'll be happy to—'

'Standard rates plus a quarter per hour for individual coaching,' said Athli firmly. 'I'll put it on your bill.' She flicked a glance at Loredan which read, *Watch yourself, this one fancies you.* Loredan interpreted it correctly and shook his head slightly.

At least, he didn't think so. But she was *odd*, no doubt about that. It wasn't that she didn't have a personality; quite the opposite, he was sure. But there was this screen up all round it, like the painted silk screen that was supposed to hide the Emperor whenever he gave an audience, so that his person would not be defiled by the eyes of commoners. Or something like that. Anyway, she was odd. 'You going to hang around?' he asked Athli, slightly nervously. She shook her head.

'I'm off home,' she said. 'Nobody's paying *me* time and a quarter.'

He let her out and locked the door. 'Right,' he said. 'Since we've got the place to ourselves, we might as well use the exhibition hall, where we can have some light.' He gestured vaguely in the direction of the tall arch opposite where they were standing. 'Bring a torch and we'll light the sconces.'

He didn't know why, but he had an uncomfortable feeling as they walked into the big empty arena. It had been built as a close copy of the courtroom itself, the idea being to get students used to the feel of the big occasion, the spectators' benches and the peculiar acoustic that could be extremely offputting if you weren't accustomed to it. They hadn't quite got that right – nowhere else did the noise of two swords clattering together sound quite so loud and brittle – but it was near enough to make Loredan feel uncomfortable.

'We'll light the place up properly,' he called out, glad to hear his voice sounding loud and confident in the empty darkness. 'Might as well, we're not paying for the wax.'

She didn't reply, and he felt rather foolish for chattering away, as if this was some social occasion. *Why did I agree to this?* he muttered to himself. *Maybe Athli's right and I've been lured here to have my honour compromised.* He thought of the girl's face. It had never occurred to him to notice whether she was pretty or not. Considered objectively she was, in an angular kind of way, but … No, he couldn't see that at all. Not that sort.

'All right,' he said, putting the last candle back in its sconce, 'let's get on with it. Use the sword in the red bag. Careful with it, mind. That's my Spe Bref.'

She nodded and untied the knot. *She bites her fingernails, I hadn't noticed that.* In her hand the sword looked strangely unfamiliar, as if its loyalty might be in question. She let the bag fall and held the sword out at arm's length, moving her feet and shoulders into position and straightening her back.

'That's almost it,' Loredan said, trying to ˉsound encouraging. 'The left shoulder a bit further back, right foot in line with the blade. That's better, you've got it. Now hold that.'

Under his breath he started to count, while he untied the second bag. For some reason his fingers were clumsy, and he caught his fingernail on the hard cord. 'You're making it hard for yourself,' he said, drawing the cut-down cavalry sword out and fitting it into his hand. 'You're gripping the hilt instead of letting it sit in the slot. Here, watch me.' He took position opposite her, slowly raising his right arm and the sword until the two blades formed a single continuous line. 'See, I'm letting my fingertips and the base of my thumb do all the work. That's the whole point of the exercise; a soft grip's much surer than a white-knuckle job, and you can move more freely. There now, that's much better. Keep it going, you're doing fine.'

She didn't seem to be listening; or rather, she didn't give a damn about his encouragements and explanations. It was that feeling he'd had before, that she didn't *want* to learn, she *had* to learn, as if this was some loathsome but necessary task. *Oh, well, takes all sorts. And her motivation is none of my business, I'm delighted to say.*

'All right, rest,' he said after a full minute. The girl frowned at him, as if she was going to argue, then lowered the blade. 'In a moment, we'll do that again and try for two minutes, but this time start off with the grip like I told you, and we'll take it from there. All right?'

She nodded. The slight movement of her head was a very precise, efficient communication, designed to limit the contact between them to the barest minimum. It was like the exchange of nods at the start of a fence, when the judge had given the word; the way two enemies communicate when they have nothing left to say except, *Now let's try and kill each other.* The recognition shocked Loredan a little.

'Right. And, now.' They raised their arms at precisely the

same moment, and Loredan found himself looking into her eyes over a causeway of steel. It was an unpleasant moment, just like being in court again, only worse. In court, when he looked the other man in the eye, he could always see that little residual glow of fear, and of course the other man would always see it in him. It was the last exchange of shared humanity, the one final thing they had in common at the very end. There was no fear in the girl's eyes, only a rather unpleasant absence of anything.

Never again, he promised himself. *And to hell with the money.*

He was counting; one minute forty-five, one minute fifty, and she hadn't wavered at all. An impressive performance, this, for someone who'd consistently muffed the manoeuvre in class. Somehow that worried him – maybe she'd been muffing it deliberately to engineer this session, though why in hell she'd want to was beyond him. Unmistakable, nevertheless, this feeling of being manipulated, combined with a distinctly spooky notion that they were being watched. *Come on, Bardas, you'll be seeing pink frogs next. Let's get this over with and go home.*

One minute fifty-eight – the girl's sword-tip wiggled, just the tiniest amount, and she made a little grunting noise, which Loredan recognised as pure agony. He could sympathise with that; his shoulder and bicep were cramped something awful, though he had the experience to keep going. Her sword-tip wobbled again, and again; a wider, more uncontrolled twitch this time. *That'll do,* Loredan decided; then, on impulse, *Let's try her on the next stage, recovery from guard. She deserves that for doing this so well.* He checked his line quickly and then lunged at her. She got the idea and parried, and they fenced two or three returns (*natural ability there, no question about that; I'm jealous*) until he knocked the sword out of her hand with a short, hard flick of his wrist that jarred the muscles right up to his elbow. The pain made him catch his breath; he bent almost double, hugging his forearm and swearing under his breath.

The girl looked furious with herself, and said nothing.

'If it's any consolation,' Loredan gasped, 'that was really quite impressive. You're getting the hang of it just fine.' He massaged the muscle on top of his forearm, bitterly regretting the urge to show off, which had done him an injury and embarrassed him in front of a student. She didn't seem to be interested in that, though.

'I failed,' the girl grunted back. 'I let you beat me.'

For some reason, that remark made Loredan feel distinctly uncomfortable. 'Be fair,' he said, trying to sound jovial. 'I'm supposed to be your instructor.'

'Being good isn't enough,' she replied, and Loredan had the distinct impression that she wasn't really talking to him. 'You can be very good and still die, if the other man's better.'

Loredan shrugged, trying rather hopelessly to lighten the atmosphere. 'You know,' he said, 'I'm so glad I retired when I did. If there's one thing I could never stand, it's perfectionists.'

The girl looked at him resentfully, her arms crossed over her chest, her fingers clawing her shoulders. Loredan had seen women do that before, and had a vague idea what it meant. He didn't know what was going on, and he rather hoped he wouldn't have to find out; even so, he felt he should say something.

'Sorry if I'm being personal,' he said, 'but why does this matter so much to you? You're making really good progress, you know, well in advance of where the others ...'

She turned her head slightly away, as if trying to get out of the way of his words. 'I want to do well,' she said.

'Well, you are. You've got a natural gift for it, which is something not many people have.' A thought occurred to him. 'Runs in the family, perhaps?'

'My uncle was a fencer.' She was looking straight at him now, as she had before, except that there were no two yards of steel to keep them apart. 'Maybe you've heard of him; Teofil Hedin.'

Loredan frowned; it rang a bell but nothing more. 'I'm hopeless at names,' he replied. 'I never forget a face, but names just go in one ear and out the other.' He grinned, rather sourly. 'Besides,' he added, 'in this business you quite often get to meet people only once, so there isn't all that much point.'

'I can *see* that.' She picked up the sword and held it by the blade, just under the hilt. 'Can we practise that one more time?'

Oh, no, do we really have to? 'Yes, why not?' he said, as cheerfully as he could. 'I won't join you this time, though. Costs me money if I sprain my wrist.'

She nodded, took the sword by the hilt and extended her arm, bringing the tip of the blade down until it touched the hard floor. 'This time I'd like to try for four minutes.'

Loredan shrugged. 'If you like,' he said. 'All right. And, now.'

She raised the sword; the point was directly in line with the hollow at the base of his throat, the perfect Old fence guard. He turned away, counting under his breath, and put his sword back in its case. When he looked back, she hadn't moved at all. *Very impressive, even if she is a nutcase.*

'When you're practising on your own,' he said, 'start off with one minute and work your way up; don't try doing three or four straight from rest. It's better for you and does more good.'

Her eyes never left him; or, more precisely, that square inch of his throat which constituted the target. It was as if she'd been doing this all her life, he reflected, and the thought crossed his mind that if she moved now – a slight bend of the right knee, a slight shift of weight and balance – she could run him through before he had the slightest chance of getting out of the way. He felt sweat in the hollowed palms of his hands, and an urge to take a couple of steps backwards. But that would be—

'Three minutes,' he said. 'Trying for four.'

And then he felt it again: an oppressive feeling of being under observation, like an exhibit or a scientific experiment. Something ought to be happening now, he was certain of it. But the girl was as still as a statue, almost as if some god had frozen her in the act of making ready for the lunge. The urge to get out of the way was becoming hard to control – *instinct*. Loredan told himself; *after ten years in the racket, every reason why I should feel jumpy having someone point a sword at me.* It was starting to bother him more than it should; apart from the sweaty hands, he discovered that he was getting what promised to be one hell of a headache. Three minutes twenty-five, and still not a twitch from the blade.

Only goes to show what a damn good teacher I am.

Three minutes fifty-five, and his eyes were starting to play tricks on him. He knew the girl hadn't wobbled at all, but it was as if he could see the present and the future as well, the sword-tip hanging motionless in the air and also lunging towards him, perfectly on line. *If she does lunge*, he thought wildly, *I'll only have myself to blame.*

Three minutes fifty-nine …

Behind him, the sound of someone clearing his throat. Loredan turned sharply, at the precise moment when the girl bent her right knee and let the sword-point drop. There was a man in the archway, watching them.

'Master Loredan?' Damnation, it was Lethas Modin, one of the governors, and he didn't look happy. 'I saw the light.'

Loredan drooped slightly. 'I was just giving this student a little extra tuition,' he said, trying to sound matter-of-fact. 'Very promising student she is too. Master Modin, my student …'

Damn. Can't remember her name. Hopeless at names, me.

The girl mumbled her name. Master Modin didn't seem particularly interested. 'I do wish you'd let me know when you intend using the facilities for extracurricular coaching,' he said irritably. 'Strictly speaking, there are additional charges; candles, ground rent and so on. I'll overlook it this time, but if you intend to do this on a regular basis—'

Loredan's brow furrowed. His headache was in full cry now, and the last thing he wanted to do was stand still and be told off in front of a student by a member of the board of governors. What the devil was the old fool doing here at this time of night in any case? Didn't these people have homes to go to? 'Thank you, Master Modin, I'll certainly bear that in mind and let you know in future. And if you'll let my clerk know how much I owe you for the candles—'

Modin waved the offer aside petulantly. 'Will you be much longer?' he asked. 'Again, strictly speaking there should be a member of the board present in the building whenever the facilities are in use, in case of accidents; the formalities, you know.' He looked at the girl, as if he'd seen something odd but had no idea what it was. 'That most regrettable incident the other week, for example. We are directly accountable to the authorities in the event that – ah – blood is shed on these premises.'

For some reason Loredan felt a cold shiver down his neck. 'My apologies, Master,' he replied stiffly. 'And we've finished for tonight, thank you. I'm sorry for any inconvenience.'

The governor made a faint snuffling noise conveying disapproval. 'Very well, Master Loredan. Miss,' he added, nodding rather reluctantly at the girl. 'Good night.'

As he locked the side door of the Schools behind him, Loredan felt rather better. His head was still pounding like a drop-hammer, but it wasn't as bad as it had been. *Now then, what was all that about? Well, at least we can knock Athli's theory on the head.* He pulled out the key, dropped it in his pocket and shouldered the equipment bags. It was a cold night, and he could smell rain.

Thank heaven for small mercies, he added.

Purple to blue; blue to green; watch the colours in the steel as the heat of the furnace soaks into it. Wait for the last change, green darkening almost to black but catch it before it goes over—

'That'll do,' Temrai said, wiping his forehead with his sleeve. 'Now quench it, quick.'

The long, flat ribbon of steel hissed in the water and became invisible under a blanket of steam. Once the hissing had stopped they pulled it out, and he examined it carefully.

'All right,' he said, trying to mask his apprehension. 'Now bend it double.'

Two strong men couldn't quite do that; but it bent like the limbs of a bow and didn't snap. 'That'll do,' Temrai said, relieved. 'That's all right, then. Now we know how to temper long saw-blades.'

He left them to sharpen the teeth, using splinters of sandstone knapped into wedges, and walked back along the bank to the main logging camp. With six- and eight-feet saws instead of axes, adzes and drawknives they could fell timber and cut it up into logs and planks at twice, maybe three times the pace. Just as well, if all the timber he needed was to be assembled at the downriver station before the winter came on and froze everything up. Carting the stuff, especially over snowed-up passes, would be a complication he could do without.

The whole valley was full of noise and movement. On the hillside, above the belt they'd already cleared and turned into a stubble of tree-stumps and lopped branches, the forest was ringing to the sound of hundreds of axes and the shouts of the lumberjacks and drovers as the teams of horses and oxen were hitched up to the trimmed logs. Below, on the rafting stages, logs were being unhitched and rolled down to the water to be prodded and cajoled together into rafts, while the rafters scampered from log to log, swearing, yelling, getting the job done somehow. *We're making this all up as we go along*, Temrai reflected with a mixture of wonder and panic. *Well, now we've got saws, and we can dig saw-pits. It'd have been interesting to try and build water-powered saws like the ones I saw in the city, but I don't think we've got time. And besides, there's being clever and there's being clever for cleverness's sake.*

What worried him most of all was the guesswork. The first week they'd been here, all he and his people had done was count trees, cutting marks in the bark of the ones tall and straight enough to be worth felling, trying to estimate how many good planks and beams each tree would produce, double-guessing how many planks and beams they'd need to build an unspecified number of engines and machines. At the end of the week he'd given up and told them to fell anything that looked halfway useful. It was either going to be far too little or far too much.

There was also the problem of keeping the clan stationary in a generally unsuitable spot for an unprecedentedly long time. Already they'd had to send the herds off upriver to fresh grazing, and too much badly needed manpower with them. That meant detailing yet more men to carting supplies and hunting game in the back end of the forest, away from the noise and disturbance. Add to that the parties he'd had to send away to forage for iron ore and lime, the charcoal-burning details, the contingent sent to guard the women who were gathering and twisting reed for the quite staggering quantities of rope they seemed to be getting through – somehow, there were always enough people left to do the work. This clan is *big*, he was beginning to realise. *There's more of us than I thought.*

'I gather the saw worked.' Jurrai had appeared behind him, mud-splashed and dishevelled from supervising the dispatch of the latest log raft. 'That's good. Shall I take the smiths off nailmaking and put them on saws?'

Temrai shook his head. 'I've already seen to all that,' he said. 'The nailmakers are now making arrowheads while the arrowmakers start making the saws. The grinding crews are teaching the spare five to seven year olds how to grind arrowheads, so they'll be available to grind the saws. And I've put the flintcutters onto shaping and dressing grindstones, which means the— Anyway,' he added with a tired grin, 'it's all in hand.' He stopped and looked around at the thousands of busy dots moving about the scarred and unreal-looking landscape. 'We must be mad,' he said, 'even trying to do all this. It took the city people hundreds of years to figure out what they know—'

Jurrai shrugged. 'Good of them to do the boring bit for us,' he said. 'And in the long run it'll serve them right.' He too spent a moment looking about him; maybe he didn't particularly like what he saw. 'Gods alone know what this is doing to us,' he said quietly. 'There's been muttering about it already. People are saying it's not right.'

'I bet,' Temrai grunted. 'What's it this time? Offending the river gods, offending the forest gods, offending the fire gods—'

'All of that,' Jurrai replied cheerfully. 'But what they're saying now is, if the city folk are evil and have got to be put down, why exactly are we running ourselves ragged trying to be like them?'

'Ah.' Temrai smiled, rather sadly. 'I don't know the answer to that one. Imitation being the sincerest form of flattery, maybe. They try and wipe us out; we learn by their example.' He rubbed his face between his hands. 'I'm not exactly happy about it myself. Still, it's got to be done. I think we're all agreed on that, down where it matters. And anybody who thinks we can bust through the walls of Perimadeia with a cavalry charge is welcome to see me and tell me how it can be done. I'd love to hear.' He yawned, stretched and stood up. 'Now then,' he said briskly, 'arrow-shafts. I'd better go and see how they're getting on with the pole lathes.'

The lathe-making detail was busy in a small high-sided combe just over the brow of the nearby hill, which had already been cleared of timber. As he walked over the crest, Temrai could see what looked like a plantation of saplings; except that these saplings had been felled, trimmed and fixed in the ground to act as the springs for the hundred or so arrow-making lathes that Temrai hoped to have up and running in the next day or so. It was very basic stuff, by city standards; the bent sapling had a rope tied round its top, which was in turn wrapped round a spindle mounted on two trestles and then fed through to a hinged treadle. The arrow-turner pressed the treadle down with his foot, pulling in the rope and turning the spindle in one direction. Then the sapling pulled it back, turning the spindle the other way. The end of the spindle was fitted with two prongs which went into the end of the length of branchwood destined eventually to be an arrowshaft; the other end was supported by a tailstock, which held the branch level. As the spindle turned, so did the branch, and the turner pressed a sharp steel blade against it, shearing off spirals of wood and eventually producing a uniformly straight, slender shaft—

(*But we're mostly using green timber, which at best makes lousy arrows, which'll fly crooked and slow even if they don't break on the bowstring. It's quite possible we're wasting our time and energy doing all this. If only we could take a little more time about it, make sure we get it right. Except we'd all be long dead before it's as right as it should be. All I can do is try and make it the least wrong I can.*)

'As to how many arrows we're going to need,' Temrai commented ruefully as they walked between the rows of three-quarters-finished lathes, 'I really don't want to know. Think about it. A man can aim and shoot twelve arrows a minute; one of these machines can make maybe twenty a day, if these men are prepared to work until they drop. We'll never have enough, even if there's enough wood to make the wretched things from. And it's the wrong sort of wood,' he added. 'And it's green. As to where we're going to get the feathers from—'

'I was coming to that,' Jurrai said. 'One of my people says there's a lake up in the next range of hills that's covered in ducks.'

'Ducks,' Tumrai repeated. 'Right.'

'Which isn't a bad idea even if we forget the feathers,' Jurrai went on. 'I gather we've run the last of the deer out into the hills, and if we don't want to have to start culling the milch herd—'

'Don't. All right, how many people do you need to go duck-hunting? Not that I ever heard of anybody fletching arrows with duck feathers, but we haven't got anything else.' True, he reflected as he said the words. Green wood and duck feathers, and we're meant to be a nation of mighty archers. Looks like we're doing our best to lull the enemy into a true sense of security.

At midday the noise and movement stopped, or at least

became less obtrusive as the food was handed round and the clan gathered in groups to eat. Temrai had just enough time to bite a mouthful out of the wedge of hard cheese before they descended on him; the puzzled, the exasperated, the querulous, the offended – *How do we do this? What were we meant to be doing? What in hell are we going to make that out of? How are we expected to do this and that without the proper tools? Do you seriously expect us to do that with this?* He fended off the enquiries and complaints as best he could, smiling, shaking his head, sympathising, promising he'd think of something or it'd all be seen to, until at last they all went away and it was time to start work again. He threw the rest of the cheese to a passing dog, and plodded away to see what was the matter with the raft ropes, which kept breaking.

Ah, well, he comforted himself, *the gods must feel like this all the time. And to think I used to envy them.*

Halfway through the afternoon, he'd just managed to convince the raft crews that the ropes were fraying because they were putting too much strain on them when he noticed something on the other side of the river; a party of horsemen, up against the skyline, watching what was going on. For a moment, he was seven years old again and terrified; he wanted to run through the camp and warn them, *Run for your lives, it's the cavalry!* But then he counted them, and thought about it, and called to his cousins Mesbai and Pepotai, who were working their way through the camp enlisting duck hunters.

'Quick as you like,' he said, 'get twenty men and go up round the back of that rise there—' He pointed to where the riders were. 'Don't do anything, just get the other side of them, make sure they don't notice you until you're in position, then come up on the crest and let them see you. If they move off, shadow them but don't make contact. Got that?'

Pepotai, a short, square youth with a long, wispy beard, nodded. 'We can bring 'em in if you like,' he said. 'Or shoo 'em off, if you'd rather.'

'No.' Temrai shook his head emphatically. 'I don't want that. For all they know, we love them dearly and wouldn't dream of hurting them. Let's keep it that way for now. Plenty of time for the other stuff later.'

When they'd gone, he allowed himself another look across the river. Ten riders from the city, sent to keep an eye on him, try and work out what he was up to down here among the tree-stumps. If Maxen was still alive, there'd have been none of this respectful watching from afar. Instead, the first they'd have known of it would have been heavy cavalry cascading down on all sides, flooding the camp, shooting, slashing, burning before anybody had a chance to get to a bow or a horse. *There's another thing I've got to do*, he decided, *post lookouts on all the approaches, and along the riverbank, too. Maxen'd have blocked the river by now, and slaughtered the men downstream* ... An unpleasant thought, that. A few men up there armed and ready, just in case they did try anything? Or would that be counterproductive, put them on their guard by showing men-at-arms as well as peacefully industrious lumberjacks?

Gods above, I shall be glad when this is all over, and we can go back to doing what we were always meant to do. He turned his back on the obtrusive presence of the city and walked away.

CHAPTER NINE

The man knocked, came in, hooked up the chandelier and went away again. Alexius, who had been asleep, yawned and sat up. Couldn't be that time already, could it? Well, presumably it was. He lit a candle from the small lamp, found his place in the book he'd been reading, and tried to concentrate.

When we consider the essential universality of the Principle, observing it as a whole and not merely the sum of its multifarious perceptible effects (which by definition cannot be taken to be true paradigms of the larger image, diluted as they are by the material and the purely fortuitous), we can at last begin tentatively to approach a state of awareness in which the infinite and the individual gradually cease to be capable of differentiation...

It wasn't much better the second time he tried to read it; it was still like trying to catch a runaway goose in a thicket of brambles. He didn't put the book down, but he allowed the page to go out of focus. Not long afterwards, he was asleep again—

—And standing on the city walls, up on the top platform of one of the towers that guarded the Drovers' Gate, looking out across the place where the river forked out towards the plains. In the distance the clouds met the horizon; there was a keen wind blowing them towards the sea, like a young sheepdog rounding up the flock, but these were clouds of dust.

Standing beside him, for some reason, were Bardas Loredan the advocate, Vetriz and her brother and a man he didn't know; another Islander by his rather appalling taste in clothes, but a city look to him nevertheless. They were staring out at the clouds of dust like spectators at a horse race or a lawsuit. After a while, Vetriz nudged her brother in the ribs.

'Two gold quarters on this lot,' she said.

Her brother pulled a face. 'No chance,' he replied.

'Give you ten to one.'

He shook his head. 'I don't take sucker bets,' he said.

'But on past form—' Vetriz started to say. Venart shook his head and grinned. 'Oh, well,' Vetriz said, smiling angelically, 'it was worth a try.'

The curious thing, Alexius couldn't help noticing, was that the dust clouds were now rising up out of the sea—

(*'Gannadius? Is that you?'*

'In your dream, I know. I would have come here in a dream of my own, but I have to stay awake this evening. Official reception for the archimandrite of Turm, you know. I promise I'll be as unobtrusive as possible.')

—And that they were not so much dust clouds as sails; thousands of grey-black sails, fat in the harsh wind that was now blowing directly in Alexius' face, making the sails crowd in at terrific speed; and the woman Vetriz was saying, 'Three gold fives at twenty-five to one,' and was finding no takers.

'This is most bizarre.' Bardas Loredan was talking to him, though he was looking straight out to sea. 'I know you, of course, by sight. I suppose almost everybody in the city does. But why am I having a dream about you? I suppose you must symbolise magic or something.'

'With respect,' Alexius replied, 'I'm the one having a dream about you. And it isn't magic, it's philosophy.'

'Oh.' Loredan shrugged. 'I'm sorry, but all that stuff's way above my head. Gorgas is the mystic in our family, aren't you?'

The man Alexius didn't know stared straight ahead, and nodded. 'And for your information,' he added, 'this is my dream and you're just figments of my—'

* * *

Vetriz woke up with a start.

Light was beginning to seep in through the shutters, and the face beside her on the pillow was glowing pale gold, the intensity of the light showing up the marks and flaws on the skin. With his eyes shut and the frown that people tend to wear when they're deep asleep, he looked older, somehow rather cruel. Vetriz yawned and brushed the hair out of her eyes.

'Gorgas,' she said.

'Go 'way.'

'Gorgas. It's time to get up.'

'Mbz.'

Vetriz slid out of bed and opened the shutters. Below the window, the sea was dark blue, almost black, with a smudge of red and gold where the clouds joined the water. From her window, Vetriz could look directly down on her and her brother's three ships, moored slightly apart from the other ships in Haya Morone, the best anchorage on the Island. She struggled into her gown, knotted the belt and pulled a comb through her hair.

'Gorgas,' she said, 'you really do have to get up now. Venart's ship's in the harbour. He could be here any minute.'

The big, thickset man in the bed opened one eye. 'You silly cow, why didn't you tell me?' he snapped, swinging his legs out and groping for his clothes. 'Didn't I tell you—?'

'Hurry.' Vetriz turned away from him, wondering what the hell she'd seen in the man the night before. It wasn't, after all, the sort of thing she usually did. 'And there's no need to be rude. He's got to get through customs and see to the unloading, anyhow. You needn't *panic*,' she added scornfully.

Gorgas Loredan didn't say anything to that; he was preoccupied with pulling his boots on over his extremely large feet. Vetriz didn't want to look at him now. Last night's wine jug was on the windowsill; she tilted it, but it was empty.

Her head hurt. Served her right for behaving like a slut.

Not that she was afraid that Venart actually might get violent if he came back early. In the unlikely event of the door flying open to reveal him standing there with drawn sword and a face like thunder, all she'd have to do was giggle or say, 'Ven, what *do* you think you're doing with that thing?' and he'd get frightfully embarrassed and back away, growling, like a dog from a red-ants' nest. And besides, if he came right in and killed Gorgas Loredan in front of her eyes, it wasn't exactly likely to ruin her life. What she couldn't face was the prospect of Ven nagging and rebuking and drawing his breath in through his teeth in a pained manner for the next six months, and insisting on taking her with him or leaving her in the charge of their gods-accursed aunt.

'Are you dressed yet?' she said. 'I thought it was women who were meant to be slow in the mornings.'

'It's all right, I'm going,' the voice behind her replied. 'Is there a side door to this place?'

'I'll show you,' Vetriz replied. 'Come on.'

And yet last night, it had all seemed so *meant*, somehow; at the dinner party, where she'd been boasting about how she'd met the Patriarch of the city – such a strange man, though really quite sweet – and been to a real swordfight in the lawcourts … and her neighbour had nudged her in the ribs and pointed to the top of the men's table and said, 'Don't look now, but see that big, chunky one at the end? His brother's a swordfighter in Perimadeia.' And then she'd said the name, and it was the same man she'd seen, *and* the same man who'd been in that very funny dream she'd had at the Patriarch's palace, or whatever it was called…. And the wine had been passed round three or four times too often, and the man she'd gone with had been dying to give her the slip and go off with that Morozin trollop (good luck to both of them) and then…

Well. It hadn't been that bad *then*, but now she wanted it over, done with and put away neatly. She closed the door after Captain Gorgas Loredan – nearly trapped the hem of his cloak in it, now that'd have added a redeeming touch of comedy to an otherwise rather dreary episode – and went through to the courtyard to have a bath.

It was nearly midday when Venart finally came home, looking tired and rather cross.

'I know we're descended from pirates,' he grumbled as he kicked off his boots, 'and I'm all for keeping alive old traditions. I just think the customs office shouldn't feel obliged to rob me blind just out of a sense of cultural identity, that's all. Is there any food?'

'Of course there is,' Vetriz replied. 'What do you think I've been doing while you were away, throwing wild orgies?'

'You might as well,' he said, massaging his feet. 'Better to blow the lot in dissipation and decadent frivolity than see it all go down the throats of those sharks down at the pool. I'll be lucky to break even on that malted barley, what with the tariff they stung me for.'

'Bread, cheese and an apple do you? Or are you going to insist on hot soup?'

'Anything that isn't fish,' Venart said, with feeling. 'If any fish comes in this house for the next six weeks, I'm leaving. There is nothing, I repeat *nothing*, to eat in Psattyra but raw bloody fish, unless you count the raw yellow fungus stuff as food, which I don't.'

'You poor lamb,' Vetriz said absently. 'Have a lie down for an hour while I get you something.'

The headache wore off quite quickly, helped on its way by willow bark steeped in rosewater and an orange, and the bath more or less removed Captain Loredan's fingerprints from her person. Even so, she felt tired and listless – not enough sleep, only yourself to blame. No wonder you had nightmares, mixing mead, cider and strong wine.

Not exactly nightmares. A proper nightmare would have been better, somehow.

Bardas Loredan woke up sweating and cursing, saw the light through the shutters and scrambled for his clothes. His head was splitting; filthy, rotten, cheap, industrial-grade red wine on an empty stomach. Now then; if he really hurried, he could get to the Schools in time to be only a quarter of an hour late. Damn that wretched, weird, crazy girl for making him need a drink.

In the event, he was only ten minutes late; rather an achievement, all things considered, and he should have received the congratulations and admiration of his class rather than all those frosty stares.

'All right,' he said, 'settle down, sorry I'm late. Now then, the footwork of the Old fence. Positions, please; not like that, Master Iuven, not unless you intend to confuse your opponent by falling over. Front foot in line with the blade, back foot square, come on, we've done this a hundred times ...'

Why should I dream about him, after all these years? And that foreign girl and her brother from the tavern? And the Patriarch, of all people? That is definitely the last time I try and economise on a heavy-drinking session.

The girl, the sullen, unnerving pain-in-the-bum who was the cause of all this, was fencing magnificently today. Her movements were beginning to take on that deadly, graceful poise that all the best advocates had, something he'd seen in others but never himself. He'd always tended to associate it with a perverse pleasure in the act of killing and he didn't really hold with it, but it certainly boded well for the girl's future in the profession. For his part, he'd always fenced exactly like what he was, a highly skilled and intelligent coward who knew that his only way of staying alive was to kill someone else.

'Hello.' Athli had materialised behind him while he was watching the class do semicircles. 'How did your tête-à-tête with little Miss Hatchet-face go last night? Did you still respect each other in the morning?'

'Please don't be arch at me, Athli, I have a slight headache. And for your information, you couldn't have been further from the mark if you tried. I don't know what that bloody woman's after, but I'm delighted to say it's not me.'

'You sure about that?'

'Convinced. As far as she's concerned, I'm just someone who's teaching her how to carve people up. Talking of which, you just watch her this morning. I hate to say this, but she's going to be good.'

'Teacher's pet, huh?'

'Oh, go away and count something, there's a good girl.' A thought occurred to him. 'There's one thing you could usefully do,' he added. 'Go and smile bewitchingly at Governor Modin. He doesn't love me any more, and I can't be doing with aggravation from the likes of him. You could do that little girl standing on one foot and twirling a lock of hair between your fingers act, like you used to do for that dirty old man from the palm-oil people.'

'I never—' Athli sounded offended, then relaxed. 'All right,' she said. 'Quits?'

'Quits. But if you could try soothing Modin for me, it'd be a help. Apparently I've been abusing the governors' trust by doing individual coaching after hours without permission.'

Athli nodded. 'All right,' she said. 'I'll tell him a dying-grandmother story and offer to pay money.'

'Just so long as you don't pay money.'

Athli grinned. 'Trust me,' she said, 'I'm a lawyer.'

It was quite true, she reflected after she'd sorted out Governor Modin, about the standing on one leg and twirling a lock of hair (and fancy him having noticed). *I shouldn't really do that sort of thing, only it does make things easier sometimes, when there simply isn't* time *to win an argument or make a case on its merits. I suppose all's fair in love and litigation ...*

'Excuse me.'

She turned round and managed not to squeak with surprise. She wanted to say, 'Should you be up?' or, 'Oughtn't you to be in bed?' but of course she didn't. What she did say was, 'Patriarch, what can I do for you?'

'I'm sorry to trouble you,' the Patriarch said, 'but are you Master Loredan's clerk? The man on the door pointed you out to me.'

'That's right,' she said. So the rumours had been true, she

said to herself; he must have been ill, because he looks awful, poor man. 'Would you like to see him? He's teaching a class right now, but I'm sure it'd be no problem if—'

The Patriarch smiled. He had a nice smile. She was taken aback; usually he seemed so dignified and grand when he was taking part in some ceremony or civic function. But then he would, wouldn't he?

'That's all right,' he said, 'it's not urgent. Would it be in order for me to wait until the midday break?'

'If you're sure you don't mind …' Athli felt rather flustered. She now had the responsibility of keeping a frail dignitary amused and comfortable for the next hour. Would she have to stand there making small talk, or would he rather just sit in a quiet corner and read a book? Always assuming she could find him a chair; further assuming he wanted to sit down. Damnation, Athli thought. My mother didn't raise me to be a diplomat.

'No, not at all.' The Patriarch gestured for her to lead the way. (If he opens doors for me I'll die of embarrassment.) 'I do hope I'm not being a nuisance. I'm afraid I'm rather ignorant of the workings of this establishment.'

After she'd offered him everything she could think of, he finally agreed to accept a chair next to a pillar and a view of the class. 'And if I could trouble you for a drink of water,' he added, 'that would be very kind. I'm afraid I woke up this morning with rather an unpleasant headache.'

Oh, gods, where am I going to find him something to drink out of? 'No trouble at all,' she said firmly. 'I won't be a moment, if you're sure you're all right there.'

'Perfectly comfortable, thank you,' Alexius replied. 'You really are most kind.'

Once he'd got rid of the clerk – a sweet girl, but inclined to fuss; or maybe she's afraid I'll turn her into a frog – Alexius slumped into the chair and caught his breath. He felt dreadful, quite apart from his headache, and he knew he shouldn't have come; but it would have been equally impossible not to, after the dream he'd had last night.

Loredan's brother. He felt an irrational surge of

resentment towards Gannadius for not being there, although he knew perfectly well that his colleague had a meeting he couldn't get out of that would last until the middle of the afternoon. But he desperately wanted to know what Gannadius had made of the dream, and whether he'd seen the same things. Still, that couldn't be helped. More important to speak to Loredan himself, something he should really have done long before now, except that he couldn't face having to tell Loredan what he'd done. But there really wasn't any choice in the matter now. Heaven alone knew what he was going to say.

He opened his eyes and found he was looking at Loredan's back, masking the group of energetic-looking young people who were hopping and prancing round in a semicircle in response to his brisk commands. He'd decided he'd seen enough of that when the semicircle turned and he could see the faces of the students—

Hell and damnation! Her!

With an effort, Alexius made himself stay calm and keep breathing, though the pain in his chest and arm was enough to make him want to cry out. One of Loredan's students was that girl, the one who was the cause of all the trouble—

The one who wanted Loredan maimed; who'd been practising fencing exercises with him in that vision he'd had from the Islander woman – of course, how stupid of me not to have thought of it.

The one who was pointing a sword at Loredan's throat right this very minute.

Well, of course; she was learning how to fence. She'd have to learn, if she wanted to be skilled enough to mutilate an experienced and highly talented swordsman. The logic behind it all made him feel cold down to the soles of his feet.

That decided him; he'd have to tell Loredan everything, warn him of the danger. Once he'd done that, it might be possible, with Gannadius helping, to lift the curse and get this dreadful mess cleared up once and for all. *If only I'd had the sense and the courage to do it in the first place, instead of rushing off looking for naturals*— Best not to think of that. And now this horrible puzzle of Gorgas, the intellectual who dressed like an Islander and turned up in his dream along with the only other two Islanders he'd had dealings with recently. If ever he did manage to get clear of this, it would make a wonderful case study: something that could be included in the foundation course as a dreadful warning of the dangers of misusing the Principle.

'Here you are.' It was the fussy girl again, holding out to him an incredibly ornate silver cup. 'I'm sorry I was so long.'

He smiled, took the cup - heavens, it was some sort of fencing trophy - and drank deeply. 'Might I ask,' he said, 'who that young lady is? The one in Master Loredan's class.'

'Oh, that's—' Athli froze. It was on the tip of her tongue, but however hard she tried she simply couldn't remember the horrid girl's name. 'That's our star pupil,' she went on. 'Bardas - Master Loredan thinks very highly of her. A natural talent, he reckons.'

'I see,' Alexius replied, trying not to react to her unfortunate choice of words. 'And she's a regular member of the class?'

'Very much so,' Athli replied, nodding vehemently. 'We hope she'll be a credit to us in years to come.'

A sharp crash of colliding metal made them both look up. Loredan was teaching a back-foot parry in the Old fence. To demonstrate it, he'd got the girl to lunge at him, while he flicked her blade away, took a neat back-foot step to the right and counterattacked in the same movement. But it hadn't quite worked like that; the girl's thrust had almost beaten his defence, and he was off balance, holding her blade off by brute strength.

'Sorry,' he said, 'my fault. We'd better do that again.'

The girl disengaged her sword; Loredan resumed his position. Alexius could feel the pain of his fingernails digging into the palm of his hand.

'And, now,' Loredan said. This time he caught the blade perfectly, turned it, made his sideways move and brought the tip of his sword precisely up under the girl's chin, all in a fraction of a second. It was quite beautiful to watch. He lowered his sword and turned to the class to explain.

The girl lunged again.

The speed of Loredan's reaction was astounding. There was very little to see; a blur of reflected light, a clank and a bump and a crack as the girl's sword was knocked out of her hand and landed on the flagstones. The tip of Loredan's blade – it was the Spe Bref; Athli knew he kept it so sharp that it could pass through your skin into your flesh before you felt anything – was touching the soft, smooth skin just under the girl's chin, applying enough pressure to prick without drawing blood. He gave her a long, puzzled look down the length of the blade, withdrew it with a short, economical movement, and turned back to the class.

'As I was saying,' he began, 'it's vitally important to keep the wrist and elbow level throughout the manoeuvre ...'

The girl was white as a sheet and trembling, both hands around her neck. The rest of the class were staring at the two of them in fascinated horror, hardly daring to breathe. Athli, who'd have screamed if there had been time, had dropped her satchel, and the lid of her portable inkwell had come off, letting dark-brown ink seep through the cloth onto the floor. As for Alexius, it was only several seconds after the affair was over that he realised how bad the pain in his chest and arm had become. He tried to get up out of his chair, but that quickly proved to be impossible. He was about to panic when he felt the pain ebb rapidly away, like water out of a punctured skin. As if to redress the balance, his head was even more blindingly painful.

In a roughly similar way, though rather more slowly, the tension ebbed away too, as the brains of all present set about the task of revising what they'd just seen to make it more credible, fit to be stored in the memory. Even Alexius wondered for a moment whether he'd made it all up, seen what his melodramatic imagination secretly expected or hoped to see, rather than what had actually taken place. It might even have been a momentary relapse into the dream, a fragment of his vision interpolated like a scholar's note scribbled in tiny handwriting between the lines of a book. He had heard of such phenomena, particularly among the mentally disturbed and those who tried to enhance their meditations by chewing peculiar herbs; while you're speaking to him, a man's head can suddenly turn into that of a lizard or a bird, and then become human again in a fraction of a second. There were fortune tellers who reckoned that they saw into the future that way, and other charlatans and mystics who claimed they could tell if a man was guilty of murder, because there would be a split second when they could see the dead man's blood on his slayer's hands. Maybe it was something like that, Alexius told himself comfortingly. And maybe, he replied, it wasn't.

At midday the class rested as usual. The girl walked quickly away towards the drinking fountain; the rest of the students immediately formed a close, whispering huddle. Loredan, looking painfully weary, sat down on a kitbox and stared at the floor, rubbing his forehead with his fingertips.

'Bardas—' Athli began.

'Don't tell me I imagined it,' he interrupted savagely, not looking up. 'She tried to kill me. I just don't understand it. Why should ...?'

'Bardas,' Athli repeated. 'The Patriarch is here to see you.'

Loredan looked up, frowning. 'Don't be silly, Athli,' he said. 'What on earth would the Patriarch want to see me for?'

'Come over here and ask him for yourself.'

Before Loredan could argue further, he caught sight of the man sitting in the chair in the shadows of the colonnade. 'That's him?' he asked. 'This is turning out to be quite a day.'

Athli nodded. 'Shall I tell that girl to get lost?' she said. 'I'll get her bill ready and—'

She broke off; Loredan was grinning. 'You're going to protect me from a crazed assassin with an invoice, are you? Don't you dare. Fairly soon, that strange creature's going to be a first-class advertisement for this school. Right fool I'd look slinging her out now.'

'But she tried—'

'Unsuccessfully. Now then, shall we go and find out what the wizard wants?'

He knelt beside the Patriarch's chair while Athli (rather reluctantly) made herself scarce. Loredan was just about to launch into a general to-what-do-we-owe-the-honour babble when Alexius leant forward, close to his ear.

'Excuse the question, but have you got a headache?'

Loredan looked puzzled. 'Why, does it show?' he said. 'Actually it's better than it was. Earlier on I felt like a road gang was splitting rocks just behind my eyes.'

Alexius took a deep breath. 'Also,' he said, 'may I ask, do you have a brother called Gorgas?'

This time Loredan recoiled, like a man who's just put his foot down on a snake. 'As a matter of fact I do,' he replied. 'Or I did; he may be dead by now, for all I know. Or care, come to that.' He shifted his weight, to stop his leg going to sleep. 'In return,' he said, 'could you do something for me?'

'If I can.'

'All right. Could you tell me as much as you possibly can about the dream you had last night? I have a feeling about that, actually.'

'I will indeed,' Alexius replied. 'Finally, would you kill an old man who can barely walk, but who's desperately sorry and is trying his best to clear up the mess?'

'I suppose not. Why d'you ask?'

Alexius explained. When he'd finished, Loredan, who had been frowning as if trying to follow a conversation in a foreign language he could just about speak, nodded his head and said, 'I see.'

'I thought I'd better tell you,' Alexius continued. 'I should have done it long before this, of course, but …'

Loredan shrugged. 'Well, you've told me now.' He rubbed his chin. 'I'm sorry,' he said, 'but I'm badly out of my depth here. I've never had much to do with magic and that sort of thing, you see.'

For once, Alexius didn't even try and explain that it wasn't actually magic. 'It seemed – well, quite innocent at the time,' he went on, knowing that he was making things worse with every word, but unable to stop. The truly galling thing about it was that he had the feeling that Loredan simply didn't believe in any of this; the Principle, curses, naturals. A moment later Loredan, rather apologetically, confirmed this impression.

'I'm sorry if that sounds rude or disrespectful,' he added diffidently. 'It's just that I've always reckoned there was enough aggravation in the real world without making up a whole lot of spooky supernatural stuff as well. And so as far as I'm concerned, you've got nothing to apologise for.' He smiled. 'I'm sorry if I've offended you,' he added. 'If my neighbours heard me talking like this to the Patriarch, they'd dip me in a tar barrel for blasphemy. But thank you for telling me about *her*. I knew there was something seriously wrong there, but it hadn't occurred to me it might be personal. It's odd,' he went on, 'but in all my years in the business I never came across anything like that; I mean, advocates' families all know the score, you just don't get blood feuds and nonsense like that. If you did, the whole system'd be unworkable.' He sighed. 'Just my luck, really. The only half-decent student I've got, and she's only learning the trade because she wants to kill *me*. Well, she's wasted her money, because I've retired. If she kills me it'll have to be good, honest murder, and you said you reckoned her principles wouldn't let her do that.'

Alexius nodded. 'So she said. But when she tried to kill you just now ...'

Loredan shrugged. 'Actually, I don't think that was anything premeditated, just a student losing her rag. It happens. Only the other week we had a student go berserk in a tutorial, got himself killed. It's a damn nuisance when it happens, it makes terrible trouble for the Schools for a month or so until it all blows over. I'm getting my clerk to draw up a disclaimer for the students to sign before they start the course, just as a precaution.' He stood up. 'Anyway, many thanks for telling me all this, and, like I said, please forgive me if I've insulted you. It's nothing personal; I really admire what you people do, it's just I don't happen to believe in it.'

'I ...' Alexius stopped, and nodded. 'Please,' he said, 'don't worry about that. I do believe in it, and I'm still extremely concerned, but,' he added, as a flicker of alarm crossed Loredan's face, 'I'm certainly not going to preach at you or try and convert you to the true faith.' He smiled, and shrugged his shoulders. 'It occurs to me that if you really have retired from legal practice then the curse is comprehensively defeated, since the duel I saw can't ever happen. So it must have sorted itself out,' he added, 'somehow or other. Certainly with no help from me, which puts me in my place. What are you going to do about her, if I might ask?'

'Hm.' Loredan rubbed his nose against the palm of his hand. 'That's a tricky one. The obvious thing would be to throw her out on her ear, but I'm not sure I can do that. I mean, she's paid for her tuition.' A thought occurred to him, making him grin. 'If I was to tell her to sling her hook now,' he said, 'that'd be a breach of contract, for which she'd be fully entitled to take me to law. If she did that I'd have to conduct my own defence – think how it'd look for me professionally if I hired a lawyer, me being a trainer and all – and then I would be giving her a chance to kill me in the courtroom; counterproductive, yes? At the moment, of course, I could beat her with one hand tied behind my back, but at the rate she's going, if she joined another class she'd be a real threat inside a year, which is well within the statute of limitations on a contract dispute.'

He took a deep breath and sighed. 'More to the point,' he went on, 'slinging out good students for no readily apparent reason isn't exactly the best way to build up a good reputation in this business, and I'm doing this for a living. I'd be better off accidentally killing the wretched girl, as far as that side of things is concerned. Not that I'd do that,' he added, as the Patriarch's eyes widened. 'I may be a lawyer, but I'm not that bad. No, I think the safest way would be to let her finish the course and just keep an extra-special eye on her at all times. When I was in the army we used to have a saying: the enemy you can see is the least of your problems.'

'Well,' Alexius pushed against the arms of the chair. Loredan helped him up and handed him his stick. 'You know your own business, and I'd better leave you to it. My attempts to interfere in your affairs so far haven't exactly done any good to anybody. The best thing I can do, as far as I can see, is go home and read a book.' He smiled. 'Do you sometimes wonder what on earth possessed you to take up your particular career? I know I do.'

'All the time,' Loredan replied. 'Well, sometimes. But then, what the hell else would I have done with my life? It's not as if I was ever exactly spoilt for choice.'

Alexius wondered if he should offer him his hand, or pat him on the shoulder by way of informal benediction. He decided against it. 'One last thing,' he said. 'Your brother – he lives on the Island?'

'I don't think so. It's been a long time since I last had anything to do with him.'

'Is he – involved in my line of work in any way?'

'I have no idea. To be honest with you, I don't get on with him, never did. He left home some time before I did, and I don't think any of us were heartbroken to see him go.' Loredan grinned bleakly. 'He isn't a terribly nice man, my brother.'

'Ah.'

'So I don't think I can help you much there. Sorry about that. And now I'd better be getting back to my class, before they start grumbling about refunds. I was late in this morning, which doesn't help.'

Alexius changed his mind and put out his hand. 'Thank you, Bardas Loredan. For what it's worth, I really am very sorry.'

Loredan laughed, and took his hand. 'Listen,' he said, 'I've been forgiving people who've tried to kill me since before I started shaving. It's nice to be able to do it to someone who's still alive.'

'Now then,' Temrai said, taking a deep breath and fixing a smile on his face. 'I *think* we do it this way.'

Uncomfortably aware that he was being watched by several thousand people, he picked up a twig and started sketching lightly on the surface of the mud.

'First,' he said, 'we make the frame, which is really nothing more than four big bits of wood joined together into a square. These bits—' he skimmed the mud carefully, marking out the shape '—are the sides, and these bits join the sides together. Then we've got the uprights, with a beam across the top; oh, yes, and two struts like so, to keep it from getting knocked out of shape when the arm bashes into it.' He paused for a moment, trying to picture it in his mind's eye. 'And there's a roller back here, axles for the wheels, the arm itself, of course. Now, is there anything I've forgotten? Can't remember. Winding gear, of course, and the slip; but that's metalwork so we'll leave that for now. I think that's about it. All right, gather round and I'll tell you how it works.'

The clansmen drifted up and formed a circle, almost reluctantly, around the crude sketch of a middleweight torsion engine. Temrai had based it on the one he'd passed every day as he walked to work; *catapult, fixed, medium heavy duty, class four,* to give it its proper nomenclature. It had looked elegantly simple back in the city, where far more complex and sophisticated engines were an everyday sight. Here, on a riverbank beside a mountain of newly sawn unseasoned timber, it all seemed rather different. His people, the clan, the men and women he'd grown up with, were staring at him as if he was proposing to build a bridge to the moon, or catch the winds in a bag. On reflection, he could see their point.

'The idea is,' he went on, 'that when you twist a piece of rope – horsehair's supposed to be the best material, but we're going to use ordinary rope to start with and see if that'll do instead – it makes a sort of spring—'

'Temrai, what's a spring?'

Oh, gods, this isn't going to work. 'A spring is – well, you know how the lathes work? When you bend over a sapling and then let it go it flies back? Or a bow, come to that. That's a spring. Something that bends and then snaps back the way it was.' He paused. 'Am I making any kind of sense, or should I start again?'

'No, that's all right,' someone said. 'Go on, please.'

'All right. Look, take it from me, if you twist a whole lot of rope together and put a pole in the middle like so, and then you pull it down like this–' he did his best to demonstrate with his hands '—and then let go, it'll shoot forwards; and if you put a stone on the end of the pole—'

'Wouldn't it fall off?'

'Not if you hollow out the end of the pole, like a spoon. Right,' he said, as inspiration struck, 'let's think of it like this. You know when you get a spoon and dip it in yoghurt or whatever, and then you pull it back and flick it, and the yoghurt flies out? We've all done that when we were kids, right? It's exactly the same principle, only what does the flicking is the rope.'

Silence. *They must think I'm out of my mind,* Temrai reflected wretchedly. *They're thinking I've made them cut down all those trees and build all those rafts, just so that we can sit under the walls of the city flicking yoghurt.*

'Believe me,' he said, with all the authority he could muster, 'it works. You see that rock over there? One of these things can throw a rock that size – oh, easily as far as that tree there, probably even further. I've seen it myself.'

Nobody spoke; probably just as well, because if they had, they'd have said, *If you say so, Lord Temrai,* in that tone of voice exclusively reserved for humouring idiots. *The only way I'll convince them,* he realised, *is to build the bloody thing and show them. So that's what I'm going to have to do.*

'Right,' he said, 'now you all know the basic principle, let's get on with it. Now then, we'll start with the sides. I want two beams of heartwood, ten feet by two by one. You lot, saws and adzes.'

The group he'd pointed to got to their feet and trudged towards the timber pile, with the air of men who've been sent to gather moonbeams in a jar. He turned back to the diagram.

'You lot, I want you to rough out these struts here. Heartwood again, six foot by one by one. I'll want tenons cut out on the ends; I'll explain what a tenon is later,' he added quickly before anyone could ask, 'after you've made the beam. Now, you lot can cut me out the beam that's going to be a fiddly bit, but we'll start with a beam seven and a half by a foot by six inches, leave the sapwood on because it'll want to have some bounce in it. Now, the uprights I'm going to have to think about, because they're a funny shape.'

For the time being, he reassured himself, it's still just a big game, they're all entering into the spirit of the thing and enjoying themselves. With any luck I'll have a machine finished and working before that wears off; and once they see one actually hurling a big rock, that ought to do the trick.

I hope so, because otherwise I'm going to be in trouble.

Things didn't go quite as well as Temrai had hoped. In the event, several parts turned out wrong and had to be done again, and it took a week rather than a day to make the components of the prototype. On the positive side, morale in the joinery squad stayed high and proved to be contagious; a large excited crowd, full of good humour and very anxious to help, comment and generally get under the joiners' feet, gathered to watch the parts being put together and the finished machine tested.

They've come to watch it fail, Temrai told himself gloomily, as he listened to the bee-hum of conversation and watched the women spreading rugs and cushions and setting out food, as if this was Temrai's funeral games. *Or maybe not*, he reflected. *I think they'll enjoy themselves either way.* He took a moment or two to survey the scene; colour and noise and movement; families and friends sitting together, children running about and shrieking as they jumped in and out of the river, mothers chasing them with towels and hauling them out of their wet clothes. A strange way to greet the birth of a terrible new weapon.

He walked to the top of the rise and stood there; that was enough to get the crowd's attention. Children were shushed, plates passed round, mead and milk poured. He wondered if he should make a little speech, decided not to. Time to make a start. He cleared his throat and started giving orders.

The largest and heaviest components were the two sides of the frame, cumbersome slabs of timber ten feet long into which most of the other components were going to have to fit. His mother's uncle Kossanai, whom he'd appointed as head joiner on the project, organised a team to line the sides up and hold them steady while the crossbars were slotted into place. First snag: the tenon on the front crossbar was too big for the mortice in the left-hand frame panel. At once a heated argument broke out between the crossbar makers and the team who'd made the sides, one party insisting that the tenon was the right size but the mortice was too small, the other side maintaining that the mortice was perfect to within the thickness of a hair, but the tenon was a sloppy piece of work and the whole crossbeam was only fit for firewood. After a brief interlude for despair, Temrai quietly got up, found a drawknife, a chisel and a cupful of soot for marking, beckoned to a couple of spectators from another team, and set to work paring down the tenon. When the crowd saw what was going on they started laughing and clapping, and the argument quickly broke up.

'Right,' Temrai said quietly, straightening his back and dusting off his hands. 'Now listen up, because I won't say this again. One more performance like that, and I'll have the whole lot of you dunked in the river. Understood? Now then, let's have the other crossbar.'

Mercifully, the back crossbar was a good fit, and the joiners started grinning and slapping each other on the back, as if the job was finished. Temrai ordered them to take it apart again.

'Lord? But it fits, you can see for . . .'

Patiently, Temrai explained that they still had all the other bits to slot in, and they couldn't do that without dismantling it. 'First we're going to check all the joints, piece by piece,' he said. 'Then we're going to put the whole thing together and drive in the pegs. All clear?'

The windlass roller came next. It had been too large to make on an ordinary pole lathe, and Temrai had had to design a whole new type of lathe to turn it on. He was rather proud of it, for it was the first part of this project that he'd thought up for himself, rather than just copying something he'd seen in the city. The roller slotted neatly into place, but it was three inches too long; it had to go back onto the lathe to be trimmed, twice, before it was right. Next came the cross-bracer for the uprights; that was a reasonable fit, only needing a little skilful whittling. With a sigh of relief, Temrai ordered the pegs that locked the tenons into the mortices to be driven home. The joiners did so, and stood back. When they let go, it didn't fall apart.

Well, that's all right, Temrai muttered to himself. *Now for the uprights.*

It was only when the two massive lumps of carefully worked timber were hauled out and held up by Kossanai's men that he realised he'd forgotten something. He swore under his breath.

The uprights, which supported the beam that the catapult arm slammed into, were supposed to slot into mortices cut on the top face of the two side pieces, where they were held in place by three-quarter-inch iron bolts. The mortices looked as if they'd been cut neatly enough; likewise the tenons cut on the bottom end of each upright. The problem he'd overlooked until now was how to lift the two solid, heavy uprights up over the side pieces so that they could then be lowered into position (assuming they were going to fit; let's assume that for now, shall we?) and bolted into place. He put his hands to his face, rubbing both sides of his nose with his fingers. Some sort of crane, it'd have to be; or a scaffolding, and lift the pieces into position by brute force. If they got clumsy and dropped one of those things onto somebody, there'd be one hell of a mess. He shut out the buzz of impatient excitement from the happy picnickers and tried to visualise the best way of doing it.

Cranes ... Yes, that'd do it.

'Kossanai, I want the new lathe taken to bits and the A-frames brought up here,' he said. 'Lasakai, Morotai, get me a couple of poles ten feet long by eighteen inches across, or as near as you can find; something with a bit of spring in it, but not too bendy. Panzen, I'll need forty foot of rope, not the good stuff we're keeping for the engine.'

By leaning the two A-frames together and tying them top and bottom, they made a firm base for the crane. One of the poles was then hauled up and tied in to act as the lever, and there was no shortage of willing helpers when Temrai called for volunteers to work the thing. He himself stood on the engine frame and guided the tenon carefully into the mortice; it went nearly halfway in before it stuck.

'Damn,' he said. 'All right, lift. That'll do. Hold it steady, for pity's sake.' He knelt down, his head directly under the dangling upright, and brushed soot inside the mortice, so that when the tenon went in again the soot would mark the places where it was sticking. 'All right, let's try that again. Down – hold it. Right, out again, and hold it there.' He turned and faced the leader of the crane gang. 'Just keep it steady like that while we trim this tenon back a bit. We'll be as quick as we can.'

At the fourth attempt the tenon went down all the way. Kossanai jumped forward with an augur and brace to bore the holes for the bolts, while the crane gang continued to hold the weight of the upright on their ropes. Temrai had chosen the right man for the job; Kossanai worked quickly but carefully, apparently not too bothered by all the fuss and excitement. It took him half an hour to drill the two holes, by which time the joyous enthusiasm of the crane gang had evaporated rather.

'Let's get the bolts in,' Temrai said, grabbing the hammer

and tapping them home himself. 'Thank the gods for that, the damn things fit. Pasadai, get the cotter pins in those bolts so we can slacken off the crane.'

And so on; after the uprights, they fitted the two bracing struts that supported them, and then the thickly padded crossbar at the top which joined them together and took the impact of the catapult arm itself. By this stage the holiday atmosphere had ebbed away and been replaced by a tense, impatient excitement, as the machine slowly and incredibly began to look like the sketch Temrai had traced in the mud a week before. Now at last the clanspeople were beginning to understand; there in front of them was something that looked real, something that would actually work and which they'd built themselves. Temrai fancied he could hear the mood of the clan changing; it was like a child growing up, terribly fast. He wasn't quite sure he liked it.

'Good work,' he said as the joiners stood back from the completed frame. 'Now let's get the metal fixings and the ropes in.'

This stage he supervised personally, since even now he was the only man in the clan who really understood how it all worked. He'd made the two ratchet assemblies himself; one for tensioning the rope, the other for locking the windlass roller so that it could be wound back in stages. There were no problems with the fit; he made them all go together more by sheer effort of will than anything else, but go together they did. While he was busy with the tensioning ratchet, Kossanai's men brought up the catapult arm – *it still looks just like a bloody great big spoon*, Temrai admitted to himself – and held it in place until Temrai had threaded in the ropes. As soon as he gave the word, another team fitted levers into the slots in the tensioners and began the slow job of winding up the rope.

Those ropes are going to break, I know it. But they didn't; nor did the ratchet mechanism or the tensioner axles, or any of the parts Temrai had shaken his head dubiously over as he dunked them in the water to quench. At last, the tensioner crews gave up their attempt to coax the winders round one more click; the levers were taken out, and someone roped up the arm to the windlass.

It was finished. All that was left was to wind it back, put a stone in the bowl of the spoon and loose the slip.

Temrai stood up. He was exhausted, filthy with mud and sawdust, bleeding from several small cuts and two sets of skinned knuckles. More than anything, he wanted not to have to give the order to loose the slip. Everybody was looking at him.

It can't work first time. Nothing ever works first time. Gods, we can't use up all our luck this early, we need it for later. What if the arm snaps, or the uprights are too weak and the whole thing just smashes itself to pieces? I ought to make everybody get back, people could be hurt by bits of flying timber if this thing breaks up.

If I do this, nothing'll ever be the same again.

'All right,' he called out. 'Let her go.'

The slip operator, someone Temrai knew by sight but not by name, tugged sharply on the rope in his hand, drawing a loop off the end of the carefully shaped hook that connected the windlass rope to the arm. The enormous wooden spoon shot forward, smacking against the felt padding wrapped round the top crossbar with a noise like a giant mother slapping a giant child. The whole engine hopped six inches in the air and landed again like a cat.

And the stone flew.

Temrai watched it rise, slow down, stop and fall, gathering pace as it came down. It didn't fall where he'd expected; it was well over to the right and a good ten yards further out, and when it landed, he could feel the impact through the soles of his feet. It pitched on a small rocky outcrop, made a cracking noise that echoed off the hills, bounced and landed in the river with a splash and a dramatic curtain of spray.

There was dead silence. After a moment or so, Kossanai's people began swarming all over the machine, peering and checking, telling each other with joyous disbelief that this, that and the other was still in one piece, that this bolt hadn't bent and that dowel hadn't snapped; that it worked, gods damn it, the bloody thing actually worked!

They were the only ones moving or speaking; the rest of the gathering were staring in silence, estimating in their minds the weight of the stone and the distance it had travelled, imagining the force of the impact, what it could do. Temrai could hear what they were thinking: *you want to be careful with that thing, it could do someone an injury.*

Well, yes. That was the point, wasn't it? Or hadn't you realised?

With an effort, Temrai snapped himself out of the communal trance and went over to the machine. The clan watched him step by step; it was as if standing near it was a political act, a statement of a new and rather dreadful policy. All at once he wanted to say he was sorry and shout at them for being wet and woolly-minded; he wanted to order them to break the machine up as quickly as possible, but he'd have attacked anybody who laid a hostile finger on it. He didn't know what to think. Above all, he was afraid.

Of what, Temrai? You can't very well sack Perimadeia by pelting them with flowers. Do you really want to sack Perimadeia? Kill all those people?

We don't do that sort of thing. They do.

What harm have they ever done you?

Slowly, he looked round until he found Kossanai, who was tapping a wedge carefully into place with a beech mallet. 'Any damage?' he asked.

'No,' the older man replied. 'Apart from a few wedges and pins that moved a bit, she's as sound as a bell. We did it, Temrai. Isn't that something?'

Temrai smiled, reached out a hand and patted the catapult arm as if it was a favourite horse. 'That's all right, then,' he said. 'Now all we've got to do is make up another three hundred of these beauties and we might just be in business. Come on,' he added, raising his voice so that everyone could hear, 'don't just stand there hugging yourselves, we've got work to do.'

CHAPTER TEN

Early one morning a man walked across the Drovers' Bridge into the city, leading a string of donkeys heavily laden with dried figs. He was tired and fed up, having lost a shoe while taking a short cut through a bog to avoid a tollbridge. His feet hurt, his detour had added to his journey instead of making it shorter, and although he had indeed avoided the tollbridge, he'd had to spend the night in a squalid and extortionately expensive inn, with the result that he'd spent twice as much as he'd saved. More than anything in the world, he wanted a stiff drink and a nice hot bath.

For the latter, he'd come to the right place. There were no fewer than seven public baths in the city to choose between, all of them within easy limping distance of the bridge. Having left his donkeys with a friend, therefore, he headed straight for the nearest one, paid his copper half plus another half for a jug of cheap red wine, and spent the rest of the morning wallowing in magnificent luxury.

The bath left him feeling relaxed and rejuvenated, but also rather ashamed of the scraggy state of his hair and beard. Before going to the market to collect his donkeys and set up his stall, therefore, he stopped off at a small barber's shop where there happened to be an empty chair just when he was passing the door. He flopped into the chair, put his feet up on the footstool and urged the barber to do the best he could.

What with the wine and the warm bath, he was feeling benign and at ease with everything around him, and it so happened that he was the sort of man who talks when he's happy. This was another reason for having a shave and a haircut, because its universally known that barbers, by the sacred code of their ancient and venerable craft, are obliged to listen.

He started off with, 'Nice day,' expanded that into a brief account of his journey, enlarged on that so as to make it a detailed account of his journey, with special reference to the predatory nature of bogs and the iniquitous cost of tollgates and inns, digressed at length on the subject of his life, times and philosophy of business, spoke for four minutes with scarcely a pause for breath about his wife's nephew (who she'd forced him to take on as an assistant, and who was no more use than a butter kettle), and was just commiserating with the city folk on the latest problems they were having with the plainspeople, when the barber stopped him.

'Problems?' said the barber. 'I hadn't heard about any problems.'

The fig merchant raised an eyebrow. 'You know, the things they're up to upriver. All those things they're building.'

'What things?'

'You mean to say you hadn't heard?' At once the fig merchant embarked on a colourful description of what he'd seen as he passed along on the opposite bank of the river; huge stockpiles of timber, the river jammed almost solid with rafts, enormous saw-pits, all sorts of funny-looking machines with people running around shouting and ordering each other about. And, he added, all them catapults.

'What catapults?'

The catapults, of course; the ones the plainspeople were making at this ford he'd gone past. Well, when he said making, what it looked like they were doing was making them, putting them together, testing them – bloody great big rocks they were chucking about, like a lot of kids with snowballs – and then taking them to bits again and packing the bits onto wagons. Surely, he insisted, the barber had heard about the catapults.

The barber asked him if he was sure. The fig merchant replied, sure he was sure. Seen it with his own eyes, hadn't he? The barber asked to be told again. The fig merchant told him again.

'Oh, shit,' the barber said, and immediately sprinted away, still holding his razor and leaving the fig merchant sitting in his chair with half a beard and a towel round his neck.

The reason why the barber took the news so much to heart was that as a young man, before he was old enough to know better, he'd spent eighteen months on the plains as one of Maxen's cavalry army before getting in the way of a clansman's arrow and being left for dead. It had taken him two years to get home, and even all these years later it wasn't often he slept without dreaming about it.

When he burst into the market waving a razor and yelling, 'The savages are coming, the savages are coming!' the city people drew the obvious conclusion, knocked him down, took away his razor and threw him in a coalshed to sleep it off; one kind soul even had the presence of mind to relieve him of his purse in case he cut himself on the sharp edges of the coins while thrashing about in his drunken rage. It was only two or three hours later, when the owner of the coalshed opened it up to get some coal, that the barber was able to escape and make his way, rather more sedately this time, to the nearest guard post.

Fortunately the guard sergeant knew him and was prepared to listen to what he had to say; which was how the first news of Temrai's preparations reached the city of Perimadeia, fourteen weeks after he had left the city and embarked on his life's work.

The sergeant, like most of the guard, was a part-timer, a soldier one day in ten and an innkeeper the rest of the time. When he'd finished making his report – a long business; he had to keep repeating his report to an apparently endless succession of officers of one sort or another, all of whom then insisted on hearing exactly the same thing from the poor terrified barber – it was well past the end of his duty shift, and high time he was back in his tavern, where his wife and daughter would be busy with the evening rush. Pausing only to dump his gear in the guard house he scurried home, quickly tied on his apron and started drawing off jugs of cider.

Once the rush had subsided a little, however, and he'd had time to catch his breath and help himself to a couple of hard-earned drinks, he lost no further time in making known the extremely rich gobbet of news he'd been fortunate enough to come across. This time, with the news coming from a highly respected member of the community instead of a drunken barber, people listened. Then, having listened, they panicked.

There seems to be a perverse law of nature that the larger the city, the quicker a rumour spreads among its population. The sergeant's customers, running home to make sure their houses were still there and weren't being looted by fur-clad savages, shouted the news to any acquaintances they happened to meet. Since it was about the time of day when the citizens were accustomed to take an after-dinner stroll round their own particular square with their wives and families, it wasn't long before the streets and courtyards were full of people running wildly in all directions, each one in turn shouting the news to anybody who might not have heard it yet. Meanwhile, the original disseminators of the news, having reassured themselves that their homes were unburnt and their possessions and loved ones still more or less intact, started streaming back in the opposite direction on their way uptown to find a government building to stand in front of and demand that Something Be Done.

Quite soon, the streets were an exciting place to be, what with crowds forming, people running and bumping into each other, the rumour mutating and conjuring up illusory parties of savages at the gates/already inside the walls/coming up through the main sewer/laying waste the tanners' quarter with fire and the sword. As always, scuffles and fights started springing up like mushrooms, someone managed to set fire to the carpet-weavers' quarter, and a number of the more level-headed opportunists took advantage of the general chaos to do a little cash-free shopping.

The city Prefect called out the guard to restore order; but since it was at the end of the day shift, the daytime guards had all gone home and the night shift were either trying to struggle through the packed streets or joining in the fun with their friends and neighbours. The city Prefect then called on the Lord Lieutenant to send in the regular army. The Lord Lieutenant reminded the city Prefect that apart from the Prefect's own full-timers there wasn't a regular army. After a moment's thought the city Prefect, the Lord Lieutenant and their respective general staffs quietly made their way to their private gate into the second city and locked it behind them.

Next morning the lower city was a sorry sight, and those citizens who had fallen by the wayside during the festivities and spent the night where they fell might have been forgiven for thinking that the city had indeed been sacked by the enemy while they'd been asleep. The fire had spread from the carpet-weavers' quarter and made quite a mess of four adjoining districts before reaching the river and burning itself out. A remarkable number of shops and stalls had been visited by the merry bands of opportunists, taverns and vintners having taken the worst of it. There were groaning bodies all over the place, and quite a few that neither groaned nor moved. By the time the city guard had managed to get together a quorum and found the courage to venture outside their posts there was nobody left to arrest apart from a few sleeping drunks, so they sent a message to their betters in the second city to let them know it was safe to come out, and made a start on clearing up the mess.

One of the few people who'd stayed at home all night and hadn't realised that anything unusual had been happening was Bardas Loredan. The day before, his class had taken its final guild examinations and every one of them had passed. This small miracle had called for a modest celebration, which started around midday and lasted until Loredan himself, the last survivor of the revels, had woken up in a tavern in the soap-boilers' quarter at about the time the barber had been let out of the coalshed, and had made his painful way home to bed. The first he knew of the night's festivities was when he struggled down the stairs to the baker's on the corner, only to find that it wasn't there any more.

He stood for a moment rubbing his eyes; then a man he knew by sight happened to pass by, and Loredan grabbed him by the arm.

'The baker's,' he muttered. 'What in hell's name happened to it?'

The account he received was a fifth- or sixth-generation variant on the original story, to the effect that some lunatic had started an entirely false rumour that the savages were at the gates, and everybody had gone briefly and flamboyantly insane. That ought to have been good enough for a man with a morning head, but once Loredan had ascertained that the notional savages referred to were the plainsfolk, he decided to go in search of harder news. This commodity proved somewhat elusive, and he'd heard four or five different versions, all wildly contradictory and none of them remotely convincing, when he turned a corner and found himself facing a four-man squad of guardsmen in full armour and with arrows nocked on their bowstrings.

'Bardas Loredan?'

'Yes, that's me,' Loredan admitted, bewildered. 'What …?'

'We've been looking for you,' the corporal said grimly. 'You've got to come with us.'

'But I didn't – I was asleep the whole time.' He took a step backwards. 'Look, what is this?'

'Orders,' the Corporal said. 'Come on, look lively.'

Although he felt strongly that looking lively was probably way beyond his limited capabilities this morning, Loredan did as he was told, and shortly afterwards found himself standing outside the gates of the Patriarch's lodgings. He was about to protest when the door opened and a splendidly dressed officer in gilded armour who came up to round about his shoulder brusquely ordered him to step this way. He followed, up several flights of stairs and along about a mile of corridors, until he was brought to a halt outside a small door in a covered cloister surrounding a rather charming green with a fountain in the middle. The splendid officer knocked on the door, and pushed Loredan into the room.

It was pleasantly cool and dark inside. He'd never been inside the building before, but from what he'd heard he guessed this was one of the chapter houses. Once his eyes became accustomed to the dim light, he saw that there were fifteen or so people there, some of them sitting on the stone benches that ran all the way round the circular room, while others were standing in the middle, talking in low voices. He recognised the City Prefect, a short elderly man with fuzzy white hair, and a couple of officers from the Lord Lieutenant's staff; and there, at the back, on a white marble throne, was Patriarch Alexius, talking to a long, thin man sitting on his right. Alexius looked up, noticed him and waved to him to join them. Before he could do so, however, another even more splendid officer swept him up and marched him over to see the Prefect.

'You Loredan?' the Prefect demanded.

Loredan nodded.

'Thank heaven for that,' the Prefect replied. 'All right, I'll get straight to the point. The rumours about an attack from the plains are true.'

'Ah,' Loredan said.

'More to the point,' the Prefect went on, frowning slightly as if to suggest that Loredan somehow failed to meet the required specifications, 'it seems they've got hold of a lot of heavy equipment from somewhere. Siege engines, catapults, we don't know exactly what, or who's supplying them with the stuff. The point is, we're taking this threat seriously, and we've decided to launch a pre-emptive strike.'

'Excuse me,' Loredan interrupted. 'Who's *we*, exactly?'

The Prefect paused, as if he'd just been asked a question he didn't know the answer to. 'The civil authorities,' he replied. 'Myself, the Lord Lieutenant, the various heads of offices, the Patriarch, naturally.' He scowled, and then went on. 'Our problem is that, as you well know, we don't have a suitable force of heavy cavalry immediately available to make the strike with. Now, you were the last man to command the heavy cavalry, so it seems logical to involve you at the outset. I've already assigned you a basic staff—'

'Excuse me—'

'And you can work from one of the rooms we've taken here until you're assigned a permanent office. My people will be doing the bulk of the actual recruiting, but you'll be able to have a certain amount of direct input at the selection stage, and we'll be looking to you to be quite heavily involved in training and *matériel* procurement, although of course control of the procurement budget will rest with the appropriate civil—'

Loredan held up his hand. 'Wait a minute,' he said. 'Slow down, please. Are you seriously suggesting that I join in this expedition of yours?'

'Don't be stupid, man. You're an officer in the Perimadeian army. It's your duty—'

It was a mistake for Loredan to shake his head, given the state it was in. 'No. Sorry, but absolutely not. You can't make me do that. I retired, remember?'

The Prefect looked as if he was about to explode. 'Colonel Loredan,' he said, and he would have sounded tremendously soldierly and authoritative if his voice hadn't been quite so high-pitched, 'you don't seem to understand. I'm ordering you—'

'Go to hell,' Loredan snapped. Startled, the Prefect stepped backwards, treading on the toes of someone immediately behind him. 'And don't call me Colonel. I'm going home, before I lose my temper.'

'Now you listen to me,' the Prefect squeaked. People were turning round and staring. Loredan started to walk towards the door, but there was one of those splendid officers in the way. Loredan decided he really wasn't up to a fist-fight, and subsided.

'Really,' he said, 'you don't want me. It's been twelve years, and look at me, I'm a mess. There must be hundreds of your men—'

As he spoke, he caught the splendid one's eye, and the truth dawned on him. *There aren't, though; just these peacocks and the part-timers. Oh, hell...*

'Hang on, though,' he said. 'What about the Emperor's guard? Come to that, what about the Emperor? Shouldn't he be doing something about—?'

Everyone around him had gone suddenly quiet, as if he'd just said something incredibly foolish. *They're doing their best not to laugh,* he realised. *What did I say?*

'Colonel Loredan,' said the Prefect with a sigh, 'there is no Emperor. Didn't you know?'

Infuriating...

But it had to be done, and nobody else could be trusted to do it properly. With a deep sigh, Gannadius kicked off his too-tight slippers, trimmed the wick of the lamp and sat down to do the accounts.

Confounded jack-in-office auditors ... Briefly he was tempted to do a little cursing on his own account. A broken leg or a fit of temporary blindness, just enough to keep them at bay without actually causing loss of life or permanent mutilation - no, maybe not. If he'd learnt anything from this sorry business, it was that the Principle wasn't a cost-effective weapon.

He opened the cedarwood box that held his reckoning counters, pulled out the velvet bag and poured the shining counters out in a pile. It was an old and valuable set which had belonged to his grandfather, who had been a substantial wool-merchant; the counters were fine silver, rather worn now but still legible, little white pools of moonlight on the dark wood of the table. On the obverse of each counter was an allegorical female figure representing Commerce, seated on a throne with a pair of scales in one hand and a horn of plenty in the other; a stout lady in a revealing dress, her face worn away by three generations of painstaking arithmetic. The reverse was the traditional ship and castle crest of the city, with PRUDENT DEALINGS AUGMENT PROSPERITY in grandiose lettering around the edge. Gannadius picked one out and studied it for a while; there was something reassuringly solid and respectable about grandfather's counters that somehow took the sting out of an otherwise loathsome chore.

With a lump of chalk he drew the lines on the table top; five horizontal lines like the rungs of a ladder right across the board. Although he wouldn't have liked it to be widely known, Gannadius was only really comfortable with the basic lines-and-spaces method of accounting, as used by traders, innkeepers, farmers and the like. Scribes, scholars and clerks used a far more elegant and complex system, involving not only lines and spaces but different coloured squares on a permanent board (usually a work of art in itself), stationary counters with abstruse technical names, and a truly fiendish concept called the Tree of Numeration which he had never been able to make the slightest sense of. As far as he was concerned, arithmetic was bad enough without garnishing it with gratuitous mysticism.

In comparison, the common accounting was child's play. Each rung of the ladder represented a multiple of ten; the bottom line was units, the second line tens, the third line hundreds and so on. The spaces between the lines were multiples of five; five, fifty, five hundred, five thousand. You laid out the first number to be added along the rungs, and then chalked a verticle line down the right hand side and laid out the next number; then you did the calculation, drew another line and laid out the next number. It took rather longer than the professional method, but it was reasonably foolproof, and the longer you stuck at it, the easier it seemed to get.

Having prepared his board, he opened the account book at the page headed *Receipts* and started to set out the counters—

Item: received on account of rents, the following sums:
           Ducas Falerin;   *2,659*
           Leras Beron;   *8,342*

Two thousand, six hundred and fifty-nine. Gannadius took a handful of counters and laid them out; four on the bottom line, one in the first space, nothing on the second line, one in the second space, one each on the third line and the third space, and finally two on the thousand line; then double-check, draw the line and lay the next number to be added down in the next column. When he'd laid out the second number he set about the rather simpler task of merging the two – four units plus two units makes six, no more than four allowed on a line so carry one up to the five space, leave one, sweep the rest away; that makes two in the first space, no more than one allowed in a space, makes one to carry up to the ten line, one to sweep away; carry across four and one on the ten line makes five, no more than four on a line makes one to carry up to the fifty space, none to sweep away; that makes two in the fifty space, no more than one allowed in a space ...

He chanted the workings under his breath like a super-stitious blacksmith reciting luck charms as he hammers a horseshoe; gradually he stopped having to think, his eyes and fingers doing the work, the counters keeping the score. Before he knew it he'd finished the page of rents and had moved on to tariffs and tithes, while his mind gently dis-engaged and wandered into a pleasantly soporific trance.

A wretched business, to be sure. He'd allowed himself to be drawn into it by the prospect of advancement; he had never allowed himself to be ruthlessly ambitious, largely because ruthless ambition tended to be counterproductive in the long run. A man who scrambles to the top of the ladder before he's forty has nothing to look forward to except thirty years of fending off a succession of equally ruthless younger men, and Gannadius could never see the point in that. Far better to move slowly and securely, cultivating lasting alliances and making as few enemies as possible, doing good work that would be remembered rather than playing politics and thereby inviting the cloister conspiracy and the secret coup. By helping the Patriarch to clean up a rather unseemly mess, he'd be laying up a solid foundation of gratitude and obligation on which he could build the next stage of his progress with a reasonable degree of confidence. A thoroughly sound career move; the mark of a mature and seasoned campaigner.

Well; that was why he'd got involved at the start. He'd certainly achieved that objective, but none of that seemed to matter quite as much as it did. No doubt about it, on one level there was an intellectual fascination to the business that intrigued him enormously; at times he'd rediscovered the fierce excitement he'd felt as an enthusiastic young student, revelling in strange and bewitching concepts. And no false modesty, please; he and Alexius had stumbled on a whole new aspect of the Principle, an area that hadn't been tamed and trampled flat by generations of meticulous scholars intent on scratching out every last flake of significance. Rather, they were like two men shipwrecked on an entirely unknown continent; everything they came across was new and unknown, which they could spend a lifetime studying if they weren't so entirely preoccupied with staying alive and somehow getting home again.

That was the point, Gannadius admitted to himself; most of all, he wanted it to be over and done with, because deep down he was afraid. He was luckier than his colleague, because he wasn't the one directly threatened. It was Alexius who had fallen ill and now could hardly walk, and despite his best endeavours Gannadius desperately wanted to save him, if he could. He could rationalise it by arguing that if Alexius died too soon, he'd never have an opportunity to cash in all that goodwill and obligation, he wouldn't be guaranteed the succession. That was still part of it, he supposed, because he did still want to be Patriarch, one day, in the fullness of time.

Maybe it's just because I like the man. Well, I do. But that's

*still not all of it. There's something important in all this, and
I need to know what it is.*

Which made it more than usually aggravating to be stuck
behind a table pushing a pile of counters around when he
wanted to be in the chapter house, listening to the news and
trying to work out what the connection between the
Alexius-Loredan business and this new threat to the city
might be. There was one; there had to be one, although for
the life of him he couldn't work out what it might be. There
was something, some spitefully oblique clue, in that strange
dream of Alexius' he'd inadvertently wandered into; the
clouds of dust becoming sails, that confounded pest of an
Island girl and something about Loredan having a brother.
Alexius hadn't been able to get anything useful out of him
(*I should have gone with him and asked the man myself;
Alexius is too emotionally involved with all this to be left to
investigate on his own*), but his description of the advocate's
manner when the subject was raised convinced him that
the brother had something important to do with all this.
Writing it all down to coincidence would be thoroughly
poor book-keeping.

Talking of which— He double-checked, dipped his pen in
the ink and wrote in the total receipts: twenty-nine
thousand and ninety-seven gold units, a disturbingly large
sum to have to account for. (*And what possible justification
can there be for a contemplative order raking in thirty
thousand smilers, let alone spending them ...?*) Then he
braced himself for the expenditure accounts, which were
fiddly, awkwardly recorded and most likely wrong, not to
mention being written up in Brother Pelagius' unspeakable
handwriting. It was enough to put a man off positions of
authority for life.

Item; beer	*- 2/3*
Item; cider	*- 1/2*
Item; smoked fish	*- 12/3*
Item; three silver napkin rings,	
* finely engraved with small deer*	*- 7/3*

Item; to cleaning latrines	- 1/3
Item; barrel staves	- 2/1
Item; [illegible]	- 9/2

Twelve and three-quarters on smoked fish for a week; he was going to get asked about that, sure as anything, and he didn't even like smoked fish. And if the auditors didn't raise hell over seven and three-quarters for three napkin rings, he would. It was high time his brothers in science were made to understand that membership of the Order wasn't to be construed as a licence to ape the follies of the nobility. It'd be different if they were his napkin rings, but they weren't. He splodged a dot in the margin and made a note to shout at somebody when he had a moment to spare.

| Item; books | - 5/3 |

That was rather more like it, unless of course it was simply Pelagius' mistake for boots. He tried to recall what the brother provisioner wore on his feet; he'd noticed more than one of the brothers hobbling around the place in the latest long-toed, brightly coloured fashion footwear. If they had any sense they'd stick to sandals until the audit was well and truly finished with for the year.

He carried on down the page, right hand tracing the column of figures, left hand laying out the counters. Most of these small, fiddling entries he could do in his head, only bothering to carry forward the subtotals for each week to the main calculation on the counting board. Some of the entries he could clearly remember; for example—

| Item; purgatives | - 12/1 |

—which commemorated the nasty bout of food poisoning when the cook experimented with those devilishly expensive imported mushrooms; closely followed by—

> *Item; to cleaning latrines*   - 1/3
> *Item; retainer (new cook)*   - 1/-

—an entry which might just be taken as evidence that Pelagius had a sense of humour. Gannadius groaned softly, remembering the mushrooms, and moved on down the page.

> *Item; arrowheads*   - 5/1

Arrowheads? What in blazes did they want with five smilers' worth of arrowheads? Frowning, he looked across at the date of the entry. Last week. Well, yes. It did make some sort of sense. The City Academy, like most of the city's institutions, was responsible for the payment and outfitting of a company of the guard. So; arrowheads. Just so long as nobody expected *him* to dress up in steel knitting and tramp up and down the walls in the pouring rain.

Gannadius shivered, wondering what was going on in the chapter house, where he ought to have been instead of crouching here doing sums. Yesterday the Prefect had announced that Bardas Loredan's expeditionary force would be ready in three days' time, and that he felt sure that firm pre-emptive action would see an end to the matter. The Prefect had sounded confident; but then, he always did. Loredan himself had looked depressed, rebellious, embarrassed and scared. Being entirely ignorant of such things, Gannadius didn't know how to interpret that; for all he knew, that was exactly how a responsible commander should look on the eve of a major expedition. It stood to reason, Gannadius argued to himself, that anybody who wanted to lead an army probably shouldn't be allowed to for that very reason.

These and similar reflections occupied his mind so effectively that he was through the expenditures almost before he knew it. Now all he had to do was subtract the expenditure total from the receipts total and be left with the figure for cash in hand, and he could call the job done and go to bed. He swept off the counters, re-drew the lines an set out the numbers. It would be so immensely gratifying if, just for once in his life, the blasted thing worked out first time.

It didn't, needless to say; and for the next two and a half hours Gannadius forgot all about the Patriarch, Bardas Loredan and the army, the barbarian hordes and the antisocial by-products of philosophy while he ground his way through both sets of figures and compelled them to agree, like a mother forcibly reconciling her warring children. As he pinched out the lamp and rolled into bed, he spared one last thought for his sadly afflicted colleague and fellow-discoverer; then a great surge of weariness swept over him, he yawned and fell asleep.

The scouts found Temrai supervising the packing up of the first consignment of trebuchet parts. The trebuchets had proved easier to build than the torsion engines, but their sheer size and weight was causing an entirely new class of problems, to which Temrai was too tired and drained to find immediate solutions.

'Now what?' he said, as a man appeared behind his shoulder, just as he was about to eat something for the first time in twenty-four hours. 'Look, if it's something you can possibly deal with yourselves ...'

'Message from the scouting party.' The man turned out to be Hedasai, until recently ex-officio commander of the duck-hunters. Now that there were no gullible ducks left anywhere within a week's ride, he'd been reassigned to lookout duties. It occurred to Temrai that Hedasai shouldn't be there.

'Well?'

Hedasai paused for a moment before answering. 'We think you should come and take a look for yourself. It could be trouble.'

Temrai looked up at him, a wedge of salted duck forgotten between his fingers. 'What kind of trouble?' he demanded. 'More observers from downriver?'

'We think it's more than that. It looks like it might be an army.'

What a ridiculous thing to say, Temrai thought. *Either it's an army or it isn't; it's not exactly something you can mistake for anything else.* And then he thought, *Oh, gods*.

'Well, I suppose I'd better see for myself,' he said. 'Jurrai, Modenai, I need you for something. Could you get my horse and my bow and meet me by the saw-pits?'

Nobody said anything much as they forded the river and rode up the winding road into the hills. From the highest point, where they'd built a signal beacon, it was possible to convince yourself that you could just see the tallest tower of the upper city; it was a splendid vantage point, and Temrai had had it in mind when he chose this place for the construction camp.

'Well?' he said, catching his breath. They'd had to dismount and lead the horses for the last half-mile, and he'd spent too long sitting and standing around over the last few months. 'Where's this army of yours?'

Hedasai pointed. A good way off in the distance, maybe fifteen miles, something flashed in the light. Temrai looked hard; was that his morbid imagination or a cloud of dust? 'Jurrai,' he said, 'you're the one with the eyesight. What do you make of it?'

'Not good.' Jurrai cupped his hands round his eyes and concentrated. 'I'd say that's a large body of men, cavalry by the dust they're putting up and the speed they're going at. Assuming they know where we are, they could be here in three hours or so.'

'Damnation.' Temrai scowled. To his surprise, there wasn't much fear, very little compared to the anger. Of all the things he didn't need, a pitched battle against heavy cavalry in front of the construction camp, where he had two hundred dismantled catapults and fifty trebuchets in the process of being fitted together and taken apart again – as if he didn't have enough to worry about. 'Oh, well, we'd better get ready for them. Modenai, get back to the camp, have the men saddled up and ready. Hedasai, take your scouts and go with him; I don't want stray riders wandering about where they can be seen, I want these people to think we're careless and stupid. Jurrai, you're with me.' Suddenly he grinned. 'Do you know how to plan a battle? I don't.'

'You didn't know how to build catapults, either.'

The two of them rode down a little way under the skyline and sat in silence for a full quarter of an hour, learning the landscape by heart and considering the implications of what they saw. Then Temrai's face softened into a smile.

'It's perfect,' he said. 'Jurrai, we can do this if we keep calm and don't try to be too clever.'

Jurrai nodded. 'I know what I'd be doing if I was their man. What had you in mind?'

'Well.' Temrai collected his thoughts; it would help him clarify matters in his mind if he explained to someone else, and there was always the chance he'd missed something obvious that Jurrai had noticed. 'He's over there, with nothing much except open country between him and us except these hills. Now, our camp is on the other side of the river, on the flat between the river and the high ground over there; which means he's got to cross the river to get to us, and there's only two places he can do that.' He stopped, rubbed his chin. 'There's the main ford down below us, opposite the eastern ends of both ridges, with our saw-pits and the jetty right beside it. Then there's the bend in the river, with those two little copses, and the other place you can just about ford the river, which is maybe a mile and a half from the camp. What he'll want to do is creep up on the other side of this ridge here, hoping that we don't see him behind the ridge until he's actually on the ford. Agreed?'

Jurrai nodded. 'Mind you,' he said, 'if I was him and wanting to do things properly, I'd be trying to make some use of that higher crossing. It'd be a crying shame to let all that natural cover go to waste.'

Temrai thought about that for a moment, trying to make believe he was the other man, whoever the other man was. 'I think you're right,' he said, 'which makes it even better for us. What if he splits his army in two when he reaches the eastern point of the ridge? He sends the best part of his forces up to the higher ford, to sneak round between the two copses and behind the head of the ridge on the camp side of the river – he'd reckon there was a better than even chance of getting into position there without being seen since we wouldn't be expecting an attack from *our* side of the river. *Then* he sends the rest of his people over the main ford; we charge off to meet him there, and his main force pops out from behind the ridge on our side and hits us from behind. Next thing we know, we're surrounded, the only way to run is back downstream, and he's got control of the camp and can destroy the engines at his leisure. Good plan.'

Jurrai nodded. 'Assuming he's counting on us not having seen him coming,' he said. 'Although we'll know soon enough by the direction he takes. He can't cross the river downstream of the camp for about ten miles, to the best of my knowledge.'

'I didn't know that,' Temrai nodded. 'But let's assume he does, it forces his hand even more. Now then, here's what we do. You take, say, two-thirds of the men and split them into two, one lot behind each of the two copses. You ambush him, one in front and one behind so he'll have nowhere to go except to run due east, which'll take the best part of his forces out of the reckoning entirely.' Temrai stood up in his stirrups, staring at the ground beyond the river bend, trying to imagine it swarming with shouting men and panic-stricken horses. 'He'll see all that, and it'll make him think that all our men are up that end of the field and the camp's unguarded. He'll then make a dash for the camp, which'll be a big mistake from his point of view, because I'll have one detachment over the river actually in the camp ready to meet him, and my main force on this side, just below where we are now, all ready to jump out and cut him off from behind. If we're really lucky we might even be able to catch him while he's crossing the ford and squeeze him into the river from both ends.' Temrai stopped, and stared at Jurrai, his eyes wide. 'Gods, Jurrai, what if it doesn't go like that? We'd have our people split up into four groups. I don't like it.'

Jurrai shook his head. 'Better than being all bunched up in the camp,' he replied. 'And your contingent's got a back door if things don't work out; you can just run for it downstream and hope you're faster than he is. If I were in his position I don't think I'd risk an extended pursuit. The same goes for my lot,' he added. 'We can always split and run east, then double back behind the ridge and join up with you downriver.' He bit his lip, and added, 'It does all seem a bit too perfect, doesn't it? Or maybe we're just brilliant tacticians and never knew it.'

Temrai sat back into his saddle, his eyes fixed on what was now quite definitely a cloud of dust far away on the flat plains. 'You've been in battles,' he said. 'What's it like?'

'Messy,' Jurrai replied. 'Mostly, you get frightened because you don't know what's going on. Usually – at least, all the fighting I've ever been in – you start off with a long, boring wait, which is when the nerves get to you and you end up convincing yourself that you're going to get killed and it's going to hurt, and you tell yourself you can't possibly keep your nerve, you'll run away at the first sight of the enemy and everybody'll despise you for ever.

'Well, you're just about ready to kill yourself there and then and save the other side the bother when the action starts, and in my experience you don't have the time or energy to be scared after that; either you're in the line and you're desperately trying to hear the orders over the shouting and keep up with the others and do what you're supposed to be doing, or else you're in command yourself, and you're so busy trying to make yourself heard, trying to keep your men together and doing what they're told, you probably wouldn't notice if you had arrows sticking out of you like prickles on a hedgehog.

'And the actual fighting; well, that's even more of a mess. You can forget all your sword training and archery practice; you're loosing off arrows as fast as you can draw, you don't think about aiming, or if you do, that'll be the moment you drop the arrow or the string breaks or the enemy suddenly change direction and ride off out of range.

'As for the hand-to-hand stuff, you're riding forward, usually too fast to be in any sort of control, and suddenly there's people all round you, yours and theirs; if you really want to, you can usually ride straight through a mêlée and nobody'll try and stop you, because the chances are the other side are just as scared and confused as you are, and nobody really wants to fight if they can help it. If you do fight, it won't be a five-minute fencing match. You hit and he hits, and perhaps one of you'll make contact, and then you'll be past him and either dead or onto the next one. If you're hit, you may well not know it. If you get killed, it'll probably be by someone you hadn't even seen. It's a bloody dangerous hobby, sure enough, but don't imagine it'll any of it be *deliberate*. It's ninety-five parts luck, and the other five depends on the generals. That's what fighting's like. Is that any help?'

'Not really,' Temrai replied. 'It sounds like what I remember of when the camp got attacked when I was a kid, except we weren't even trying to fight back. The crazy thing is,' he added hopelessly, 'I started all this. I must be out of my mind.'

'As Your Majesty pleases,' Jurrai replied politely. 'Let's get back to the camp.'

When the enemy reserve suddenly appeared out of nowhere and came crashing into the rear of the column, trapping them half in and half out of the river and throwing the whole party into utter confusion, all Loredan felt was a vague sense of relief; the worst had happened, there were unlikely to be any more unpleasant surprises; all he had to do now was fight it out and it'd all be over for the day. Even as the men behind him dropped off their horses into the water, dead before they fell, he knew that he wasn't going to be killed; not here, not this way. It was strange, this calm, this sensation of not being involved except as a spectator; perhaps it was because he'd been expecting something like this ever since they left the city. Now things were going the way he thought they'd go, at least he knew where matters stood. It was starting to make some sort of sense. Just as the old man always said; the enemy you can see is the least of your problems.

His greatest and most insoluble problem, namely his five so-called co-commanders had been solved for him. Two of them were dead already, to his certain knowledge. As for the other three, well, if they were still alive, there wasn't much damage left for them to do. He tugged hard on his left rein, lifted his sword and selected one of the enemy to take out his anger on.

It had been, of course, all his fault. If he hadn't whined and complained solidly about being put in charge of this ludicrous venture, in the hope of being replaced by someone else, he wouldn't have had five deadheads foisted on him the day before the expedition was due to set out, each one of them apparently convinced he was the commander-in-chief and the other five were only there for decoration.

Six generals, for crying out loud. Sheer lunacy under any circumstances. Six generals in charge of five thousand untrained volunteers meant they'd never stood a chance.

The plainsman rode straight at him, spear levelled. Loredan pulled up, watched him come, dragged his horse round at the last minute and severed the other man's spine just above his shoulders with a short-arm cut as he flashed past. Something hit him six inches or so above the left knee; it felt like a sword or an axe, wasting its force on the heavy-duty mail and the thick padding underneath. Damn fool of an amateur; never hit unless the blow achieves something, you should kill 'em or leave 'em alone. He'd estimated where the other man would be before he'd finished turning round; the enemy horseman was almost past him, his back turned, but not so far past that he was safe from a long-arm thrust under his armpit, where there was a gap in the boiled-leather armour just nicely convenient for a sword to go in and reach the heart. The dead man's own forward momentum pulled him off the sword; Loredan watched just long enough to see him topple forwards, then spurred his horse on and rode for a gap in the mêlée. He wasn't achieving anything by just sitting there killing people, and he needed time to think.

He couldn't see very well for all the people in the way, but it seemed fairly certain that they were hemmed in back and front, with the deep water of the river on either side. That meant there was nothing for it but to force a way through either front or back. Chances were the main force of the enemy were behind them, since that was his logical line of retreat. In which case, he'd have to go forwards, try and break through to the camp and perhaps throw them off balance by getting between the camp and the ridge. If only he could keep things mobile, there was even a chance of outrunning the force behind them, coming up on the enemy detachment who'd ambushed the flanking party, spooking them, rescuing what was left of his people upriver and getting out of this shambles with some vestige of order.

First things first. He pulled his horse round and forced a way through the mass of terrified men that formed the centre of his column. A more useless congregation of human beings would be hard to find, but enough of them followed him to give him a little impetus, just enough to give him a chance of reversing the flow of the mêlée on the east bank of the ford. Luckily the enemy were slackening off, starting to think they'd done enough and that it was now just a matter of finishing the job. He killed seven men and carved up another four before he finally made it through to the other side; his right arm ached so badly he could hardly breathe, and his head was splitting after a bash on the side of his helmet from something he hadn't seen.

The wedge of men behind him forced a breach in the enemy line – not so much a line as a mob, jammed tight by weight of their own numbers, certainly no longer in the mood to fight after they'd decided in their minds that they'd already won. If you've won, why risk getting killed? More amateur thinking. At long last, something resembling a survival instinct led his column to push through the gap. The enemy let them go, too busy with their own sudden and unexpected panic to initiate any further hostilities. They wanted to be left alone now, and Loredan was happy to oblige them. When he looked back over his shoulder at the ragged stream of horsemen emerging from the slaughter of the ford, he was pleasantly surprised to see that he'd managed to get nearly four-fifths of his people out. The rest were as good as dead; the hell with them.

Still in business, he congratulated himself. *Now then.*

His assumptions held good. The last thing the enemy were expecting him to do was attack, and so when he rode up between the head of the ridge and the southernmost of the two little copses, he had a clear run straight into the rear of the happy throng of slaughtermen who were surrounding what was left of his flanking party. Once they realised what was happening, they cleared off without even making a pretence of a fight, heading upriver to cut him off from the high-river ford across which they were expecting him to go. Reasonable guess, but amateur thinking nonetheless. What he needed most at this point in the proceedings was time, space, peace and quiet; they were going to let him have some, and that ought to be enough grace to save all their lives. As soon as he was sure he'd got as much of his flanking party with him as he was likely to get, he signalled a right wheel and led the column off east at the double.

CHAPTER ELEVEN

Having realised he was still alive, Temrai opened his eyes and yelled. After a minute or so, his dead horse was pulled off him and he was lifted up out of the water. It occurred to him that he was shaking like a man having a fit, but there was nothing he could do about it.

'What happened?' he gasped. 'I thought we'd won.'

'We have,' replied the man who was holding his right arm. 'They've got away from us, and they're running for it. Are you all right?'

Temrai nodded. 'What happened?' he repeated. 'Everything went like we wanted it to, and then the next minute they were all over us.' He shuddered, remembering the sudden terror that had paralysed him as the other man, the one who'd started it all, burst out through a solid wall of Temrai's guard and came straight at him, his face so completely calm, almost serene, that for a moment Temrai had taken him for Death itself.

He remembered how there had been no time at all – the man was on him, his sword-arm through with the thrust before Temrai could even make up his mind what to do, but it had all gone so slowly, so that he'd had time to think all sorts of things before the other man's sword-tip came out through the other side of his horse's neck, and he'd felt both of them gradually toppling over into the water. He remembered the extraordinary feeling of calm and resignation after that – *oh, well, here goes, that was that* – as he waited to hit the stony bed of the ford, feel the hooves of the oncoming enemy landing on his face and chest— And here he was, apparently alive and not hurting, nothing broken, no blood he could definitely say was his own. Just like Jurrai had said: a mess ...

'Where's Jurrai?' he asked, already knowing the answer.

'Didn't make it,' the man replied. 'Same man as got you got him. I think he was trying to save you—'

Nice thought, Temrai said to himself, but I was there, remember? He simply didn't know what hit him, same as me. So Jurrai's dead. Well, we'll have to deal with that later. Dammit, the battle isn't even over yet, I ought to be doing something—

'Are they safely away from the camp?' he asked.

The man nodded. 'Far as I can see. They lit out for the upper ford; maybe we'll catch them there, I don't know. Do you want to stay here talking in the middle of the river or shall we move on?'

Temrai allowed himself to be frogmarched onto dry land. They had to step over bodies – some dead, rather more still alive but probably past saving. That was a bad thing; all these men in the most desperate moment of their lives, scrabbling with their hands for help because they're too weak to cry out, their voices won't work any more, and we step over them as if they were cowshit in the road. 'Get a message through, call it all off.' Temrai's voice was harsh, as if he was attributing blame. 'I want everybody back to the camp, and then let's see about clearing this lot up.'

The man who'd hit him – hadn't he seen that face before? Quite possible; after all, it as less than six months ago that he'd been working in the city arsenal, perhaps some of these swords that were lying discarded on the grass were ones he'd made himself. Maybe even the one that had killed Jurrai, and nearly done for him. That'd be an amusing coincidence; but all that seemed so long ago and far away as to be part of some dream-time, and he was as different now as the moth is from the caterpillar. The hell with all that, too. Right now, there was work to be done.

Someone brought him a fresh horse – *oh, hell, Thunder's dead, my poor old friend, and I didn't even think of that until now; I used to cry myself to sleep about losing a horse when I was a kid* – and he hauled himself up into the saddle, suddenly aware of bruises, wrenched muscles, traumatised and shredded skin where he'd been ground against the stony bed of the ford. As he looked round he was subconsciously collecting faces, every face recognised a further piece of salvage, one less dagger in his conscience when the time came for him to face up to what he'd deliberately set in motion. But there wasn't time for all that now; too much to organise, so many things to be sorted out before he could say this day was over.

'Kossanai.' The Chief Engineer was a sorry sight; soaked to the skin, one of the shoulder straps of his boiled-leather breastplate flapping loose and a raw cut underneath. But he was a reliable man and still on his feet; someone else could do some work for a change. 'Get yourself over to the higher ford, make sure we're pulling out and nobody's gone dashing off in pursuit. Tell whoever's in charge up there I need those men down here now.' Kossanai nodded, wearily hauled himself into the saddle. 'Stilchai, you're in charge of picking up the wounded. Get hold of Nimren, tell her to organise the healers. And put someone in charge of prisoners. The sooner they're rounded up the better, just in case there's any that don't know the battle's over yet. Maltai, get some scouts out and let's know for sure where everybody is instead of guessing.'

It was some time before the scouts came back. The enemy were long gone; they'd doubled back behind the ridge and disappeared downriver, presumably heading for the lower crossing. Nobody had shown the slightest inclination to chase after them.

Casualty figures gradually came in; for the enemy, nine hundred killed and a further three hundred and fifty captured, half of them cut up to a greater or lesser extent, as against the clan's losses, currently standing at a hundred and seven dead and seventy-odd wounded, twenty or so seriously. It was, by any standards, a glorious victory; and if it should have been more glorious still as regards the body count, nobody seemed in too much of a hurry to dwell on that. On the contrary; for the first time in living memory, the clan had taken on the dreaded riders from the city and seen them off in no uncertain terms. Men and women whose mothers had terrified them into obedience with the threat of Maxen and his raiders had seen those same bogeymen pinned down and surrounded, caught in a pitfall and tethered for the slaughter. The fact that somehow they'd managed to slip away before their throats were actually cut was something the clan could afford to overlook; and besides, the more survivors who went home to tell the tale, the greater the panic and confusion of their enemies. A wholesale slaughter would only have served to stiffen their resolve, and made the rest of the job that much harder. As for Temrai; well, they'd always known he had the right stuff, hadn't they? It was good to know they'd been right all along, but it came as no surprise.

(There was also the somewhat discordant note struck by the families and friends of the hundred and seven dead, and the rather ungrateful attitude of the badly injured, who would rather have had their legs and hands back than all the generous praise of a grateful nation; Temrai wondered if he had time to deal with all that yet, and decided it would have to wait until the burial details had reported in and the horses had been seen to.)

The final task of the day was to finish dismantling the last seven trebuchets, so as not to fall too badly behind schedule. There were any number of willing volunteers, most of whom got under the engineers' feet and made the job take half as long again as it should have done. Once that was out of the way, everybody was at liberty to go back to their tents and campfires; except for Temrai and his heads of department, who had the long and tedious business of thinking the whole thing through and deciding what had to be done about it.

'They may try again,' Uncle Anakai said, 'but I doubt it. Not immediately, anyway. They'll be too busy deciding whose fault it was, if I know the city people.'

He was talking slowly because of the ball of cotton waste pressed to the side of his face; an arrow had slit his cheek open for three inches directly in line with his mouth. It had almost certainly been friendly fire, since the enemy had loosed off relatively few arrows.

'Let's assume they don't,' Ceuscai replied. 'I had a good look at them, after all. They didn't know what hit 'em.' He shook his head, as if unable to accept what he'd seen. 'That can't be their real army,' he went on. 'For all we know, it could just have been some privateer outfit; you know, if the Emperor won't do anything about it, we will. I can't believe the city's main field army's as easy to beat as that lot was.'

Ceuscai was reasonably undamaged; slightly stiff in one knee after an awkward fall from his horse (he'd led the ambush party at the higher ford; his misadventure had come about when he was caught in the press of his own men surging forward to massacre the encircled enemy.)

Temrai grunted in agreement, nodded slightly. 'I think you may well be right on the first count,' he said, 'not so sure about the second. Whether or not that was their proper army, I reckon we've got to expect some sort of attempt on the engines when we unload them at the final camp downstream. That's what I would do; strike hard and close to home. We can't rely on that, however. From now on we'll have to work on the principle that they could come at us at any time, which'll mean having to take people away from making and moving the engines and put them on escort duty. That'll slow us down, and won't that make us still more vulnerable?'

'What about a punitive expedition?' Shandren interrupted. 'Think about it. They've just been badly beaten in the field, for almost the first time ever. Isn't it likely they'll want to set the record straight, if only for the sake of their own self-image? They'll need to do something to restore morale.'

Anakai shook his head. 'Far more likely to take it out on their own people,' he said. 'Punishing the General'll make it so they can feel good about themselves again, and they won't have to risk a second defeat. No, I think that if they want to intercept the engines, they're most likely to do it while they're on the water. There's several places where the river's pretty wide between here and the final camp, and they know how we feel about boats. If they launch a few barges full of soldiers, they could sink the rafts or tow them off without ever coming within bowshot. We'd pursue along the bank, and either fall into an ambush or leave the construction camp exposed for a hit-and-run attack. Thinking about it, that was the obvious thing to have done instead of what they actually did; more support for your theory, Ceuscai, about this lot not being the regular army.'

'I don't think there is a regular army,' Temrai put in. 'I've said this before and nobody's paid any attention.' He shifted his weight off his painful side before continuing. 'There's a few permanent guards on the walls, and a part-time levy who're supposed to be trained men and aren't. As far as most of them are concerned, the part-timers treat their training allowance as a sort of state handout to the needy and feckless, and the rest of them look on it as a sort of drinking club. Oh, I'm not saying they won't do their best when the walls are actually under attack; I just don't see them being used as a field army away from the city. It'd be lunacy, and they know it.'

'Maybe,' Ceuscai conceded. 'But so was this.'

The glow of the fire lit up the ring of faces; twelve people who knew each other well, talking calmly and rationally about something that might well have been the end of the world. There were also places where someone should have been, but wasn't; Jurrai as leader of the horse archers, Pegtai and Sorutai as members of the chief's household – *I broke Sorutai's flute when we were children, and now I'll never be able to make it up to him; he doted on that flute, and I broke it because I was jealous. Why did I do that?* – but the gaps could be filled with others just as good, it was in the order of business for tonight's meeting, together with formal thanks to the gods for letting our losses be so light. Had Sasurai ever had to do this, Temrai wondered, carry on as if nothing had happened, accept a loss because it couldn't be helped and things might have been a whole lot worse? And what were his friends in the city thinking, as the first reports came in? Nine hundred empty beds in the city tonight; would they be filled so easily, and without the comforting reassurance of victory to let the rest of them declare that it had all been worthwhile? To die for one's people is bad enough; to die for one's people and lose as well must be a dreadful thing.

'Let's sum up then, shall we?' Temrai said, swallowing a yawn. 'We don't think they'll attack again, or at least not for a while, but it'd still be sensible to have a mobile reserve just in case. I'm not sure that's quite the answer; a reserve that's too small to make any difference is worse than no reserve at all, because it's taking people away from the jobs they should be doing. My own view is that they're not going to risk another humiliation by attacking us here, but they might have a go at the camp downstream, simply because it's nearer, it's got less people to defend it and – let's face it – that's where all the finished engines are, or will be soon enough. So I've decided that we'll have a fairly strong force down at the bottom camp, which can serve both as a guard and an early-warning post to let us know if a substantial army's on its way here. Ceuscai, I'd like you to think it over tonight and let me know tomorrow what you'll want by way of men and supplies; once I know what you're taking down there, I'll be able to reassign people here to cover.' He yawned again and stretched, wincing as his stiffening muscles protested. 'I think that covers it, don't you? Right, next, we've got vacancies on this council to fill. Nominations, please.'

Under any other circumstances there would have been a certain amount of debate, politicking, trading favours and remembering obligations; but it was too late in too overwhelming a day for anybody to have the patience or the stamina to play games. In consequence, the nominations were sensible and the debate mercifully short; even so, Uncle Anakai's head was starting to nod forward by the time Temrai declared his decision, and the pad of bloodsoaked cotton fell from Anakai's hand onto the rug, revealing the full ugliness of the wound, the crudeness of the chewed-sinew suture it had hastily been sewn up with. My fault again, Temrai reflected; all the sinew they'd normally have used had been requisitioned by the bowmakers for strings and back-facings, so the healers had to unwrap old stuff from tools and furniture and chomp it soft in their mouths in order to stitch up wounds.

That's something else we'll have to deal with; we can't go into battle again with nothing to patch the casualties up with. He thought for a moment about the word *casualties*; a nice technical term, suitable for military use. You didn't talk about people slashed open and bleeding, people with arms and legs missing, people with holes in them or scars that made their own children frightened of them; you said *casualties*, and after a while you talked about *acceptable losses* and then *expendable forces*, and pretty soon it all became a game of chess, observed from the top of a hill, part of a sequence of games, a tournament. And then you wonder why your friends don't talk to you the same way any more, and after that you start worrying about conspiracies and treason; and after that, the chances are you'll really have conspiracies and treason to worry about. And to think; there's people who actually *want* this job. Crazier still; there are places where people who want this sort of job are allowed to do it.

Which is how wars start; or, at least, how they're caused.

'Next on the agenda,' he heard himself saying, 'is the formal vote of thanks to the gods for keeping our casualties down to an acceptable level. Uncle, if you'd care to do the honours.'

Loredan didn't mind. If anything, he was glad of the peace and quiet, relieved to be on his own. He stretched out, hands behind his head, legs extended, feet crossed. The stone bench was cold, but not unbearably so. *I could get to like this*, he said to himself.

If he'd felt it was unjust, that he didn't deserve to be here, it'd be a different matter. As it was, what had the Prefect called it? *Culpable negligence, dereliction of duty, gross errors of judgement*; he couldn't really argue with that. A thousand men dead or in the hands of the enemy, because he'd been too busy sulking to notice that they were walking into a trap. Culpable negligence was putting it mildly; it couldn't have been more obvious if they'd cut the word TRAP in eight-foot letters in the chalk. *If Maxen was alive, he'd have pulled my lungs out for what I've done.*

Yes, but Maxen was dead. Hence all this.

Held pending an immediate inquiry, the Prefect had said. Loredan hoped it wouldn't be too immediate. A week or two here in the quiet and the dark would do him the world of good, let him get rid of the horrors before he had to go out and explain himself to people. Right now, a stone bed in a cell under the council chamber was infinitely preferable to getting yelled at in the chapter house; he could easily imagine the panic inside and the hysteria outside, the mobs baying for someone's blood, rioting down at the docks as people fought for berths on outgoing ships, a wonderful pretext for another night of looting and breaking down the doors of unpopular neighbours.

As to what happened after that, he couldn't really summon up the energy to worry about it. Maybe he'd be put to death, here in his cell or in some quiet guardroom on the wall. That kind of death he could accept; somehow it wasn't nearly as depressing as the thought of dying in the courtroom had been, when he'd been facing the prospect of fighting Alvise for the greater glory of the charcoal people. That would have made very little sense, his last dying thought would have been, *Gods, how stupid.* This way? Well, fair enough, in context. He owed a death to the people of the plains. This way he'd been able to get four-fifths of the army home and still pay off his debt to the enemy.

Someone walked past in the corridor outside; heavy boots, a jangle of metal, keys probably. Were there other prisoners down here, or was he the only one? Other enemies of the state, out of sight and mind? He wondered what they'd done. You had to be pretty fair-average wicked to end up in the cells; mere piracy, rape or murder weren't enough to get you free board and lodging in this town.

Fancy there being no Emperor, he said to himself, still not quite able to believe what he'd heard. The Prefect had been very matter-of-fact about it, as if he'd been talking about the tooth fairy or the headache elves, things you grew out of believing in when you turned seven. According to the Prefect, there hadn't been an Emperor for the whole of Loredan's lifetime – *but didn't we always pick flowers for his garland on his birthday when we were kids? What did they do with all those hundreds of flowery garlands that got handed in with such ceremony at the upper-city gate each year? Disturbing, somehow, to think of all that love going to waste, like water draining into sand.*

When Callelogus IV died with no heirs and the succession stood to be disputed between three distant cousins, foreign princes who couldn't speak the language and whose table manners alone would have rendered them entirely unacceptable to the city, it occurred to the City Prefect and his cronies that if the people weren't told the Emperor was dead, then nobody would know, and what they didn't know wouldn't hurt them. Since then, the upper city had been empty except for a few caretakers and some officials who had offices there; Callelogus had lived to be ninety-six, and on his death the diadem passed to an entirely made-up nephew, the son of a wholly fictitious sister who'd supposedly been married off to an unknown princeling in a far-distant land just long enough ago that nobody could be expected to remember it happening. Meanwhile, the government of the city stayed in the hands of the people whose trade was governing cities, quietly and piecemeal; secretaries of state, officials, middle-city men who knew how to repair roads and negotiate trade agreements. The more Loredan thought about it, the more he favoured it as a system of government. They had, after all, done a good job.

Up till now, at least.

Gods, Loredan thought, *what if the city is going to fall?* Unthinkable; the wall still stood, after all, and nobody could ever get past that. But he'd seen siege engines in the plainsmen's camp, catapults and trebuchets, sections of siege wall, mobile housings for battering rams, sections of siege towers, and he couldn't help thinking that if they'd managed to make such things, homeless savages who lived in tents, then there was a will and a determination there that wasn't going to be put off by the city's reputation for being impregnable. That thought disturbed Loredan far more than the prospect of his own death.

And yet it would be fair enough, all things considered. It wasn't a matter of right and wrong; even if such things existed, they had nothing to do with the life cycle of cities and nations. The city's dealings with the people of the plain were no more reprehensible than the lion's relationship with the deer, but that worked both ways. If it was the clan's turn to be the lion, that was the way it was meant to go. You couldn't *disagree* with something like that. All you could sensibly do was leave and find somewhere else to live.

More footsteps outside, coming this way, stopping outside the door, A slim blade of light slit the darkness, then turned into a flood. There were two outlines in the doorway.

'Just give me a shout when you're done, Father,' said a voice Loredan recognised as the warder's. 'I'll be right outside.'

The door closed, but the light stayed inside; yellow and warm from a small lamp. It turned the other outline into Patriarch Alexius. Taken aback, Loredan swung his legs off the bench and stood up.

'Here,' he said, 'sit down.'

'Thank you. I will,' Alexius replied. In the melodramatic light of the oil lamp he looked like a corpse, and it took him a while to hobble the length of the small cell. 'That's better,' he said. 'Just let me catch my breath, will you? Stairs,' he added.

Loredan sat on the floor, his back to the wall, waiting for the Patriarch to say something. He didn't want to be rude, but he was in no mood for small talk.

'You'll be out of here fairly soon,' Alexius went on after a minute or so. 'We've just had a rather annoying meeting, lots of foolish people saying stupid things; the gist of it is that I'm to address the crowd and tell them to calm down and go home, and they're letting you go. You'll have a chance to have a bath and a shave before the next meeting.'

Loredan's mouth dropped open. 'Next meeting?' he repeated. 'What, you mean I'm still—?'

Alexius nodded. 'I had an idea at the time you wouldn't be overjoyed about it. It's all a matter of expediency, you see. We need scapegoats for the defeat, but we also need a hero for the people to trust.' He sighed; the marks of fatigue on his face were as clear as the portrait on a newly minted coin. 'That'll be you,' he continued. 'I shall tell my fellow citizens that the five generals responsible for the disaster were the ones who died in the battle; Bardas Loredan, on the other hand, saved the day, snatched four-fifths of the army out of the jaws of death, turned a humiliating defeat into a moral victory—'

'Oh, for pity's sake!'

'Don't be so ungrateful,' Alexius replied. 'And besides, it's near enough to the truth. And if you're determined to be a martyr, you might yet get your chance. You haven't heard the funny bit yet.'

'Tell me the funny bit,' Loredan said.

Alexius stiffened as a cramp came and went. 'This is our illustrious Prefect's idea of a compromise,' he said. 'At an unspecified date in the future, you're to stand trial in a court of law.' He paused, then continued: 'Until then, you're appointed Deputy Lord Lieutenant, with responsibility for organising the defence of the walls and the lower city. Don't say it,' he added quickly, 'I think everyone thinks so too. It only goes to show: who needs an Emperor when we can be imbeciles all by ourselves?'

'I think that's the most glorious piece of idiocy I've ever

heard in all my life,' Loredan said, his eyes closed. 'What if I refuse?'

Alexius shook his head. 'I don't think that's allowed,' he said. 'Put another way, if you don't do it, it won't get done. They didn't like my idea,' he added. 'A pity. It was a good one.'

'Really? What as that?'

'I wanted you made Commander-in-Chief,' Alexius replied. 'I may not know anything about tactics and battles, but I can recognise a natural leader when I hear of one.'

Loredan didn't say anything to that. 'So when do I get out of here?' he asked. 'Not that I'm in any hurry.'

'Once the crowds have been told you're a hero. Until then, you're better off here. There's a mob several thousand strong demanding your head on a pole at the lower-city gate. If they get through and break in here—'

'I see.' Loredan nodded. 'Your idea also?'

Alexius shook his head. 'One of the pointy-faced types from the Office of Supply,' he replied. 'They're all fools, but some of them are surprisingly cunning.' He leant back and rested his head against the wall. 'If I may,' he said, 'I'd like to stay here until it's time for me to go and make my speech. It's agreeably peaceful. How up to date are you with the news?'

'Not very. What's the situation outside?'

'Quiet,' Alexius said. 'There hasn't been any activity upriver; as far as we can tell, they're carrying on with building engines and rafting them down the river. All they've done is put a cavalry escort – three or four thousand, no more – on the downstream camp where they're landing the engines.'

'That puts them no more than five miles from the city,' Loredan said thoughtfully. 'Gods, I wish we hadn't mounted that stupid expedition. Now's the time we should be making sorties, and of course we won't, for fear of another good hiding.' He looked up. 'I assume the Lord Lieutenant's in command of external operations.' Alexius nodded. 'What about what's left of the task force? With four thousand men, provided we think about what we're doing this time, we could still cut out those engines at the landing point without too much trouble—'

'He won't hear of it,' Alexius replied. 'And he has got a point. If we were to suffer another defeat, particularly one so close to home, the city'd be ungovernable. You can't imagine what it's like down there.'

'So we sit tight and wait for a siege. What about supplies and the like? It won't be long before the news crosses the sea, and then we'll have the harbour crammed with people come to sell us grain at sky-high prices.'

'Sky-high or not, we've authorised the Prefect to buy everything he can lay his hands on. Not that food and supplies will be a problem; there's nothing the clan can do to interfere with shipping, so there's no reason we can't have business as usual. But it'll reassure the people if they see us stockpiling, and then maybe they'll stop looting the bakeries.'

Loredan shook his head. 'They *like* looting bakeries,' he said, 'It's only afterwards they start complaining, when they can't get their usual orders because the place has burnt down.' He smiled. 'It's times like these that bring out the best in people. What are they doing about recruitment? Has anything been organised yet?'

'Not really,' the Patriarch replied. 'At the moment, we've got old men and boys by the thousand demanding to be allowed to volunteer, while most of the able-bodied men are busy smashing the city and beating up the guard. And of course everyone wants to know why the Patriarch isn't using his arcane powers to avert the danger. I anticipate quite a lot of that when I go out to make my speech.'

'Well, quite.' Loredan grinned. 'What's the point in having all these wizards if they can't even launch a few fireballs and turn the enemy into frogs? Makes you wonder whose side they're on.'

'I think the Prefect and the Lord Lieutenant are going to ask me that quite soon,' Alexius said mournfully. 'I've even started thinking that way myself, may I be forgiven. Thanks to my recent researches, I now know rather more about curses and the way they work. It occurs to me that if we had that girl from the Island here, the one we think might be a natural…'

Loredan held up his hands. 'Don't,' he said. 'Not if you want me to leave this nice safe cell.'

'I thought you didn't believe in all that.'

'I don't,' Loredan replied. 'But there's healthy agnosticism and there's sitting up and begging for trouble. Not for the city, I mean. For you, personally. You look as if you died a week ago and they gave you to the apprentice embalmer to practise on.'

Alexius laughed; more appreciatively than the joke deserved. 'That's the nicest thing anybody's said about me in a long time,' he replied. 'I must confess, I've felt better. But it's all right,' he added, with a slight grin, 'because it's just honest-to-goodness ordinary illness, not any more of those confounded side effects from – let's say – our little adventure into the unknown. Ordinary illness doesn't worry me so much.'

Loredan nodded. 'The enemy you can see is the least of your problems. That was a favourite saying of my old commander, rest his vicious soul. It's like the joke about the two men in the middle of the battlefield; one of them gets hit by an arrow and falls to the ground moaning. The other one takes a look at the fletchings on the arrow and says, 'It's all right, mate, it was one of ours.' What's that expression they have for it these days? Friendly fire?'

Alexius nodded. 'That's more or less the way I feel,' he said. 'Physical illness might not be much fun, but at least you don't feel it's out to get you, in the same way the other stuff did.' He sighed. 'I suppose you'd say it was a self-inflicted wound, and I should stop imagining things.'

'No,' Loredan replied, 'because we're going to be working together and I do still have a modicum of tact.' He rubbed his chin thoughtfully before continuing. 'Actually,' he said, 'I did give the matter a certain amount of thought, back when you first told me about it all. I still don't believe in this all-pervading Principle of nature you people talk about – or at least I don't *disbelieve* in it either, it just seems too wishy-washy to be of any importance ...'

'It is, usually,' Alexius interrupted, smiling sadly. 'Most of the time, in fact. All this business with curses and benedictions is just a minor and irrelevant by-product, like oak-apples on oak trees.'

Loredan nodded. 'I'll have to take your word on that,' he said. 'Another thing I don't believe in, though, is co-incidence; not on the grandiose scale we were getting back-along. I'm prepared to concede that *something* was going on; I just don't reckon any of us had the faintest idea what it was.'

Alexius nodded his head. 'There, my sceptical friend, I agree with you entirely,' he said.

'But why can't I *see* him?' Athli demanded for the sixth time. 'I'm his clerk, he's got a business to run. I've got students asking for their money back. If you'd care to explain to them why they can't have the instruction they've paid for ...'

The clerk frowned. 'I'm sorry,' he said, 'but there are important matters of state involved; rather more important,' he added unpleasantly, 'than your colleague's coaching practice. In fact, I would suggest that you refund any money you may be holding on account without further delay. I would think it highly unlikely that Colonel Loredan will be free to resume his private work for the foreseeable future.' He stood up, to indicate that the audience was ended. 'And now,' he said, 'if you'd be good enough to excuse me.'

'All right,' Athli said, not moving from her seat. 'Could you pass on a letter for me, and forward the reply? I know he's in the city,' she added. 'I saw him come back myself. And he wouldn't have left again without letting me know.'

The clerk studied her objectively through dead-fish eyes, noting that she was young and attractive and exhibiting more concern for her principal than a normal business relationship would warrant. Athli read the interpretation in his face, made a mental note to have him horribly murdered at some convenient future date, and played up to what he was thinking. She simpered a little. 'Please,' she added. 'It'd mean so much to me if you could.'

'I might be able to send a message,' he said, his voice lightly spiced with contempt and a little self-conscious compassion. 'I'm not sure about a letter, though; it would have to be passed by the Committee for National Security, and there would inevitably be a delay. Any reply from Colonel Loredan would be similarly subject to—' He paused, and smiled bleakly. 'To review,' he concluded. 'If that's not acceptable—'

'That'll be fine,' Athli replied firmly. 'Can I borrow your pen?'

The clerk sighed and sat down again. 'Help yourself,' he said. 'But please, if you could hurry it up a little. I have to attend a meeting which will be starting very soon.'

'Won't keep you a minute,' Athli said.

This is just to see if you're all right, and if there's anything you want me to do. We've got enough punters for two full classes now, presumably thanks to your recent publicity stunts, so I'm putting the charges up by a third. I've been to your apartment and made sure everything's all right there; and I had a man put a lock on the door, so don't be surprised if you can't get in. I'll send you the key if they'll let me. Cheer up. It must be fun to be famous.

She hesitated. Should she add anything else? She wanted to say *something* to let him know that she understood how he must be feeling. (Not that she did, and they'd both know it.) No, she'd only embarrass him. Instead, she scribbled her name, folded the scrap of parchment and handed it to the clerk. 'You're sure you've got my address?' she added.

'We know where to find you,' the clerk replied with a slight emphasis she was supposed not to like. 'And now, I really must—'

She allowed herself to be shooed out of the office, and watched the clerk scuttle off at a dignified half-trot towards the main cloister; then she made her way slowly back towards the gatehouse. Nothing to do, and all day to do it in. Again.

Rather than mope about at home, she decided to go down to the stationers' quarter and buy something. It was traditional that clerks should have something of a stationery fetish; good for business as well, since the tools of a clerk's trade lent themselves to elegant splendour, and clients tended to assume that the costlier and more magnificent the pen and inkwell, the higher the quality of the words that issued from them. Athli was only too happy to conform to the stereotype. When she stopped to think about it, the amount of money she'd frittered away on such things appalled her (though, she reassured herself, since she'd only ever bought quality she could probably get her money back on them with no trouble at all if she had to.) Which reminded her of something else.

Odd, she mused as she strolled through the chairmakers' quarter towards the Chandlers' Gate, the fact that he never seems to have any money. The mathematics of it simply don't make sense. I get twenty-five per cent of what he makes, and I can live in a nice part of town and afford to waste money on marquetry writing boards and solid-silver counters. He lives in the slums and owns nothing. I know he goes out drinking quite a lot and that must cost a bit, except he seems to go to places where you can drink yourself to death for the price of a glass of wine in a decent inn; what does he do with all his money?

Strange, to work with someone so closely for so long and now know the first thing about him. We get along all right; better than all right, in fact, it's always been great fun. I've never known a man who I can talk to so easily, one who doesn't make any difficulties ... But what do I actually know about him? He was in the army – well, everybody knows that now, of course; in fact, everybody knows rather more than I did before all this started – and he was brought up on a farm and he's got an unspecified number of brothers and at least one sister. He doesn't talk about his parents, so maybe they're dead; or maybe he just doesn't talk about them. And he had lots of acquaintances, in the trade of course, but I've no idea if he has any friends. Of course, he knows all about *me* – not that there's too much to know. He always seems quite interested when I tell him about things, can't quite seem to understand why I haven't got married and don't see anybody. I don't suppose he's really interested, though. Why should he be, after all?

She frowned, remembering the clerk's knowing leer. He'd been wrong, of course, though she'd be lying if she said the thought hadn't crossed her mind once or twice. But never seriously; not much future in a relationship with a man in that line of work. Worse than loving a sailor; at least they come back sometimes. Not that he's in that line of work any more; except he's *Colonel* Loredan now, and that's scarcely an improvement.

She stopped opposite a stall selling rather garish painted wooden bowls. If he's going to be Colonel Loredan for any length of time, she thought, he won't be teaching people how to fence; and then what am I supposed to do for a living? That's odd, too; when he was working in the courts, I always had my contingency plans ready, just in case anything happened. Now I'm at a loss to think what I'm going to do next. I can't carry on the school on my own and I don't think I could bear to go back to clerking for advocates. Oh, damn and blast, what is *wrong* with me?

Slowly and deliberately, Athli calmed herself down; and as she did so, a small but persistent voice in the back of her head began chanting, *When all seems lost, buy stationery!* It seemed like the best advice she was likely to get. She took it.

The atmosphere in the stationers' quarter varied between picturesque bustle and hell on earth, depending on the time of day and year, supply and demand, the health of the economy and the mood of the city. The feverish intensity of the activity under the rich awnings reflected the influence of the last factor on the list; the clerks of Perimadeia had decided that the end was probably nigh, in which case they might as well indulge themselves while they still had money and their money was still worth something; and if it wasn't the end of the world, they had cause for celebration, best effected by buying things. The stationery trade had risen to the occasion; Athli had never seen so much good stuff, or such high prices.

There were lignum vitae and rosewood writing boards and accounting boards, lavishly carved and inlaid with ivory, mother of pearl and polished lapis lazuli. There were inkwells; gods, the inkwells – silver inkwells, gold inkwells, inkwells with jewelled lids and little jewelled feet, patent inkwells with little ribs for knocking off the excess ink after you'd dipped your pen, inkwells hollowed out of elephant tusks and walrus tusks, inkwells in the shape of roses, pigs, kneeling figures, skulls, horses, the backsides of women and boys, the Patriarch's ceremonial crown.

There were cedarwood tablets, hinged and inlaid, with the creamy yellow wax as inviting as sand on the beach after the tide has just gone out, crying out to be marked. There were styluses of breathtaking beauty and nauseating vulgarity, pens cut from the feathers of eagles and peacocks, so long that you wouldn't be able to use them without wiping your eye with every stroke. There were counters (counters beyond number; joke) of silver and gold, tiny counters for the secretive, huge counters like saucers that probably took two men to lift, fancy counters with every conceivable kind of decoration, including some that were hastily whisked away before Athli could look at them (spoilsports!), plain counters on which your name, titles and favourite platitude could be engraved by our highly skilled craftsmen while you wait, counters that cost more than the sums they'd be used to calculate.

There were cuff protectors and eyeshades, magnifying lenses for the short-sighted, lamps and candle holders, abacuses and tiny sets of portable scales that came in the most delightful little ivory boxes. There was parchment – was there ever parchment! How could there be enough sheep in all the world to supply so much parchment – and every square inch of it scraped and pumiced smooth, thin and softly translucent, so that it glowed like a cloud at sunrise.

There were little jars of powdered ink in every colour you could dream of; turquoise and cobalt, crimson and purple, coroner's green and government black, chamberlain's azure, works orange, army blue, shipyards brown, even the incredibly expensive and highly illegal imperial gold – in theory, a clerk could have his hand cut off for using it without express authority; the way round that was to dilute it with a tiny amount of silver in vitriol, which cost as much as the gold ink and burnt you to the bone if you splashed it. There were tiny knives for trimming pens, their blades as thin as leaves and ten times sharper than the average Perimadeian razor; bigger versions, too, that swaggering young clerks liked to display on their belts as a way of getting round the prohibition on carrying arms in the council building.

There were enamelled ink stirrers and gold-wire ink strainers, parchment stretchers and beautifully wrought pumice scrapers for scraping parchment clean of old letters to use again. There were seals, seal-cases, sealing-wax cases, tiny chafing dishes and miniature spirit burners for melting wax, tiny thin blades for unlawfully lifting seals without breaking them, little pots of specially fine clay for taking impressions of seals for the purpose of forgery. There were portable writing chests and little cabinets to hold all your gear (the lid folding out into a writing and counting board, with little hinges and fine silver chains) that stopped your heart with the glory of the workmanship and cost slightly more than a fully equipped warship.

After a while, Athli had to stop looking and sit down, her eyes dazzled by so much glitter and sparkle. One of the things city people loved to boast about in front of foreigners was that in Perimadeia almost everybody could read and write. What she'd seen today made Athli wonder whether literacy wasn't in fact some kind of vice.

Once she'd got her breath back she moved on to the bookstall, where you could buy any number of manuals of forms and precedents; letters for every occasion, every possible vicissitude of human life. She lifted down a small, squat volume and squinted at the minuscule writing on the title page:

> *Letters from creditors to debtors*
> *Letters from debtors to creditors*
> *Letters from superiors to juniors*
> *Letters from juniors to superiors*
> *Letters from poor students to rich uncles imploring assistance*
> *Letters from rich uncles to poor students refusing assistance*
> *Letters from lovers (male) to married women, beseeching*
> *Ditto, despairing*
> *Letters from married women to lovers (male), ambiguous*
> *Ditto, encouraging*
> *Letters from tradesmen respectfully demanding payment*
> *Letters from gentlemen to tradesmen tactfully postponing payment*
> *Letters from tenants of state farms to district commissioners requesting leave to transport pigs to winter pasture on public commons*
> *Letters from district commissioners to tenants of state farms declining leave to transport pigs to winter pasture on public commons and reminding said tenants of their obligations to provide said pigs with adequate fodder during winter*
> *Letters proposing marriage*
> *Letters declining marriage*
> *Letters to a beloved (female) threatening suicide*
> *Letters to an unwanted suitor (male) encouraging suicide*

> *Letters from military officers informing parents of death of a son*
> *Other sundry letters.*

—All with the first word of the title picked out in red, the page number, the appropriate cross-references, and the occasional scribbled addition where the previous owner had added in a few well-favoured precedents of his own; the whole thing for only one and a half gold quarters, guaranteed to make it so you'd never again have to think what to say, no matter how bizarre the circumstances. Athli couldn't resist that, so she bought it, having first negotiated half a quarter off the price and bullied the stallholder into throwing in the carrying case for nothing.

She sat down on a stone bench in the shade of an awning and was just about to see what her guide recommended for *Letter to unmarried niece politely declining request for contribution to dowry* when a shadow fell across the page and she looked up.

'Hello,' said a voice coming out of a black shape silhouetted against the sun. 'Excuse me, but aren't you Master Loredan's clerk?'

The voice was female, foreign and quite pleasant; Athli blinked and squinted a little. 'I know you, I think,' she replied. 'You're the na—' She recovered in time and swallowed the rest of *natural*. 'You're the merchant's sister, from the Island. We met in the tavern the day Loredan fought Alvise. Vetriz?'

'That's right,' Vetriz nodded and sat down on the bench beside her. 'Fancy you remembering.'

'Necessary skill of the clerical profession,' Athli replied, budging up a little. Ordinarily, of course, she'd have forgotten the dratted female completely by now; but Loredan's account of his weird conversation with Patriarch Alexius in the Schools not long before the cavalry expedition had vividly refreshed her memory. Now, of course, she was filled with a strange mixture of instinctive revulsion and insatiable curiosity; unlike Bardas, she had no doubts at all about the existence and power of magic, and wasn't this female somehow supposed to be the most powerful witch in the world? Something like that, anyway.

'I came here to buy an inkwell,' Vetriz said, with a trace of bewilderment in her voice. 'But there's such a choice I don't know where to start. At home there's plain inkwells and fancy inkwells, and that's about it.'

Athli smiled politely. 'So long as you remember never to pay the asking price, you won't go far wrong,' she said, and then remembered that this female was a merchant's sister, probably a seasoned trader in her own right; certainly not the sort of person who needed advice on bargaining techniques from a fencer's clerk. 'How long are you staying?' she went on.

'I'm not sure,' Vetriz replied. 'We brought in a load of preserved fruit, and prices are extraordinary; because of the invasion, of course. If only we'd known, we'd have filled two ships. Anyway, we sold the fruit in no time at all, and my brother's going round trying to decide what to take back. We spent all of yesterday and most of today looking at rope—'

'Rope?'

Vetriz nodded. 'Rope,' she repeated. 'And there comes a point where one shed full of coils of rope begins to look *exactly* the same as all the others, and Ven said that having me standing about looking bored and yawning wasn't really helping him terribly much when it came to getting the best possible price, so perhaps I should go back to the inn and wait for him there. So I came down here to buy an inkwell.'

'I see,' Athli said. 'Well, don't let me keep you.' *Foremost witch of the known world she might be, but she's starting to get on my nerves. Go away, witch.* 'There's cheaper ones on the stall over there by the fountain, or some really nice carved ivory stuff on the one with the purple and white awning.'

Vetriz turned and smiled at her. 'You obviously know about this sort of thing – well, I suppose you would, in your line of work. Would you mind awfully advising me?

Otherwise I'll have no idea whether what I'm getting is a bargain or a piece of junk.'

If only she hadn't been painfully aware that she had absolutely nothing else to do, Athli would have made an excuse and left. As it was, she could truthfully have pleaded a slight headache. Instead, she muttered that of course, she'd be delighted, and led the way to the cheap stall. Once she'd started advising, however, she slowly found herself getting carried away by the excitement of the enterprise. When asked roughly how much she had to spend, Vetriz had named a sum which immediately caused Athli to transfer the search to the purple-and-white-striped stall; and the quiet thrill of serious shopping with someone else's money soon blanked out her vague dislike of the female herself. In fact, she listened so attentively and seemed so genuinely interested in the valuable information she was getting that Athli gradually revised her opinion. The revision speeded up considerably when Vetriz, having secured a terrifyingly valuable and desirable gold and pearl inkwell for a sum that was only moderately obscene, insisted on buying Athli a small present by way of thanking her for her help. In Vetriz's terms, a small present consisted of a chiselled steel and walrus-tusk penknife whose value would have fed a family for a month.

'Thank you,' she said. 'It's very nice.'

'My pleasure,' Vetriz replied, and she did seem genuinely pleased that her new friend liked the present. 'Oh, aren't there a lot of lovely things! I think we should get Venart down here and then you could tell him what to buy. You could name your own price for things like this back home; I'm sure they'd bring a much better return than mouldy old rope.'

'Well ...' Athli started to say, visualising a new career as an assistant stationery buyer. 'But I wouldn't have the first idea about what's saleable on the Island; I don't know what they like.' She massaged the side of her head with her fingertips; the headache was starting to annoy her. 'I think that sort of thing's better left to people who know what they're doing,' she said, realising as she said it that she was probably being insulting.

Vetriz shook her head. 'If I'm to learn business, I've got to practise,' she said. 'Properly speaking, I've got a half-share in everything, and Ven's only managing it on my behalf. I know I'll never get the hang of sacks of flour and jars of oil and so forth, but there's no reason why I shouldn't specialise in fancy goods; that's just as much trade as bulk commodities, after all, and quite possibly there's more profit in it. The only thing that was putting me off, now I come to think of it, was not knowing the markets here.' She stopped, turned to Athli and beamed. 'You know, I think it was fate or something, bumping into you like that. What do you say? You advise me, I'll do the buying and we split the profit three parts to one.'

'I'm not sure,' Athli said. It was getting increasingly difficult to concentrate, because of the pain in her head; in addition to which, she had the strangest feeling of being pushed, or rather of drifting on a current that wanted to go downstream when she was heading up. On the other hand, it did seem like a sound commercial venture (though she wasn't sure about the value of her proposed contribution). 'I suppose so, if you're really serious. But won't you need to get some money from your brother first?'

'Actually,' Vetriz replied, lowering her voice and smirking slightly, 'no. For heaven's sake don't tell Ven, but I brought a bit of my own money with me on this trip, just in case I happened to find something to invest it in. I've been thinking along these lines for a while now, in very general terms. No, what I think I'll do is pretend to Ven that all the stock I buy this time is things I want for myself. Then if I do make a loss getting rid of it when we're back home, he'll never need to know. And if I make a go of it, I can plough the money back in – less your share, of course – and buy more stock the next time we come over; which ought to be quite soon, with prices the way they are. Come on, let's shake hands like proper business partners and call it a deal.'

'All right,' Athli said, and as they shook hands, she couldn't help wondering what on earth she thought she was doing. *And what's this strange fascination Loredan and I hold for these people? Here's this woman I've only met once before, and already she's freed him from a curse and taken me on as a business partner. And didn't Bardas say something about headaches? I could probably remember if my head didn't hurt so much.*

CHAPTER TWELVE

Loredan got the letter just as he was being led out of the cells to his first council meeting as Deputy Lord Lieutenant. He read it, felt vaguely guilty, folded it up and tucked it in his belt.

The chapter house was full this time, and there were scarcely any faces he knew. He hoped that was a good sign; even if the strangers turned out to be nothing more than stray passers-by they'd dragged in off the streets, they couldn't help but be an improvement on the Committee for National Security.

To his extreme embarrassment he was led right the way up the steps to the bunch of seats that had arms and backs, instead of simply being stone shelves. This was where the high-ups sat; each place had the office of its customary occupant carved into the stone – Patriarch, Urban Preceptor, Dean of Offices, City Archimandrite, Archimandrite of Elissa and so on. There was an empty place marked Archdeacon of the Chapter that he was clearly supposed to sit in. He lowered himself into it, wondering vaguely who the Archdeacon of the Chapter was and what he did for a living, and waited for someone to say something.

The City Prefect stood up, looked around and nodded to the two sergeants, who closed the doors of the chamber and bolted them. 'I think we're all here at last,' he said. 'I'm pleased to be able to tell you that Colonel Loredan's agreed to accept the post of Deputy Lord Lieutenant, so we can get started on the main business of the day, which is quite straightforward: what steps ought we to take to ensure the security of the city?' He turned to Loredan and nodded. 'Colonel,' he said, 'you have the floor.'

Loredan waited for a moment, just in case the Prefect had meant some other colonel, and then stood up. His knees felt a little shaky, until he considered that usually when he stood up in a place as crowded as this, there would be a man with a sword trying to kill him. The worst this lot could do was throw apples. He didn't feel nervous after that.

'Gentlemen,' he began. *Oh, gods, what am I going to say?* 'I suppose I should thank you for having faith in me; I'm not sure I agree with you, but let's not bother with that now. The point is, I think, that you're asking me, because of my knowledge of the clans, to suggest ways of improving the defences of the city. Well, I do have an opinion on that subject, if you'd like to hear it.'

He paused for a moment, took a deep breath and continued. 'Everyone in this city,' he said, 'is brought up to believe that because we've got the walls and the harbour, we don't really need to worry about attacks from inland. The people on the plains don't like us much, maybe with good reason, but they're just a load of savages with never a hope in hell of breaching the walls or scaling them, and a siege won't work because all our supplies come in by sea anyway; the clans don't know the first thing about ships, so all we have to do is sit tight and wait for them to go away.'

He looked round and nodded. 'There isn't much wrong with thinking like that,' he continued. 'That's why we've never bothered much with a field army, at least not since we gave up any ideas of building a land empire between here and the Salimb mountains. There was Maxen, of course; while he was alive, he kept the clans in a permanent state of terror and they never dared come within sixty miles of the city for fear of getting cut to pieces. We were pretty smug about that at the time, I seem to remember. Well, it's easy to be wise after the event, but if it hadn't been for Maxen and the Pitchfork, we wouldn't be in this mess now. As it is, it looks like we've got a young fire-eater of a chief who wants to make sure nothing like Maxen can ever happen again by wiping us off the face of the earth. This wouldn't be a problem, except it appears that he's got city people with him who are teaching his people how to build heavy engines and siege equipment. Now *that's* worrying.'

Nobody was moving, or whispering to the person sitting next to him, or even looking out of the window. Loredan was surprised and impressed; maybe they were going to take this thing seriously after all.

'Now then,' he continued, 'I may not be a scholar of history, but I can't call to mind any occasion when these magnificent walls of ours have ever been put to the test by a properly equipped assault force. Maybe they're impregnable, maybe not; we just don't know. I suggest we assume they aren't, and try and get inside the other man's mind. How would we go about attacking the walls of Perimadeia? Any suggestions?'

He folded his arms and waited. There was a long silence, as his audience tried to work out whether it had been a rhetorical question. Then a short, broad man with a beard stood up somewhere near the back, more or less opposite Loredan. The face was vaguely familiar; some kind of engineer, at a guess.

'The answer to that's quite simple,' he said. 'There's three ways. One, knock the walls down. Two, climb over them. Three, dig under them. Simple,' he added, 'but not easy, if you get my meaning.'

Loredan nodded. 'All right,' he said. 'Let's go through them one at a time. Knocking them down; I take it you're thinking of torsion engines, mangonels, trebuchets and so on, right?'

The engineer nodded. 'And rams,' he said. 'But in order to use rams they've got to get across the river, which means building a causeway or floating a ram down the river on pontoons. Neither way's easy, but both are possible.'

'Right,' Loredan said. 'And you're …?'

'Leucas Garantzes, Deputy Municipal Engineer,' the bearded man replied. 'Responsible for maintaining the walls, guard towers and stationary engines on the landward side.'

'Pleased to meet you,' Loredan said. 'Here's what I want you to do. I don't actually know how effective rock-chucking engines are against heavy masonry, so I want some facts and figures – ranges, capacities, rates of fire, some indication of what each class of engine is capable of. Now, we don't actually know anything about what they've got, but we can start by assuming they're copies of the government pattern. Once we know what they can do, we'll know what we need to do to counteract them. Agreed?'

Garantzes nodded. 'I'll see what I can do,' he said, and sat down.

Loredan drew a deep breath. 'Now we're getting somewhere,' he said. 'Anybody here who can provide me with scale plans of the defences?'

Nobody moved for a while; then a very young man near the front stood up and said, 'I think I can help with that.'

'And you are?'

'Timoleon Molin,' the young man replied. 'Surveyors' Office. Really I'm in charge of drainage and flood precautions, but we've got lots of detailed maps in the office, which ought to do.'

'That's good,' Loredan said, and Molin sat down again with obvious relief. 'Anybody here from the arsenal?'

The man who stood up was short, bald and slightly stooped. 'Teodrico Tiron,' he said. 'I make catapults.'

'Just the job,' Loredan said with approval. 'I want you to get together with Timoleon over there and Deputy Garantzes and draw me a plan of the walls showing the fields of fire of all the stationary engines we've got in place already, and any blind spots or places where we could do with upgrading the artillery cover. If their engines look like they're going to be a threat, our best chance is to be able to knock them out before they get going.' He turned to his left. 'City Prefect,' he said, 'while we're on the subject, I'd like to talk to all the full-time artillery captains about what they're capable of at the moment, and sort out some intensive training. I want us to be able to hit what we shoot at, otherwise we'll just be wasting our time.' He paused to draw breath, going over in his mind what had been said. 'Now, unless anybody can show me something I've missed, we've covered their first option. Let's turn to the second option, scaling the walls.'

As he continued, he could feel the mood of the council changing; from curiosity to a kind of stunned acceptance of all the work they were being so high-handedly assigned; and he wondered, *Why are they taking all this like it was words of wisdom from some great general? Can't they see I'm making it all up as I go along? Or hadn't it even occurred to them to do any of these things? Why's it all suddenly up to me, for gods' sakes?*

'Now then, food distribution,' he heard himself saying. 'I know we've got a fair bit put by, and the Prefect's Office is adding to that by large-scale purchasing on the open market, so that's fine; but I think it'd help if we knew exactly how many people we've got to feed, and how we're going to go about organising distribution. Anybody here from the Chancellor's Office? Good; now, I know it's been a long time since we had a proper census …'

Just listen to yourself, will you? Since when were you a born leader of men? If truth be told, you don't know spit about the corn supply. Which is why it makes sense to find out, I suppose.

And what happened to all the politics? Why isn't anybody arguing, for pity's sake?

Things must be serious.

He suddenly realised he'd run out of things to say. He felt awkward; he didn't know how to wrap up a speech and sit down again – *well, of course I don't, I'm a fencer, for gods' sakes* – and wasn't sure how to work it out from first principles. So he nodded, again, and turned to the Prefect.

'I think that's all I wanted to say,' he said. 'City Prefect, over to you.'

The Prefect got up, looking slightly startled. 'Thank you,

Colonel Loredan,' he said. 'Well now, it seems that we all have a great deal of work to do, so I suggest we adjourn until this time tomorrow. Gentlemen.' He dipped his head in a shallow nod, and everybody stood up and started chattering at once; the abrupt swell of noise and surge of movement put Loredan in mind of a flock of rooks suddenly put up off a field of wheat stubble. He stayed where he was, hoping he'd be left alone while he tried to make sense of it all.

'My congratulations, Colonel.' It was that damn fool of a Prefect, glowering at him from under his spectacular eyebrows. 'You've contrived to make yourself the most important man in the city.' He paused for effect. 'After myself, of course. I do hope you'll bear that in mind.'

Oh, good, threats. Now I know where I am. 'You want to give this job to someone else, City Prefect,' he said wearily, 'please, be my guest. I'm still trying to figure out where all that stuff came from.'

The Prefect raised an eyebrow. 'I imagine from your time on General Maxen's staff,' he said. 'Where, I assume, you learnt to use your common sense in dealing with matters of administration.'

'Ah.' Loredan couldn't help grinning. 'So that's what we were doing. Odd; all I can remember is a lot of sleeping rough and fighting people. I suppose you're right, though; it *is* just common sense, and recognising the fact that we don't know how to go about this, so we'd better try and work it out before we start. Is that really why I got lumbered with all this?'

The Prefect sat down beside him and leant close to his ear. 'Partly,' he said. 'Mostly, it's politics. I think I've been guilty of sloppy thinking; I assumed you'd have realised. It's quite simple; you used to be a military officer, and now you're nobody. If someone has to be given extraordinary powers to co-ordinate the defence of the city, a political nonentity like yourself is obviously the safest bet.' He smiled unpleasantly. 'No chance of you siding with one faction or the other and setting yourself up as a military dictator. We have to bear these things in mind, you see.

And,' he added graciously, 'you would appear to be reasonably competent. As I said a moment ago, it's mostly just common sense.'

The Prefect wandered away to talk to someone else, probably unaware of the heavy load of savage curses he'd suddenly accumulated. Loredan put him firmly out of mind, and had decided to try sneaking out into the city and maybe even going home for an hour or so when he noticed Alexius beckoning him. With a soft sigh he made his way across the chamber.

'The Prefect's just been explaining why I got the job,' Loredan said. 'Apparently it's because I'm a person of no consequence whatsoever. With men like him in charge, it amazes me that we haven't tried sorting out this business with diplomacy. He'd make a marvellous ambassador.'

'It never ceases to amaze me how clever the fools are in this city,' Alexius replied. 'I've known Bolerun for fifteen years on and off. He'd spent his entire life getting to the stage where he can be an abject failure in the most public manner imaginable.'

Loredan looked puzzled. 'Bolerun?' he asked.

'Meinas Bolerun. The City Prefect.'

'Oh.' Loredan shrugged his shoulders. 'You see? I don't even know what these people are called. In fact, I don't know if he's been Prefect for years and years, or if he only took office last month. I don't suppose most people do, come to that.'

Alexius muffled a yawn with his knuckles. 'If it's any consolation,' he replied, 'by sunset tonight everybody in the city will know who you are.'

'No,' Loredan said bleakly. 'It isn't.'

Feeling slightly dazed, Venart found his way back to the inn (follow your nose till you come to the river, second turning and then immediately left) and asked for a small jug of cider.

There was more to rope, he'd discovered, than meets the eye. Rope, in fact, had turned out to be a subject of such multifarious complexity that a hundred scholars devoting their lives to its study would never obtain more than a faint and misleading shadow of understanding of the great miracle that was rope. Perimadeian rope, at any rate; back home, rope came in thick, medium or thin, hairy or smooth, cheap and nasty or good but expensive, and that was all you needed to know apart from how much of the stuff you wanted. Two whole days touring the ropewalks of the city, however, had opened his eyes, with the result that he knew rather less than he did when he'd started, but was at least properly aware of the scale of his own ignorance.

He also hadn't bought any rope. First thing tomorrow, he promised himself, he would go out and buy some rope. Any rope, so long as it was cheap. After all, if he didn't understand rope, neither did the people he intended to sell it to.

On the other hand, he mused as he put the jug on the fender to mull, thanks to his guided tours he now knew something he hadn't known before, and knowledge is never wasted. Now he knew that there was flax rope, reed rope, rope made from a mixture of flax and reed, rope made from the hair of any number of different animals (except that it wasn't called rope, and what it was called he couldn't now remember), there was silk rope, which was surprisingly cheap, and there was cheap rope, which had turned out to be more expensive than he'd bargained for; above all, there was bulk rope, which was what he wanted to buy and what everybody wanted to sell him. It was only the incidental details, such as price, that were holding up the clinching of the deal.

He poured out half a mug of cider and drank a couple of mouthfuls, relishing the unfamiliar flavour of the nutmeg; a typical city refinement that he liked very much. There was something else, he realised; something he was missing.

Namely, one sister.

He put the mug down and got to his feet, uncertain what to do. His first thought was that something had happened to her; an innocent girl, on her own in a decadent and

sophisticated city. What had he been thinking of, letting her
loose on her own? Even while he was caught up in the first
surge of panic, a rational voice inside him pointed out that
Vetriz wasn't entirely innocent, and it was a matter of cold
fact that Perimadeia was a much safer place to wander
about in, especially at night, than the Island. There was also
the problem of where to start looking, in a place this size.
He sat down again, and had another swig of cider to clear
his mind.

*She was supposed to come straight back here, and that
was four hours ago. By now, she's either dead or shopping.*

Either way, continued the irritatingly rational inner
voice, the chances of finding her by just wandering up and
down are depressingly slim. Far more sensible to sit down,
keep calm and stay put until she finally turns up. Venart had
no answer to that; so he shooed away the mental image of
his sister lying bleeding to death in an alleyway (feebly
calling his name with her dying breath, needless to say) and
finished off the cider, which it would have been wasteful to
leave now that he'd paid for it. It was particularly good cider,
robust without being heady, and he was just about to get
another jug when he heard a loud, musical and familiar
voice coming from the other room. He jumped up, tripped
over a sleeping dog, swore and went through.

There was his sister; and with her another girl, pretty,
vaguely familiar. Relief, good manners in the presence of a
stranger and a small jug of good cider dissipated his
fraternal wrath; he waved and joined them.

'Hello, Ven,' Vetriz said. 'Sorry, I completely lost track of
the time. I've been shopping.'

'I thought as much,' Venart replied casually. 'Er ...'

'This is Athli,' she went on. The pretty girl smiled politely.
'You remember, we met her in that tavern the day we went
to the lawcourts.'

Ah, yes, that was it. The fencer's clerk. 'Hello,' Venart said.
'Nice to see you again.' *Quite decidedly pretty,* Venart said
to himself, while Vetriz explained that they'd bumped into
each other in the stationery market and Athli had been

kind enough to help her with her shopping, so she'd asked her back for something to eat. Venart agreed that that was the least they could do, and made some feeble joke about maintaining the Island's reputation for hospitality. Another part of him was wondering whether it was usual for unmarried girls in this city to go out dining in taverns after dark with chance acquaintances; a futile reflection, he decided, since here one was, doing just that.

It was a good meal, as one would expect from one of the best inns in the city; a dish of roast quails with soft white rolls followed by a fair-sized red mullet with capers and a wine sauce; then the inevitable Perimadeian main course, the 'table' – a round, flat, thin sheet of unleavened bread made exactly the same diameter as the table they sat round, onto which the serving boys ladled dollops of strange and colourful mixtures out of huge steaming cauldrons. Venart and Vetriz eventually managed a third of the thing between them, while their guest effortlessly dealt with the rest. In fact, she finished before they did and was happily recommending the sweet dumplings in cranberry sauce while they were nerving themselves to swallow the little dough shovels still between their fingers. However often I come here, Venart told himself, I'll never get used to the amount they eat; which would make a siege interesting, as well as a once-in-a-lifetime business opportunity.

The first priority was to head Athli off before she could return to the subject of sweet dumplings. Accordingly, Venart launched a pre-emptive strike and asked how things were in the legal profession.

'Oh, about the same as always,' Athli replied. 'Actually, we're not in the law now. What I mean to say is, Loredan's retired and opened a training school, teaching young advocates how to fence, and I'm his clerk.' She frowned. 'Well, that's a bit out of date too. He's working for the Security Council now,' she added, a bit doubtfully. 'You see, we mounted an attack on their camp, where they're building the siege engines. It all went wrong, unfortunately, and a lot of our people were killed. It was mostly thanks to

Loredan that we didn't lose more than we did.'

Vetriz looked up sharply. 'How wonderful,' she said. 'Oh, gods, listen to me, I'm sorry. What I meant was, how wonderful that he should be the hero of the hour and so forth. We'll be able to tell everybody when we get home that ...'

'Please excuse my sister,' Venart interrupted. 'I only bring her on these trips in the hope of starting a war.' He scowled across the table, and went on, 'How serious is the situation, do you think? Everywhere I've been people are talking as if it's the end of the world, but they're acting as if nothing's happened. Except for prices, of course; and even there it's as if the whole thing's just a way of stimulating trade.'

Athli shrugged her shoulders. 'I simply don't know,' she said. 'We've never been in this situation before. It's hard to imagine anybody being able to storm the walls, let alone a bunch of people who are, let's face it, little better than savages. That said, we'd be crazy not to take it seriously.' She turned her head and looked away. 'After all, they did make our expeditionary force look pretty silly. They're saying now that that was because our generals made a complete mess of things and strolled into an ambush, so it can't be taken as proof either way of whether they're capable of giving us a hard time when we're *not* making silly mistakes, if you see what I mean.'

Venart nodded. 'Well,' he said, 'I suppose only time will tell. Do you know very much about these plainspeople? I assume you must do, if you've had trouble with them before.'

'Not a great deal, no,' Athli admitted. 'The truth is, we aren't ever anything more than mildly curious about anyone except ourselves. Up till recently, we'd never have dreamed anything like this could happen. We were quite friendly with them, in fact. There were some of them living and working here – after all, people from all over the world come here, and we don't think anything of it.'

Venart nodded. 'The legendary Perimadeian tolerance,' he said sententiously. 'Looks like it hasn't done you any favours in this instance. After all, if they're basically savages and now they're building siege engines, it must have been someone from here who taught them how to do it.'

He got a cold look in return for that. 'What are we supposed to do?' she retorted. 'Keep all our knowledge and skills deadly secret in case they get used against us? We're a nation of traders and manufacturers; if we did that we'd starve. The same goes for if we took against foreigners. You, of all people, should appreciate that.'

Fair point, Venart admitted to himself; at least she'd had the good manners not to point out that the Islanders were at best the third-generation descendants of pirates who'd several times tried to attack the city. He decided to change the subject.

'Talking of trade,' he said, 'you wouldn't happen to know anything about rope?'

Athli looked at him and giggled. 'Oddly enough, I do,' she replied. 'We had a regular client in the rope business. What do you want to know?'

Vetriz had felt her attention wavering while the conversation had been about politics; as soon as they started talking about rope (horsehair for elasticity; pure flax is cheaper and almost as good, but don't let them fob you off with anything made from what they call sailmaker's twine, it isn't really pure flax) she let her mind wander. Fairly soon, what with the warmth of the room and the comfortable weight of the food, she was starting to doze...

And was suddenly somewhere else – rather disconcerting, until she subconsciously registered that it was a dream. The confusing part of it was that she was also still in the dining room of the inn, sitting at a table covered in crumbs and little morsels of escaped food; and there were Ven and her new friend Athli, still busily chatting about rope and oblivious to anything else. But there were other people sitting round the table as well, and she recognised them easily, as if they were people she knew well. The tall, worried-looking man was Bardas Loredan; well, she did know him, and also, regrettably, his brother Gorgas. Now that she could see them both together the family resemblance was obvious; she hadn't seen it in Gorgas before, but they both had the same nose and the same heavy muscle in the jaw, and, most noticeable of all, the same alert, observant eyes. Nothing romantic or even particularly attractive about the Loredan eyes. They were hard but not cold, a rather dark brown (Athli had green eyes, curse her; some girls have all the luck) and neither of the two brothers seemed to blink as often as most people did. Another curious thing: Gorgas had told her he wasn't on speaking terms with his younger brother, and yet here they were talking quite easily, just the way you'd expect two brothers to talk to each other. It was a pity that she couldn't make out what they were saying. Whatever it was, it was bound to be more interesting than rope.

And there was a woman sitting on Gorgas' left, between him and Ven; she was a Loredan too, the same nose and jaw (it doesn't suit her) and unmistakably the same eyes. She was older than both of them but too young to be their mother, so Vetriz deduced she was either an older sister or a youngish aunt. Probably a sister; the resemblance was too marked for it to be anything but a direct blood line. She wasn't saying anything, and when Vetriz decided to talk to her, she suddenly wasn't there any more. Instead she saw a young man she didn't recognize at all. He was no more than eighteen, shorter, fairer and slighter than the rest of them, and his features were small and a little pudgy, making him look younger still. For some reason she knew he was one of the plainspeople, and she decided he was here in the dream because they'd been talking about them and she'd fallen asleep after a heavy meal.

She studied him with interest, never having come across a genuine barbarian before. He wasn't much to look at, certainly not very barbarous; his hair was a little greasy but neatly combed – maybe the grease was some kind of dressing; not being able to smell anything in this dream she couldn't tell if it was some variety of scented oil or pomade – and he was wearing a rather plain-looking shirt with full

sleeves, which closer inspection revealed to be made of very
fine buckskin. She couldn't see what he was wearing on his
legs because the table was in the way. At any rate, his
manners seemed acceptable enough; he was sitting quite
still, hadn't even got his elbows on the table, and appeared
to be listening to the great rope debate with every sign of
polite interest. He looks like somebody's apprentice, Vetriz
decided, who's been allowed to come to dinner as a special
treat.

Since she had nobody else to talk to, she decided to strike
up a conversation with the young barbarian. She smiled
and caught his eye. He smiled back, rather pleasantly.

'Don't say you're a rope fancier too,' she heard herself
saying.

'Most of it's going over my head,' he admitted. 'But it's
always worth listening when people are discussing
something they know about. You can learn things that way,
and knowledge is never wasted.'

Vetriz grinned. 'You sound just like my brother,' she said.
'That's a favourite saying of his. In fact, that's probably why
I just dreamed you saying it.'

'You may well be right,' the barbarian replied. 'As it
happens, rope's something I need to learn about. You see,
we're building a whole lot of torsion engines – catapults,
that sort of thing – and it's the rope that powers the arm and
makes them go. None of us have the faintest idea what sort
of rope's best for the purpose. I imagine we want something
tough and springy.'

'Ah.' Vetriz nodded. 'I might be able to help you there,
because just before I lost interest in what they were saying,
that girl there told my brother that horsehair's best for
elasticity – does that make any sense to you?'

'Very much so.'

'Oh, good, because it's wasted on me. Anyway, horsehair's
the stuff, and if you can't get that, pure flax is meant to be
almost as good, though apparently you should avoid
sailmaker's twine like the plague.'

'Oh.' The barbarian's brow creased a little. 'That's odd,

because a man I talked to at the arsenal said sailmaker's twine was what he used himself. That didn't mean an awful lot to me, because I wouldn't recognise sailmaker's twine if you wove it into a noose and strung me up with it.'

Vetriz giggled. 'Perish the thought,' she said. 'And now, if you don't mind, let's put the subject of rope firmly on one side and talk about something else, shall we? In fact, I'd like to ask you a question, if it won't offend you.'

The barbarian shrugged. 'Be my guest,' he said.

'All right. I was just wondering: what is it about this city that you don't like? I mean, you must hate it an awful lot if you're going to all this trouble to destroy it. Or is that what you people do, sort of a fundamental part of your cultural identity?'

'Not really,' the barbarian replied. 'I mean, we do fight among ourselves sometimes, but on the whole we're quite peaceful. Certainly we aren't ones for plunder and loot, like your ancestors were; all that gold and silver and furniture and stuff'd be just so much dead weight to lug around with us. No, the thing with the city's personal. It's something that's got to be done, that's all.'

'Really?' Vetriz raised an eyebrow. 'And why's that?'

The barbarian pulled a face. 'I'd rather not say,' he replied. 'If you really must know, why don't you ask those two?'

And before Vetriz could ask him which two he meant, he wasn't there either, and Venart was prodding her shoulder with his forefinger (exactly the way he did when they were children, and she'd hated it then) and telling her to wake up because it was late.

'Don't want to wake up,' she mumbled sleepily, aware that the Loredan brothers had gone too. 'Sleep when it's late. Wake up when it's early.'

Venart sighed. 'Like I said before,' he said to Athli, who was grinning, 'you really must excuse my sister. I can't take her anywhere.'

Temrai, who'd been dozing by the fire, suddenly woke up. 'Horsehair,' he said.

Uncle Anakai looked at him over his cup. 'What did you just say?' he asked.

'For the catapults,' Temrai explained. He shook his head, felt dizzy; too much to drink, he decided. 'I've just remembered, I think. Anyway, that's what we should be using.'

Anakai shrugged his shoulders. 'You're the boss,' he replied. 'And it's something we've got plenty of, though people are going to take some persuading before they'll let you take a pair of shears to their prize bloodstock.' He rubbed his chin. 'We'll have to start a fashion for bobbed manes and tails. They'll agree to anything if it's fashionable.'

'Good idea,' Temrai said. He was dimly aware that he'd been dreaming; but he never remembered his dreams for more than a split second after he'd woken up. 'We'll get onto it first thing in the morning,' he yawned. 'Right now, I think I'll go to bed. I seem to have woken up with something of a headache.'

Uncle Anakai smiled. 'You sleep it off, then,' he replied. 'You've earned a good night's rest. Oh, by the way, who's Loriden?'

'I don't know,' Temrai replied with a frown. 'Should I?'

'You kept muttering the name while you were asleep. Some girl, obviously,' Uncle Anakai added with a grin. 'It's a girl's name, after all.'

Temrai thought for a moment, then shook his head.

'Never heard of her,' he said.

CHAPTER THIRTEEN

Next morning, his head buzzing and his belt heavy with money, Venart set off for the ropewalks.

It was one of the sights of Perimadeia; a spacious district with wide streets, one of the few places in the city where you could see the buildings without an endless procession of carts and wagons getting in the way. Because there was so little traffic, it had a peaceful, almost park-like atmosphere, spoilt only by the disgusting smell of tar. Although the streets were broad you couldn't walk down the middle; you had to creep along the sides, trying not to get in the way of the ropemakers as they twisted their skeins of cord, stretched on short wooden pillars from one side of the street to the other, winding ten, twelve, often as many as thirty strands of fine line together to make one strong, pliable rope. At first sight it looked like the web of a huge and slovenly spider.

In the light of his new-found expertise, Venart had decided to place his order with one Vital Ortenan, who he remembered as having boasted of his skill in making long rope from horsehair. He found Ortenan sitting outside his shop, his feet up on one of the wooden pillars and a mug of cider in his hand.

'Good morning,' Venart said briskly. 'I expect you remember me. I'd like to buy some rope.'

Ortenan looked at him. 'You'll be lucky,' he said.

'Excuse me?'

'I said, you'll be lucky,' Ortenan repeated, scratching his ear. 'No rope today, sorry.'

Venart frowned. He knew most of the standard bargaining gambits, but this one was new to him. 'How do you mean, no rope?' he asked. 'You had tons of the stuff in there yesterday.'

'I did,' Ortenan said. 'Yesterday. Then, round about an hour before closing up, a bunch of government men came by and took the lot. Every last bloody inch.' He scowled at the thought. 'Gave me a bit of paper saying I'd be paid according to the official tariff in due course. In other words, I've been requisitioned. Marvellous, isn't it?'

'But ...' Venart let his hands fall to his sides. 'What about everybody else?' he said. 'Surely there must be some-body...'

Ortenan shook his head. 'Went through this district like a cloud of locusts,' he said darkly. 'Cleaned the lot of us out. Said it was for catapult ropes,' he added, as if that was the most idiotic notion he'd ever heard. 'So I'm afraid you're out of luck, mate. Should've done a deal yesterday, like I told you. Then you'd have your rope and I'd have my money.'

Venart thought for a moment. 'All right,' he said. 'Why don't you make some more rope, instead of just sitting there? Did they take all the raw materials as well?'

'No,' Ortenan replied. 'But why the hell should I bother? Anything I make's got to be sold to the government, otherwise they'll sling me in the coop and fine me to buggery, because of this so-called state of emergency.' He curled his lips and spat. 'Well, they know what they can do. When I see some money – real money, not this paper stuff – *then* I might just consider making some more stock. Till then, they can go play with themselves. My materials won't go off for sitting in the bins for a week.'

A brief tour of the district confirmed what Ortenan had said. There was nothing to be had, except a few hundred yards of soggy and mildewed mess which the government buyers had rejected, and Venart decided he didn't really want that. Dejected, he went back to the inn.

'That's a nuisance,' Vetriz said when he told her. 'And after you spent all that time and energy researching the subject. Whereas if you'd just blundered into it and bought the first stuff that came your way, you'd now have the next best thing to a world monopoly of the rope trade and be able to name your own price.'

Venart scowled at her, which made her giggle. 'I'm glad you think it's so amusing,' he snapped. 'I hope you'll still be laughing your silly head off when we sail home with an empty hold.'

'But we won't do that, will we?' Vetriz replied. 'Because all we've got to do is buy something else. Or hadn't that occurred to you?'

Venart sat down and took off his left boot; he'd got something sharp in it on the way back from the ropewalks. 'Oh, yes, and what exactly did you have in mind? Or have you been secretly studying the markets while I've been out frivolously working my fingers to the bone to keep you in—'

'There's plenty of things we can buy,' Vetriz said, with a truly aggravating air of patience. 'So long as we get the right price.'

'Right, then. Suggest something.'

Vetriz nodded. 'Carpet,' she said promptly.

'Carpet?'

'Carpet.' She studied her fingernails for a moment, then continued, 'Where does all the carpet on the Island come from?'

Venart thought about it. 'Blemmyra,' he said. 'Direct,' he added.

'Very good. But what you haven't noticed, because you've been too busy mugging up on twelve-ply pure flax this-that-and-the-other is that the Blemmyra carpet they're selling here is better than the stuff we get at home and about a third of the price.'

'Oh.' Venart scratched his head. 'You sure?' he added.

'Sure I'm sure. I was looking for some yesterday to replace that mouldy bit of rag I've got on the wall of my bedroom. I happened to notice the price and mentioned it to Athli and she explained it to me. You see, the Blemmyrans buy all their wine in the Mesoge, but they ship it in their own barrels to save money, and barrel staves are so much cheaper than at home because the Hesichians bring them in as ballast on their big bulk freighters. So the barrel staves cost the Perimadeians next to nothing, which means they can sell the carpets they get in exchange from the Blemmyrans much cheaper than we can; *and* they're much more fussy than we are, so they insist on the good stuff, and we get all the carpet the Perimadeians don't want.' She yawned. 'It's called international commerce,' she added insufferably. 'You should find out about it when you've finished studying rope.'

'Carpet,' Venart said. 'Fine. And have you thought about how much carpet we can actually get rid of in our quaint little backwater home? It's not exactly a high-volume seller, is it?'

'It could be,' Vetriz replied, 'if it was nice stuff and the price was right. I don't blame us for not wanting to be robbed blind for second-rate rubbish. Proper carpet, on the other hand—'

Venart shook his head. 'I'm not gambling our working capital on some theory you and your new chum cooked up while you were out shopping,' he growled. 'What I *am* going to do is go and see this man Loredan, if I can.'

'Loredan?' Vetriz looked up sharply. 'Why?'

'He's the only person we know in the government,' he replied. 'Think about it, will you? They're buying up all the rope in the city; but a lot of that rope's no good for catapults, so presumably they'll sell off the stuff they can't use on the surplus market. Unless,' he went on with a smug grin, 'someone makes them an offer for it first. Cheap government surplus rope, best quality, one careful owner? The secret of international commerce is being able to see the opportunity that lurks inside every disaster. Plus,' he added, 'knowing something about the commodities you deal in. In my case, rope. See you later, don't wander off.'

It had seemed a conclusive argument when he'd been explaining it to Vetriz. It was still a good argument by the time he reached the council buildings. After he'd spent an hour waiting outside a clerk's office only to be given a chit that would allow him to see another clerk at the opposite end of the building, it was nothing more than a hare-brained scheme, and he'd reached the point where he would gladly have traded all his notional future earnings from the rope business in exchange for a floor plan of the building with the exits clearly marked when he nearly walked into someone he thought he recognised.

'Sorry,' the man said. 'Wasn't looking where I was going.'

'You're Bardas Loredan,' Venart replied. 'I was just coming to see you.'

'Well, here I am,' Loredan replied. 'I think I know you from somewhere, but I can't say exactly—'

'We met in a tavern,' Venart said. 'I was with my sister. You'd just fought a case against a man called Alvise.'

Loredan smiled. 'That's it,' he said. 'I had an idea it was something to do with a tavern, but most people I meet in taverns I deliberately try and forget. What can I do for you?'

Suddenly, Venart's tigerish trading urge wilted. What he was going to suggest was probably illegal; certainly bad form and morally repugnant. Terribly short-sighted, too; here he had a contact at the highest level of the city government, and he was proposing to alienate him on the offchance of making a quick quarter on a load of rope. It was too late to back out now, however. He took a deep breath and started into his sales pitch, doing his best to lard it solid with *if you think it'd be all right*s and *so long as it'd be in order*s. Eventually he ground to a halt and stood nervously on one leg, waiting for Loredan to summon the guard.

'Well,' Loredan said after a moment, 'it'd certainly help me out of an awkward position. The clowns in the Quartermaster's Office were only supposed to take an inventory, not bring the stuff back with them by the cartload; so we were facing the prospect of either giving back the stuff we can't use, which wouldn't be easy since they didn't bother to mark on the barrels where each lot came from, or else pay up on the assignats when the ropemakers present them for payment. Either way it's a bit of a shambles, so selling the stuff on seems a fairly good idea.' He paused. 'Did you say you wanted the lot or only part of it? To be frank with you, I'd be rather more inclined to agree if I could get rid of all the unwanted stuff in one go.'

Venart licked his lips, which had become rather dry. 'Certainly I'd be interested in taking the lot,' he said, ignoring the frantic protests from the back of his mind. 'It would of course depend on the, er, price.'

Loredan nodded. 'That'd have to be strictly by valuation,' he said. 'Quartermaster's valuer puts a price on what we're going to have to pay. You give us that and we can balance our books and forget it ever happened. I understand that standard practice for government purchasing is to split the difference between cost price and what the seller would have got for the stuff selling to the trade. I hope that's all right, because I daren't go any lower.'

All the medium- and coarse-grade rope in Perimadeia, at less than trade… 'That's fine,' Venart muttered. 'Yes, I'd be quite happy with that.'

Loredan actually looked relieved. 'That's one less thing for me to worry about then,' he said, rubbing his temples as if he had a headache. 'Good thing I happened to bump into you. Oh, one other point. If you could let us have a quarter, say, up front and the balance in a month's time, that'd help things along a bit. You know, I'm starting to get the enemy and the auditors muddled up in my mind. I'm terrified of both of them, but the auditors know where I live.'

Venart, who had been wondering how quickly he could raise a hundred per cent mortgage on his ship, swallowed hard and said, 'That's no problem at all.'

'You're sure?'

'I can probably give you a quarter now, if it's any help. Subject to valuation,' he added quickly.

'Splendid,' Loredan said. He closed his eyes and opened them again, as if the light was bothering him. 'Bit of a morning head,' he explained. 'Look, if you can spare the time we can go over to the Quartermaster's Office right now and get the paperwork drawn up. Is that all right, or are you in a hurry to get somewhere?'

Gods bless the government service, Venart said to himself as he followed Loredan through the rat's nest of corridors and cloisters. *The inefficient, bungling, inexhaustibly rich government service. I can have the whole lot sold before I need to pay the balance. I wonder if there's anything else they've got too much of?*

'They'll do the valuation today,' he told Vetriz, when he got back to the inn, 'and release the stuff to us tomorrow. They're even going to cart it down to the docks and load it for us, would you believe? And they accepted the cash I had with me as the quarter up front, so as soon as the stuff's on board, we can get home and start selling. It's unreal,' he added. 'The way it's worked out, it's enough to make you believe in miracles.'

'Oh, good,' Vetriz replied. 'So you've spent all the money, then?'

'Of course I've spent all the money. D'you think I was going to let an opportunity like this slip through my hands for the sake of trying to shave a bit off the deposit?'

Vetriz nodded. 'I see,' she said. 'What it comes down to is, you've agreed to buy all the rope in the city, except for all the good-quality stuff they're keeping for the catapults, and you don't even know yet what the price is going to be. And now there's nothing left in the box to try out my idea about the carpets. Fine. You're the businessman.'

For the sake of a quiet life Venart decided he hadn't heard that. 'And if this works,' he went on, 'who knows, we might be able to do it again with something else. Apparently the Quartermaster's Office is virtually out of control; they're grabbing stuff right, left and centre and handing out paper to all the merchants. Just think of what they might buy up next; timber, nails, pig-iron—'

'Did you say Loredan had a headache?' Vetriz interrupted.

'What? Oh, yes, I think he did. Probably explains why he wanted to get it all over and done with quickly, so he could go and lie down. What the devil's that got to do with anything?'

Vetriz shrugged. 'Just interested, that's all. I seem to remember I had a bad head the day we went and saw the Patriarch.'

'Huh? Well, hard luck, I'm so sorry. It's probably something to do with the weather; thunderstorm on its way, something like that. Damn it, Vetriz, I thought you'd be *pleased* about this deal.'

'Oh, I am, really', she replied absently. 'Jolly well done, and let's hope it doesn't go wrong, with all our money at stake. It's funny, you mentioning miracles. We do seem to be having something of a run of luck.' She grinned. 'Maybe that nice Patriarch put a spell on us. Wouldn't that be fun?'

From the top of the slope overlooking the new camp, Temrai could see the city. In a strange way it was like coming home.

In his hand he jingled a couple of reckoning counters; loot from a caravan of merchants who'd made the mistake of assuming the rumours of the clan's advance were the usual irresponsible scaremongering. It had been a stroke of luck; a set of counters and a counting board were likely to prove as useful as five hundred archers once the job began. He'd learnt simple accounting while he was in the city; the wages clerk in the arsenal had been only too happy to show off his skills to someone prepared to take an interest. An endearing and very helpful Perimadeian characteristic, this urge to disseminate useful knowledge.

Pretty things they were, too. On one side, the city arms; on the other, more or less exactly the view he was looking at now, the city in all its picturesque strength, smug as a landlord behind its guaranteed-secure walls, with the sea behind and the river as a moat keeping the unruly elements from the interior at a respectful distance. Well, he said to himself, I'll keep these safe, just in case someone in years to come wants to know what the city looked like, before Temrai pulled it down.

Temrai; Temrai the what? Temrai the Great, Temrai the Magnificent, Temrai the Terrible, Temrai the Cruel – he'd be happy to settle for Temrai the First, or just plain Temrai. But just-plains don't destroy the greatest city in the world.

Assuming it turned out to be possible, of course. No guarantee of that; the thought that he might fail was almost reassuring, because if he failed he wouldn't have to be Temrai-Sacker-Of-Cities, Temrai the Butcher.

How about Temrai the Engineer? He could fancy the sound of that, rather more than Temrai the Great, certainly more than Temrai the Slaughterer. As for Temrai-Who-Bit-Off-More-Than-He-Could-Chew, that wasn't the kind of immortality he was keen on.

Below him, in front of his tent, a group of children were weaving carpet (carpets, soaked in water and slung over the frames of the siege towers, were going to counteract the enemy's attempt to set them alight with fire-arrows, or, at least, that was the plan). They were working on a large vertical loom, squatting on a plank that rested on the rungs of two ladders, so that it could be raised as the work progressed. The children passed the weft thread between the rows of knots, their small hands moving quickly and neatly where a grown-up's couldn't go. At the front the old woman in charge of the job sang out the stitches, and the children repeated them after her as if learning a lesson. Even though it was a purely military artefact, designed to be shot through and scorched, the old woman couldn't help laying a pattern into it; probably she knew no other way of doing the job – it'd take longer to work out how to make it plain than it did to make the pattern. A strange situation, Temrai couldn't help feeling, when even old women, children and soft furnishings go to war.

Temrai the Carpet-Weaver… He turned back and gazed at the city, as if he could melt those walls with his fiery glance. Maybe one day they'd say that's exactly what he did. Quite; and if wishes were siege engines, he'd be a great big

log. That was enough daydreaming for one morning; work
to be done.

*Tell us again, Grandmama; tell us how, when you were a
little girl, you helped weave the carpets so Temrai could sack
the city...*

On the river side of the camp, there was something he
felt he could really be proud of; a row of trebuchets, still
glistening with the pitch that would keep the wet out and
stop the joints from springing. They stood like a herd of
thoroughbreds in a pen, waiting to be broken in, the
pitching arms standing high in the air with the sling that
held the stone furled round like a banner at rest before the
charge is signalled. Each of them could hurl two and a half
hundredweight the best part of two hundred and fifty yards,
although the rate of fire was slow compared with a torsion
engine, and it took an awful lot of men pulling on ropes to
haul up the two-hundred-hundredweight of rock that
formed the counterweight. The torsion engines would be
ready soon (just as soon as we can make the ropes; oh, hell,
how are we going to make the damned ropes? So much
horsehair, so little time) and the component parts of the
rams and towers were stacked neatly, ready for assembly.
The rest of the gear, the things the enemy mustn't see until
later, was on its way down the river, trussed up in bundles
to disguise the shape. Pretty soon, they'd have almost
enough arrows (green wood and fletched with duck; we'll be
a laughing stock), enough bows, enough armour, enough
horses, enough food, shirts, boots, belts, helmets, swords,
crockery, helmet-liner laces, enough of every damn thing
that went to make up a war. Now he even had something to
count them all with; there would be a full census of the clan,
for the first time ever. Soon, this great engine he'd built and
wound up would slip its catch and go off, and nothing would
ever be the same again.

It could be worse, he reflected soberly. I could still be
living in the city when it got attacked.

Someone coughed politely behind him; it was the young
lad, can't remember his name, who was drawing maps. He

seemed very proud of his handiwork, as well he might - neat, clear, accurate information carefully set out on parchment, everything you need to know about the lie of the land at a glance. He smiled encouragingly; the boy thanked him and carried the maps down the hill to the command tent, where the council of war was waiting. Time he was joining them himself; yet another meeting, the third today...

Boy? Lad? Gods above, that kid is older than I am; and yet he was so deferential, so full of respect. Exactly what am I turning into, in all this historic activity?

Uncle Anakai stood up when Temrai pushed through the tent flap. That seemed *very* strange and not quite right, but Uncle An had done it instinctively. *Maybe he knows something I don't,* Temrai reflected, and made up his mind not to let it worry him. He sat down on the floor, yawned and asked if there was anything to eat.

'Anything except salt duck,' he added, as Mivren leant forward to unfasten the lid of her basket. 'Too much of a good thing's bad enough; too much salt duck is ... Come on, there must be some cheese or something.'

Someone handed him a wedge of cheese and an apple. He attacked them while the heads of department reported progress. By and large, the news was good; problems that had seemed insurmountable yesterday were looking rather more manageable today, the various work parties were managing to co-operate and nobody had yet asked, *Why are we doing this?* The fletchers had somehow managed to turn the green wood into arrows that flew straight. Just when it looked like they were about to run out of hides for roofing over the battering rams and the siege towers, a hunting party everybody had forgotten about weeks ago had suddenly turned up at the downriver camp with forty mules laden with raw buckskins - by pure chance they'd happened upon a herd of some kind of large deer that only showed up on this side of the badlands once every forty years or so; the deer were completely unused to humans and stood still to be shot, gazing with blank incomprehension as their fellows dropped all around them.

Another party had found a substantial bed of osiers in a small combe that the clan had been passing for years without ever realising it was there; the perfect raw material for weaving shields and baskets, more than they could possibly use in a generation. A flash flood some way upstream had led to a blockage in the river; where the dry bed had been exposed for the first time ever, a scouting party had stumbled across a seam of best-quality clay, just right for making the close-grained, thin-walled jars Temrai had been demanding for this secret weapon of his that nobody was allowed to know about yet. Just when they'd been on the point of giving up on their search for a source of bulk naphtha, a raiding party had ambushed a merchant caravan carrying ten cartloads of the stuff. When the merchants realised that not only were they not going to be horribly killed, they were being asked to name their own price for a reliable supply, they'd been delighted to co-operate; the result was a thoroughly satisfactory deal, unpolished amber for naphtha, and the merchants had made the first delivery at the lower depot the day before yesterday. It was enough, someone remarked, to make you believe in miracles.

Temrai listened to all this good news, thought about it for a while, and then announced that at this rate, they'd be ready to move on to the assault camp in a week or two. Someone else said two weeks was pushing it, could he make it twenty days? Someone else said they ought to be able to meet the two-week deadline if everybody really knuckled down. There was a brief discussion; compromise, sixteen days from today, which would also be the full moon, ideal for the night march they were going to have to make if they wanted that extra advantage of surprise. At the full moon, then; agreed? Agreed. And that was that; Temrai the Great had spoken.

And that, Temrai told himself as the meeting broke up, *is how things happen. Odd; I suppose I made the decision, though as I recall I was sitting with a mouth full of cheese at*

the time, when someone else said, 'At the full moon, then.'
And now it's decided, and one way or another, what's going
to happen will happen. And it'll still all be my doing. Or fault.
Whichever.

He pushed through the tent flap and blinked in the bright
daylight; and a moment or so later a man came running up
to tell him he was needed urgently to sort out a technical
problem with the mangonel winding ratchets. *Ah. More*
tinkering. That's more like it. He nodded, threw away his
apple core and asked the messenger to lead the way.

'And what's that supposed to be?' Loredan asked.

The engineer gave him a wounded look. 'It's the derrick
for the drawbridge windlass,' he replied. 'It's in perfect
working order. I checked it myself only the other day.'

'I see,' Loredan replied, and gave it a gentle kick. The
wooden frame shuddered and a bit fell off. 'Get it fixed,' he
said wearily. 'Properly, this time. And don't explain why
that'll be difficult, because I don't want to know.'

From up here, on the top of the western-side gatetower,
he could see a flash of light from the high ground five miles
or so away downriver; a spearhead or a helmet, or maybe
just a brightly scoured cooking pot, happening to catch the
sun at a moment he happened to be looking in that
direction. His mouth twitched, and he mimed raising a hat
in polite salutation.

Aside from odds and ends, like the heap of junk he'd just
noticed and a few other bits and pieces, they were as ready
as they'd ever be. From where he stood, he could see the
masons dismantling their scaffolding around the new
bastions, daringly sunk into the hard rock of that part of the
river bed; it had been a bold, confident design, and it seemed
to have worked (at least, it hadn't fallen down yet). Two
engines on each side of those clean, new wedges of stone
could command a much broader field of fire, taking care of
two notorious blind spots and effectively pushing the safety
zone back by another fifty yards. That meant that anything
within three hundred yards of the wall was within range;

and not many bowmen could shoot over two hundred and fifty yards in a tournament, let alone in the middle of a battle, with half-hundredweight engine shot falling all around them.

He allowed himself a moment to admire the new masonry; unweathered, all the edges still sharp and uneroded, the mortar between the stones still slightly dark where it hadn't quite dried out. His bastions were the first major addition to the walls in – what, a hundred years, a hundred and fifty? It'd be nice to think that in another hundred years' time, they'd point them out as Loredan's defences, maybe tell the awed and fascinated visitors a bit about Loredan's war and how the enemy hadn't stood a chance from the very beginning—

Listen to yourself, will you? You're even starting to think like them. He knelt down and gripped the wooden batten that was part of the mounting for a new engine, to be installed this afternoon. He couldn't shift it; it'd do. He stood up again, looked out, visualised the arc of fire from this point, tried to imagine what it'd be like on the wall when the engine and the hoist for lifting up ammunition were in place, whether there'd be enough room to pass comfortably on the rampart walkway; traffic jams on the wall in the middle of an assault were a complication he didn't want to have to face later. As Maxen used to say, *the worst thing a general can ever say is, I didn't anticipate that.*

And then he remembered Maxen; so clearly that he could almost see him, as if he was standing there on the wall beside him. He remembered his broad, somewhat round face and his beard that never grew more than three-quarters of an inch, with an almost bald patch in the middle of his chin where it scarcely grew at all. He remembered his way of staying silent for a second or a second and a half after he'd been told something; then the invariable slight nod of the head, down and a bit to the side, always the same whether you'd just told him the camp was being overrun or the soup was ready. He wondered what Maxen would be doing now if he were commanding these walls, and hoped it would be pretty much the same as he'd done himself, though he doubted that.

And then he thought, all this is Maxen's fault, when you come right down to it. Maxen's fault, for doing his job, doing it as well as it could be done and with the resources available to him, doing it *heroically* well; but suppose that job didn't need doing, shouldn't have been done at all? If it's safe to hide behind the walls now, it'd have been safe then, there was no need to take the war out onto the plains, there was no need to do what we did. And once we'd stopped doing it, nothing suddenly got worse; we weren't suddenly up to our knees in shrieking savages, bashing down the gates to get at our wives and our table linen.

But Maxen did his job, never suggested to anybody that his job might not need doing; because that's what Maxen was, the city's one and only general. Did he stay out there in the plains, pouring away his life and the lives of others, simply because there wasn't anything else he could do? Because he couldn't face having to quit the army in his mid-fifties and try and find a proper job? What kind of man does a thing like that, entrench himself in the business of ending lives just because it's the only way he knows of making a living?

Loredan considered the implications of that. *Yes, but I retired. Or I tried to. I made an effort to get out of that line of business, and here I am with the lives of all the city and all the clans in the palm of my hand. Gods, if I still had a sense of humour I'd find that amusing.*

He heard someone behind him; big, clumping boots. He recognised the sound.

'Nearly done,' said the engineer, Garantzes, puffing from the climb up the stairs from ground level. Too much cider and sitting at a drawing board. Loredan reflected smugly that he'd run up the steps two at a time and not even broken into a sweat.

'Good,' he replied. 'I don't think it's a moment too soon, either.' He pointed to the horizon, where a light was flashing. 'How long before all the new engines are in place?'

Garantzes shrugged. 'The day after tomorrow, at the latest. They're all put together and ready to go – we're turning them out at a rate of two a day in the arsenal; the big problem's going to be finding enough wall to fit them all onto. The other problem is that we've only got two cranes big enough to lift them into position.' He grinned sheepishly. 'Forgot about that, in all the excitement. We're building another two cranes, they'll be ready tomorrow, with any luck.'

Loredan nodded. 'The day after tomorrow will do fine,' he replied. 'The same goes for the fences.'

The fences had been his idea; or, rather, something he'd read about in a book, many years ago. According to the book, just before a sea battle a century and a half ago, the pirates of the Island had prevented the Perimadeian marines from boarding their ships by rigging up an arrangement of posts, projecting some way from the sides of each vessel, along which heavy-duty cables were strung like the bars of a post-and-rail fence. The result was that the marines' boarding ladders had come to rest on the cables, not the sides of the ships, and all attempts at boarding had failed. Loredan figured the same technique might serve to protect the walls against scaling ladders. There was now a line of six-inch-diameter posts, each post seven feet long, projecting out of the wall all along the vulnerable zone where ladders might be set up. Over the next few days an iron chain would be strung along the line, and the workmen from the Office of Works were arguing fiercely among themselves as to who should, and shouldn't, have the dubious privilege of shinning along a seven-foot pole like a monkey to hang upside down over a sheer drop into the river to attach the chain to the staples.

'We'll do our best,' Garantzes sighed. 'Oh, and while I think of it, I've got a message for you from Filepas Nilot, from the Quartermaster's Office.' He frowned. 'I don't know if I've got this right, but what I think he said was, he's managed to get hold of the two million bees you wanted and he's seeing the joiners about making the chutes tomorrow.'

Loredan smiled. 'Splendid,' he said. 'Well, then, I think we're more or less there. Now all we need is an enemy.' He turned back towards the point where the light had been. 'And I might just know where I can lay my hands on one of those.'

After the Chief Engineer had gone away, Loredan made a circuit of the top of the tower, trying one more time to see the city as his enemy would see it. It was an exercise he'd put himself through every day since this wretched business had begun; a productive one, but he still couldn't help feeling he must have missed something. As far as he could see, there wasn't a weak spot; all he'd done was strengthen the existing strengths. And yet there must be something he'd missed but the other man hadn't, or else why was the other man coming at him with such exuberant confidence? Deep down he wanted the attack to begin, to have the enemy under his eye (because the enemy you can see is the least of your problems); but until that happened he knew he had to keep nagging away, searching and speculating until he saw that one missing factor that would make him curse himself and say, *Of course! How could I have been so stupid!* He wanted so much to say that before the enemy were under his walls ...

But he couldn't see it. What he could see, from the highest point of the defences, was the sweep of the land walls, forming the two arms of a V whose point was the gatehouse tower he was standing on, and which faced the mouth of the river, the point at which it forked to flow round the island on which the city stood. Directly below the tower was the drawbridge of the Drovers' Bridge, which spanned the eastern branch of the river a hundred yards or so from the point of divergence, where the river was narrowest and deepest. The causeway on the other side extended into the water to within fifteen yards of the tower (the length of the drawbridge itself), but long before the enemy were in position that causeway would be a tangle of broken planks; the big trebuchet whose frame he was leaning on was sighted in on it, and it was reckoned to be the most accurate engine on the wall. Given the strength of the gatehouse tower and the depth of the river at that point, he could rule that out as a likely pressure point.

On either side of the river-fork, the river gradually widened; a hundred yards at the fork, a hundred and thirty at the apexes of the two bastions, over two hundred where the two branches met the sea. The bastions were so placed that their three-hundred-yard arc of fire covered the whole of the area where the river was less than a hundred and seventy yards wide, and before any attack began he planned to cram as many engines as he could, long-range trebuchets if he could get them, onto the bastion ramparts. Thanks to his one major innovation, the secret that he hadn't shared with the council or even most of the engineers (and the engineers were people he *trusted*), he felt he had control of that three-hundred-yard semicircle on either side, and that was the only logical place from which to launch an attack. As for the rest of the wall, he had towers every hundred and fifty yards, each one soon to have two torsion engines and a trebuchet backed by a fifty-man garrison plus engineers; and below the towers, a minor engine every twenty-five yards, on a tilting carriage that would enable it to throw its stone as much as two hundred yards or as little as fifty. He could see no weak point along the whole length of the land wall; either the river was too wide, or else he could lay down a barrage for at least fifty yards inland that nothing could survive.

He'd even considered the ludicrous options. Suppose the enemy were capable of digging a tunnel right under the bed of the river, to come up beneath a tower and undermine the wall; it was impossible, but he'd provided for it nonetheless. Suppose they could bring enough long-range firepower to bear on the walls that they knocked out all his engines in one sector; with the arsenal turning out engines at the rate of two a day and long cranes almost as fast, he could replace a smashed engine within the hour, just about giving the engineers time to shore up the wall using the convenient stockpiles of materials assembled at the foot of each tower.

If they managed to lob in fireballs, he'd have his firefighters standing by. He'd even entertained the notion of enemy soldiers catapulted alive out of trebuchets and floating down into the city with artificial wings strapped to their arms, and made plans accordingly. Now that *would* be a sight to see...

Or suppose they simply intended to wear him down; massed engines battering the walls day and night, until there was no firm place left to shore onto, nothing left to shore with; well, they could try it, but they'd be disappointed. Before the dust had settled, his masons would have thrown up dry-stone pocket walls on the inside of the breach, backed by scaffoldings on which engines could be deployed; and as for materials, the whole world lay on the other side of the sea, waiting to rush in timber and mortar and ready-dressed ashlar blocks in return for universally respected Perimadeian ready cash.

A child of ten could direct this defence; and women and children could hold these walls for ever, provided there were enough of them to work the windlasses. The whole thing's so tight, not even smoke could get through.

Which is probably why I'm so worried; there's nothing obvious to worry about. Something obvious would be the least of my problems.

Yes. Well. Very good.

So why is the bastard still coming?

Ironically, it was while Loredan was making his inspection that a man presented himself to the sentries at Temrai's camp, bringing with him the final confirmation Temrai needed; not that he'd been worried, but it was nice to be absolutely sure.

It'll be there, the man assured him. On time. As specified. Just the way we discussed it, that day we first met in the city.

Never doubted it for a minute, Temrai replied truthfully. And you can leave the rest to us.

The man looked doubtful. Temrai didn't bother explaining.

He didn't much like these people, for all that the whole venture depended on them. But he trusted them. Doubt the gods, or the love of wife, mother and daughter, or the loyalty of friends; but always trust the profit motive. A lever based on that one firm place was about to move the world.

'Admit it,' Gannadius said, his voice only just audible over the hum of conversation in the main room of the tavern, 'you're regressing. This is the sort of prank I'd expect from a second-year student rather than the Patriarch of the Order.'

The Patriarch of the Order who's also seriously ill and horrendously overworked, he could have added but didn't. No need to say what they both knew.

'That's why,' Alexius replied, addressing the unspoken part of the rebuke, 'I needed a change. This is a change.' He grinned under the floppy overhang of his broad-brimmed hat. 'I'm enjoying myself. It's a distraction.'

'I thought you always said you were too easily distracted,' Gannadius replied, sipping the rough, unpalatable wine. 'Why go to all this trouble to invite it?'

Alexius shrugged. 'Indulge me,' he said. 'I haven't been in a place like this for over twenty years. Besides,' he added, in what he hoped was a rather more grown-up voice, 'it enables me to monitor at first hand the mood of the city.'

Gannadius didn't dignify that obvious piece of nonsense with a reply. 'If anybody recognises you—'

'They'll point and say, "There's a tramp in that corner who looks just like the Patriarch." And their friend'll say, "Don't be ridiculous, the Patriarch's ears don't stick out like that." People only see what they can cope with.' He finished off his wine and put down the cup. 'One more,' he said, 'and that'll have to do. The days when I could put down five of these and still recite the thirty-two cardinal suppositions are long gone, I fear.'

'Stay there,' Gannadius sighed, getting up from the table. 'If anybody tries to talk to you, pretend you're a leper.'

Perhaps Gannadius is right, Alexius said to himself; perhaps this is second-childishness brought on by stress and an excess of responsibility. For the Patriarch suddenly to yield to an urge to dress up in scruffy clothes and go drinking in the lower city, even in a reasonably salubrious tavern such as this, is more or less unthinkable. I should be in my cell, lying on my back calculating extrapolations of pure theory and staring at those confounded mosaics. But this is a much better place to come and clear my head.

It needed clearing. The wine or the noise or something of the sort was making the sides of his head throb; but he had grown used to headaches recently, since he'd been hustled onto the Security Council and made to spend his days keeping the Prefect and the Deputy Lord Lieutenant from each other's throats. Correction; keeping the Prefect occupied while the Deputy Lord Lieutenant did his job. That was, he knew, the best thing he could do for his city, and he'd worked more diligently at it than anything he'd done before in his life. Thank goodness he had Gannadius to run the Order for him in the meantime. Or thank enlightened self-interest. Now he'd been officially declared Vice-Patriarch, his succession was assured. Somehow, though, he doubted whether Gannadius cared too much about that. It was a curious thing, but he genuinely believed that Gannadius, whose company he'd actively avoided not all that long ago, was now the nearest thing he'd had to a friend since he'd been appointed Patriarch.

Another correction; Bardas Loredan, the man he'd cursed, was a friend too, someone he could talk to freely, admit his fears and aggravations to. Remarkable, that so near the end of his life he should suddenly and quite unexpectedly discover friendship. It was like being able to see for the first time at an age when everyone else is starting to go blind.

'Here you are, and I hope it chokes you,' Gannadius muttered, plonking down a cup and sliding awkwardly back onto the bench. 'I might point out that if you wanted to drink excessive quantities of cheap wine, we could have gone to the Academy buttery and done so for free.'

'Yes, and where'd be the fun in that?' Alexius objected mildly. 'And, as I told you just now, we're here on business. Note the apparent air of normality, the lack of brittleness and panic. Clearly the morale of the city remains encouragingly high.'

Gannadius sniffed. 'The fools haven't yet realised what a desperate mess we're in. Or they've forgotten, or assumed it's gone away. It's not that long since they were rioting in the streets.'

'We had a riot when I was in my third year,' Alexius said dreamily. 'A group of freshmen had stolen a pig from the cattlemarket, painted it blue with raddle from the auctioneers' yard and dressed it up in the robes of the Commissioner of Fair Trading. Then they chased the poor creature down the city promenade until they came up against a detachment of the watch. That should have been the end of the matter, only we – I mean, a contingent of reprobate students who'd been drinking heavily to celebrate the end of their third-year examinations – happened to pass by, saw their comrades in the hands of a hostile agency and immediately hurried to the rescue. Nobody was seriously hurt,' he added defensively, 'and the Order paid for the damages. And it taught the watch a lesson in the tactful exercise of their powers when dealing with over-privileged young drunks.'

'I see,' Gannadius said drily. 'And what'd you do if a gang of our first years did the same thing? Declare a day's holiday and treat them to a dinner in Hall?'

'Certainly not,' Alexius replied. 'I'd throw them out of the Order and hand them over to the civil authorities. We can't be doing with that sort of thoughtless behaviour.'

'I'm delighted to hear it.' Gannadius took a sip of wine and made a face. 'You can have mine, too, if you like. I've got a bad enough head already without drinking myself another one.'

Alexius looked at him. 'You too?'

'Why? Have you …?'

'Ever since we came in here. I put it down to rough wine and the ambience, but if you've got one as well—'

'Our Island friends? Oh, not again, please. Haven't we got enough to contend with already?'

'Apparently not.'

Surreptitiously, Gannadius peered round the room. 'I can't see them,' he said. 'It must be the wine. Headaches can occur from natural causes, you know,' he added, 'and I'm flattering this sheep-dip by calling it natural. I think honest grapes and yeast had very little to do with its manufacture.'

He saw Alexius relax. 'I'm sure you're right,' he said. 'Bad wine, too much of it and an over-active imagination. Perhaps we should go home now.'

They got up, as unobtrusively as they could; in their anxiety to be thoroughly disguised, they'd turned themselves into the class of person not usually welcome in this class of establishment. Getting slung out into the street was scarcely the best way of staying inconspicuous.

It would probably have been all right if Alexius hadn't tripped over a small leather bag that someone had left lying between two tables, sending him lurching into the back of a customer just returning with a full jug of hot mulled cider. As the contents of the jug slopped down his leg, the customer yowled with pain and swirled round.

'You idiot,' he snapped. 'Look what you've done.'

Alexius stammered an apology, but not quite loud enough to be audible. The customer attached a broad hand to his collar. 'You realise these breeches are ruined,' he went on. 'And someone's going to pay for them.'

'Of course,' Gannadius said, in his most conciliatory tone, battle-tested in a hundred faculty meetings. Unfortunately, he'd forgotten that his best diplomatic voice didn't quite accord with his disguise. The customer could hardly fail to notice the discrepancy, which Gannadius made worse by oozing more soothing assurances and reaching for the purse in his sleeve. Before his hand was halfway there, the customer had grabbed it and twisted it painfully aside.

'Who the hell are you?' he demanded. Heads began to turn.

'Does it matter?'

Alexius looked round to see who'd said that, and saw a burly figure directly behind the customer; big, tall and bald, with a foreign but familiar accent. Very familiar, somehow.

'The gentleman's said he'll pay,' the stranger continued. 'Now mind your manners.'

The customer released Gannadius' arm and pressed the side of his own head, as if in pain. 'All right,' he said, 'there's no need for anybody else to stick their nose in. So long as I get my money—'

Gannadius produced a sum that would have clothed the man in ermine from head to foot, grabbed Alexius by the elbow and hustled him out into the cool night air. 'Damn it, Alexius, I knew this nonsense would land us in serious trouble. We could so easily have been recognised—'

'We were,' Alexius replied wearily. 'Oh, don't worry, we won't be the laughing stock of the city by this time tomorrow, if that's what you're thinking. But we were definitely recognised, be sure of that.' He realised he was standing in a puddle of something that wasn't just water, and stepped out of it. 'Come on, let's go home before we find something even more stupid to do.'

He set off down the street, his pace quicker and steadier than Gannadius would have thought possible, as if he were too preoccupied to remember his own infirmity. Gannadius scuttled after him.

'It's all very well saying we were recognised,' he hissed, 'but you can't just leave it at that. Who the hell by?'

'Our rescuer,' Alexius replied over his shoulder. 'That big bald man.' He sighed. 'Just think,' he added, 'I honestly thought matters were sorting themselves out. We've hardly seen the beginning of it yet.'

'Alexius, if you're going to turn oracular on me I shall give you up as a lost cause. Explain, for pity's sake.'

The Patriarch smiled bleakly. 'Gannadius, you surprise

me, I always thought you were an observant man. I was sure you'd have recognised him.'

'Recognised who? The bald man, you mean? I thought you said *he'd* recognised *us*.'

'He did.' Alexius halted for a moment to catch his breath. 'He recognised us, and I recognised him. And, since I don't believe in coincidences to the point of blind idolatry, I can only conclude that somehow or other he caused us to be there.' He shook his head sadly. 'I suppose it explains my sudden urge to go drinking in taverns after twenty years. I wonder how he managed it?'

'Alexius…'

'He was in that dream we all shared. You really don't remember?' Alexius took a deep breath and let it go, slowly, through his nose. 'That was Gorgas Loredan.'

CHAPTER FOURTEEN

War preparations meant more trade. More trade meant more litigation. More litigation meant more lawyers. And, since the turnover in the profession was necessarily high, newly qualified advocates were getting their chance to stand up in court for the first time rather earlier than usual.

Because justice must be seen to be done, the court listings were pinned up on the courthouse door every morning, four hours before the first session, to give the general public a certain amount of notice of the cases to be decided, to enable them to exercise their civic right to witness the proceedings and lay their bets.

Since Venart and Vetriz had gone home, taking with them enough rope to tie the Island to the city several times over, Athli had nothing in particular to do. When she happened to pass the courthouse and glance at the listings and the names of the advocates, she rapidly revised her plans for the day and joined the queue. There was a certain advocate making her first appearance in whose career Athli was personally interested.

The case was a rather complicated matter concerning a shipload of beans. The plaintiff alleged that the defendant, a ship's master who had contracted to carry the said beans from Perimadeia to Nissa for the sum more particularly specified in the charter party, had failed to exercise proper care and attention in stowing the said beans during the voyage, in that he had allowed the said beans to become damp, with the result that they had sprouted and become valueless, thereby rendering the plaintiff in breach of his contract to supply the said beans to a third party in Nissa, in consequence of which the plaintiff had lost the value of his contract and of the said beans, and further was liable to the said third party in damages.

The defendant alleged that the said beans had sprouted as a result of the plaintiff's own negligence in packing the said beans in barrels that were badly fitted and inadequately sealed; further or in the alternative it was a term of the plaintiff's contract with the said third party that risk in the said beans passed to the said third party on the ship's departure from Perimadeia, and that accordingly the said plaintiff had not breached the said contract and had suffered no loss at the hands of the defendant even if (which was not admitted) the defendant had been negligent in his stowing of the said beans.

While this rigmarole was being read out by the clerks, the audience sat in good-natured silence, broken only by the usual gentle coughing and the furtive munching of apples. It was a large crowd; lady advocates weren't exactly a novelty in the courts, but they weren't an everyday spectacle either, and a rumour had spread that this lady advocate was also young and pretty. On the strength of this rumour, several large bunches of flowers and baskets of fruit had already been handed in at the side door of the courthouse.

Not pretty, exactly, Athli said to herself; striking-looking. The girl – even now Athli couldn't remember her name, though she'd recognised it immediately when she'd seen it written down – was dressed for the occasion in the traditional court costume of a male advocate; not what lady fencers usually wore, and the defendant's clerk had tried to argue the point to the judge before the boos and hisses from the spectators had drowned out his words. The judge, an ex-fencer whom Athli recognised, had threatened to clear the court if the disturbance continued, but had disallowed the point of procedure. The trial was therefore about to begin.

The defence advocate was the first to take guard, adopting the bent-knees crouch of the City fence. Athli knew of him; he was no novice, and his reputation was for an energetic style of fencing that relied as much on the edge of the blade as the point. He was no more than average height, but his broad shoulders and thick forearms suggested that his wristwork would be strong and fast. The girl took her guard in the Old fence, standing up straight with her heels almost together and her sword-arm extended, the point held steady and unwavering. Athli put her apple core in her pocket and sat up straight. This was going to be interesting.

The woman next to her, middle-aged, red-faced, brightly dressed and fat, nudged her gently in the ribs. 'Silver quarter on the bloke,' she whispered. 'Seen him last week, he's mustard.'

'Bet,' Athli replied, as the defendant hop-skipped a pace forward, lifting his sword and aiming to push her blade aside in a pre-emptive parry that would leave her open. The girl watched him come; at the last moment she turned her own wrist over, bringing her blade up inside the parry, at the same time taking a step to her left. It was an intelligent gambit; he was now on a completely different line to her, and if she'd had the physical strength to deflect him safely, she could have counterthrust and finished the matter there and then. As it was, he was the one who counterthrust; she avoided it easily with footwork, but couldn't reach far enough to thrust back. She reverted to guard; he did the same. She had the moral victory, of course; but, as Loredan was so fond of saying, moral victories feed no crows. It was still all to play for.

In the next encounter, the defence displayed a little more intelligence. Because she was using the Old fence it was obvious the plaintiff was waiting for him to come to her; logical enough, since he was bigger and stronger. He did no such thing, guessing that her relative inexperience would lead her to make an attack simply to relieve the tension. She stayed put, however, her sword-point as still as a star in the clear night sky, and in the event he was the one who lost patience first. Taking a gamble on her inexperience, he deliberately lowered his guard a little, creating an opening for her. She would take advantage of it, he would be ready for her, and that ought to be that.

The girl refused to oblige. Even from where she was sitting, Athli could see the sweat glistening on the man's forehead; but the girl's face was pale and dry as paper, and her eyes were fixed on the other man's sword, exactly as they were supposed to be. It was almost, Athli realised, like watching Loredan fence; that total concentration on the ribbon of steel in the other man's fist, that alert stillness which implied a dogged refusal to make assumptions until the other man's sword was actually moving. *If she had her back to me*, Athli thought, *I might even think it was him.*

The battle of temperament was almost over. The defendant lowered his guard a little more, provocatively, like a woman hitching her skirt over her knee. The girl ignored him, continued staring down her blade at his. The crowd were beginning to murmur – hadn't paid good money to see two people standing still – when the man closed up his guard and made a good, orthodox lunge, leading a true line and angling his blade down to make the parry as hard as possible.

The next development happened very fast. The girl took two steps to her right, circling, stepping out of his line, the fundamental ploy of the Old fence. Her movement took her out of striking range for a counterthrust of her own, but it allowed her to turn her arm and fend his blade away, opening him up on his right side so that he couldn't easily recover in time to parry. He reared back, trying to get his sword inside hers to be in a position to use the strength of his wrist to make up for his disadvantage in position. But before he could even touch his blade to hers, she was inside him again; the counterthrust he'd anticipated she'd make hadn't happened, and he was parrying a sword that wasn't there. Before he had time to get back out of it, she'd stabbed him under his right arm. He fell off her blade, hit the ground and died.

'Oh,' said the fat woman. 'Damn.' She shrugged her big round shoulders, dug in her sleeve and produced a rather worn silver quarter. 'Double or quits on the next case?' she asked hopefully, still gripping the coin. Athli shook her head and held her hand out for the money. Then she stood up and walked out of the courthouse.

By the time she reached the street, she was trembling a little.

Wonderful advertisement for the school, she told herself. *Wonder if she's looking for a clerk?*

It was purely force of habit that led her to the usual tavern, just round the corner. She'd just watched a lawsuit, and so she felt thirsty, in need of a stiff drink. It was the first time she'd ever been in the place on her own, and even though it was the sort of establishment where unescorted women wouldn't expect to encounter difficulties, she nevertheless felt rather apprehensive until she saw a female figure sitting alone at a table by the window. A moment later, she realised who it must be.

Coincidentally, it was the same table she used to sit at with Loredan; out of the way of the through traffic to and from the back room, handy for the long-established matted sheaf of cobweb in case there were cuts to dress. Was it conscious imitation, or simply an inherent fencer's instinct that had led the girl to it?

I'll tell him when I see him next. He might be amused.

There was, of course, no need for her to go over and make conversation; she didn't even want to. But she stood there looking in the girl's direction for a minute or so longer than she should have. The girl looked up, caught her eye and recognised her. Good manners deprived Athli of the option of silent withdrawal. She went over.

'Hello,' she said, smiling. 'I've just been watching you in court. Well done.'

The girl nodded a perfunctory acknowledgement. In front of her was a small glass of wine, the smallest measure that the house provided. Athli asked if she'd like another. She shook her head, the minimum of movement necessary to convey her meaning. Rather appalling to think that, even in partial jest, Athli had contemplated clerking for this person. She decided to persevere a little longer.

'Your first case, I gather,' she said. 'Rather a substantial client to get for your maiden brief.'

'I'm related to him,' the girl replied, turning her head away and staring out of the window. 'On my father's side. And it wasn't as if they expected me to do anything; they were sure they were going to settle before it got to court.' She looked round, straight into Athli's eyes. 'Neither side wanted it to go to trial,' she went on. 'They wanted to carry on doing business together, and all this stuff was just in the way.'

Athli was intrigued, in spite of herself. 'What went wrong, then?' she asked.

'I knew there was going to be a cancellation in the listings, so I went to the court clerk and had this case brought forwards. It was such short notice they didn't have time to settle. So I got my fight.'

'I see,' Athli replied slowly.

The girl grinned at her. 'One of the advantages of not having a clerk,' she said. 'I can do things like that.'

'Well, it'll be good for your career,' Athli replied. 'You shouldn't have any trouble finding work now.'

The girl shrugged. 'I need the practice,' she said. 'Schoolwork's all very well, but I need to get the feel of the real thing. Actually kill people in open court a few times, build up my temperament.'

It was a reasonable attitude for a professional, and it wasn't the first time Athli had heard the gist of it, though never put quite in that way. Nevertheless, she found the girl's attitude rather revolting, and decided not to say anything.

'You were a clerk, weren't you?' the girl went on, looking away again. 'So you'll know about these things. If I wanted to get work from the State Prosecutor's Office, are there any particular advocates I should be trying to get a case against? As I see it, if I target particular advocates, the

Prosecutor'll notice me far quicker than if I just flounder about in general practice.'

Athli thought for a moment and suggested a couple of names; established advocates who picked and chose their work and charged high fees. 'If you beat any of them,' she went on, 'you'd certainly make a name for yourself. And obviously, the Prosecutor's always looking out for new advocates.' She paused, not wanting to know the answer to the question she was minded to ask. 'Why do you want to work for the Prosecutor, particularly? The money's good but nothing special, you'd do better in commercial practice. In fact, being a woman you'll probably find divorce would be a good field to be in.'

The girl shook her head, dislodging one of the combs from her hair; it fell on the table with a clatter. 'Divorce is a waste of time,' she said. 'Thanks for those names; I'll bear them in mind.'

Athli felt a great urge to go away, and decided to give in to it. 'Well,' she forced herself to say, 'well done once again and the best of luck.' She stood up. 'Clearly all that extra tuition wasn't wasted.'

The girl looked up sharply at that. 'No,' she said, 'I intend to make sure it wasn't. Goodbye.'

She said the word like a military officer saying *Dismissed*, and Athli walked away without looking back. She had decided not to say anything to Loredan; after all, he was through with all this, and he had a city to defend. Besides, she found she couldn't even now remember the wretched girl's name.

The enemy camp appeared under the walls of the city one morning like a mushroom, or a suspicious lump under one's skin not previously noticed. Later, the Security Council decided that they must have sneaked their rafts downstream as far as the gorge where the river cut through the low hills, a mile or so from the fork. Then, during the night, they somehow managed to make the last mile in pitch darkness, land their gear and set up camp no more than a third of a mile from the Drovers' Bridge; all in utter silence, setting up tents by feel without a sound or a gleam of light. Practice, the Council supposed, makes perfect, and for nomads pitching and breaking camp must be second nature. Nevertheless, it was an impressive achievement.

That was what was said in retrospect. When the first light of a grey and rather chilly day illuminated a vast expanse of ghostly grey and brown shapes apparently growing out of the low slopes on the left bank of the river, the city's reaction was rather less analytical.

This time, however, there were no mobs or riots; not even the anticipated mad rush to the harbour that Loredan had carefully provided against in his first-stage plans. That was just as well; even his plans hadn't covered the possibility of the enemy simply being there one morning. Instead, the city was quite unnervingly quiet, with groups of people standing out in the streets as if they were waiting for something to happen but had no idea what it was likely to be.

The first Loredan knew of it was when someone he didn't know burst into the small, cold room in the second-city gatehouse that he'd been using as a bedroom since his return from the cavalry raid. He jerked awake and was scrabbling for the hilt of his sword when the intruder spoke.

'We've got company,' the man said.

Loredan forgot about the sword and concentrated on getting his eyes open. He'd been up late the night before going over some discrepancies in the Quartermaster's accounts.

'What?' he mumbled. 'What's going on?'

'They're here. The enemy. They're camped outside the gates. Sir,' the man added as an afterthought. 'You're needed right away.'

Loredan swung his legs off the stone shelf that served him as a bed. 'Who the hell are you?' he asked.

'I'm Captain Doria of the change watch. With respect, sir, are you coming or not?'

Loredan studied him sourly through barely functional eyes. 'All right, Captain,' he said. 'Hold your water just a minute while I get dressed. Whatever the enemy may have done to us, they don't deserve to be greeted by the sight of me without my trousers on.'

As he rode down through the lower city, past endless faces staring up at him from every inch of pavement, he had the feeling of being late for some important ceremony that couldn't proceed without him; his wedding, for example, or his funeral. He was aware that he hadn't shaved, his hair was a mess and his clothes looked like they hadn't been changed for a week (which was true). He got a stitch in his side climbing the bridgehouse tower, and arrived uncharacteristically short of breath.

'All right,' he panted, resting for a moment against the frame of a trebuchet. 'What's going on?'

Then he noticed that almost the entire Council was there; the Prefect, the Lord Lieutenant, the clutter of officeholders that he hadn't even bothered to sort out in his mind; even Alexius and the Chief Governor of the Fencing Schools. *Always the same*, he muttered to himself, *the General's always the last to know.*

They made room for him on the rampart, and he looked out. At first, he took the grey shapes for low mist, such as sometimes drifted up from the river; but it was the wrong time of year and besides, he'd seen the clan's tents before.

'Well, well,' he said, very quietly. 'How did that get there, I wonder?'

The bridgehouse Captain told him what had happened in a low voice, and Loredan nodded. 'Possible,' he replied. 'A good night's work, if that's the way it was. I'm impressed.'

'We think it's the only way they could have done it,' the Captain murmured. 'The implications ...'

'Quite.' Loredan nodded. 'By the way, why are we all whispering?'

Actually, it seemed reasonable enough; don't make any loud noises, you might wake them up. 'People in the city are saying it can only have been done by magic,' said the

Prefect, with a quick scowl at the Patriarch. 'We're putting a stop to that kind of talk, of course; terrible effect on morale.' He paused and gazed out at the awesome sight in front of him; from his expression, it was quite possible that the Prefect subscribed to the magic theory. 'I shall want an explanation of how this was allowed to happen,' he added. Loredan ignored him.

'Has it occurred to anybody to ask them what they want?' he said.

'I'd have thought that was obvious,' the Lord Lieutenant drawled. 'I don't believe they're here to try and sell us carpets.'

'It's worth a try,' Loredan replied evenly. 'At the very least, we might get a good look at this remarkable young chief of theirs. I'd be interested in seeing what he looks like.' He stopped talking and rubbed his chin, feeling the bristles against the ball of his thumb. 'Talking of which, has anybody actually seen one of them yet? Looks to me like they're still in bed.' He looked round. 'Where's Garantzes? Is he here?'

The Chief Engineer stepped forward. Damn it, how come he was looking so spruce and military at this unholy hour?

'Chief Engineer,' he went on, 'how far away would you say those tents are from here?'

The engineer frowned. 'Six hundred yards,' he replied, 'possibly a fraction less. Well out of range, if that's what you were thinking.'

'Right.' Loredan nodded. 'Pity. Still, we might as well say good morning, while we're here.' He beckoned to the bridgehouse Captain. 'Get that new trebuchet wound up, will you? Quick as you like. And someone send down for a twenty-five-pound stone and one of those big wicker baskets with straps on the lid.'

Trying to aim an underweight missile from a trebuchet over twice its normal operational range wasn't an experiment Loredan had bothered to conduct. Fortunately, the camp was a large target. The stone flew from the hemp and rawhide sling, shedding the basket (which was only there to make it big enough to fly cleanly out of the sling) and rising almost impossibly high before plummeting down and landing destructively on an empty wagon just inside the extreme western edge of the camp.

The effect was quite satisfying. The thump and crash brought men running from the nearby tents; a pity they were too far away for their faces to be visible, but the way they stood for a moment before running off again in all directions was eloquent enough. They had been confident that they were well out of range, and here was evidence that they weren't. It was quite some time before it occurred to them that it had been a fairly small stone, and there hadn't been any others, whereupon they came out again. *Now, with luck, they'll go and wake the chief,* Loredan said to himself. *We might even find out where his tent is. I don't see why he should have a nice lie-in if I can't.*

'Temrai,' gasped a voice in his dream, 'they've started shooting.'

He woke up, lifted his head, opened his eyes. It wasn't a dream any more; there was a young lad he didn't recognise standing half-in and half-out of the tent flap. 'What do you mean, shooting?' he asked blearily. 'And who the hell let me go to sleep? There's so much I ought to be ...'

'They're throwing rocks into the *camp*,' the boy interrupted frantically. 'From that big tower over the bridge. I saw it with my own eyes.'

Temrai was up out of his chair in a matter of seconds. 'That's impossible,' he said. 'We're well out of range. They can't have anything that powerful, surely.'

The boy led the way. Already the place was like an ants' nest, just after the first slosh of boiling water has hit it. The scurrying people stopped in their tracks when they saw Temrai coming, and fell ominously silent. *Gods, they're blaming me,* he thought, quickening his pace. *But it's still impossible. Nothing could pitch a two hundredweight block of stone over six hundred yards; it'd have to be a trebuchet, and you couldn't make one with an arm strong enough to bear the counterweight, not to mention the devastating stresses on the frame. The thing would have to be as tall as a mountain; you'd never find trees tall enough to make it from.*

'There,' the boy said excitedly, and Temrai saw that he was pointing at a wagon. It wasn't exactly an inspiring sight; one side was splintered, an axle was cracked and the rear wheel on that side was missing a couple of spokes.

'Well?' Temrai said.

'There!' the boy repeated. Temrai looked more closely, and saw that there was a small rock partially buried in the ground beside it. For a moment he stood looking at it, wondering if there might be a connection. Then he realised what had happened.

'Is that all?' he said, relieved.

Everyone was looking at him.

'Well,' he went on, 'just look at it. It's nothing more than a pebble, compared to proper trebuchet shot. Think, will you? It takes twenty minutes to wind those things up, and the best they could do with stones that size would be pick us off one by one. They'd all be old men before they did us any significant damage.'

They carried on looking at him. Nobody actually said it – *Yes, but suppose I'm the one the next rock hits* – but they didn't need to. Temrai went closer, picked the rock up and dropped it again. Most of all he was thinking about what he'd just said; significant damage, a military expression meaning thousands of dead people rather than just hundreds. It wasn't all that long ago that one old woman being swept away when they crossed a river constituted a national disaster.

'All right,' he said, 'here's what we'll do.'

The second shot of the war sailed over the city wall, clearing the rampart by a few inches, dropped in the gutter and was buried in horse manure up to its blue and white duckfeather fletchings. It was an arrow from the bow of a fast-moving mounted archer, riding a zigzag pattern directly under the arms of the wall-mounted engines, right up to the causeway opposite the drawbridge. He'd loosed his arrow at the gallop, wheeled flamboyantly round and hurtled back. Nobody shot at him, loosed off a catapult or even called him a rude name; the towers of the city seemed as indifferent to his escapade as the trees of a forest are to the scamperings of a squirrel.

'What was all that in aid of?' somebody asked, breaking the silence.

'Bravado,' someone else replied, picking the arrow fastidiously out of the dung by its nock and handing it at arm's length to a clerk from the Office of Records. 'Go and put that in a museum somewhere,' he said with distaste. 'One of these days it might be worth something, if you wash the horseshit off it first.'

Loredan nodded. 'First round to us, anyway,' he said. 'We win the opening exchange of melodramatic and futile gestures. Now we've got their attention, let's go and see if they want to talk.'

While the Security Council were bickering about who should make up the embassy, things started to happen down on the plain. A line of huge rafts appeared on the river, each one tying up as close to the camp as it could get. The rafts were laden with stacks of timber; you didn't need to be an engineer to recognise the components of torsion engines.

Somebody on the wall noticed, and the word was passed down to Loredan, who left the squabbling diplomats and scampered up the stairs to the nearest tower.

'Right,' he said. 'We can do something about that. Run to the harbour and get three light cutters ready for immediate action. We can sink those rafts where they stand; or rather,' he added, 'we can tow a couple upstream and scuttle them, so the river'll be blocked. We'll see how they get on if they've got to carry all that stuff five miles on their backs.'

He'd hardly finished speaking when someone tugged his sleeve and pointed. One of the rafts had pulled in on the right-hand bank, not far upstream of the bridge causeway. As Loredan watched, the rafters unshipped one end of a thick, heavy chain. Other men from the same raft set about sawing through a substantial oak tree that grew beside the water. *Hell*, Loredan muttered to himself, *they're ahead of me again. They're going to block the river off with that chain so we can't get at the rafts.* 'Tell 'em to forget about the cutters,' he called down the stairs. 'These people are brighter than I thought.'

The embassy rode out across the drawbridge; ten members of the Council escorted by thirty heavy cavalry, with a captain of the guard riding ahead with the flag of truce.

'I suppose they know what a white flag means,' muttered the Lord Lieutenant nervously. 'We know what it means, but do they?'

'Well, I don't know, do I?' the Prefect muttered back. 'You'd better ask Loredan, he's the one who knows these people.'

Loredan pretended he hadn't heard; let them worry, it might encourage them to keep quiet while he tried to parley. Not that he had much hope of success. It didn't seem likely that this large and splendidly equipped army had come all this way and gone to all this trouble just to negotiate more favourable tariffs on imported manufactures. As far as he was concerned, there was only one thing to be achieved, but it was quite possibly the key to the defence of the city. He wanted to see the other man.

Because the enemy you've seen is the least of your problems.

The approach of the embassy caused a stir in the camp, where the clan was only just calming itself down after the shock of Loredan's pebble. Another boy – a different one this time – came running full tilt to the landing area, where Temrai was going over the unloading routines with the men he'd put in charge.

'Horsemen,' the boy said, thereby gaining the attention of everyone present. 'Forty of them, heading this way.'

Uncle Anakai broke the silence. 'Either they're being mean with their resources today, or they want to talk,' he said. 'Are they carrying a white flag?'

The boy looked uncertain. 'I don't know,' he replied. 'They've got a standard, I think, but I didn't notice what colour.'

'A white flag means they want to talk,' Temrai explained. 'It's some sort of primitive Perimadeian belief – a bit of old shirt tied to a stick makes you arrowproof. One of these days I'd love to test it scientifically.'

Uncle Anakai grinned. 'Are you going to talk to them?' he asked. 'There doesn't seem much point to me.'

Temrai, who had been crouching on his knees drawing a diagram in the mud with a stick, stood up and wiped his hands off on his trousers. 'On the contrary, Uncle An,' he said. 'This is a stroke of luck I hadn't expected. It gives us a chance to take a good look at who we're up against.'

One of the engineers raised an eyebrow. 'You mean that's their leaders out there? Why don't we kill 'em now? Take out their entire high command before the battle starts.'

Temrai shook his head. 'And then we'll be back where we were, fighting against generals we know nothing about. No, let's go and talk to them, get an idea of how their minds work. Best behaviour, everyone. Remember, ears open and mouths shut.'

The two parties met just in front of the camp. Not to be outdone, Temrai had brought with him fifteen counsellors, fifty horsemen and three white flags, hastily manufactured out of captured bedlinen. At the last moment, he nudged his cousin Kasadai in the ribs and whispered, 'You be me, all right?'

'What?'

'Pretend you're me. Don't want them to know who I am. All right?'

Kasadai shrugged. 'You're the boss. What shall I say if they ask me things?'

'Whatever you like. Thanks, Kas.' Temrai dropped back, shifted his otterskin cap a little further down over his face and let Kasadai ride to the head of the party.

As the two groups converged, Loredan spurred ahead, dropped his reins and folded his arms across his chest. 'All right,' he said in a loud voice. 'Which one of you monkeys is in charge here?'

After only a tiny moment's hesitation, Kasadai rode forward. He cleared his throat. 'I am Temrai Tai-me-Mar,' he said impressively, 'son of Sasurai. What do you want?'

Loredan smiled at him contemptuously. 'No, you're not,' he said. 'You're too old. The new chief's a snot-nosed kid, everyone knows that. Must be you, the one wearing a dead rat on his head. Come over here where we can talk without bellowing.'

After a long embarrassed silence Temrai rode forward. 'I'm Temrai,' he said. 'Who are you?'

Loredan squinted at him. 'I know you from somewhere,' he said. 'Hopeless with names, but faces I don't forget. Got it; you're that clumsy kid from the arsenal, the one who bust my sign.'

Temrai nodded slightly, his eyes as cold as steel in winter. 'That's right,' he said. 'I remember you, too. I'm pleased to see my enemies have a drunk for a general.'

Loredan grinned broadly. 'That's a good one,' he said. 'I must remember that. Anyway, enough small talk. We'll let you withdraw in good order on two conditions. One, you burn those contraptions you've got over there before you go. Two, you pay me what you owe me for my sign. Deal?'

He was trying to maintain eye contact, stare the other man down; but it wasn't easy. Just then, he'd have preferred it if Temrai had been looking at him down a sword blade, even if he'd been unarmed himself. He'd have known where he stood. But the boy's eyes were painfully steady, as unwavering as that head-case girl's sword-tip that night in the Schools.

'I don't forget faces either,' Temrai said at last. 'Since you won't do me the courtesy of telling me your name, I shall just have to remember your face. I hope we'll meet again.'

Loredan yawned. 'I'm going to have to take that as a no, I think,' he replied. 'Pity. You haven't a hope in hell, and an awful lot of your people are going to die. Not that I care a stuff about that; but some of mine'll get hurt too, and I'd rather have prevented that, if I could. Ah, well, on your head be it.'

'Accepted,' Temrai said.

'One last thing, though,' Loredan went on, 'since I've got you here and you'll probably run away before we capture you, so we may not meet again – out of interest, why are you doing this?'

Temrai stared at him for a long time before answering. 'It's personal,' he said.

'Personal? That's it? You're leading your tribe to certain death because you're miffed with us about something?'

Temrai nodded. 'That's about it,' he said. 'Actually, I'm grateful to you for reminding me. I was beginning to ask myself the same question; now I find I can remember the answer.'

Loredan pulled his horse's head round. 'Be like that, then,' he said. 'See if I care. You still owe me for my sign.'

'You'll get what's owing to you,' Temrai said. 'I'll see to that myself.'

To his credit, the City Prefect waited until they were out of earshot of Temrai's party before he launched into his attack.

'What in hell's name did you think you were playing at?' he hissed furiously. 'If that's your idea of diplomacy—'

'It was a gambit,' Loredan replied mildly. 'An aggressive opening, like taking guard in the City fence. I found out what I wanted to know.'

'I'm so pleased,' the Prefect replied. 'Perhaps you'd care to share this priceless intelligence with the rest of us, because I'm damned if I can see what was achieved back there. And what was all that nonsense about owing you for a sign?'

Loredan smiled wanly. 'All perfectly true,' he sighed. 'And that's five quarters I won't see again in a hurry. You want to know what I've learnt? I'll tell you. First, there's no traitor who's been selling arsenal secrets to the enemy; six months or so ago, that kid was working in the arsenal as a swordsmith. Now we know why. I guess we can say we taught him all he knows.'

The Prefect started to say something, but didn't. Loredan nodded.

'Second,' he said, 'that boy is clever. Grown up a lot, too; well, I suppose becoming chief of the clan might do that to a kid. Anybody who's capable of carrying away the full specifications of all our major military engines in his head and then getting a tribe of nomads who've never done anything like it before to build a collection of engines like theirs is clearly not someone to be taken lightly. Now *that's* justified this trip on its own.'

The Prefect bit his lip, and nodded. 'I agree,' he said.

'Good. Now, third. Here's a history lesson for you. Twelve years ago, Maxen attacked the chief's caravan – that was when this lad's father, Sasurai, was in charge – and we wiped out most of the royal household. To be honest, we thought we'd got the lot, all his living relatives in one go, all part of Maxen's destabilisation policy; leave no obvious heir to the throne, result – civil war when the old man dies. Obviously we didn't get them all, because the lad who pretended to be our man called himself Temrai, son of Sasurai. Also, when I asked him why he was doing this, he said it was personal.' Loredan sucked his lower lip thoughtfully. 'He wasn't kidding, either. If he's Sasurai's son, then we killed his entire family, except for him and the old man. The fact of the matter is, he's got no choice. He's *got* to do what he's doing, and the clan'll know that. Which means they aren't going to get bored and go away if they don't carry the city at their first attempt.' He shook his head. 'I'd already guessed this was all to do with Maxen's war. I hadn't realised till now it was this serious.'

'Anything else?' the Prefect asked.

'A bit more. Our boy isn't impressed by bluster, and he doesn't lose his temper. That's worth knowing. He's in full control, as far as I can judge; there were plenty of clan dignitaries there, but none of them said anything apart from Temrai. That implies they'll do what he tells them to. We might try and figure out whether there's a way of breaking that, something we can do to turn them against him, but I wouldn't hold out much hope of that.'

As soon as they were inside the city, Loredan called for Garantzes and told him to break up the causeway opposite the drawbridge. Soon afterwards, four torsion engines on the eastern bastions were let slip, and the causeway became a tangled mess of splintered logs and planks. It was an impressive display of artillery work, and Loredan hoped that Temrai had been watching. On the other hand, he felt it was a little depressing to think that the first part of the destruction of the city had been accomplished on his direct order. He rather hoped it wasn't an indication of what was to come.

'Of all the stupid, cowardly things to do,' the Lord Lieutenant raved, 'breaking down the causeway so we can't mount a sortie. So now we're going to sit behind the walls and watch while they assemble their engines completely unhindered. It's criminal.'

'We can't very well watch if we're *behind* the walls, surely,' his daughter replied. The rest of the family managed not to giggle.

'Don't be flippant,' he said. 'You know perfectly well what I mean.' He tore the crust off a slice of bread, crushed the middle into a hard knob of dough and bit into it. 'I wouldn't be surprised if money was changing hands somewhere in all this,' he added melodramatically.

'But I thought—' His wife stopped herself and returned to her embroidery.

'Well?'

'Take no notice. Just something I must have got wrong.'

'I'll be the judge of that.'

'Well,' she said, squinting to thread her fine bone needle, 'it's just that I thought it was you who'd insisted – very sensibly, I thought – that after the, what's the word, exploratory force or expeditionary force or whatever it's called, after they made such a mess of things, we weren't going to have any more going outside the walls to fight them, we were going to sit tight and let them come to us. I think that's what you said,' she added. 'Can you remember what Daddy said, Lehan, dear?'

Lehan, who was seven, nodded gravely. 'I think so,' she replied. 'That was more or less it, anyway.'

The Lord Lieutenant scowled. 'That's not the same thing at all,' he replied through a mouthful of bread. 'Going outside and looking for another pitched battle is one thing. Harrying them while they're setting up their confounded siege engines is something else entirely. Sheer folly to deprive ourselves of the chance of doing that.'

'But you said their engines wouldn't work anyway,' Lehan pointed out. 'You said it stood to reason that a mob of ignorant savages—'

'That's not the point. The point is, while they're weak and disorganised, with their minds occupied with unloading the engines, now's the best time to attack them. And that fool—'

The Lord Lieutenant was not, of course, an impartial observer. He was the leader of the Reform faction in the politics of the city, whereas the Prefect (the object of his fulminations; as far as he was concerned, Loredan was merely the Prefect's agent) led the Popular faction. Although to an ignorant outsider the two factions were completely indistinguishable, the rivalry between them was unremittingly ferocious, and the uneasy truce that had been in place since the emergency began was starting to take its toll of everyone in the Council.

Nevertheless, the debate in the Lord Lieutenant's household was fairly representative of what everyone in the city was saying, except that the average man tended to compromise the two positions; he derided the government for its cowardice in breaking down the causeway, while wholeheartedly subscribing to the view that the walls were impregnable and the savages would soon give up and go away.

'They should be doing *something*,' said Stauracius, the senior deacon, as he walked off his dinner in the cloister of the City Academy. 'You're pretty thick with the Patriarch,

Gannadius. You should be lobbying for some action. It's time the Order's views were given the consideration they deserve.'

'Oh?' Gannadius raised an eyebrow. 'Why? We're an organisation of philosophers and scientists engaged in abstruse metaphysical research. Why should we have a valid opinion about fighting a war?'

Stauracius looked at him oddly. 'I have to say,' he said, 'as the effective leader of the Order now that Alexius is so busy with his new duties, you don't seem to be particularly concerned with our standing in the community. Or our responsibilities, come to that. We have an obligation to guide and counsel at times like these. We should be doing more—'

'Perhaps.' Gannadius looked away pointedly. 'So you belong to the let's-zap-them-with-magic school, I presume. It's not an approach I have much time for, I'm afraid.'

'It's nothing to do with magic, as you know perfectly well.'

'That's what they're saying we should do,' Gannadius pointed out. 'Curse the savages to smithereens. Roast 'em with fireballs or turn 'em all into frogs and fill the sky with hungry cranes. I'd love to know how it's done.'

'Now you're even starting to sound like Alexius,' Stauracius replied disapprovingly. 'With all due respect, I always felt there was an underlying flippancy in his character that didn't quite accord with the best traditions of his office.'

'You mean he's got a sense of humour? Well, perhaps you're right, and perhaps it's something that gradually grows on you once you find yourself in charge of the Order. I can distinctly remember a time when I sounded just like you.'

That served its intended purpose of offending the deacon sufficiently to get rid of him, and Gannadius was able to get to his office without further molestation. He faced the cheerful prospect of a night of administrative paperwork, with a thick wedge of academic reading to catch up on if he wanted a break. He remember how Alexius had complained about such things, and how scornful he'd felt of someone who held the office but didn't fancy the work. That was all a long time ago now.

He closed the door, shot the bolts and lit his lamp from the candle he'd been carrying. The sour yellow light cast heavy shadows in the corners of the room, and the smoke from a badly trimmed wick made his eyes itch. It would have been nice to go to bed now, but if he did that all the work would still be there in the morning. He sat down and picked a sheet of parchment off the top of the pile.

Minutes of a meeting of the Joint Faculties Committee on appointments and funding.

He scanned the page, noting his name under *Apologies for absence* and translating minutes-talk into real language as he went along. The words on the page made a sort of sense; but somehow he couldn't see how any of it was relevant to him, or to anything anybody could possibly be interested in. The world had moved on too much since he'd last sat in a finance meeting.

Three days now; and so far, nothing had happened. On both sides of the wall, the air was filled with the sounds of hammers, saws, axes, winches and swearing; on both sides, men were hauling on ropes, lugging timber, bashing in wedges and slapping glue into mortices, trimming stones, shouting orders, standing around in groups while someone else tried to resolve the latest unforeseen disaster. Yet the distance between the camp and the wall was still the same, and nothing had dared set foot in it apart from the usual feeding birds and stray dogs. He hadn't seen Alexius to speak to since the first morning; the Security Council was in more or less continuous session, although what there was for them to do he wasn't entirely sure. At times he suspected they might have rigged up a couple of dice tables and one of those water-powered organs, just the thing if you're having a really serious party.

For some reason, though, his mind kept returning to their ill-fated drinking expedition, and the man Alexius had claimed was Gorgas Loredan. At the time he'd put it down

to the rather spectacular amount of industrial-grade rough
wine the Patriarch had absorbed; the idea that even if the
man was the Deputy Lord Lieutenant's brother, he'd
somehow managed to lure them into a tavern just so as to
have a look at them had struck Gannadius as too
far-fetched to be worth considering. Why bother? And even
if he'd done everything Alexius claimed he had, so what?
And yet the Patriarch had seemed convinced that Gorgas
Loredan was somehow a bird of very ill omen, for the two
of them and possibly the whole city as well.

*And now I'm worrying about it too. I wonder if there really
is anything in it? Or is it just a more entertaining subject for
contemplation than these truly awful minutes?*

To break his train of thought, he stood and made up a fire
in the room's small hearth. Lately, he'd found a certain
degree of pleasure in doing this sort of thing for himself
(strange; not long ago, he'd regarded not having to do this
sort of thing as evidence that he'd made something of his
life) and he lingered over the job, taking pains to lay the
wood properly. Once he'd lit the kindling and got it going,
he sat down again, not at his desk but in the fat, comfortable
visitor's chair, with his feet up on a large cedarwood
clothes-press. He had the sheet of minutes in his hand and
he was looking at it, but he wasn't reading. Soon his eyelids
began to feel heavy, and he let them close—

—And found himself in front of a different fire, something
very hot and painfully bright; he was several yards away
from it, but he could feel his skin tingle from the heat. It was
like being in a forge, except that he was outside, not in. In
fact, it was the building itself that was on fire.

He looked more closely, and recognised the arsenal; not
a place he knew well, although he'd wandered in there
once when he was a second-year student with time on
his hands. Now it appeared to be burning to the ground;
and outside it, using the flames to work with, was a man
standing over an anvil, with a small hammer in his hand
and a glowing orange strip of metal gripped in a pair of
tongs. It was—

'Gorgas Loredan?'

The bald-headed man turned his head and nodded affably. 'Hello,' he said. 'Fancy seeing you here. Would you mind making yourself useful for a moment?'

'Of course,' Gannadius replied. 'What do you want me to do?'

'Work the bellows while I mix the flux for the solder,' Gorgas replied. 'Won't be a jiffy. But if it cools down I won't be able to get the solder to run.'

'What do I do?'

'Just pump these handles up and down – there, you've got it. Nice and steady, and that'll be fine.'

'All right.' Gannadius pushed the handles and raised them again. 'By the way,' he said, 'how come I know all these technical terms? I don't know the first thing about metalworking.'

'Knowledge is never wasted,' Gorgas replied, his back turned. He teased out a small pile of white powder onto a sheet of slate, spat into it and mixed up a paste with a bit of stick. 'Valuable stuff this,' he said, 'got to be careful with it. Can't use anything else with the silver solder.'

'Ah,' Gannadius replied, wiping sweat out of his eyes with his sleeve. 'I thought we didn't know how to use the silver stuff.'

'That's right,' Gorgas replied, 'but the plainsmen do. Marvellous stuff. Right, that ought to do it. Got to be the right consistency, like a cross between spit and snot, or it won't take. Keep pumping while I do the business.'

Gannadius nodded and carried on working the bellows. 'My friend Alexius suspects you of being at the root of all this,' he remarked as he pumped. 'I don't see it myself. What do you think?'

'I think Alexius may have a point,' Gorgas replied. 'But wouldn't it be easier just to ask my brother, rather than guessing yourselves silly and losing sleep over it?'

'True,' Gannadius replied. 'Or you could tell me yourself, come to that.'

Gorgas smiled. 'I'd love to help,' he said, 'but I'm only a

dream, sort of like a belch of undigested wind from your own subconscious mind. If you don't know the answer, then how can I?'

'Ah, but you're not,' Gannadius said, 'because if that was the case, how come I know all this stuff about silver-solder flux and keeping the metal just the right shade of cherry red so the solder'll take? That didn't come from my memory; therefore, neither do you. So you can answer my question.'

Gorgas nodded. 'Good point. Obviously you've learnt a thing or two since you've been hanging around with our esteemed Patriarch. Either that—' Gorgas lifted his head and grinned; he was bright red in the glow of the flames, '—or I'm running you, like Alexius says I am. Come on, then, now you're so clever, you tell me which it is.'

'Why's the city on fire?' Gannadius asked.

'Search me.' Gorgas was bent over the strip of orange steel, delicately touching the stick of solder to the joint. 'On that subject, you'd have to ask my sister. She's the clever one in our family.'

'I didn't know you had a sister,' Gannadius said, waking up with a start as the pile of papers slid off his lap onto the floor. Someone was tapping on the door. He grunted, picked up the documents (which were now all mixed up and out of order) and said, 'Come in.'

A young girl's face appeared round the door; not someone he recognised. 'There's someone to see you,' she said. 'They say they're friends of yours. Foreigners,' she added meaningfully.

'Hm? Oh. Send them up here, will you? Did these foreigners have names, or are they too outlandish and foreign for you to pronounce?'

'Oh, I didn't ask,' the girl replied, and her face vanished again.

Gannadius rubbed the sleep out of his eyes, reflecting on the girl's emphasis on the word *foreigners*. He took it to mean that the visitors were either clan agents to whom he was about to hand over the keys to the city, or else incredibly powerful wizards who had come to help him cook up the really devastating magic by which the clan were soon going to be hexed to oblivion; probably, he decided, both. He regretted entertaining the second hypothesis when the door opened again and Venart and Vetriz were standing in the doorway.

Venart cleared his throat. 'I'd just like to say,' he announced, 'that this was entirely her idea.'

His sister gave him a scornful look over her shoulder and perched on the edge of the desk. Venart stayed where he was, close to the door.

'Please come in,' Ganadius said. 'Would you like something to drink? Please, help yourselves.'

'Oh, thanks.' The girl leant across the desk, neatly gathered the winejug and a cup, and poured. 'Mm, this is delicious,' she said. 'What is it?'

Gannadius smiled. 'Speciality of the house,' he said. 'It's a sweet wine from the south, with honey and cinnamon. But that's gone cold, and it should be warm. I'll ring for some more.'

'Thank you,' Vetriz said, ignoring her brother's pleading look. 'I'm sorry to barge in on you like this, I can see you're busy. But we wanted to see Captain Loredan—'

'*Colonel* Loredan,' her brother muttered.

'Colonel Loredan, and nobody knows where he is. Ven went to his office, but he wasn't there, and the clerks were terribly unhelpful, and Athli, that's his clerk, she's in business with us now, she happened to mention that the Colonel's on very good terms with Patriarch Alexius these days, so we went to find him to see if he knew where the Colonel was, and when we asked at the palace—'

'Warden's lodgings.'

'—they said you might know, since you were filling in for him while he was busy with the invasion and everything. Isn't that a terrible thing, by the way?'

'Shocking,' Gannadius replied with a smile.

'Isn't it? Anyway, we were wondering, if it's not too much trouble, do you think you could pass a message on to the Patriarch to tell the Colonel that we're back in the city, arrived here just this morning, and if he could spare us five minutes—'

'Vetriz,' groaned Venart. 'Shut up.'

'Oh, shut up yourself. Do you think you might?' she went on. 'We'd be ever so grateful if you could.'

There was a knock at the door; the young girl again. Gannadius placed an order for a large jug of warm spiced wine and three clean cups. The girl nodded, took a long look at the two Islanders, and went away.

Experimentally, Gannadius touched his fingertips to his forehead. It didn't hurt. He wondered about that for a moment, and made up his mind.

'I don't see why not,' he replied. 'Venart – that's right, isn't it? – do please sit down, I think you'll enjoy the wine. Yes, I should be able to pass a message through to Colonel Loredan. It may take a day or two, of course. You'll appreciate that with the recent developments—'

'Oh, that's all right,' Vetriz replied. 'We've got to be here for at least a week to load the rest of the rope – Ven's bought up all the surplus rope from the government, a very good deal for us. That's what we want to see the Colonel about. You see, last time we were here he mentioned they're very short of seasoned lemonwood staves for making bows, and while we were home this time we managed to get hold of a rather substantial quantity – cancelled order, actually, but please don't tell the Colonel that.'

'Of course.' Gannadius nodded conspiratorially. 'And I'm sure he'll be delighted. Of course, if you wanted to deal with the matter quickly rather than wait around to see the Colonel personally, I believe the Quartermaster's Office is allowed to do purchasing without the Colonel himself having to be involved.'

Vetriz smiled. 'Oh, we knew that. But when you've got a contact high up in an organisation, it does no harm to deal personally. Isn't that what you keep telling me, Ven?'

Venart, who was balanced on the edge of a hard straight-backed chair, nodded glumly and said nothing. For once, it seemed, he was perfectly happy to leave all the talking to his sister.

'In return,' Gannadius said, 'perhaps you might care to do something for me.'

Vetriz beamed with pleasure. 'Well, of course,' she said. 'Is it something you want brought in?'

Gannadius shook his head. 'It's more to do with the circumstances of our last meeting,' he replied. 'I have to confess, Alexius and I were rather less than honest with you.'

'What, you mean— How absolutely fascinating! You're talking about the magic, aren't you? Oh, I forgot, I mustn't call it that.'

Another tap at the door; the girl bringing the wine. 'Thank you, we'll pour for ourselves,' Gannadius said firmly. The girl left, looking cheated.

'Are you sure you won't join us, Venart?' Gannadius asked.

'No thanks, really. Spiced wine always gives me a headache.'

Gannadius poured wine into two cups and passed one over to Vetriz. 'I'll come straight to the point,' he said. 'When Alexius and I tried that experiment, the first time we met you, Alexius told you it had effectively been a failure. He wasn't telling the truth. There was—' He hesitated, stared into his cup. 'Something there,' he continued. 'Something we'd neither of us come across before, which is probably why we kept quiet about it. More embarrassment than anything else, I suppose; after all, we're supposed to be good at this sort of thing. And perhaps we both thought we'd imagined it, I don't know,' he added with a straight face. 'On reflection, however, I'm sure there was something; so, with your agreement, I'd like to try again.' He stopped fiddling with his cup and put it down before he spilt it. 'I don't think Alexius would approve, I have to say; but to be honest with you, now that we have this emergency on our hands, I feel that every avenue that might conceivably be productive has to be explored; and if it comes to nothing, well then.'

Vetriz's eyes were big and round and shining like sunlight reflected on a distant glass. 'Oh, yes,' she said, 'do let's. You're not going to be stuffy about this, are you, Ven? Because if there really is something we can do, I think we owe it to them, since they've been so helpful about everything.'

'Go ahead,' Venart said resignedly. 'I take it you mean my sister,' he added to Gannadius. 'I seem to remember that I fell asleep.'

Gannadius stroked his chin. 'The indications at the time did suggest that it was your sister who was, um, having an effect on things. But that may not mean anything. You see, I'm sure that whichever of you it is doesn't consciously know what she or he is doing. On that basis, it could quite easily be you.'

Venart shrugged. 'I'm game, then, if you think it'll help.'

'Splendid.' Gannadius sipped his wine. Still no headache. 'Perhaps it'd help if I very briefly explained how the Principle works in this regard – or at least, how we think it works. As I said a moment ago, this is effectively new ground for us as well.'

He started to explain, and although he did his best to keep it simple and reasonably lively, his monologue was inevitably rather abstruse and full of long unfamiliar words; and the room was comfortably warm and the wine was heavy and sweet, and before he knew where he was—

—He was standing on one of Loredan's new bastions, apparently in the middle of a battle; there were men rushing about all round him, carrying ropes and levers and sheaves of fresh arrows with bits of straw still stuck in the feathers of the fletchings, and they were stepping over the bodies of dead men, and others who weren't dead but groaning or weeping, and some of the casualties were city people and others were plainsmen. Every now and then he could feel the walkway shake beneath his feet; he guessed that heavy stones were hitting the wall below the level of the rampart. There was a big engine, a trebuchet, over to his left and there were men fussing over it, some of them scrambling up the side of the frame or sitting on the crossbars, others handing them up tools and lengths of rope.

There were arrows sticking in the wood, their shafts facing outwards towards the plain, and other arrows sailed across the wall from time to time, some clattering against the stone and others carrying over into the streets below. There were archers on the wall, standing up straight to bend their long, stiff bows; they didn't seem to be worrying about the incoming arrows, but Gannadius saw one man fall to the ground with an arrow sticking out of his ear, and another suddenly drop his bow and clutch at an arrowshaft sticking in his upper arm. Two other men hurried up and helped him to the stairs, while a third picked up his bow and started to shoot.

Gannadius looked round, trying to see Vetriz or Venart, or anybody else he recognised, but he couldn't. An arrow flew past him, so close that he imagined he felt the feathers brush lightly across his chin. It was terrifying, but it had happened so fast and so quietly that at first he'd taken it for a breath of wind or an insect.

Damn, he thought, *so now what do I do? I must have come through on my own.*

He peered round, but it was hard to see anything for all the running men in the way. Presumably he'd come through at some crucial moment – that seemed to be the way it worked, you found yourself at the turning point, the moment where you could reach out and grab hold, and by so doing change the course of events. He wished he knew something about military affairs, tactics and the like. It all looked to him like a confused mess; if there was something vitally significant going on he didn't have the first idea what it was supposed to look like. That didn't help; for all he knew, he might miss it completely, or change it the wrong way out of sheer ignorance. Suppose this was the moment when the battle was going to swing decisively in the city's favour, and he was about to change that simply because he didn't know what he was doing?

Someone was running up the stairs; Bardas Loredan, with blood soaking through his hair and a bow in his hands. Instinctively, Gannadius stepped back to let him past, although logically Loredan should have been able to walk straight through him.

'The chain,' he panted. 'Which of you clowns forgot to raise the chain? Gods, we'll have to do it in the middle of all this. Right, you and you, get ready to shin out along the pole and haul on the ropes. I'll do this one here. All we've got to do is get it up onto the hooks and make it fast.'

The men he'd spoken to stepped back with terror in their eyes, not saying anything. Loredan grabbed one by the arm, but he pulled away.

'Someone's got to do it, for pity's sake,' he shouted. 'They'll have those ladders up here any minute.'

An arrow swished past Gannadius, hit Loredan's mailshirt just above his hip and glanced off. The two men turned and ran. Somehow Gannadius couldn't find it in his heart to blame them.

Oh, gods, he's going to try and do it on his own. Gannadius concentrated, wondering how exactly he was supposed to go about changing the course of events. Then he thought, *Yes, and suppose Loredan succeeds, and that's what saves the city? If I stop him, we'll all be killed. Oh, why don't I know what to do?*

Loredan was on the rampart, swinging one leg over, looking down to find the pole. Gannadius caught his breath. *Do something!* he told himself—

'Hello?' It was the Islander girl, Vetriz, and she was gently prodding at his shoulder. 'You fell asleep,' she said.

'What?' Gannadius opened his eyes. 'Good heavens, so I did. I'm so sorry. What was I saying?'

He completed his explanation; and then they all tried very hard to fall asleep and couldn't manage it. When it had started to be embarrassing, Gannadius thanked his visitors very much, promised again to pass their message on and shooed them out. Then he sat down on the edge of his bed, steadily drank his way through the rest of the wine (which was stone cold) and lay on his back, feeling ill.

He was exhausted. He didn't have even the slightest trace of a headache.

He was a very worried man.

CHAPTER FIFTEEN

The next morning, Temrai gave the order to hitch up the mules and bring forward the first battery of trebuchets.

Half an hour after they'd entered the three-hundred-yard zone, all five engines were so much firewood and the ground was littered with smashed timber, stones, dead mules and dead men. In reply they'd managed to loose off precisely one shot, which had landed in the river. Very pale in the face and trying his best not to let his people see that he was shaking, Temrai ordered the next two batteries forward simultaneously. The assault had begun.

Seven engines survived the next volley from the eastern bastion; and trebuchets take time to wind and load. Say twenty minutes between volleys, enough time if they looked sharp about it. He sent in another ten engines, and nobody on the wall had anything left to shoot at them with. When it eventually came, the next volley from the city smashed another two engines, but this time Temrai's engineers had fifteen trebuchets ready to return fire. He shouted to them to take their time and remember the sighting drill. They waved back at him; *don't bother us, we're busy*. The first engine let slip, and its stone hit the wall somewhere near the base. There was a great cheer from the clan, but Temrai yelled for quiet. The engineers adjusted the trajectory by tightening the winch a precisely calculated number of turns. Another machine let slip, and its stone sailed over the wall, clearing it by a matter of five or six feet. The other engineers slacked off their winches a little. The third engine let slip, and this time the clan really did have something to cheer about.

'Close,' Temrai called back, 'but close isn't good enough. Keep that mark, and sooner or later we'll get those engines.'

They managed to hit one before the next volley from the bastion, which smashed another of Temrai's engines and dropped a stone onto the crew of another. That wasn't a pleasant sight, by any means; there was a man still miraculously alive under the stone, and he was screaming for help. Temrai waved a party of men forwards; eventually they rolled the stone away, but by then the man was dead. Meanwhile the artillery duel went on; and every stone that missed an engine on the bastion hit something else, while the unlucky shots from the bastion simply dug holes in the ground.

This is how it's going to be, Temrai said to himself, *and we've got hours of it still to go before we know whether it's going to work. Oh, well. At least we aren't making complete fools of ourselves.*

The dreary business went on for a long time. In a way it was absurd; the engineers were working at fever pitch, hauling on ropes and manhandling boulders, trying to keep the mules that drew the lines that raised the counterweights from breaking their traces in panic when a stone landed, trying to get them to move at all the rest of the time. And the remainder of the army watched, like spectators at a Perimadeian lawsuit, while the men in the middle worked and died. Once he'd managed to conquer the urge to drag his men out of the danger zone, Temrai found it was rather like a very boring event at someone's funeral games; presumably his own. It had the same strange contrast; frantic and desperate effort in the arena, silence and stillness in the crowd, the occasional shuffling of feet cramped from standing too long in one place, even here and there the crunch of an apple, an overheard snatch of conversation about something quite other.

Fairly early on in the exchange, Temrai realised where

there was an advantage to be had, and ordered the engineers to move the engines rather further apart. He'd noticed that although his men had only scored two direct hits in ten volleys, the city engines were shooting far more slowly and less accurately than they had been. He thought about that, and realised that although his shots weren't smashing engines, they were mostly landing on or around the bastion itself, and the bastion rampart was so crowded with machines and engineers that it'd be hard to drop a stone on it without hitting something. What his engines were doing was killing or injuring the city engineers; the trained men who knew how to work the machines properly. In their place came men who knew less about managing trebuchets than Temrai's people did, hence the poor quality of their work. Accordingly it made sense to space his engines out. It worked; such shots as did land on target and break bone or wood were merely lucky, the practical application of the laws of averages. His men, however, were getting better at it as they went along.

Over and over again the mule-train stopped, the engine-master engaged the slip that connected the arm to the windlass, the captain of engineers checked the aim and adjusted the tension so that the witness-marks scratched on the windlass drum lined up exactly with the equivalent scratches on the frame opposite before giving the order to the master to let slip; whereupon the master tugged on the cord that pulled the steel hook out of the loop fitted to the underside of the arm; the counterweight, a huge plank crate full of rocks, swung back to rest and flipped the arm up into the air, making the massive beam bend like a sapling in a high wind; the sling on the end of the arm snapped out and forwards, whipping the two hundredweight stone out as if it was a pebble flung at a bird, and the stone lifted and became smaller and smaller as it flew, until it dwindled down to a dot, small and distant as a shooting star, visible only by the line its motion drew across the sky, and eventually dropped out of sight onto the faraway prospect of the wall.

Even at this range, the sound of its impact could be plainly heard; a solid, painful thump, a chunky noise that promised damage, like the sound of a rider's bare head hitting the ground after he's fallen from a moving horse. It was easy to imagine the force of its blow, because when the city's stones landed they made the ground shake; watching them coming down was horribly fascinating, seeing them grow in the air, trying to guess which way they'd fall, trying to figure out their looped and irregular trajectories, sometimes guessing right, sometimes not. Temrai watched one man watching a falling stone; he ran from where he'd been standing, stopped, ran back, ran forwards, his head right back and his eyes fixed on the swelling dot; stopped, waited, ran back, waited, at the last moment jinked sideways; managed to get it completely wrong, so that the stone landed directly on top of him, obliterating him so thoroughly that it was hard to believe he'd ever been there.

The arm snapped on one of the trebuchets, its crack a sharp and deafening noise; cheated of its momentum the sling flopped down, sweeping horribly through the engineers who were working the machine. Nobody killed, but arms and legs and ribs broken like the branches of a dead tree, the sort that give way suddenly when you put your weight on them. Then there were people running forward, hauling and scrabbling at the stone; screams from the men pinned down by it – *no, stop! You're rolling it the wrong way! You're crushing me, get it off me* – and then more men running in, getting in the way of the first rescue party.

A stone lands ten feet or so away from them; it hits a previous shot and splinters, flinging sharp edges of stone that slash skin and jar bone. And as more people run up to help, an engineer with red-raw hands and hair soaking wet waves his arms, yells, 'Get these people away from here!': The rescuers stand confused, not knowing what to do. Someone yells, *Look out, coming in!* and before they have time to move a stone whistles down, pitches fifteen feet away from them, neatly nipping off the foot of the man

who'd shouted the warning. He stares down, too surprised
to speak; tries to move, falls over. And all the time Temrai
watches, doesn't move, says nothing.

On the wall, it was a nightmare of shouting, blood and stone
dust. There were large gaps in the walkway, a mangled
trebuchet dangled by its counterweight, draped over the
battlements while the frame hung and swayed in the air.
Men stepped over bodies and hopped over gaps, scrambled
to untangle ropes and knock back wedges shaken loose by
the vibrations of discharge, lost their grip on levers and
spanners that fell over the parapet. Engine-masters fought
with tongs and hammers to straighten bent loosing-hooks,
captains blocked out the noise and movement as they
concentrated on the witness-marks, or yelled at their men
to realign an engine that had shifted from its place.

Engineer Garantzes was down on his knees, hacking at a
tangled rope with a belt dagger far too flimsy for the job,
while Loredan went from engine to engine, trying to make
himself useful and getting in the way. He saw men nudging
corpses off the walkway with their feet to make a little
room, engineers shouting and cursing at the untrained men
who had taken the place of the dead men who'd known
what they were doing. He heard screams from down below,
as a winch rope broke and a two hundredweight stone fell
back on the hauling team, watched another man step out of
his shoe and observe helplessly as it fell off the walkway,
then put his bare foot down on the jagged stone of the
splintered parapet, not looking down as it sliced his skin like
a knife, all his attention on a twisted ratchet iron he was
trying to replace while his team held back the impossible
bulk of the counterweight; if they let go or the rope broke,
his hand would be chopped fine by the spinning ratchet, or
the spanner would fly up and go into his ribs like an arrow.

It's because I can't see the enemy, he told himself. And it
probably looks far worse than it really is.

This isn't working. We're going to lose if this goes on.
Do something.

A stone had clipped away the first six steps of the stairway, and he had to sit and slide down on his backside to get to sound footing. There were wounded men on the stairs, men who'd managed to crawl this far and reckoned that that would have to do. He stepped over them, an awkwardly placed heel landing on an outstretched hand; no time to apologise or even look back. He made it to the bottom of the stairs and walked quickly – mustn't be seen to run – up the street and into the town.

It was as if there was a line drawn across the road; the war stops here. On the other side of the line, people were shopping, sitting in their doorways making things (a shoemaker cutting leather, looking up, staring at the bloodstained, dusty, dirty man in armour walking past his door) as if there was no small hell a few hundred yards away; as if all you had to do was leave, turn your back, no longer be a part of it.

Quite.

He walked into the council chamber and headed straight for the Prefect, who was sitting under the window with a pile of documents spread out in front of him. He looked up – how spotlessly clean his white gown looks by comparison – and started to say something.

'We need to send out a sortie,' Loredan said. 'We can use a ship, sail out of the harbour as far as the chain, put the men and horses ashore on the west bank. They'll have rafts on the river; we can grab a couple of those upstream, get across and come up on them from behind the cover of the hills. So long as we get their engineers, the raiding party's expendable.'

The Prefect shook his head. 'Out of the question,' he said. 'No sorties, no hand-to-hand fighting. We've all agreed.'

Loredan took a deep breath. 'We're being smashed to pieces on the east bastion,' he said. 'And if we lose that, we lose the three-hundred-yard zone. I need that sortie.'

The Prefect shrugged. 'I had my doubts about the bastions from the start,' he said. 'Now, obviously, they aren't viable. We'll have to write the experiment off as impractical and go back to the original plan of defence in depth on the walls.'

Loredan managed to control his temper. 'If we lose the zone,' he said, 'they'll be able to bring up their minor engines, and then they'll drive us off the old wall as well. And we'll be in bowshot, and they've got more archers and bows that shoot further. If we ride down their trebuchet crews we'll slow their rate of fire, give ourselves a chance to sort out the mess up there on the bastion; we'll be able to match them and the zone'll be safe. Please, I need that time.'

The Prefect thought for a moment. 'How many men would you need?'

'A hundred, a hundred and fifty. It'd be speed and surprise rather than numbers; the whole bloody clan's out there watching the show from the edge of the zone.'

'And you think you can manage to get in position without being seen? Won't they see your men landing and wonder what they're up to? And surely they've got detachments stationed deep to guard the rafts.'

Loredan shrugged. 'Possibly,' he said. 'Personally, I rate the chances of rolling them up like a carpet and getting the boys back into the city by dinner time as very slender indeed. But unless you want to give Temrai control of the wall by nightfall, we're going to have to try something. If you've got a better idea, I'd love to hear it.'

'There's the mercenary horse-archers,' said a voice behind Loredan's head; Liras Fanedrin, something or other high up in the Office of Establishments. Loredan still wasn't quite sure what exactly it was that the Office of Establishments actually did. 'They're expendable, and it sounds like their sort of work.'

Loredan shook his head. 'Mercenaries don't do suicide missions,' he said. 'It'll have to be city troops.'

The Prefect looked annoyed. 'Oh, very well,' he sighed. 'Liras, your department. What about the ship?'

'Different department.' Fanedrin shook his head. 'Requisitioning ships is Office of Supply, not us,' he replied. 'Get

Teo Oliefro onto it. I think I saw him around here a moment ago.' He turned to Loredan, and said, 'Any ideas about who's going to command? You'll want someone good, but not that good.'

Loredan was about to object; he'd assumed he'd be leading the force himself, since he was in charge. It hadn't occurred to him to send somebody else.

'Piras Muzin,' he said. 'He'll do what he's told, and he hasn't got the imagination to realise he won't be coming back.'

Expendable – yes, like advocates in the lawcourts. If it was Muzin or me, out there in the centre, I wouldn't hesitate for a moment. And besides, if I went I'd probably lose my nerve and run away.

'Good choice,' said Fanedrin. 'You'd better brief him. We should be ready to go within the hour.'

Fanedrin and the Prefect went away, and Loredan collapsed into the window seat. Suddenly he felt very tired, and he didn't want to have to go back up on the wall, where the stones came crashing down and everything seemed to be going wrong. It would be nice to stay here for a while; much easier to think things through clearly in peace and quiet, and there wasn't anything useful for him to do up there. And as for Piras Muzin – well, people died every day, and he couldn't be held accountable for that. A little time; patch up the bastion, clear away the mess, replace the smashed engines, *make it so we can start again from the beginning.*

His head was splitting; noise and dust and fear and exertion. A drink would be a good idea. A drink would *not* be a good idea. Dangerous enough up on that wall without a spinning head. He stood up while he still could and walked slowly to the bridgehouse, where he could watch the fun.

Piras Muzin, a man Loredan had spoken to six or seven times, handled things very well. He'd been in charge of a wing of the cavalry during the mess upriver; he'd shepherded his people through the gap in the line that Loredan had opened, gone on to help relieve the ambush at the upper ford, stayed with it through the retreat and the return to the city. He'd have made a reasonable regular officer, something near the bottom of the chain of command in Maxen's army.

From the bridgehouse it looked rather more like a game, and Loredan kept himself amused while he was waiting by keeping score. The advantage was still with Temrai, but his rate of fire had slowed down; hard to tell at this distance, but his engineers looked as if they were having trouble with the engines shaking themselves to bits after so much continuous use. The city engines were keeping up a better, steadier rate, but only one in fifteen shots was having any effect. The other side scored about one hit in twenty, but a good third of their shots were hitting the bastion there or thereabouts, and even the clean misses were mostly clearing the wall. Odd, to be a spectator for a change; he could see how people got to like watching. He wondered if any of the other men on the tower with him would be interested in a small bet.

When the time came, the cavalry action was short and not particularly spectacular. Muzin did exactly as he'd been told; his men came out from behind the cover of the hills and rode through the engineers, cutting and slashing downwards from the saddle at men who hadn't been expecting anything of the sort, working as quickly and efficiently as farm workers harvesting a crop. At least half of them stayed at it until Temrai's horsemen reached them; the rest tried to get out, but there wasn't time. Although it was largely irrelevant and not part of the mission, they put up a fine show against the plainsmen before they were overwhelmed. It was all in the very finest traditions of the service.

And, once the mess had been sorted out, the mule-trains came and pulled the trebuchets out of the zone. Of the thirty-five enemy engines that had been used, eighteen were still working or capable of being repaired. Looking across at the bastion, Loredan could see nine catapult arms silhouetted against the sky; nine out of sixteen, not so bad after all. Of course, tomorrow would be another day.

Loredan yawned and stretched; no rest for him tonight, not until the bastion had been patched up, as far as that was possible, and new engines hauled up to replace the losses. He'd already decided where to get the replacement engines from; four from the western bastion, one from the gatehouse, and two straight from the arsenal with the pitch still wet. He would have to organise teams to recover as many of the enemy's stones as were still fit for use; chances were that the day had produced a net profit as far as ammunition was concerned. The main problem would be trained engineers; he was going to have to strip the rest of the defences, certainly most of the western side, if he wanted to be sure of having enough men on hand to replace tomorrow's losses without slowing up the rate of fire. On the other hand, Temrai would be facing the same problem.

By and large, then, an evenly balanced day; nothing significant gained by either side, the whole job to do over again.

Ah, well. At least we didn't make complete fools of ourselves.

He'd have liked to have stayed longer, high up and out of it all, but a messenger from Garantzes summoned him back to the bastion – problems with structural damage requiring a policy decision. He walked slowly and found climbing the stairs a great effort. When he was two-thirds of the way up, he noticed a long slit across the left knee of his trousers, surrounded by a wide bloodstain. He paused to examine the wound, which he hadn't noticed until now. It was a long, deep cut, quite clean and made by something extremely sharp, probably a splinter of stone. It must have happened several hours previously because the blood was dry on his skin, just starting to flake off. He made a mental note to deal with it later, if he got the chance.

'Not good,' Garantzes reported. 'This whole section of the wall's taken one hell of a pounding, gods alone know what's holding it up. We can shore it with beams and try and get some mortar in, but it really wants pulling down and doing again.'

'Fine,' Loredan said wearily. 'And maybe you could ask the enemy to hold the ladder for you while you're doing it.'

Garantzes didn't think that was particularly funny. 'All I can think of,' he said, 'would be to tear down some other bit of wall and use the blocks to build an inner wall to line this one with, give it something to lean against. It'd take time, of course, but it'd be a damn sight quicker than getting new blocks cut, even if we've got that much raw stone in the city. If we put it in dry-stone it'd save time, and we can use the trebuchet cranes to do the hauling. If we stuck with it day and night and had enough manpower, I could do a reasonable job in a couple of weeks.'

Loredan shook his head. 'Think about it,' he said. 'My guess is they'll try and move their engines back into the zone during the night so they can start the barrage again at first light. That's how long you've got.'

'Impossible. In that case, my advice to you is to get all these engines shifted off here tonight; that way, when the bastion goes down tomorrow it won't take the best of our artillery with it.'

So it had all been for nothing; the heroic cavalry charge, Piras Muzin laying down his life for his city, all the effort involved in building the bastions in the first place. Now he was going to give the order to take down the engines they'd just hoisted up and put them back on the old wall, abandoning the advantage of the three-hundred-yard zone and inviting the enemy to come in close enough to let their archers sweep the defenders from the walls. As simply done as that. 'All right,' he said.

'Pity,' Garantzes said thoughtfully. 'Now, if we'd had a series of these bastions all along the wall it'd have been a damn good idea. Just one, and all we did was give them a single target to aim at.'

Removing the engines without bringing the wall down took most of the night. One of Garantzes' men had his leg crushed – he'd shouted, 'Hold it!' to the people feeding out the rope, but they hadn't heard him – and another put his foot on a bit of wall that wasn't there any longer and broke an arm and several ribs. When the sun rose, it revealed a line of trebuchets just inside the three-hundred-yard zone, their arms back and their slings loaded.

Temrai gave the word, and the line advanced.

Thanks to his census, Temrai knew how many men walked with him towards the city; three thousand, the best archers in the clan, each man carrying two quivers of twenty arrows each. A hundred and twenty thousand arrows (green wood, fletched with duck) which his men ought to be able to loose off in under ten minutes. Temrai had once heard a friend of his mother's complaining about preparing a special meal to celebrate someone's birthday; a day and a half she was going to have to spend getting everything ready and it'd all be eaten in an hour or so, all that time and trouble for something that'd be all gone so quickly and then forgotten.

Overhead, the latest volley from his trebuchets flew like a flock of geese, trailing fleeting shadows behind them that raced along the ground, showing them where they had to go. A little to the rear of the screen of archers were the mule-trains, hauling the torsion engines. Very soon, the batteries on the wall would open up, and this time he wouldn't be watching from a safe distance.

He glanced up at the clouds, trying to read them. Rain would complicate things horribly; wet bowstrings, engines bogged down, torches refusing to light, leather armour absorbing water and swelling, water running down inside the armour and making every man in the line feel wretched, rain beating into the eyes of the archers as they lifted their heads to take aim. The clouds were low, fat and grey; as soon as they reached the hills, there was a fair chance they'd let go and drench everything.

He was still looking up when the first stone came swinging down. He watched it, noticing how its trajectory decayed and its descent steepened. Clean miss, twenty yards or so in front. Ranging shot.

Nearly there now; he could make out details of the men on the walls he hadn't seen before. Theoretically they had an advantage in range because they'd be shooting down, but Temrai knew the city bows; self longbows cut from a single stave of wood, as opposed to the short, heavily recurved composite bows of the clan. In practice, their advantage of angle was more or less exactly cancelled out by his advantage of superior construction, just as the fact that the city people habitually used arrows that were too stiff to be accurate was offset by his disadvantage of having to make his shafts out of unseasoned wood, feathered with inadequate fletchings. It was as if someone was deliberately trying to even up the odds – we have more men, they have cover and better armour; we have the sun in our eyes, they have the wind against them; we're in the right, they're defending their homes and families. A very carefully designed, precisely manufactured war this was turning out to be.

It didn't take the city artillery long to find the range. The first accurately sighted volley gouged out gaps all along the line, obvious as footprints in clean snow. Temrai called a halt and gave the orders; nock arrows, draw, take aim, loose, the cycle repeating smoothly and without pause. He shot in time with his own commands, hoping he'd judged the elevation correctly – at maximum range, raise the arrowhead an inch or so over the target and in line, not aiming off to the side as you have to do at shorter ranges.

The physical effort of the work was absorbing, enough to take his mind off what was actually happening. At the moment of the draw, push with the left hand against the bow handle, pull back the string with the right, until the shoulder blades feel as if they're about to touch behind your back. Head still; wait for the touch of the string against your nose and lip, the feel of your hand under the point of your chin. On the command *loose*, take away the strength that curls the fingers of the right hand, so that the string can travel easily and without interference. After the shot, hold your position for a heartbeat before letting your right hand drop onto the quiver and feel for the nock of the next arrow. Above all, look at the target and not the bow, keep your eyes fixed on the faraway objective, the distant spot where your work and effort will have its effect.

Away there, on the wall, the arrows would be falling like rain, anonymous and impersonal, not like the intimate business of hacking flesh close in with an edged weapon. Back here at the two-hundred-yard line, there was still a deceptive sense of taking part in a great game, a staged event, with the wall as combined target and audience. Funeral games; what fun, to be able to watch one's own.

One quiver empty already; Temrai looked round and saw the runners hurrying up, shuffling like hedgehogs under a great burden of prickly bristles. Another twenty thousand arrows or so; enough to keep the war going for a whole minute.

Participants and spectators; Temrai was reminded of the lawcourts in the city. He'd been to see a couple of cases, sitting so far back he couldn't even make out the faces of the advocates, and it had seemed to him a remarkable way to do business in a city that otherwise seemed to have worked things out so well. On the other hand, there's nothing to beat trial by combat for an unarguable result.

Beside him, a man dropped his bow and pitched forward onto his knees, an arrowshaft standing out of the right side of his chest. Lung-shot; he was fighting for breath, wondering why he was inhaling but still choking. He turned to Temrai, the subject to the lord, and opened his mouth, but nothing came out except blood. Before Temrai could say anything he flopped down on his face, the arrow making him lie slightly askew. Then someone handed Temrai a bunch of arrows, and he stuffed them awkwardly into his quiver, the heads of the new arrows catching in the fletchings of the old.

Gods alone know if we're doing any good. One minute the wall looks empty, the next it's bobbing with heads. His right arm and back were beginning to ache, and every time he loosed the string it slapped his left forearm in exactly the same place, making him wince. Steady work; before he knew it his quiver was empty, and he left his place to go forward and pick up some of the other side's arrows (longer and stiffer than ours, fletched with goose and peacock, tipped with narrow triangular heads that punched through armour with the maximum efficiency). While he was bending down, a stone landed on the exact spot he'd been occupying. He felt rain spotting the back of his hand.

'That's all we need,' groaned Teofil Leutzes, captain of the archers of the east wall. 'Strings soggy, fletchings wet, and these bows break for a pastime in the damp.' He beckoned to a man on his left. 'Send runners down the line, tell 'em to wax their strings quick, before it starts pissing down. Not that they will, of course,' he added. 'All they want to do is shoot off all my arrows as quick as they can and get their heads down.'

Soon the rain was falling in fat splodges, dripping off the back edges of helmets down the necks of the archers, making their leather gloves sticky and the bow handles slippery. Loredan pulled his hood up over his helmet and ducked inside the frame of an engine. Rain's wet in war as well as peace, and only a fool stands out in it unless he's got to.

It was going abysmally. Basically the same problem as before; the enemy were spread out, his men were packed together. The cover of the battlements was doing no good at all, since the arrows were coming in from above, slanting in like rain on a windy day. Some of the men had two or three shafts sticking out of their armour, where the clan's broad-bladed arrowheads had cut through the chainmail but hadn't made it through the padded jerkin underneath; they were still shooting, too preoccupied to spare the time to wrestle the arrows loose. The engines were letting fly at longer and longer intervals, as more and more engineers were hit and their places were taken by untrained men.

And now the rain; too wet to keep a torch burning. The walkway was slippery, slowing up the runners who were supposed to be handing out fresh supplies of arrows. The winches that raised the barrels of arrows up to the tower were running slow as well; too easy for a rope to slip through wet fingers and let a heavy barrel drop on the winding crew. Worst of all, there was nothing he could think of that might improve matters; it was a slow, remote kind of warfare that couldn't be hustled or bounced into victory by acts of flamboyant valour. Just hard, gruelling work in the rain. For this, Loredan reflected, he might just as well have stayed home on the farm.

'They're bringing something else up now,' sang a voice above his head; some young enthusiast who'd scrabbled his way up onto the crossbar of a disabled engine to get a better view. He'd been there a while. The arrows seemed to avoid him, like fastidious cats who won't sit on the knees of strangers. 'I can't see what it is, but it's big and bulky; they've got about thirty mules hitched to it.'

'You want to get down from there,' Loredan replied. 'You're asking for trouble. We'll see whatever it is soon enough without you risking your neck.'

'All right, I'll be down in a minute. I think it may be some sort of tower, on its side. Or a bridge, possibly. A bridge'd make more sense than a tower.'

Ah, yes, the last problem; how were they planning to get across the river?

The rain had set in for the day. It was that hard deliberate rain that sends men running down the street with their coats pulled up over their heads, or strands them in doorways or under trees. Already the ground underfoot was the clinging consistency of wet dough, making each step an effort.

On the lower slopes of the hill that overlooked the bridgehouse, Temrai huddled under a quickly improvised hide canopy. He was holding the piece of parchment on which he'd sketched out a plan of what was going to happen next, but the rain had long since washed the charcoal away, leaving him with a sodden piece of thin leather that was no use for anything. No matter; he knew what he was doing.

Behind him, the river above the fork was full of rafts; a hundred and twenty-six of them, each one twelve feet long by ten feet wide. He raised his arm, and the raftmen started to pole forward, heading for the chain stretched across the mouth of the river fork.

It'd be nice if this could be made to work. Well, we'll soon see.

From where he was sitting he had what should have been a good view of the engagement below the walls, but there was so much rain in the air that he could only see shapes and vague colours instead of precise details of machines and men. Still, by all accounts it seemed to be going well. He now had just over ten thousand archers drawn up under the wall, and the return fire from the city was feeble and sporadic. Nearly all of the city engines had stopped shooting, while his own catapults and trebuchets were scientifically pounding away at a hundred-yard section of the wall that overlooked the narrowest point of the river. Unlike the bastion they'd been engaged with yesterday (which was recent work, badly designed and shoddily built), the main wall was too solid and massive to breach with artillery; but his engineers were concentrating on battering the ramparts and battlements, breaking up the towers and chipping off the castellations that his men would otherwise have had to scramble over when the moment came.

'All right,' he said, and beckoned one of the runners who were sitting wretchedly half-under the small canopy. The poor lad was soaked to the skin and water was running in clear streams down his face, like tears. 'Get over there and tell them to lower the chain, quick as you can. Then get back up here.'

The young man nodded and set off, skidding and sliding as he tried to run down the muddy slope. *Gods, he'll slip and break his neck, and we'll be held up even more.* He shouted after the lad, 'Slow down, look where you're going,' but he was already too far away to hear.

* * *

'They're lowering the chain!' yelled the spectator above Loredan's head, still miraculously unkilled and as enthusiastic as ever. For a moment or so, Loredan couldn't think what he was talking about – chain? What chain? Oh, *that* chain.

Dear gods, they were lowering the chain, and that's how they're going to get across the river.

They must be out of their minds.

Please ...

He looked round for someone to carry a message, but they were all busy; shooting arrows, squeezing themselves under narrow ledges of wood and stone to get out of the arrow-rain, falling and dying. Loredan was just about to go himself when he thought, yes.

'You,' he said, 'get down from there. I need you to take a message.'

'Coming,' the boy replied. 'I'll just ...' And then a body flopped down a couple of inches from Loredan's feet, an arrowshaft broken off in its chest. *Damn*, he thought.

Someone scuttled across to see to the fallen man. Loredan grabbed at him as he went past.

'That one's dead,' he said. 'Carry a message to the harbour. I need marines in small boats – small, mind, they've got to be able to get along the west river past the bastion – to take out rafts coming downstream. Top priority. Anybody makes trouble, smash their teeth in. Got that?'

The man stared at him, shook his head. 'I can't go,' he said. 'I'm an engineer, not a runner.'

'Get moving or I'll sling you over the wall.'

The man hesitated a moment longer, then ducked away and slithered/ran to the stairs. He had to climb over broken timber and a pile of fallen masonry to get there; the tower overlooking the stairs had taken several hits too many and was falling apart, littering blocks and lumps of shattered mortar all over the walkway.

They must be out of their minds. But so far, everything they'd tried had worked, and everything he'd tried had been a disaster, so who was he to criticise?

The unwilling messenger must have done his job well, because four flat barges, oystermen by the look of them, appeared from behind the western bastion and were suddenly up against the jostling mass of rafts, spilling out men like a jar of grain dropped on a hard floor. Temrai saw them and swore, immediately aware of his error – somehow he'd assumed that once he'd set up the chain, the threat from the harbour would cease to count for anything. In his mind's eye there would be a smooth transition, from a chain stretched across the fork to a chain stretched from the foot of the bridgehouse to the ruins of the causeway. He hadn't imagined they could get boats ready and out so fast.

There was one raft that was bigger than all the others, thirty feet long and solidly built out of timbers he'd been at great pains to find. Mounted on it was a tall cradle of A-frames, from which hung the huge battering ram on which so much was going to depend. A lot of work had gone into that raft; calculating the height the ram would have to be so that it'd be level with the gates rather than the stonework of the drawbridge causeway, making and fitting the hide-covered shields that protected the ram-workers top and sides from arrows and stones, making the thing solid enough to work the ram from, yet not so unwieldy that it couldn't be moved.

Now all he could do was watch while enemy soldiers swarmed all over it, like ants on uncovered food. They had killed the ram-workers already; now they were breaking up the raft, cutting the cables that held it together, cutting the ropes that held the ram, poling the poor, helpless thing away from the rest of the rafts into open water, so Temrai's men couldn't try and stop them. Very soon it began to come apart. Two of the barges collected the soldiers from the wreckage and the water, while the other two landed their men by the ruins of the land-side causeway. Nothing anybody could do to stop them; by the time his men got there, the landing party had cut the cables that held the chain, and that beautiful, brilliant artefact slid down into the water and was lost for ever.

There were more boats on the way, rounding the western bastion, their decks lined with men. Temrai sent another runner; get the reserves from the camp, I want those boats cleared, don't care what it costs. Everything was suddenly going wrong, all because of one mistake, like a woodpile collapsing when one log is pulled out from the base.

As the raft sank, Teoblept Iuven looked round and saw he had nowhere to go. He'd stayed to make sure, insisting on cutting the last bond himself; since he'd assumed, somehow, that they'd never pull it off and they were all going to die, it had seemed like a waste of time and energy to work out an escape route. He stood balanced on one bobbing log like an acrobat, feeling rather foolish, the victim of his own success.

He'd broken his sword cutting the last few twists of cable; the ancient and incredibly valuable Fascanum that'd been in his family since the human species began had never been intended for chopping wood and slitting string (we have people who do that sort of thing for us) and he'd had to saw through the last half-inch with the splintered end. He swore, drew back his arm to throw it in the river, changed his mind.

There were men on the riverbank now, enemy archers. They'd been running, slipping and sliding and falling over in the mud. As they stopped to draw their bows and take aim, he could see them fumbling, clumsy and cack-handed in the wet. It was, he decided, high time he wasn't here. Although there was precious little chance of his being able to swim more than a yard or so in all this ironmongery he was wearing, it was better to drown than stay put and get shot. Presumably.

He positioned himself for a graceful dive off the log and in doing so lost his footing and fell face first into the river. Instinctively he still held onto the broken sword, until the weight of his armour began pulling him down faster than he could compensate for by kicking and thrashing with his feet. The river came up over his face before he had a chance to close his mouth.

So ended his first command, which he was sure he'd only been given because he was a Iuven and because he'd been a pupil at the fencing school run by the man who was now the Commander-in-Chief, Bardas Loredan; no experience, no natural ability, no innate qualities of leadership to justify putting him in charge of such an important mission. He'd done the job, though, so perhaps they'd chosen the right man after all.

As his head ducked under the water for the second time, it occurred to him that he might improve his situation if he took the bloody armour off. This he managed to do, just about; the standard city mailshirt had its buckles at the side, where a man could reach them, but a nobleman has a squire to help him on with his armour, so his buckles were up the back. When his head bobbed up for the fourth time, an arrow splashed into the water no more than twelve inches from his nose; he took the hint and a deep breath and went under again, kicked and pawed at the water until he was facing west (he hoped) and struck out for the shore.

When he couldn't hold his breath any longer, he pushed upwards and burst back into the light and air, unable to think about anything except the pains in his chest and the desperate need to breathe. Something slapped against his arm; he turned his head and saw an outstretched hand, the side of a boat. Amazing; he was being rescued.

A thick-set, middle-aged man with wisps of grey hair plastered to the side of his head by the rain grabbed his wrist and pulled, nearly jerking his arm out of its socket. With his other hand Iuven clawed at the side of the boat, but there wasn't anything to hold onto. 'It's all right,' the man shouted, 'I've got you.' And then something happened, and Teoblept Iuven found he was having difficulty breathing, which didn't make sense now that he was out of the water. His arm encountered some obstruction; it reminded him of walking in a wood, with branches and briars getting in the way. There was an arrow sticking out of him. Oh, he thought. Then he closed his eyes and died.

A qualified success, Loredan said to himself, as he watched the six or so remaining boats turn back; we've sunk the battering ram and got rid of the chain – and killed a lot of people, of course, though there's plenty more where they came from. We haven't managed to do anything about the main flotilla of rafts, but there's other things we can do about them. In theory, at least.

Best of all, though, the rain was slowing up. At this time of year it seldom rains for more than an hour or so—

(Only an hour or so? I feel like I've been here all my life. Did I have a life before all this started? I assume I must have done, or I'd be too young to be a general.)

—And as soon as it stopped raining, he could spring his surprise, the one thing he still had in reserve that could really make a difference.

Bad cramp in his legs from crouching for too long, and there were pools of bloodstained rainwater all around. He extracted himself from the shelter of the catapult frame, stepped over the body of his dead observer, and made his way to the head of the stairs.

Damn.

He looked round, and saw Garantzes. The engineer was sitting on the frame of an engine, his back to the uprights; not dead, as Loredan first assumed, but fast asleep.

'Wake up.'

'Huh?' Garantzes' eyes jerked open. 'What's …?'

'The chain,' Loredan said. 'Get the chain up while there's still time. If they're going to use those rafts to stand scaling ladders on—'

Garantzes shook his head. 'Waste of time,' he said. 'They've beaten the shit out of this part of the wall, I don't suppose there's more than a dozen posts still in there. There's nothing to hang the chain from. Sorry.'

'Oh, hell.' Loredan scowled. 'Well, can't you improvise something? Get some timbers and run them out over the battlements? We've got the bloody chain, we might as well use it.'

The engineer took a deep breath as if to argue, then nodded. 'See what I can do,' he said. 'Gods know, there's enough bits of timber lying about the place we can use, with all these bust engines; it's really just a question of how we can fix them to the walkway so they won't come away. Leave it with me, we'll sort something out.'

'Good.' Loredan left him and scrambled over the wreckage and rubble to the stairway. 'And get these stairs clear,' he called back, though he doubted very much whether Garantzes had heard him.

Cramp all gone now, but *very* bad headache. Never mind; I'll feel dreadful later, when I've got time.

It had stopped raining.

The rafts nuzzled and bumped each other like sheep crowded together in a dipping pen. Fortunately, there was nobody much left on the wall to interfere with the raft crews from above; they had enough trouble as it was coping with the innate malignity of inanimate objects without any of their fellow humans deliberately trying to make things worse.

The idea was good and simple. Fix a series of strong cables to the masonry of the wall, and stretch them across to the riverbank opposite. Attach the rafts to these cables back and front, and to each other at the sides. The result would be an artificial floor bobbing on top of the water on which the scaling ladders could stand, the bottoms of their legs fitting into prefabricated sockets. Once the ladders were in the sockets and held fast at the base by steel pins, the ladders could be walked upright and placed against the wall.

It was a good idea. It might work. It wasn't necessarily doomed to failure.

It had worked more or less when they'd rehearsed it in relative peace and quiet upstream. They'd found a place where the river passed between two sandstone cliffs, where they'd been able to practise hammering tethering pins into the rock, drawing the line taut, herding the rafts together and securing the fastenings. They'd reached the stage, they reckoned, when they could do it all blindfold.

Gazing at the confused scrum of rafts and their scampering crews, Temrai wondered if that was where they were going wrong; no blindfolds. Wherever he looked there were men tangling ropes, dropping tools in the water, breaking or letting go of poles, falling in the river and having to be fished out again. *Thank the gods we cleared the wall*, he muttered to himself. *If we had defenders dropping rocks on us, we'd have no hope at all.*

He'd pulled the cordon of archers in, right up to the riverbank, no more than a hundred yards or so from the wall; at this range and given enough arrows, they ought to be able to pick off individual targets, should the need arise. He'd stood down the engineers, however; there wasn't anything the engines could do that the archers couldn't, and the last thing he needed was for a couple of hundredweight stones to fall short and sink any rafts. The odd arrow bouncing off the stonework and falling among the raft crews was bad enough.

Just when he was considering pulling the rafts out and starting all over again the next day, the first ladder sat up, spindly and unsteady as a newly born foal, and slumped forward into place. Almost immediately it was pushed away; it hung in the air for what seemed like a very long, drawn-out half-second, then toppled magnificently backwards and crashed onto the riverbank, smashing itself to pieces as it landed. But almost before it had completed its fall, the next ladder was up and then the one beside it; then two more, standing perpendicular as the previous pair came to rest against the chain that ran round the top of the wall.

A nice idea, the chain, but poorly executed. The improvised posts it was slung from simply couldn't take the strain; they snapped, bent sideways or folded down under the weight, merely slowing the ladders up and preventing them from hitting the parapet dangerously hard. The climbing parties were standing by, ready to swarm up the ladders and meet the enemy face-to-face inside their own city for the first time. It was—

It wasn't over yet.

Loredan grunted, staggering a little under the weight of a smooth-sided earthenware jar. There wasn't anything much to grab hold of, making it difficult to hold onto. Embarrassing if he were to drop it ...

Many years ago he'd read in a book about a liquid compound of sulphur, asphalt and naphtha which was supposed to catch fire easily and stay alight, even (so the book claimed) on water. It could be set alight and poured from the walls of a city, loaded into pottery jars, lit and shot from catapults so that when the jar landed it shattered, spraying fire in all directions; it could even be forced out in a jet from the nozzle of a specially designed bellows, catching fire from a torch or a red-hot billet of iron fixed in a holder in front of the nozzle. Bolts of cloth could be dipped in the stuff and wrapped round hand-sized stones, which were then piled in the spoon of a catapult arm, lit and sent flying in a wide and lethal pattern, enough to set light to a whole enemy encampment. Once something was covered in the stuff, water wouldn't put it out; stamping on it would simply set your feet on fire, smothering it with a cloth would set the cloth alight. Until all the liquid had burnt itself away, nothing could be done about it.

The book went on to offer suggestions for the safe handling of the compound; after being mixed, it should be stored in stone jars covered with freshly scraped rawhides, and the men who handled it should have their clothes and gloves impregnated with talc; to ignite it, use a torch on the end of a very long pole, and stand well back ...

Also contained in the book were clear and concise instructions as to how to annihilate enemy armies by smashing clay models of them with a mallet; how to create panic by blotting out the sun by means of incantations; how to supplement your own depleted army by bringing the recently dead back to life using secret charms and arrowroot. It was not considered to be required reading for aspiring young officers, and was generally only taken down from its shelf by young novices who'd heard there were pictures of naked women in one of the later chapters.

Nevertheless, once he'd found out what naphtha was and where it could be bought, he'd set a team of engineers to experiment with mixing the stuff, trying different quantities and purities of ingredients. The results had been startling; so much so that he was tempted to try and find the book again and have a go at some of its other recommendations.

Throwing the stuff from catapults had turned out to be impractical. The jars had an alarming tendency to shatter at the moment of release, setting fire to the engine and showering its crew with blazing potsherds. With this in mind, he hadn't even tested the small stones wrapped in impregnated cloth. Instead, he'd ordered the Quartermaster to buy up all the raw materials his department could lay its hands on, and commissioned the potters to produce tall thin-walled jars with high, narrow necks that could be stuffed with rag and set on fire; one of which he was now frantically trying to keep hold of while an engineer touched a lighted torch to its neck.

'Ready,' the engineer said, as the rag flared up and started to burn ferociously a few inches away from his face. Cursing, Loredan hoisted the jar up onto the battlement, held it out into space and let go.

'Next,' he said.

Suddenly, the crew of one of the rafts seemed to be wearing fire.

From head to foot they were alight, like torches. Screaming, they barged into each other, slipped up, fell over, scrambled to their feet, still burning. Everything they touched caught fire, or was already alight. Some were consumed almost at once, dropping as black man-shaped cinders into the flames that danced on the deck of the raft. Others launched themselves into the water, went under and came up still burning. A few were still alive as they scrabbled onto the adjacent rafts, whose crews jabbed at them with spears and fended them off with raft poles, only to find that the fire had spread and was now flaring up around their feet. Meanwhile, more pots were being dropped from the walls; as they smashed they spread more fire, splashing the stuff everywhere so that the surface of the water was covered in hissing flames.

The ladders caught fire and toppled back onto the men below; the crews of the rafts that weren't alight yet were furiously hacking at the cables, trying to cut the bonds that held the manmade island together and pole away before the fire reached them. Flames licked up the walls, almost reaching as high as the battlements. Swirling clouds of black smoke rose and hovered over the scene, so that from his place on the high ground Temrai could only catch intermittent glimpses of fire and movement to help him interpret the sounds that were coming from the river, the screams and shouts and crashes.

It was like some visible plague spreading uncontrollably, and the men on the bank kept the raft crews from coming ashore, afraid that the contagion would spread. Men were diving off the rafts, swimming a few yards underwater and coming up to find their heads emerging through a horizontal curtain of fire that kindled their wet hair and dripped down their faces, scorching out their eyes and being sucked into their lungs as they panted for air. Some of the archers had started shooting at the rafts, either to put the burning men out of their misery or to stop them coming ashore. More pots were falling, although the rafts they fell on were already on fire; when these shattered, all their contents lit up at once, creating great gusts of swelling, billowing flame that rose high in the air. Steam rose and met the clouds of smoke, until a translucent curtain closed the spectacle off like the flap of a tent.

Many things crossed Temrai's mind as he watched; among them the thought that someone in the city had read the same book he had, and the slight consolation that the reserve secret weapon he hadn't yet had time to develop properly could, quite evidently, be made to work.

CHAPTER SIXTEEN

'Right,' said Loredan, wiping talc from his hands, 'that'll do. Get the rest of that stuff back to the stores, and for gods' sakes be careful with it. You two, casualty lists. You and you, inventory of engines still operational or capable of being repaired. You, organise clean-up and get these dead people out of here. Garantzes—' He paused. 'Anybody seen Garantzes? Last time I saw him—'

Someone made a gesture, a finger across his throat. Loredan scowled.

'Oh,' he said. No time now to ask how it'd happened, whether he died bravely in defence of his city or just lost his balance and fell off the wall; the engineer would still be dead later on, and he could deal with it then. 'In that case, where's Faneron Boutzes? Still alive? Good, because you're now Chief Engineer. I want a report of structural damage to the walls and how soon it can be patched up. If anyone wants me, I'll be in Council.'

Miraculously, someone had found time to clear the head of the stairs, and he managed to get down them without falling over. If he could somehow persuade his feet to carry him up the hill and through the second-city gate to the chapter house, he'd reward them by sitting down. It had been one of those days.

We came close, but we're still here. Didn't make fools of ourselves. And tomorrow is another day.

It was a very strange feeling to walk through the city in the middle of the afternoon and see nobody in the streets. Where were they all? There were lots of houses in the lower city of Perimadeia, but somehow Loredan had always suspected that there weren't enough of them to accommodate all the thousands of people he was used to seeing in the streets. Subconsciously he'd somehow assumed that they worked it by shifts; the day people came home about the time the night people went out, and somehow they shared living quarters.

A few courageous souls were starting to poke their noses through the shutters. A solitary wheelwright had opened the top door of his shop, and was ostentatiously planing a spoke held in a wooden vice. As he passed through the silversmiths' quarter he heard voices from behind the closed door of a tavern he'd been to a few times. A few dogs wagged tails and sniffed here and there; a horse trailed its reins slowly through the overflow of a blocked gutter.

He passed another tavern, a favourite. They served good cider, not cheap but not too expensive, and a wicked half-distilled sweet wine that left you asking complete strangers who you were and where you lived. Probably just as well it was shut. *Am I allowed to go into taverns?* he wondered. *Is it in order for the Commander-in-Chief to pop in to a boozer for a quick one on his way home from the war? Probably not.*

Ah, well. There'd be something to drink when he got to the chapter house (mustn't start thinking of it as home). And possibly even food, maybe a place he could lie down and get some sleep. All of those things would be nice, except that tomorrow was another day.

When he arrived at the chapter house, he found the place almost deserted. There were a few clerks, people who had specific jobs to do and no time to stop and chat. He asked where everybody had got to; the Prefect, the Lord Lieutenant, the heads of department. The clerk looked up, shrugged and said he didn't know; some of them may have gone down to the harbour early so as to avoid the mad rush for a place on a ship, some had hurried away when word came through that the rafts had been dealt with – gone to their offices, presumably, to deal with matters of importance.

The others, for all he knew, might well have gone off to celebrate. After all, it had been a victory, hadn't it?

Loredan's brows furrowed. Victory? What's that? Well, he supposed you could call it that.

'So nobody needs me for anything?' he suggested.

'I don't know,' the clerk replied guardedly, obviously unwilling to take responsibility for giving the Commander-in-Chief the rest of the day off. 'I'm just making copies of these minutes, like I was told to.'

'Right,' Loredan said. 'If anybody comes looking for me, tell them I'll be in my quarters.' That sounded sufficiently military, he decided.

A wave of relief hit him as he pushed open the door of the room in the gatehouse where he'd been sleeping since the emergency began; also a feeling of anticlimax, and guilt, of course, for skiving off when there was undoubtedly work he should be doing. None of them lasted very long, however. No sooner had he put his back to the stone ledge than he was fast asleep.

Loredan never remembered his dreams after he'd woken up, so that was all right.

Two and a half hours later, he came round to find someone waggling his foot backwards and forwards. 'Wake up,' he was saying. 'Everybody's looking for you.'

Gods, but I wish that just for once somebody would talk to me as if I was something other than a hired entertainer. 'Go away,' he grunted. 'Be with you in a minute.'

'The Prefect wants to see you, now,' the man replied. 'It's important.'

Loredan toyed with the idea of kicking him across the room, but he wasn't sure he'd have the strength. Virtually every joint in his body had seized like a rusted hinge. 'All right,' he sighed. 'Do I get to wash my face and hands first, or have I got to go along looking like something found on a sausage-maker's midden?'

'Urgent is what I was told,' the messenger replied. 'And that was an hour ago. Come on.'

As threatened, the Prefect wasn't happy about having

been kept waiting. He'd chosen to meet Loredan in one of the side cloisters that radiated away from the chapter house like the spokes of a wheel, and when Loredan got there he was pacing up and down with a ferocious scowl on his face.

'I'm not blaming you,' were his first words. 'I know the situation was grave, and I believe you were doing what you thought was best for the city. But it's caused the most awful uproar on the political front.'

Loredan sat down on a stone lion and held up his hand. 'Excuse me,' he said, 'but what are you talking about?'

The Prefect looked at him as if he'd caught him asleep in class. 'This magic-fire weapon of yours,' he replied. 'I'm afraid we've played right into the opposition's hands by using that.' He gave Loredan a reproachful look. 'If only you'd given me some warning, at least I could have paved the way, done some groundwork at grass-roots level.'

'I still don't know what you're talking about.'

The Prefect glared at him. 'This fire stuff. They're saying you shouldn't have used it like that. Partly because it's magic, and that's a red rag to a bull as far as the Rationalist lobby are concerned. Mostly, though, they're saying it's inhumane. By using it we're acting like savages ourselves. They're talking about implications, possible reprisals. I'm afraid you've really stirred up a hornet's nest in Council.'

Loredan opened his mouth; but there wasn't any point saying the things he could get away with saying. He closed it again and sat still.

'I've done my best,' the Prefect went on. 'They wanted an outright ban, but we've compromised on the position that we won't use the stuff again without formal advance authority from the Council, and then only in certain rigidly defined ... Where do you think you're going?'

Wearily, Loredan sat down again. 'Please,' he said, 'let me have a wash and get something to eat. I think I need to throw up, and that's hard to do on an empty stomach.'

The Prefect made a faint tutting noise that could easily have cost him his life under different circumstances. 'I was rather hoping you'd be sensible about this,' he said. 'After all, we've had our differences before now, but you've done a good job over the last few days and I was hoping I could spare you this, not to mention the embarrassment it'll cause us.'

Loredan tried to find a few last scraps of patience, but there wasn't any left. He got up slowly and started to walk away.

'I'm relieving you of your command,' the Prefect said to his back. 'Effective immediately. I'm sorry, but this witch-craft business on top of that fiasco with the cavalry raid—'

Loredan turned round. 'You agreed to that,' he said. 'You agreed it was necessary to take out their engineers—'

'Not that one, the other one. Before they even got here.' The Prefect folded his arms across his chest. 'I'm sorry,' he said, 'but I think the only way out of this shambles is to bring the trial forward to the earliest date acceptable to the prosecution. Then, assuming you win—'

'Trial?' Loredan looked blank. 'What trial?'

The Prefect looked as if he was about to lose his temper. 'Your trial, man. For culpable negligence in your handling of the raid. If I can, I'll try and persuade the Prosecutor's Office to add on these new witchcraft charges so that it can all be dealt with in one go.' He sighed. 'It won't be easy, since strictly speaking they're different jurisdictions, but in the circumstances they might agree.'

'Witchcraft,' Loredan repeated. 'I see.'

'I'm glad you do,' said the Prefect sharply. 'Anyway, if we can bring the date forward, then – assuming you win, as I said – we'll be in a position to reinstate you in a week or so, provided the Council can be made to agree. I trust you appreciate the fact that I'm sticking my neck out for you, Loredan. You'd do well to remember that the next time you choose to take the law into your own hands.'

Loredan thought for a moment. 'If I'm relieved of command,' he said, 'does that mean I can go home?'

'I suppose so,' the Prefect said. 'You can do what the hell you like, provided you vacate your office and sleeping quarters within the next three hours; and, of course, you lose your right of attendance to Council meetings. We'll need to know where you can be reached, of course, in case the Council want you for any reason. If you'd take my advice, I suggest you get back to work at your fencing school, get yourself in shape and on form for your trial. If you were to lose that it'd reflect very badly on us. Very badly indeed.'

'I'll try to remember that,' Loredan said, and walked away.

'I think we should go home now,' someone said.

There were four new faces at the council of war in Temrai's tent, and he didn't know the names of two of them. He shook his head.

'No,' he said.

'Temrai.' Uncle Anakai leant forward and laid a hand on his arm. 'It was a disaster. We were comprehensively beaten. We've lost the rafts, the ladders and the battering ram, not to mention just over fourteen hundred killed. Carrying on simply isn't an option if you want to remain as chief of this tribe.'

'We're staying,' Temrai said quietly. 'We're carrying on until we win. That's all.'

'Temrai.' His aunt Lanaten, seventy years old and nearly blind, knelt painfully beside him. 'There's no need. You've done your best, nobody will blame you for not doing what isn't possible. Perimadeia can't be taken, it's protected by magic. You can't fight the gods.'

'Magic be damned,' Temrai grunted, his eyes closed. 'That wasn't magic, it was a recipe out of an old book. I read the book myself. But they weren't making the stuff while I was there, of that I'm certain.'

'A book?' someone queried. 'You mean it's something people can make, not magic at all?'

'Of course,' Temrai said. 'It's just naphtha, pitch and sulphur. Why do you think I've been buying up every jar of the filthy mess I could lay my hands on?'

Uncle Anakai's eyebrows shot up. 'You think *you* can produce this fire-oil?' he said.

'Of course. Anybody can make anything if they've got the knowledge and the tools. It's just a matter of trial and error till we get the proportions exactly right.'

'So we could use it against them,' said someone else. 'Are we going to?'

Temrai nodded. 'Yes, eventually,' he said. 'When we get to that stage. More to the point, I know how we can protect ourselves against it in future rather more effectively than we did today. It's only a matter of time.'

'Temrai, fourteen hundred people *died* today.' That was Ceuscai, sounding angry; he's starting to presume a bit too much, Temrai said to himself. 'That's more than die in a year under normal circumstances.'

'We're at war, Ceuscai. People get killed in a war, it happens.'

'Not like that they don't.' Ceuscai was definitely angry now. Temrai remembered that he'd been in charge of the archers, he'd have had a first-class view of what happened on the rafts. Even so, he was speaking out of turn. 'Temrai, I don't care if it wasn't witchcraft, people *believe* it was witchcraft and you're not going to be able to change their minds. You'll lose them, Temrai. It's not something they can be expected to do, take on the gods, everything they believe in. For pity's sake, man, you ought to be able to see that for yourself.'

Temrai stood up. 'This council is dismissed,' he said abruptly. 'And now I've got work to do, and so have all of you.'

When they'd gone he sank down onto the bed, his knees drawn up to his chin and his arms wrapped round them, his eyes wide open. He felt like a man who's stared directly into a bright sun; there were flashes and splodges of hot colour on the surface of his eyes, even when he closed them. The effect of staring at the sun fades sooner or later; but these colours came from the light of the burning rafts, and he doubted that he would ever be rid of them.

Thinking about them brought to mind other flames, other people wearing coats of fire; strong images in his mind of people running between the rows of tents, clothes and hair burning, terror and unbearable pain in their faces and voices, while horsemen rode backwards and forwards propagating the fire, deliberately making things worse instead of trying to help, the way a normal human being would surely do. He remembered seeing such things from underneath a wagon; it was burning too, but it was the only place where the horsemen might not notice him, and he'd far rather have burnt than had to endure the sheer malevolence of those men in their black armour.

Above all he remembered the face of a man illuminated in the glow of fire, the horseman who'd stopped and sat watching, easy and relaxed like someone who was at home in the saddle, one hand lightly resting on the reins while the other held a blazing torch. He hadn't been there for more than a minute, but that minute had lasted a long time; quite possibly it still wasn't over. It was so clear in Temrai's mind, the absolute horror that filled him as he lay on his stomach watching the horseman, praying he wouldn't turn his head and notice him, while the heat from the fire overhead roasted the skin on his back and his tears poured down his face in just the same way the rain had done this morning.

It was strange, after all these years, to be able to put a name to that well-remembered face; Colonel Bardas Loredan, currently in command of the Perimadeian army.

Put the steel into the fire and watch it change colour; straw to orange to brown to purple to blue to green to black. According to some smiths he'd talked to, there's a certain point at which something happens to heated steel. Make it hot enough and the flexibility changes to cutting hardness, at which point the skill lies in tempering it, quenching the heat with skill and care in such a way that the steel stays hard without becoming brittle. It's a delicate business, the perfect balance of fire and water; although there are some smiths who prefer to temper in some kind of oil, and others who use blood. Blood, they say, puts something into the steel at that crucial moment of tempering, an extra touch of hardness on the outside of the metal that doesn't effect the flexibility and resilience of the core.

The assault had failed, he admitted that. He could force them to hide under the parapet with his stones and arrows, just as he'd hidden once upon a time, but he couldn't cross the water because of the fire. He could pitch in fire of his own, so that their houses would burn and their women and children would be made to wear fire on their backs and in their hair, but if he did that, there wouldn't be horsemen; and what would be the point of fire without horsemen? If a thing's worth doing, after all, it's worth doing properly.

So they'd just have to sit there under the walls, waiting for something to turn up. Meanwhile, the people inside the city, and in particular Colonel Bardas Loredan, would have a very long minute of their own to keep still for. In fact, he reflected, bearing in mind how long that minute's already been going on for, there's no real reason why it should ever end.

On his way to the gatehouse, Loredan stopped off at the kitchens, waited till nobody was looking, and sneaked an empty flour sack under his coat. It proved to be plenty large enough to hold the contents of his sleeping quarters (one shirt, bloodstained and torn, only fit for polishing-rags; one pair of boots; one blanket, property of the state, rather less ancient and threadbare than his own; a writing tablet, bottle of ink, various papers; a set of plain brass reckoning counters; a cheap bone comb with seven teeth missing; a roll of bandage, frequently washed). He slung the now-full sack over his shoulder and left the gatehouse, heading for the Patriarch's lodgings.

'He's ill,' said the clerk, in reply to his request to see Alexius. 'Much too ill to see visitors. I'll tell him you were here.'

'That's all right, I'll tell him myself. Which way did you say it was?'

The clerk blocked his way. 'You can't go in there,' he said.

'It's restricted. State security. Patriarch Alexius is busy with important work for the Security Council.'

Loredan looked the clerk up and down, then eased him gently out of the way. 'You did your best,' he said encouragingly. 'Now get out of my way before I break your arm.'

I shall have to get out of the habit of being obeyed, he told himself, before I get to be really obnoxious. The poor lad was only trying to make sure Alexius gets some sleep.

In fact, the Patriarch had been awake for half an hour or so by the time Loredan found his door and knocked on it.

'You don't mind me dropping in like this, do you?' he asked. 'Only, there's something I wanted to tell you.'

The Patriarch welcomed him in. 'Please excuse my not getting up, but I'm feeling a bit fragile after all the excitement. There's wine in the jug and some rolls in that basket there; a bit stale, I'm afraid, but ...'

'Good heavens above!' Loredan exclaimed. 'Food. I remember food; we used to eat it when I was young. Want some?' he added with his mouth full.

'No, no. You carry on. When was the last time you had a proper meal, anyway?'

Loredan shrugged. 'You sound just like my mother. How are you feeling, anyway? Nothing serious, I hope.'

Alexius shook his head. 'Just worn out,' he said. 'When I got back from the Council meeting, that old woman of a clerk put me straight to bed, as if I were a five year old with a temperature. And then,' he admitted, 'I fell asleep. You look like you could do with some rest yourself.'

'I agree,' he said. 'Fortunately, I'm now a civilian again, so I can sleep as late as I want. They fired me,' he explained, 'for my mishandling of the defences. Nicest thing the government of this city's ever done for me,' he added, picking up another roll and tearing it in half. 'Good bread, this. Obviously the word stale means something quite other when you're this high up the hill.'

'Do you mean to say you've been relieved of your command? This is outrageous.' Alexius started to swing his legs out of the bed. 'I shall go and see the Prefect immediately. Of all the—'

'Please.' Loredan raised a hand until he'd swallowed a mouthful. 'Do no such thing. If that's the power and the glory, they're welcome to it.'

'I wasn't thinking of you,' Alexius replied. 'I was thinking of the city. Who's going to do your job? If that fool of a Prefect imagines for one moment—'

Loredan grinned. 'I think appointing my replacement was the last thing on his mind,' he interrupted. 'The poor man was fighting for his political survival.' He told Alexius what had happened, including the Prefect's firm assumption that the fire-oil had been witchcraft. 'Which is why I thought I'd better mention it to you,' he added. 'If his enemies are using this public outcry thing they've cooked up to persecute him with, he might well try and pass it off on you as well as me. I get the impression he believes that aggravation isn't something you hoard, it's something you share.'

Alexius made a rude noise, quite inappropriate for a man in his exalted position. 'I'm afraid you could well be right,' he said. 'Well, let him. I've been telling people we don't do magic for twenty-five years, and I'll carry on telling them that, because it's true. Besides, there's no such thing as the criminal offence of witchcraft in Perimadeian law; that's right, isn't it? You're a lawyer, you know these things.'

Loredan shook his head. 'My clerk knows the law,' he replied, 'I just kill people. Or I used to. But as far as I know, you're right; at least, in my ten years in the racket I never heard of anything like that. I didn't tell the Prefect that, of course, because if I had he'd have gone away and thought up something else to charge me with.' He slid back in his chair, trying to ignore the pain of exhaustion in his knees and calves. 'I'm not worried about him and his damned lawsuits,' he went on. 'In fact, I'm not really worried about anything any more. I'm too tired, for one thing.'

Alexius lay back and stared at the mosaics for a while. 'You think the danger's passed, then?' he said. 'They've given up the idea of a direct assault.'

Loredan nodded. 'For the time being,' he replied. 'They'd have to build more equipment before they could have another go; ladders and rams and engines and the like. Also, they're going to have to think of some way of protecting themselves against the fire-oil.' He grinned. 'Assuming we don't tell them we've outlawed its use, of course,' he added. 'And as far as I know, there isn't anything you can do about the stuff. Well, that's not strictly true. You can use big rawhide canopies to keep it from actually landing on your head, but I suspect that sounds better in theory than in practice. Imagine trying to climb a scaling ladder holding a burning umbrella over your head.'

'So what do you think their next move will be?'

'I don't know,' Loredan admitted. 'In their shoes, I'd probably try and find someone inside the city who'd open the gates in return for a large sum of money. Except I'd have tried that first, instead of fooling about with rafts and building all those catapults.'

Alexius yawned. 'The thing I still don't understand is why they're doing this. True, they have a legitimate grudge against us, but it's over ten years old. Why wait so long?'

Loredan didn't reply to that; instead, he finished off the last of the rolls and washed it down with the dregs of the wine. 'I think I'll go home now,' he said. 'And tomorrow I'd better see whether I've still got a business to run. With luck, in a fortnight's time all this will seem like a horrible dream.'

Venart stood on the quay, looking at his ship and not saying anything.

'It could have been worse,' his sister said, for the tenth time that morning. 'They might have sailed off in it, and then we'd have no cargo, no ship and no way of getting home. As it is—'

'As it is,' Venart replied bitterly, 'we've still got the ship. And all my beautiful rope's somewhere at the bottom of the harbour.'

'You can't blame them really,' Vetriz said. 'If you thought your city was about to be sacked by a merciless and fanatical enemy, and there happened to be a ship standing by in the harbour that could get you to safety—'

'The ship's insured,' Venart said. 'The cargo wasn't. And even if they were going to steal my ship, there wasn't any call to go throwing the cargo over the side. It wouldn't have taken them that long to unload it onto the dock.'

'Oh, well, it's done now. And we're still alive, and we can go home. Really, there's no earthly reason why we should hang about here any longer.'

Venart kicked a stone into the water. 'Somebody's going to have to pay me compensation,' he said at last, 'even if I've got to take them to law to get it.' He rubbed his chin thoughtfully. 'How'd it be if I had a word with Bardas Loredan? I'm sure he'd see that we can't be expected to bear the loss ourselves. After all, the only reason we were here was to bring in desperately needed supplies—'

'Ven.'

'Don't you Ven me. It's your money as much as mine.' A promising new approach occurred to him. 'If it was just my money I could afford to be philosophical about it, but where your capital's concerned I have a duty as your trustee—'

'Ven.'

Venart ignored her. 'I'm sure Loredan will help,' he said. 'He seemed a very honourable sort of person. If we ask him politely...'

'He isn't in charge any more. They gave him the sack.'

'What?' Venart scowled. 'Oh, damn. All right then, what about your friend the Patriarch? I'm sure that if *he* put in a word for us—'

'Oh, do shut up, Ven, before I push you in the harbour. I've had enough of it here. I want to go home.'

Venart took another look at his ship, as if to reassure himself that it was still there. 'What did he do to make them sack him?' he asked. 'I'd have thought he'd be the hero of the hour.'

Vetriz shrugged. 'You'd have thought so,' she agreed. 'But like I keep telling you, these people aren't like us.' She started to walk away, so that Venart had to run to catch her up.

'He might still be able to use his influence,' he puffed. 'He can't have made enemies of everyone in the government.'

'Actually,' Vetriz said, 'we might ask him if he wants to come with us. And that clerk of his, Athli. I like her, she's got good sense. And we could always use another clerk.'

Venart stared at her. 'You can't be serious,' he said. 'All our working capital's lying rotting at the bottom of the harbour and you're talking about taking on more staff. Sometimes I think you must live in a world of your own.'

'Well, we could at least offer them a ride to the Island. Assuming they want to go, of course. They may prefer to stay here and sweat it out. But we ought to ask.'

Venart scowled at her. 'And I suppose you want me to offer free berths to the Patriarch and his friend as well. I mean, why leave them out?'

'Good point. Though I don't for one moment suppose they'd accept.'

'Vetriz,' Venart said, his voice almost pleading, 'we can get good money for every berth we can fill on the ship; the last thing we want to do is fill the wretched thing up giving free rides to people we hardly even know. Particularly if we don't get any compensation. It'd be throwing away our only chance of getting some of our money back.'

They discussed the matter further on the way back to the inn, and in consequence it was decided that they'd ask Loredan, Athli, Alexius and Gannadius if they wanted free passage to the Island. 'And if they offer to pay for it,' Vetriz added, 'refuse. You take one copper quarter off any of them and I'll make you eat it.'

'All right,' Venart said grudgingly. 'But first we'll ask whether they can do anything about getting an indemnity for all that rope. Bloody stuff,' he added savagely. 'I wish I'd never set eyes on it.'

'Ah, well,' Vetriz said, with a deliberately aggravating smile. 'If you'd done as I said and bought carpet the last time we were here ...'

So, after a deliberately cheap and frugal meal, they went

to find Athli, who would know where to find Loredan. She wasn't at home.

'Wonderful,' Venart said, after they'd banged on the door and peered through the windows. 'Now what do you suggest?'

'We could wait here,' Vetriz replied. 'Or we could go and see the Patriarch. He'd probably know where Loredan lives.'

'What makes you think that?'

'Who?' Alexius demanded. The pageboy repeated the names, mispronouncing them both. 'Oh, them.' He exchanged glances with Loredan. 'Show them up,' he said. 'Let's see what they want.'

'I'll stay for this, if you don't mind,' Loredan said, after the boy had gone. 'They're the ones you reckon have these peculiar powers?'

'The girl,' Alexius replied. 'And I know you're sceptical. I don't know what to make of it, though; their being in the city, I mean. If I'm right about her – well, we'll see.'

Loredan grinned. 'Actually,' he said, 'it's all to do with rope.'

'Rope.'

'I sold him a whole load of surplus rope we'd appropriated by mistake,' Loredan explained. 'Presumably he came back to pick up the stuff he couldn't carry the last time he was here.' A thought struck him. 'I hope nothing's happened to their ship,' he said. 'By all accounts things got fairly lively down at the harbour yesterday.'

Alexius nodded. 'Well,' he said, 'if anything has happened to their ship, it knocks a fair-sized hole in my theory. It's a pretty poor sorceress who can't protect her own property.'

'I thought you weren't meant to call them—'

The door opened. 'Oh, isn't that lucky!' Vetriz said loudly. 'Here they are, both of them. Two birds with—'

'Patriarch,' Venart said formally, nodding to Alexius. 'And Colonel Loredan. This is indeed most fortunate. If you could possibly spare us a little of your time—'

'Can we have some wine, please?' Alexius said to the boy

before he could escape. 'And something to eat, if there's anything going? Thank you.' He propped himself up on one elbow. 'Please excuse me,' he went on, 'but I've been officially declared ill and I'm not allowed to get up even for visitors. Sit down, if you can find somewhere.'

Vetriz immediately perched on the edge of the bed, almost but not quite sitting on the Patriarch's feet. Her brother tried not to notice and remained standing.

'Sorry to barge in like this,' Vetriz said, 'but we're sailing for home and we wondered if you'd like to come with us.'

Neither Alexius nor Loredan knew what to say. The thought of leaving the city hadn't occurred to either of them before. It was like hearing some strange heretical new theory about the nature of the universe; something too wild and radical to accept, too plausible to ignore. 'That's a very kind offer,' Alexius murmured. 'I—' He stopped and looked down at his hands, resting on top of the sheet. 'That's a very kind offer. Very kind indeed.'

'And Athli, too, of course,' Vetriz went on. 'And your colleague Gannadius, Patriarch. Is he here today, or is he back at his own—' She couldn't think of the right word. 'Establishment,' she ventured.

'That's an interesting idea,' Loredan said softly. 'Are you sure? Passages out must be a valuable commodity right now. I'd have thought you could name your own price.'

Venart opened his mouth to say something, caught his sister's eye and closed it again.

'We do need to know fairly quickly, though,' Vetriz said. 'We're hoping to leave tomorrow morning, first thing.' She hesitated, rubbed the side of her head with her fingertips, and went on. 'If you like, sleep on it and we'll keep four berths empty for you on the ship, just in case you do want to come.' Venart made a quiet moaning noise, which she ignored. 'I do hope you will,' she added. 'I mean, it was wonderful the way you all rallied round and beat off the attack yesterday, really it was, but ...' Then she smiled brightly. 'That's all we wanted to say. We won't stop for the wine, thanks. Goodbye.'

'But—' Venart said, as she opened the door. 'Oh, never mind. Our ship's at the north quay,' he added, turning to follow her, 'the *Squirrel*, she's called. You shouldn't have any trouble finding her, she's the only twin-castled freighter in the docks.' He raised his hand in a vague salutation, saw that Vetriz had already gone and darted after her, closing the door behind him.

'Well, if that doesn't beat cock-fighting,' Alexius said after a long silence. 'What do you make of that, Bardas?'

Loredan rubbed his forehead with the heel of his hand before replying. 'How's your head feeling?' he asked.

'I – Good heavens, you're right. Sort of a dull, heavy ache, as if there was thunder in the air. I hadn't noticed it until you mentioned it, but it's there all right. How about you?'

Loredan grimaced. 'I wish I'd had the really good night out this is the hangover for,' he replied. 'I still don't believe a word of it, of course. How about their offer? Guilty conscience, perhaps?'

Alexius lifted his head sharply. 'That's a nasty one,' he said, 'particularly coming from a sceptic like yourself.'

'I'm humouring you. Are you going to accept?'

Alexius shook his head. 'Twenty years ago, perhaps. Maybe even ten. Now, though, the journey'd probably kill me. Anyway, I thought you said a direct assault wasn't going to work.'

Lordan shook his head. 'If I go,' he said, 'it won't be because I'm afraid of the clan. But there's nothing to keep me here except the prospect of a trial for culpable negligence. I might just go, at that.'

'Oh,' Alexius said. 'Well, yes, I suppose there's a call there for your sort of services – teaching fencing, I mean, not lawyering. I suppose,' he added, 'I'd better let Gannadius know about the offer. He's younger than me and still ambitious, still has things he wants to do in the world. I'm sure I could concoct some post for him in one of the Order's houses on the Island.'

Loredan nodded. 'That reminds me,' he said. 'I ought to tell my clerk, since she was included in the offer. Damn,' he added. 'Just when I thought I was going to get a chance to go to bed.' He stood up, wincing at the stiffness in his joints. 'If I do decide to go,' he said awkwardly, 'then I suppose – well, so long, Alexius. We could have known each other better under different circumstances, except that under different circumstances we'd never have got to know each other at all. Take care of yourself.'

Alexius nodded. 'And you,' he said. 'I have an unpleasant feeling at the back of my mind that I've interfered with your life to an extent that I'd never be able to put right if you stayed here. Maybe this business is someone or something putting it right. I'd like to think it was. If you decide to go, that is.'

'I gather you think I should.'

Alexius shrugged. 'Don't ask me,' he said. 'Another thing I can't do is tell fortunes.'

Shortly after Loredan had gone, the boy came back with wine and cakes for four. He put the tray down nevertheless, and asked if there was anything else.

'Yes, if you'll just wait a moment,' Alexius said, his head bent over a writing tablet. 'I want you to run down to the City Academy and give this to Archimandrite Gannadius, as quickly as you can. Give it to him and nobody else, please; tell him it's important. Can you do that for me?'

The boy nodded eagerly, his eyes bright with the prospect of an excuse to get outside the walls for an hour or so. Shortly after he left, Alexius could hear him running down the stairs. *Enthusiasm*, he thought. *I had some of that myself once. And look where it got me.*

Athli wasn't at home, which was a nuisance. He hung around outside her house for half an hour or so feeling painfully conspicuous – *I feel like a lovesick sixteen year old, and I didn't even do this sort of thing when I was sixteen* – and then gave up and headed for the baker's shop on the corner, which was cautiously opening its shutters.

'I know you, don't I?' said the woman in the shop as she handed him a freshly baked loaf stuffed with slices of cheese and bacon.

Loredan nodded. 'It's possible,' he said. 'I used to work for the government.'

'That's it,' the woman said, snapping her fingers. 'Weights and measures. Didn't you use to come round here checking weights and measures one time – oh, must be all of ten years ago now?'

'Fancy you remembering that,' Loredan replied, his mouth full of bread.

The woman looked at him, and edged sideways in front of the shop scales. 'You still doing that?' she asked.

'It's all right,' Loredan replied. 'I just quit earlier today.'

'Oh.' The woman noticed his armour under his coat. 'Got called up, did you?' Loredan nodded. 'It's happening to everybody,' she went on. 'Damn shame, if you ask me.'

Loredan nodded. 'I blame the General,' he said.

'What, the one who got the push or the new one?'

'Both,' Loredan replied, putting his hand out for his change.

He finished off the loaf outside the shop, then explored a little until he found an open tavern. He didn't feel quite so tired now that he'd eaten something, and the idea of a drink was very attractive indeed. Eventually he located one, in a small, rather dismal place he hadn't been to in years. It hadn't changed a bit.

'Guardsman,' said the landlord, pouring pale cloudy cider into a grubby-looking horn mug. 'Seen some action these last couple of days, I'll bet.'

'Enough to last me a while,' Loredan replied, handing over a coin. 'Your health.'

He and the landlord were the only people in the place. Loredan remarked on this.

'Don't know why I bothered opening up,' the landlord replied. 'Nobody wants to venture out of the house, just in case the savages suddenly come running down the street. That's not likely, is it?' he added.

Loredan shrugged. 'Don't ask me,' he replied. 'Last I heard they'd obviously had enough, after the General used that fire-oil stuff.'

The innkeeper nodded. 'Good work, that,' he said. 'And it's about time the wizards did something to earn their keep. Night after night we had people in here asking, why don't the wizards do something? Should've realised they'd keep the magic stuff in reserve for when it'd do most good.'

'Fine man, the Patriarch,' Loredan said.

'His health,' replied the innkeeper, tilting the mug he'd just filled. 'If you ask me, though,' he went on, lowering his voice, 'there's more to it than that.'

Loredan's face registered interest. 'You reckon?'

The landlord nodded. 'I've heard it said that the Prefect and the General've been deliberately keeping old Alexius from doing anything, because it's in their interest for the emergency to carry on as long as they can spin it out for.'

'Get away.'

'Just repeating what I been told,' the landlord said. 'Stands to reason, though; the two of them, running the whole city – because you're not going to tell me the Emperor's been running things all this while. My guess is they got him locked up somewhere.'

'That's terrible,' Loredan said.

'Too right it's terrible. And now, soon as the bastards've been defeated, look what happens. The General gets the push, just like that. Well, it's obvious, isn't it?'

'Hm?'

'Fallen out over dividing up the spoils,' the landlord said. 'My guess is, Colonel Whatsisface was getting a bit too greedy, trying to edge the Prefect out of the racket. And the next thing he knows – wham!'

'I hadn't thought of it like that,' Loredan confessed. 'Put that way, though, it does seem to make a lot of sense.' He sipped his cider, which was horrible. 'More sense than the other explanation, anyway.'

'Take that business with the rope, now,' the landlord went on. 'Should've realised then what was going on. But you never think that sort of thing goes on, though, do you?'

'What business with the rope? I've been a bit out of things lately, remember.'

'Oh, this was some time back,' the landlord replied. 'Seems that Colonel Whatever-he's-called went around commandeering all the rope in the city, and then flogged it off cheap to all his buddy-buddies from the Island.' He grinned knowingly. 'If you ask me, that's what this whole emergency's been in aid of, right from where they made a muck of that cavalry raid. You're not going to tell me we couldn't have kicked those savages back where they come from if we'd have really been trying.'

Loredan drank some more horrible cider. 'I never did like that man's face,' he said. 'Used to be a lawyer, of course.'

'Well, that says it all, really. Same again?'

'I think I'll try the wine, thanks.'

'House red? Or I got something a bit special, if you'd prefer.'

'House red'll do fine.'

The wine, though horrible, was a degree less unspeakable than the cider, and Loredan stayed for a couple more, during which time he learnt a lot more about what had really been going on up the hill. Then he decided to go home, before the landlord's booze achieved what Temrai and all his men hadn't been able to. His way home led him past Athli's house, and he decided to give it one last try. This time, she was in.

'Hello,' he said.

She stared at him, and for a moment he almost believed she was about to jump into his arms. She didn't.

'Hello yourself,' she replied. 'They let you out, then.'

'Time off for bad behaviour. I've got a message for you.'

'Come in and have a drink,' she said.

He'd been in Athli's house before, but that was some time ago. He'd forgotten how light and airy it was, with its white distempered walls and bright, cheerful tapestries, neat and well-made furniture, clean and dry floor. *Of course there are people who live like this*, he said to himself, *people who like everything to be nice. If they had to live in a cave, they'd have some flowers in a jar to cheer the place up.*

He sat down in the chimney corner while Athli took

down two silver cups from hooks over the fireplace and filled them from a jug. 'What's the message?' she said, handing him one. 'Something nice?'

Loredan nodded. 'Possibly. You remember those two types from the Island? Venart and Vetriz?'

'How odd you should mention them. I was going to tell you about them in a minute.'

'Well, they've offered us a free ride out of here,' Loredan said. 'Their ship leaves first thing tomorrow; if we want, we can be on it.'

'Oh.' Athli stood in front of the fire, holding her cup tightly. 'Are you going?'

'I'm not sure.' Loredan sipped the wine; rather more like it, if a bit sweet for his taste. 'I'm sorely tempted. What about you? And what were you going to say about those two?' He leant forward a little. 'You've obviously run into them again since I saw you last.'

Athli nodded. 'More than that,' she said. 'We've gone into business together.'

'Good gods. How did that happen?'

Athli explained, while Loredan listened very attentively. 'I'm starting to wonder about those two,' he said when she'd finished. 'Seems like we can't put our feet down recently without treading on them.'

'I thought it was rather a coincidence,' Athli agreed. 'Anyway, what do you think?'

'About their offer?' Loredan bowed his head over his cup, staring into the dregs. 'I told the Patriarch I wasn't afraid of standing trial,' he said. 'I lied. I feel like I've been in one fight too many as it is. My father used to say, luck's like a bloody great big rock balanced on a cliff above your house; doesn't do to push it too hard.' He shook his head. 'Not that that means anything in this case. For instance, if I go, maybe there'll be a storm that sinks the ship and I'll drown, while if I'd stayed put I'd have lived to be a hundred. Which is making the assumption that I want to live to be a hundred,' he added, 'which I don't. You thought about it yet?' He looked round. 'You've got something to leave behind,' he said.

'What, this?' Athli laughed. 'It'd have been nice to have a chance to sell it and get my money back, but the hell with it; basically, it's just things.'

'So you're going, then?'

'Don't know.' She looked up. 'I will if you will.'

Loredan felt uncomfortable. 'There must be a few smilers' worth of stuff in here,' he said. 'You seem to have a good eye for a bargain.'

'Always the shrewd businesswoman,' Athli replied briskly. 'Talking of which—' She hesitated, then went on, 'Can I ask you a question? Personal question.'

'Depends. You can try.'

'All right.' She took a deep breath. 'Why is it,' she said, 'when you make ten times as much money as I do, you live like a pig and always seem to be broke? No offence, but it doesn't make sense, mathematically. I've often wondered.'

Loredan looked away and Athli thought, *That's done it, I've offended him now.* But a moment later he turned back, and his expression was more or less the same.

'I send a lot of money home,' he said. 'Maybe I mentioned before, I've got rather a large family. Three brothers and a sister – my parents are both dead now, but two of my brothers are still on the farm. I've been helping them out, when I can. I owe it to them, you see.'

'Helping them out,' Athli repeated.

'That's right. My father was a tenant, in a small way; actually, he was a peasant, strictly hand-to-mouth stuff, and with the landlord taking a sixth of everything off the top, it wasn't exactly easy at the best of times. So I bought the land. Enough for all three of them to have a decent life. Like I said, it was the least I could do, all things considered.'

Athli thought, *It still doesn't make sense; if the brothers got the farm and Bardas went off to make his way in the world, shouldn't it have been the other way about? They got everything, and he started out with nothing.* 'I see,' she said. 'That explains it, I suppose. They must be pretty well off by now then, your brothers. The ones that stayed,' she added.

Loredan nodded. 'They're good farmers, by all accounts,' he said. 'Not that I hear from them very often. Anyway, that's the answer to your question. Very mundane, very ordinary, no great mystery.'

'You never talk about your family.'

'No, I don't. I don't find them a very interesting topic of conversation. Is there any more of this wine, or are you saving it for your old age?'

'Sorry,' Athli said. 'Please, help yourself.' She waited until he'd filled his cup, then went on, 'You aren't thinking of going back there, then? Home, I mean, the farm.'

Loredan shook his head. 'Too much like work, living on a farm,' he said. 'Not to mention the smell, and goats in the living room. I'm too old to go to work.'

'How about the Island, then? You decided?'

'I think you should go,' he replied. 'I know we saw them off yesterday, but I'm pretty sure they'll try again. And keep trying, till they get it right. I think the city will fall, and probably sooner rather than later.'

In spite of herself, Athli was shocked; to hear him say it, quite casually, the thing that she and everybody else had been dreading while at the same time knowing, absolutely *knowing*, that it could never ever happen. 'You really think so?' was all she said.

Loredan nodded. 'You don't realise how bloody close they came to it yesterday,' he replied. 'If it hadn't been for the fire-oil, we'd none of us be here now. There's so *many* of them; we simply hadn't imagined there could be so many. And the things they've achieved; the engines, the organisation, everything. Last time I had anything to do with them, they were – well, I suppose I'd have to call them savages, though I don't mean it the way most people do. They were primitive; like they didn't want anything more than what they'd always had, which is fair enough, at that.

'Now they're making things just as well as we can – don't believe anybody who says they've bought them somewhere or been given them; that kid Temrai came here and set about learning how to make everything he needed to take this city. He's absolutely amazing, that boy. He deserves to win, just as we— Anyway,' he went on, 'the only thing standing in his way is the fire-oil. If he can find a way of getting round that, we're done for. Given what he's achieved so far, I doubt it'll take him too long. And even if he doesn't, he's got so many men he could just push straight through anything we can throw at him, provided he's prepared to take the losses. And I think he is. He's a good chief, but for some reason taking this city *matters* to him. I saw the way he kept bringing up engines after our trebuchets had just made firewood out of the previous wave. In the end it comes down to whether we're as prepared to die for our city as they are to die for their chief. And on that basis, we're stuffed.'

Athli nodded slowly. 'So you're leaving,' she said.

'I didn't say I was.'

'But if the city's going to fall ...'

Loredan leant forward until he was very close to her. 'I think you should go,' he said. 'I'm not saying this is your last chance or anything like that, though it's got to be better than cramming onto a crowded refugee ship later, when they're on the wall. I'd—' He stopped, breathed in and out, started again. 'I'd feel happier if I knew you were out of it. You've got a skill that'll make you a living anywhere you go. You've even got friends on the Island now, you'd have no difficulty making a life for yourself. What have you got here, apart from all this nice furniture?'

'I'll go if you go,' she said.

He moved away, frowning. She wanted to reach out, but didn't.

'We could start a school there,' she said, 'just like the school here, except I don't suppose there's the competition. And what you said about me having friends there, it goes for you, too. For some reason those two seem to have taken a shine to us; we wouldn't just be refugees starting from nothing, we'd know people, they'd help us.' She tried to meet his eyes, but he was looking away, into the fire. 'You don't actually want to stay here, do you? Stay here and be killed, be a hero when there's nobody left to remember? You always said you never had any time for heroes.'

'Don't be stupid,' he said gently. 'Why the hell should I want to get myself killed? For free,' he added. 'For money'd be different.'

'Well, then. Let's go, together.' She tried to find a smile from somewhere. 'It'd be fun, the two of us. Like it used to be.'

He looked up at her now, but she couldn't see anything in his face except a faint reflection of fire in his eyes. 'That was your idea of fun, was it?' he said. 'Oh, well. Takes all sorts.'

She tried to stay calm, stay in control. 'Well, I won't go if you won't,' she said. 'That's what we in the trade call moral blackmail. Essential skill for a lawyer's clerk.'

Loredan finished his wine and stood up. 'I didn't say I wasn't going,' he said. 'Just that I haven't made my mind up.' He put the cup down on a table and did up his coat. 'Didn't you say something in your letter about having put a lock on the door of my apartment?'

Athli looked blank for a moment. 'Oh, gods, yes, the key. Hang on, I'll get it for you.' She opened a drawer in a small exquisite writing desk and took out a bundle of cloth. 'Here you are,' she said, handing it to him. 'It's a bit stiff, you have to lean on the door before you turn it.'

'Thanks,' he said. 'How much do I owe you for that?'

She was about to say, *Don't mention it.* 'Five quarters,' she replied. 'You can owe it me till tomorrow if you like.'

'No, I think I've got that in change.' He counted out the coins and handed them over; Athli imagined they hurt her hand as she took them. She put the money down; he walked to the door.

'The ship's called the *Squirrel*,' he said. 'North quay, twin-castle freighter. I'd go if I were you.'

'I'll think about it,' she said.

He left.

CHAPTER SEVENTEEN

'Mind out.'

Gannadius looked round. 'Sorry?' he said.

'Mind out. You're in the way.'

'Oh. Right.' Gannadius shuffled a few steps to one side to allow the men to get by. 'Sorry,' he continued. 'I've never been on a boat before.'

They looked at him without saying anything, and carried on with their work, which was something to do with pulling on ropes. As far as Gannadius was able to judge, most things on board the ship seemed to involve pulling on ropes, or winding them up, or throwing them.

Once he'd satisfied himself that he was no longer impeding the crew and thereby endangering the ship, he went back to staring at the skyline. He'd often heard people describing the view of the city as seen from the sea, and never once felt any great inclination to experience it for himself. Now that he was here looking at it, he wasn't sure what all the fuss had been about.

'Beautiful, isn't it?'

'Yes, quite,' he replied automatically. 'Very - impressive,' he ventured, 'seen from this angle.'

The man beside him leant his forearms on the rail, his eyes fixed on the gradually receding prospect. 'The Triple City,' he said. 'The teardrop of the gods, a glowing pearl bright in the sea-wave's tresses, far-seen, ivory-crowned Perimadeia, Perimadeia the shining, the nurse of fine women, the everlasting gateway.'

Gannadius mumbled something polite. To him, the city

looked like a collapsed sugarloaf; but he recognised the quotations the other man was reeling off, the conventional epithets and clichés that everybody mouthed without thinking what they meant. To be strictly accurate, in fact, the original line from Phyzas' *Homecoming* was 'nurse of *fair* women', not 'fine'; but everybody got it wrong except the few who'd actually waded through the turgid thing.

'Pity, really,' the man said. 'Still, when you've had your time, you've had your time.' He looked up and studied Gannadius' expression. 'First time at sea, is it?'

Gannadius nodded.

'You get used to it,' the man said. 'Eventually. The trick is, don't fight it. Once you've chucked up a couple of times you'll feel a whole lot better, believe me.'

There were a great many people up on deck, taking a final look at the city as it slowly disappeared below the horizon; like a tall, proud ship gradually sinking, Gannadius said to himself, how depressingly apt. In spite of what his neighbour on the rail had said he didn't feel nauseous (he didn't feel *well* either, but he didn't feel nauseous). Nor was he overwhelmed by grief and the pathos of it all. Mainly, he supposed, he couldn't accept that he was quite possibly seeing the city for the last time.

'Me,' the man said, 'I'm from Scona originally, only been in the city about five years. You ever been to Scona? No, sorry, of course you haven't. Miserable place, Scona. But at least people don't go around burning it down every five minutes.'

'You think it'll come to that?'

The man laughed. 'Right fool I'll look if it doesn't, after I've coughed up six hundred smilers for a ride on this tub. Well, don't you? You must do, or why are you here?'

'Actually, I'm on my way to a posting on the Island, so I'd have been leaving anyway,' Gannadius said.

'I *see*.' The man didn't need to call him a liar, or even imply it. 'Fortuitous, that. What line of work are you in, then?'

'Banking,' Gannadius replied.

'Really? Which bank?'

Gannadius winced; served him right for being a coward and not telling the truth. 'It's a small family bank,' he replied, 'you wouldn't have heard of us. Boredan,' he added as an afterthought.

'Boredan? With a B?'

'That's right. The Boredan bank. Like I said, we're very small, quite low-profile ...'

The man looked at him. 'I bet you get sick and tired of people muddling you up with the other lot,' he said. 'Must be very aggravating.'

'It is,' Gannadius replied, looking straight ahead. 'How about you?' he said. 'What do you do?'

'Oh, you know,' the man said. 'Letters of credit, bills of exchange, that sort of thing. Typical bits-and-pieces, hand-to-mouth credit trading. It's odd, though, there being a *Boredan* bank and me never having heard of it. Pir Hiraut,' he added, extending a hand. 'Maybe we could put some business each other's way sometime.'

Gannadius took the man's hand – he had a grip like a bench vice – and smiled broadly. 'That would be – I mean, yes, we must certainly explore the possibilities,' he said. Inspiration struck; he clapped a hand to his throat and made a gurgling noise. Grinning, the man wished him luck and moved away.

'Next time,' said another voice, this time on his left side, 'pretend to be a merchant. Something boring, like dried fish. Nobody ever wants to talk shop with a dried-fish merchant.'

Gannadius turned his head and grinned sheepishly. 'You – ah – overheard?'

Vetriz nodded. 'You should have told him you were a wi— a member of the Order,' she said. 'It really is very highly respected on the Island, you know. Is there really a foundation there?'

Gannadius nodded. 'There is indeed. But it's little more than a consulate, looking after our financial interests; they don't do any teaching, precious little research either. Still, it's a job. Better than landing as a penniless refugee.'

'Somehow I don't see this lot as penniless,' Vetriz confided, 'or they wouldn't be on this ship. I think you'll find there's quite a few *real* bankers, as well as traders, merchant venturers, others of that sort; people whose lives aren't completely confined within the city walls.' She placed her elbows on the rail and cupped her chin in her hands. 'That's why they're prepared to leave, I suppose,' she said. 'Don't get me wrong, we had no trouble filling the ship, but there weren't great long queues either. Most people aren't interested in getting out, not now the assault's been repulsed.'

Gannadius shrugged. 'I hope they're right,' he said. 'And if they are, I shall wait a while and then creep quietly home and try and burrow my way back into the hierarchy of the Order. I've lost my chance of becoming Patriarch, of course, but to be honest I don't much care. It isn't quite the wonderful life everybody supposes it to be.'

Vetriz furrowed her brow. '*He* stayed, though,' she said.

'Alexius' health wouldn't permit him to travel,' Gannadius replied. 'He conceals it to some extent, but he's not at all well.' Gannadius was silent for a moment, wondering if he'd ever see his friend again. There hadn't been time to say goodbye; he'd scribbled a few lines on a tablet and thrust it into the messenger's hands, but that wasn't the same thing at all. He regretted that. Anything approaching genuine friendship in the upper reaches of the hierarchy was extremely rare, something you came not to expect. Having found it, he was sorry to lose it again.

But the thought of getting out – escaping – was irresistible. And since, thanks to Alexius' last-minute improvisation, he was able to leave with a vestige of honour and a job to go to, he'd have been mad to pass up the opportunity.

The city had almost completely sunk; only the blinding whiteness of the upper city remained, glaring in the sun. It put Gannadius in mind of the old fable, about the Lost City of Myzo, the fabulously wealthy and magical island-kingdom that angered the gods and sank beneath the waves a million years ago, when there still were gods and such things were permitted to happen. These days, of course, geography wasn't quite so amenable to the demands of poetic justice, or so the city people reckoned.

Well. Possibly.

Feeling some gesture was called for, he raised his hand to shoulder height, palm facing the faraway flash of white until it was completely gone, and then let it fall.

'Saying goodbye?'

'Being melodramatic,' he replied. 'I've spent so long teaching that I have a persistent weakness for showmanship, even when it's entirely out of place. Do you know, this is the first time I've been out of sight of the city in my entire life. I'm fifty-four,' he added. 'I suppose I should feel quite lost, but I don't.'

'Pleased to hear it,' Vetriz replied. 'There's plenty of time for you to feel homesick later on.'

She left him and crossed the deck to see how her other new friend was getting on. Vetriz had been sympathetic, but tears were something she'd always found unsettling and hard to cope with; accordingly, she'd left her to pull herself together.

'I'm sorry,' Athli said. 'I didn't mean to embarrass you. It's just—' She left the sentence unfinished, her eyes still fixed on the horizon.

'You really thought he'd come? At the last minute?'

Athli shook her head. 'Oh, it wasn't that,' she said. 'But leaving the city, not knowing if it'll be there when I come back ...'

Vetriz didn't say anything; she wasn't sure she believed what Athli was trying to tell her, but there was no way of knowing. She was over-inclined, she knew, to see storytellers' romance where there really wasn't any evidence for it outside her own imagination. On the other hand, this was a situation where her instinctive interpretation could quite reasonably be expected to be the correct one.

Besides, it was none of her business.

'It'll be there,' she said, 'just you wait. It'll have to be, if we're going into the fancy-goods business. Can't let a silly old war get in the way of a good business idea.'

Athli smiled. 'Particularly one your brother didn't think of.'

'Precisely.' As she said it, Vetriz knew she was saying the opposite of what she believed. Somehow she knew the city would fall, sooner or later. It wasn't something she cared to dwell on long enough to rationalise the intuition; thinking about it, in fact, quite literally gave her a headache. She knew, that was all; just as she'd known the last time she saw her great-aunt Alamande (ninety-two years old and crippled with arthritis; for the last ten years she'd been waiting for death like an impatient traveller waiting for the ferry) that it was the last time, a proper occasion for formal leavetaking. She hadn't been particularly attached to Great-Aunt Alamande, and she wasn't particularly attached to the Triple City of Perimadeia (pleasant enough to visit but you wouldn't want to live there). Perhaps you needed to be detached to have the proper perspective; in any event, that was why she'd given in to the impulse to try and get all her new friends out of there and away to safety. It was a pity the Patriarch hadn't come; and Loredan too, of course. But it was scarcely a surprise; they were both men with a strong sense of honour and duty, not the kind to run away.

(*Honestly*, she thought. *Men!*)

Venart would be on the forecastle, looking out impatiently for the seamarks that would bring him home. She went to join him, feeling suddenly glad that she was who she was, and that the most they had to worry about was a cargo of rope at the bottom of a harbour and the prospect of a good market lost.

'Actually,' Venart said, a little later, 'it may be a – damn, what's the opposite of a mixed blessing? A blessing in disguise, or at least an opportunity. Sure, we lose a market, and a very good one. But it's not the end of the world; there's still a whole world out there wanting to buy and sell, and if they can't do it in Perimadeia, they'll have to do it somewhere else. This could be the big chance the Island's been waiting for; I mean to say, it's not that long ago we were trying to destroy the place ourselves, for precisely that reason.'

'Ah,' Vetriz said ominously. 'So that's all right, then.'

Venart clicked his tongue. 'Yes, I know it sounds callous and unfeeling, and believe me, I really do feel sorry for them, though when you come to think of it they did rather bring it on themselves, letting the enemy wander in and learn how to make engines and things, no questions asked. The fact remains, we've got a living to earn, and it's an ill wind ...'

Vetriz nodded. 'So you think we could be on the brink of a wonderful new opportunity?' she asked.

'Quite possibly. Quite possibly.'

'Splendid.' Vetriz smiled happily. 'So, with all this new business coming our way, it'd only be sensible to take on an extra clerk. I'll tell Athli, she'll be so pleased.'

'Vetriz—' Venart saved his breath for a long, resigned sigh. The truth was, once his sister had made up her mind that something was going to happen, as often as not it did and that was that. The only sensible thing to do was to accept it, and try and find some way to mitigate the expenditure it would inevitably involve without letting her realise it.

In front of him, he imagined he saw a straight, wide road leading home. To go home, with a profitable cargo, money in his pocket, something that'd be of use to him once he got there; it wasn't much to ask.

As sieges go, it could have been far worse.

There are sieges where the defenders starve; where a dead rat or blackbird changes hands for the price of a bushel of fine wheat-flour, and dark rumours of robbed graves and cannibalism spring up out of the general despair like mushrooms in the dark; where the besiegers camp in the steaming marshes outside a strong and well-supplied city, watching the guards on the wall walking off their dinners with a pleasant stroll while fever and hunger desiccate their enemies; sieges where the trebuchets of the besiegers throw rotting carcasses into the city to spread pestilence, sieges where the trebuchets of the city throw stale bread into the besiegers' camp to mock their starvation. Some cities suffer two sieges; the enemy outside and plague inside. Sometimes the plague spreads from one enemy to another, so that on both sides of the wall men evaporate like rain on hot stones. Savage heat oppresses the defenders in summer, snow and ice ravage the besiegers in winter. All in all, it can be an unpleasant business for all concerned. A stagnant war seldom does anybody any good.

Not so the siege of Perimadeia, if it could be called a siege at all. True, the city people couldn't venture out on the land side; but then again, who really wanted to? The Drovers' Bridge was where foreigners came in and out of the city; Perimadeians came and went from the harbour when they travelled at all. As for the commodities that came by land; who needed them? Food and some raw materials, nothing that couldn't come by sea, and if it meant paying a little more, that could be covered by a modest rise in prices. Once it became obvious that there was to be no fresh assault, that the rafts on the river weren't bringing in the components of more engines, ladders, rams, canopies, the people of the city gradually began to lose interest; indeed, except for the continuing debate over the ethics of using fire-oil (which the political factions managed to keep going, like the flame of a lamp with a damp wick), they put it out of their minds and went back to work.

Temrai's people also found themselves settling into the comfort of a routine. The land behind the city hadn't been grazed for over a decade, making it good country for the flocks and herds. Water was plentiful, and after the frantic activity of engine-building and engine-moving, a rest was welcome. There were still things to be done. They were rebuilding the causeway opposite the bridgehouse, there were arrows to be turned and fletched, arrowheads to be made, armour to be repaired and reinforced. Whether to increase efficiency or simply to keep his men occupied, Temrai had organised weekly archery competitions, with good prizes for the winners and compulsory training for the bottom tenth of the losers; that gave them something to speculate about and gamble on, and went some way towards repairing the damage the battle of the rafts had done to his relationship with his people. Very few of them still speculated as to what the next phase was going to be; the generally accepted view was that they were all waiting for something to happen, and until then there were worse places in the world to pitch camp for a month or so.

It was almost becoming amicable. City people wagered on the clan's archery matches, discussed the form of the various champions and contenders over spiced cider in the taverns, observed the life of the clan and found in it things to appreciate, as the city had always done in its dealings with foreigners. The clan was getting used to the view; you couldn't live under the walls for long without beginning to respect them, to wonder about the sort of men who could make such a huge artefact and make it so perfectly. Some of them sat for hours watching the ships on the water, thinking what it must be like to be carried inside a little wooden shell far out into the middle of that astonishing blue emptiness until you reached another country, another place that would be like this one but different in ways they couldn't begin to imagine. There were even a few men in the camp who considered, sometimes actually talked about, the idea of *not* destroying the city. *Deliberately to ruin such a thing would be a waste, and what could be more abhorrent than waste?* They were, however, very few. Most of the plainsmen gave it no thought, being too busy with other things.

Loredan reopened his fencing school, and soon had a full class. Litigation was still tending to increase, the demand for lawyers was greater than ever, and there were others joining the schools who didn't intend to practise law but just wanted to learn how to fence. He hired a new clerk, a man in his sixties who did the sums, collected the fees and wrote up the books. He arranged the sale of Athli's furniture, surrendered her lease and got a refund on the balance of the rent, and found a reliable courier to forward the proceeds to the Island. Three weeks later he got a receipt in her neat, clear handwriting, accompanied by a formal note of thanks copied from the usual book of business precedents.

The *Squirrel* came back with a cargo of bowstaves and peacock feathers, and left with three berths still empty; people were still leaving the city, but the price of a passage had fallen by a third. Venart came alone; he called to see Loredan with a message, but he was out and the person he was playing messenger for hadn't written a letter. He took a letter from Gannadius to the Patriarch, and came away with his arms full of books, fresh parchment, pens, two bottles of extremely good wine (one for himself, for running the errand). Alexius was out of bed, and had more or less resumed his duties as Patriarch now that the Security Council only met once a week. He asked Venart to give Vetriz his best wishes, and wondered if there might be room for a barrel or two of preserved pears aboard the *Squirrel* the next time she made the run. His doctors had absolutely forbidden them, but what did they know? And besides, where was the point in being a wizard if you couldn't eat what you fancied?

The Prefect, the Lord Lieutenant and their colleagues in government returned to their work with renewed vigour after the enforced holiday of the emergency. It was an exciting time for them, full of opportunities; during the uneasy suspension of faction politics, any number of potential weapons had been forged and stockpiled, so that when conventional government was resumed both sides were spoilt for choice when it came to subjects for debate and argument. For the first week or so the contest was fairly evenly balanced, but it wasn't long before it became apparent that the Lord Lieutenant's Radicals were gradually getting the better of the Prefect's Popularists, thanks mostly to two issues which immediately caught the imagination of the Council and thereafter refused to go away; the bungling of the initial cavalry raid, and the unauthorised use of the barbarous and inhuman fire-oil.

As far as the Prefect was concerned, his worst enemy was timing. In less than a month, he was due to be reaffirmed in office by the Council; with the Radicals baying for his blood as the officer nominally responsible for both disasters, this might not turn out to be the formality it should have been. There were precedents for the impeachment of a Prefect – the last one over a century ago, it had to be admitted; but that only increased the glamour of the situation, since it was a poor councillor who didn't want to be involved in making history – and his only line of defence, he quickly realised, was attack. By shifting the blame onto Colonel Loredan (who had been, of course, *Deputy* Lord Lieutenant, although directly answerable to the Prefect's Office), he could so engineer matters that if he were to fall, the Lord Lieutenant would inevitably fall with him. This would involve a major escalation, from which there could be no turning back; but once both of them had been impeached, they would then have no alternative but to work together to overturn the impeachments (his constitutional advisers were already working their way through the loopholes in the regulations and had promised an early report) and restore the situation to what it had been before. The best way to achieve that would be to bring forward Loredan's trial to the earliest possible date.

'I don't believe it,' muttered Ceuscai. 'Read it again.'

Temrai nodded and held the parchment up to his nose. The light in his tent was just about good enough for reading, provided the writing was clear.

'"Bardas Loredan to Chief Temrai, greetings,"' he recited. '"You will recall that we have an outstanding contract between us. Would you be so kind as to indicate when it would be convenient for us to meet, under safe conduct, to discuss how this obligation might best be discharged? I await your answer with interest."'

'He's gone mad,' Uncle Anakai pronounced judicially. 'Probably the result of his disgrace and being relieved of command. I'd sling it on the fire if I were you.'

'He must be a bit crazy if he thinks we'll go for the old single-combat routine,' Ceuscai agreed. 'For one thing, there's no evidence at all that this challenge'd be ratified by his government.'

Temrai lifted his head. 'Who said anything about single combat?' he said.

The council of war looked at each other. 'That's what he's getting at, surely,' someone said. 'Roundabout way of putting it, I know, but what else would you expect from a raving lunatic?'

'This hasn't got anything to do with the war,' Temrai said. 'It's personal. He wants me to make him a sword.'

The tent went very quiet. 'Are you sure about that?' asked Uncle Anakai. 'No disrespect, but that's rather a lot to read into a fairly short letter—'

'Actually,' Temrai said, 'he's quite right. Oh, come on, I must have told you the story. Didn't I? It was what he was referring to when we played diplomacy that time we met him. You remember.'

Ceuscai frowned. 'I remember there was a lot of stuff I didn't understand about signs and you owing him something,' he said. 'But if you explained at all, I must have been asleep or something.'

'Oh.' Temrai's face twitched into a slight grin. 'I'd better fill you in, then. I did meet this Loredan while I was living in the city; well, actually it was the night I left. Jurrai and I were just riding along the bridgehouse road, in fact, when this Loredan barged in front of me, blind drunk, and I, um, trod on him. Rather, my horse did. He wasn't damaged, but it has to be admitted, some of his property was. A painted sign. Apparently rather valuable. And he insisted on being paid for it, and for some reason or other I promised to pay him back by making a sword for him. So you see, strictly speaking, he's entitled.'

Another silence.

'This is getting ludicrous,' Ceuscai said at last. 'Stop messing around, Temrai. You make it sound like you're almost considering doing it.'

Temrai scratched the back of his head. 'Maybe,' he said. 'Maybe not. I'm in two minds about it, to tell you the truth.'

Everybody started to speak at once. Deafened, Temrai held up his hand for quiet.

'About meeting him, I mean,' he went on. 'Think about it, will you, rather than yelling your heads off. This man used to be the Commander-in-Chief of the city, but now he's been disgraced. The latest word is, he's going to be put on trial; if he's serious about this sword business, then maybe that's what he wants it for.' He paused to let the implication of what he'd said sink in. 'In other words,' he said, 'he's discontented, with a whopping great big grudge against the city rulers, possibly a bit mad as well. And didn't we all agree a week or so back that the only way we'll ever get in there is if someone opens the gates for us?'

'I see,' said Anakai softly. 'So you think that's what he's really getting at?'

'It's possible. And even if that isn't what he's got in mind at the moment, there's no reason why we shouldn't plant the idea ourselves. Or has anybody else got any addle-brained malcontents on the payroll who are crazy enough to betray the city and also in a position to be able to get hold of the key?'

'Well, *he's* not, for a start,' someone objected. 'You just said, he's been relieved of command.'

'He'll know how to get the gates open,' Temrai replied confidently. 'Come on, it must be worth a try. Mustn't it?'

The council of war considered the point. 'Try this,' someone suggested. 'Here's the disgraced Commander-in-Chief, reputation and honour in shreds, nothing left to live for, he's failed his city and he's got nothing to lose. Why not try and make up for it and become a national hero by assassinating the clan chief? It'd be a suicide mission, but as far as he's concerned it's got to be better than being put to death by his own people.'

Temrai nodded. 'That's perfectly possible,' he said. 'Which is why, if we do decide to meet him, I'll want the best archers in the clan covering him from the moment he sets foot in this camp. Then we can send his head to the rulers and tell them he came here offering to betray the city. That'll give them all sorts of things to worry about.'

Anakai frowned at him thoughtfully. 'You've made your mind up, haven't you?' he said. 'You really do want to meet this lunatic. Temrai, he's the man who poured the fire-oil on the rafts. I won't insult you by asking if you'd forgotten.'

'He was only doing his duty,' Temrai replied quietly. 'Just as we were only doing our duty putting the rafts under the walls in the first place. If you want to argue morality we can do that later, although personally I prefer chess.'

More silence, this time with an unspoken commentary; *he never used to be like this, he's changed, maybe the war's really got to him.*

'And suppose he does actually want you to make him a sword?' someone eventually asked. 'Would you do that?'

'I don't know,' Temrai replied, looking the man steadily in the eyes. 'It may be that I want this particular man kept alive, rather than getting himself killed in the lawcourts. Also, I've never made a law-sword before, it's rather an interesting exercise, technically speaking. And consider this, too,' he went on, cupping his chin in his hands. 'Suppose he wins his trial and gets back into favour. Suppose he gets his command back. And then suppose it becomes known that he won his trial with a sword made for him by the enemy chief personally. I think our friends over the river could really tear themselves apart over that.'

'And we wouldn't have to contend with their best general,' someone added. 'It's a nice idea.'

'You're all out of your minds,' Anakai grumbled. 'This is either a trick, or the ravings of a madman, or a really peculiar form of practical joke. You don't even know for sure that the letter came from Colonel Loredan.'

Temrai smiled, and yawned. 'True,' he said, 'but if I'd allowed myself to be put off by not knowing things, we'd never have started this war in the first place.' He sat still for a few seconds, then went on. 'I'll tell you something else,' he said. 'I'm prepared to bet that the man who brought this message – he's waiting in the guard tent, with ten men ready to cut him into slices if he so much as scratches his bum – is Loredan himself. Who else is he going to find to run his errands for him?'

Ceuscai shook his head, as if trying to wake up from a peculiar dream. 'Well, we'd recognise him if we saw him. Why not bring him in and see for ourselves?'

'Why not indeed?' Temrai grinned. 'Go fetch, Ceuscai. And bring plenty of guards, remember.'

Loredan sat in the middle of the circle, trying to put out of his mind the arrowheads trained on him. It was the first time he'd sat in a plains tent; he'd seen any number of them, but always from the outside. It was a clever design, he realised, efficient and comfortable. The heavy felt kept in the heat, while the oil and lard on the outside kept out the rain. The uprights were strong enough to keep it up even during the savage windstorms of the plains spring, but could be put up and taken down again quickly and easily by one practised man. Unlike so many city houses, it had adequate ventilation to allow the smoke from the fire to escape, rather than filling the room and blinding everyone inside. It would also catch fire at the least provocation, as he knew better than most; cut the guy ropes and pitch in a torch, and nobody would get out alive. Curious, that these eminently practical people had never dealt with such an obvious flaw in the design. They had some sort of blind spot where fire was concerned.

'It's very good of you to see me,' he said pleasantly, 'a busy man like yourself.'

Temrai shrugged. 'It's not every day we get visits from distinguished enemy lunatics,' he replied. 'Now then, what's all this *really* about?'

Everyone in the tent waited for Loredan to answer. He took his time about it, as he enjoyed the warmth of the fire. He was still damp after swimming the river, and with his hair plastered down over his forehead he didn't look particularly mysterious or threatening. *He looks older than I'd have thought,* Temrai said to himself, *but it's definitely the same man, the one I remember.* The thought of him getting away, dying cleanly in the lawcourts from a single thrust without knowing that his city was being destroyed and his people butchered, wasn't something that Temrai wanted to dwell on. To find his one true enemy again after so many years and then to lose him, at the very moment of consummation, would make the whole exercise meaningless. After all, it had been that last-minute meeting, just as he was about to leave the city with every part of him urging him to spare it, that had made him come here and shown him that this terrible thing had to be done.

'I'm sorry,' Loredan said. 'I can't have expressed myself clearly enough in my letter. You said you'd make a sword for me. I need one rather urgently. It's as simple as that.'

'I see.' Temrai scratched his chin thoughtfully. 'What sort of sword are we talking about?'

'A law-sword,' Loredan replied promptly. 'Do you know the design? It's a bit specialised.'

Temrai nodded. 'I know the general principle,' he said. 'But wouldn't you be better off buying one in the city? Old ones are the best, I gather, but there are supposed to be quite a few current makers turning out first-rate products. I'm sure you'd get a much better sword from them than from me.'

Loredan shook his head. 'I have this problem,' he said, 'with the wretched things breaking. It's something to do with the way the steel gets heated up when the cutting edges are being brazed to the core; the way we do it makes them brittle, and I suppose there's something in my fencing style that must put an unusual amount of strain on the weak part of the blade. I used to have quite a collection, but all the good ones have snapped on me over the last six months or so. The last one went yesterday, in fact, while I was practising. You see, I shall be fighting for my life in the courts very soon, and I have rather a bad feeling about the outcome. It's to do with who my opponent's going to be; it's all rather complicated, and I won't bore you with details. The point is, your technique with the silver solder makes a much less fragile blade, and I don't know anybody in the city who can do it. 'So,' he concluded, folding his arms, 'here I am.'

Temrai nodded again. 'And what makes you think I'd put myself out for you, of all people? You've got to admit, this whole business is extremely bizarre.'

'Oh, I thought you might,' Loredan replied equably. 'It was worth asking, anyway. My old commanding officer—'

'General Maxen?'

'That's right, General Maxen. He always used to say, *When you can't trust your friends, try your enemies.* He wasn't usually wrong.'

Temrai took a deep breath, held it and let it go. 'You could be mad,' he said, 'or extremely tired of your life. Or you could have come here to save your ruined honour by killing me, as my advisers have suggested. I was rather hoping you'd come to get your revenge on your city.'

'What, do a deal with you and open the gates?' Loredan raised an eyebrow. 'Another thing Maxen used to say was, *I like treachery but I don't like traitors.* I'll be honest with you,' he went on, 'the thought had occurred to me, too. But I don't think I will, thank you all the same.'

Temrai looked at him for a while, then said, 'Fair enough. From what I gather, you're no longer in a position to do anything about it, so I won't press the point. For the same reason, I can't be bothered to have you killed. I suggest you go away before I change my mind.'

Loredan shook his head. 'I asked you to do something for me,' he said. 'As an enemy, and because you owe me. It's embarrassing to have to admit this, but I think my life may depend on it.'

'Really.' Temrai studied him for a while. 'I can't believe

we're having this conversation,' he said. 'I keep expecting to wake up and find it's all a dream.'

'Have you been suffering from headaches recently?'

'No. Why?'

'Just asking. It's a long story.'

'We have a fairly effective cure for headaches,' Temrai said. 'Bark from a willow tree, boiled in water. When it's cool, you drink the water.'

Loredan nodded. 'I know,' he said. 'Well?'

'Do you know, I'm almost tempted to do it,' Temrai said. 'It's obvious that your habit of excessive drinking has finally undermined your wits, but it's got the makings of a very fine legend. A great chief ought to do unexpected and flamboyant things. Meghtai, get a forge heated up and find me about a dozen old horseshoes and some solder.'

Loredan watched Temrai through a curtain of fire as the young man mixed the flux, occasionally glancing sideways to watch the colours change in the steel. The wire that held the billets of hard steel to the core glowed bright orange, but the blade sections were still a dark purple.

'The trick,' Temrai observed, 'lies in tempering the edges while letting the core cool slowly. It's important to do everything in the right order,' he went on, spitting into the flux to make it smoother. 'First, solder the joints; then we pack the blade with bonemeal and dried blood while it's still cherry red, and we hold it there for as long as we dare, to let the hardness seep in through the pores of the steel. Then we've got to temper the blade, as far as possible without cooling down the core. That's difficult.'

Loredan nodded appreciatively. 'It's cooling it suddenly that makes it brittle, then?' he asked.

'That's partly it,' Temrai replied, 'though there's more to it than that. Some grades of steel don't harden at all. Also, you don't want the edges too brittle either; you actually want to soften them just a little after you've quenched off the original heat, and you do that by heating it up and quenching it a second time, except you take it to a much lower heat. You can tell the right heat by watching the colours; somewhere between reddish brown and purple's what you're after. The simplest thing to do is quench the edges only after the first heating – that's when we've got it red-hot and smothered it in bonemeal – so that the heat left in the core passes out into the edges (which we've just cooled) and brings them up to the right temperature. There, that ought to do,' he added, giving the flux a final stir. 'Are you interested in all this,' he added, 'or am I boring you?'

'Not at all,' Loredan said, 'it's fascinating. And knowledge is never wasted.'

Temrai grinned. 'Another time I'll show you how to build a siege engine,' he said. 'Here we are, look, that deep, rather attractive orange colour.' He nodded to the men working the bellows; they stepped up the rate of pumping, so that the metal glowed in the flame. 'The flux'll cool it, of course,' he added as he drew the billet out with a pair of tongs, 'so it'll have to go back in again before we can start soldering. Patience is a virtue in blacksmithing just as much as in siegecraft.'

The flux hissed and bubbled as it drew down into the joint, leaving dull grey flecks on the orange metal like clouds in a sunrise. When he judged that it was ready, Temrai pulled it out again and touched the solder stick to the sides of the joint, watching the silver disappear into the fine line between the parts of the blade. 'It only flows if it's hot enough,' he said, 'and if it doesn't flow, you're wasting your time. The flux helps, but it's the heat that does it.'

In the glow of the fire, Temrai's face shone a bright orange, like the steel he was working. Loredan mopped his forehead with his sleeve.

'It's taken,' Temrai said. 'Now we pack it with the hardening stuff and bring it back to cherry red.' He raised his head and looked Loredan in the eye. 'If the smell of burning blood and bone makes you feel ill, now's the time to stand well back. It can turn your stomach if you're not used to it.'

He sprinkled the bonemeal and dried blood, making sure

the edges of both sides were evenly covered. Loredan remembered the smell, but stayed where he was. As soon as the steel glowed red through the grey and brown crust, Temrai lifted the billet off the anvil and called for the quenching tray, a long wooden trough half-filled with water.

'A bit of salt in it helps,' he said. 'Fortunate that we're so near the sea, really. In fact, this is an ideal spot for this sort of job. Now then,' he added, as he dipped the edges carefully in the trough, moving his head away as the steam rose up (the meeting of fire and water, after the burning of blood and bone), 'here's a useful tip. When you're quenching, keep moving the metal up and down in the water, or else you'll find you get tiny cracks which'll ruin the whole thing. There,' he concluded, holding up the billet. 'Quickly scrape off this crud from the edges so we can see the colours, and there we are.'

Loredan watched the colours change, straw to mud, mud to purple; then Temrai swung the blade dramatically through the air and held it up, examining it carefully. 'That'll do,' he said. 'Now we cool it for the last time, using oil because it cools more slowly than water, and that's the job done. It isn't all that difficult to understand,' he added, 'once you know why it's got to be done that way. Like so many things in life.'

'Indeed,' Loredan replied. 'Thank you, it's been quite an education.'

Temrai smiled as he wiped sweat from his face. 'Amazing what you can pick up just by listening to people while they're working. By the way,' he went on, 'I didn't make this thing out of old horseshoes just because I'm a cheapskate; it's the best material I know for blade steel. There's something about being continually bashed about and trodden on that makes the stuff remarkably tough and hard. You'll have to provide your own hilt,' he said, wrapping a scrap of rag round the tang. 'It's too late at night to go drilling bone and messing about with skin and wire. Here you are.'

The swordsmith handed the sword to the swordsman, holding it by the blade and offering him the rag-bound tang. Loredan took it and felt the balance, then held it up and looked down it to check the straightness. Along the narrow ribbon of steel he could see Temrai watching him, as if he were the other man in a matter of justice. 'Thanks,' he said, 'it's a neat job. For a first attempt, it's very good indeed.'

'I like getting things right first time,' Temrai replied. 'And doing things I haven't attempted before. Does that make us all square, do you think?'

Loredan nodded. 'As far as I'm concerned,' he said. 'I expect you're glad not to be beholden to me any more.'

'It was the least I could do for an enemy,' Temrai said. 'Now get out of this camp before I have you crucified.'

CHAPTER EIGHTEEN

'It can't be,' said the wheelwright's wife.

'It is.'

'It *can't* be.' She frowned, and peered. 'He's bedridden, never leaves his palace—'

'Lodgings,' her husband corrected her. 'The Patriarch's house is called his lodgings.'

'Whatever. Still can't be him, surely.' She peered again. 'It looks like him,' she conceded.

'Well, there you are, then.'

'Doesn't mean it actually is him. I mean, what's the Patriarch doing getting out of bed when he's seriously ill to go watching a lawsuit?'

'Ah.' The wheelwright lowered his voice. 'He's a friend of this Loredan, by all accounts. Great friends, they were, during the emergency. They do say,' he added in a furtive whisper, 'that he's implicated.'

His wife looked shocked. 'Get away,' she said. 'Patriarch Alexius?'

'So I've heard.'

'Don't believe a word of it.' His wife scrutinised the figure on the opposite side of the spectators' gallery for a minute or so, hardly noticing the honeycakes she was munching as she did so. 'Are you sure?' she asked.

'Well, there's no hard and fast evidence, of course, though I've heard it said—'

'And there he is, bold as brass,' his wife muttered, scandalised. 'How he's got the nerve to show his face in public—'

Once every so often, the fixture lists pinned to the door of the lawcourts produced what could only be described as a dream ticket; a combination of issues and participants so perfect that they could hardly have been better if they'd been chosen by popular demand. This was just such an occasion; the gorgeous and enigmatic girl fencer who had recently been appointed Attorney-General versus the notorious Colonel Loredan on a treason charge – which meant the City Prefect would be presiding in person, dressed in all his traditional finery, with a platoon of guards in parade armour standing by and, to crown it all, *free admission*…

Needless to say, all the city dignitaries were present; the Lord Lieutenant, entitled by virtue of his rank to sit in the Emperor's own box, surrounded by the heads of all the offices of state and a buzzing swarm of magnificently costumed clerks and functionaries; the upper hierarchy of the Order, including the Patriarch himself (but where was the City Archimandrite, late Deputy Patriarch, until recently the Patriarch's inseparable companion? Rumour had it he'd either fled the city or been forced into exile on the pretext of an overseas appointment because of what he knew about the Patriarch's clandestine involvement in whatever it was Colonel Loredan was supposed to have done; the plot thickened.)

To the people of the city, whose morale had recently been so sadly depleted by the indignities of the emergency, this display of civic pomp and gratuitous justice was just what they needed to remind them of the awesome majesty and splendour of Perimadeia, the strength of her institutions and the unquestionable rightness of her cause and proceedings. At a time when it was of the utmost importance to make the citizens feel good about themselves and the city, the perfect event had suddenly materialised, almost as if it had been planned that way by some public-spirited deity.

'What's her name?' whispered the wheelwright's wife. 'You know, the Attorney-General.'

'Don't ask me,' replied her husband. 'Presumably she's got one but I can't remember ever having heard it.'

In the entrance hall trumpets blared, a signal for everyone in the courthouse to stand. While the magnificent domed roof was still reverberating with the sound, like a lover of fine wines savouring a special vintage, the main doors swung open and the Prefect entered the court at the head of a procession. In honour of the occasion he had ordered a brand-new set of official regalia; a flowing robe of gold tissue trimmed at the collar and cuffs with ermine and otter, and a tiara embroidered with gold and silver thread. In one hand he carried the lavishly embellished sword of state, while the other held the book of ordinances. He walked with a slow, measured dignity towards the place reserved for him, tucked the skirts of his gown around his knees, and sat down. Around him, his entourage filled the rest of the dais like a quart slopped into a pint jug, not quite pushing and shoving for the few available seats, while the Prefect and the Lord Lieutenant exchanged poisonous looks and the rest of the spectators plumped up their cushions and made themselves comfortable.

When the important matters of protocol had been sorted out and the ushers had hushed down the crowd, the Prefect opened his document case and nodded to the clerk; elderly, short-sighted Teofano, who had sat below the dais watching advocates die every day for half a century.

Teofano recited the grievances of the city of Perimadeia against the prisoner Bardas Loredan, customarily styled Colonel but without authority to use such title; that while commanding an expeditionary force against the national enemy he had by his negligence and failure to exercise due care allowed the said enemy to inflict on the said expeditionary force a severe defeat resulting in the loss of nine hundred and seventeen lives, injuries to a further two hundred and forty-eight of the soldiers comprising the said force and losses of horses and property both of the state and of private persons amounting to the sum of twelve thousand, three hundred and eight gold quarters; further, that while commanding the defence of the city in the capacity of Deputy Lord Lieutenant he had wilfully and without authority of the Council deployed and used an unauthorised weapon namely an incendiary compound, thereby tending to enrage the enemy and exacerbate the existing state of war between such enemy and the city and people of Perimadeia; further, that while serving in the said capacity he had negligently and carelessly performed his duties with the result that the said enemy had severely damaged the said defences and killed seven hundred and sixty-one citizens, injured a further three hundred and ninety-six citizens and caused damage to property both of the state and of private persons amounting to the sum of two million, three hundred and forty-nine thousand, five hundred and forty-nine gold quarters; further, that while charged with the duties and responsibilities of the said office of Deputy Lord Lieutenant, he had corruptly and fraudulently seized private property namely rope valued at eight thousand four hundred gold quarters; further, that while charged with the said duties and responsibilities he had corruptly sold state property valued at twelve thousand gold quarters to a third party for the sum of ten thousand gold quarters, to his own advantage and to the detriment of the state.

When Teofano had finished, there was an appropriately awed silence. Then the Prefect cleared his throat and asked who appeared for the state. A long, thin girl of no more than seventeen years of age, with a thin face and pale blue eyes, stood up and gave the court her name and details of her professional qualifications, adding that she was the Attorney-General of the city. Then she bowed to the Prefect and sat down.

'Very well,' the Prefect said. 'Who appears for the prisoner, Bardas Loredan?'

After a moment, a dark-haired, clean-shaven man of just over average height stood up and faced the bench. 'I do, my lord,' he said, a little bit too softly. He raised his voice slightly as he gave his name; Bardas Loredan, fencing instructor, appearing as a litigant in person.

'Very well,' the Prefect repeated, and he began to read the depositions. They were more than usually long and complicated, phrased in the mystical language of lawyers' clerks, and while his voice droned and droned the spectators sat in mesmerised silence, relishing the tension and studying the advocates' faces, occasionally nudging their neighbours and indicating the size and odds of their wagers with their fingers.

In his seat at the back of the spectators' gallery, Alexius gave up trying to follow the legal rigmarole and concentrated on keeping his eyelids from drooping. The Prefect's voice was a heavy monotone, and Alexius could feel sleep slowly crowding in on him. He fought it, but—

—Sat upright, to find he was exactly where he had been, sitting in the courthouse, with its high domed roof, the rows of stone benches encircling the sandy floor, the judge's platform, the marble boxes where the advocates waited for the command. He could see Loredan's back, and over his shoulder the girl on whose behalf he had once dreamed exactly the same dream; older now, grown up, somehow suddenly beautiful in a way that made him uneasy. He could see the red and blue light from the great rose window burning on the blade of her sword, a long, thin strip of straight steel foreshortened by the perspective into an extension of her hand, a single pointing finger.

He saw Loredan move forward, his graceful, economical movement; and the girl reacts, parrying backhand, high. Now she leans forward, scarcely moving her arm at all except for the roll of the wrist that brings the blade level again. Loredan's shoulder drops as he tries to get his sword in the way, but he's left it too late, the sin of an overconfident man. Because Loredan's back is to him, he can't see the impact or where the blade hits; but the sword falls from his hand, he staggers back and drops, bent at the waist, dead before his head bumps noisily on the flagstones. The girl doesn't move, and the blade of her sword points directly at Alexius, her eyes staring into his along the narrow ribbon of steel whose point hangs in the air, motionless, unwavering ...

Alexius reached out for the moment, the double handful of time he'd just seen for the second time, caught it, held onto it tightly like a blacksmith trying to hold onto the hind leg of a nervous horse while he presses the red-hot iron shoe onto the hoof, and the air is filled with smoke and the smell of burning, and steam as the hot iron is quenched—

—And woke up, to hear the Prefect's voice still droning. The woman sitting next to him was nudging him in the ribs.

'You were almost asleep,' she hissed. 'Don't want to miss the big fight.'

He smiled his thanks and sat up, trying desperately to remember whether he'd managed to catch that double handful of moment, and if he had, what he'd done with it.

'Five quarters on the girl,' whispered the woman. 'Two to one.'

Alexius considered for a moment. 'Done,' he whispered back, fumbling in his sleeve for the money.

The Prefect gave the signal, and the two fencers took guard. At precisely the same moment they both raised their swords into the guard of the Old fence, so that between them lay one continuous ribbon of steel that connected them hand to hand and eye to eye. For what seemed like a lifetime they held the position, their arms outstretched but absolutely steady, their sword-points not wavering by the thickness of a hair. One minute, a minute and a half, two minutes; they could have been an instructor and his pupil practising the oldest and most arduous exercise of all, which strengthens the muscles and trains the mind to be patient and alert. Three minutes—

Alexius' head began to hurt, very badly. He put his fingertips to his temples, closed his eyes, opened them; then the pain began in his chest and arm, and he leant forward, trying unsuccessfully to breathe. Just as he thought he was about to black out, he felt a hand on his arm; and at once the pain stopped, his head cleared, his lungs filled with air—

'You all right?' asked the man on his left; a large, thickset bald man with an accent. 'You had me worried for a moment.'

Alexius gestured that he was fine; then he recognised—

'Gorgas Loredan,' he said.

'That's right,' the man replied. 'Fancy you knowing my name.'

'I—'

'Ssh. They're off.' Gorgas Loredan was gazing intently ahead. 'You a betting man, by any chance?'

'Sometimes.'

'Five quarters on our kid. Two to one.'

Oh, well, thought Alexius. 'Done,' he said.

Then he looked down at the two small figures below. Loredan had his back to him; he was lunging now, graceful and economical in his movements. The girl parried, backhand, high, and counterthrust. Loredan dropped his shoulder to parry, realising he was late on the movement, but just in time—

(*Ah*, said Alexius to himself.)

—He caught the point of her sword on the shell of his hilt, his elbow high and cramped, his wrist turned over. Her blade passed his body, slitting his shirt; then Loredan turned his arm back, converting the late parry into an almost uncounterable riposte. The girl sidestepped; two quick shuffles forward, while twisting her thin body out of the way and frantically trying to cover herself with her sword. In mid-thrust Loredan saw she'd done enough; he aborted the thrust and sidestepped to match her movement, pre-emptively deflecting her blade before she was through with her own parry. This time, when he counterthrust, there would be nowhere for her to go.

But he was too good a teacher to have neglected such emergencies. The girl jumped backwards from a standstill, just as she'd been taught, and feinted a slash at Loredan's knees, to make him parry low and leave his chest and head exposed. He in turn anticipated the feint, starting to make the anticipated parry and then converting it into a block for the blow she'd intended to make, a short, wristy slash at his face. Having parried that, he stepped back, lowering his sword-point to cover his retreat. She circled, stepping back and to the right to defeat his intended line, but she'd failed to read the signals correctly. Instead of lunging, being parried and laying himself open to a counterthrust, Loredan bent his knees until his outstretched left hand touched the ground, simultaneously slashing with his sword at ankle height. Just in time she skipped over the blade, only to find as she landed that Loredan's sword was pointing at her heart, and she had no chance of blocking the thrust in time.

Jerking her head back she wrenched herself to one side; instead of running her through, the blade sliced into her side a hand's span above her hip. It was a sharp blade, there was very little pain, but it was the first time she'd been cut, and she panicked. Without even trying to move her feet or find her balance she slashed wildly; Loredan fended the blow away from his face with the thick part of his blade while stepping back and left, bringing his blade round to face her undefended side. Then, with a short bend of his arm and a sharp turn of his wrist, he struck her right hand, catching her fingers against the grip of her sword and shearing them off just below the knuckle. Her sword clattered on the flagstones and he stepped back to make the final thrust; hesitated—

She kicked hard. He turned away, taking the force of the blow on his thigh. Before he could line up, she had sprung back a good three yards and was scrabbling left-handed for her sword. *Damn*, Loredan thought, *I hate fighting southpaws*; he retreated a step or two and took the guard of the City fence, knees bent and sword angled up. She'd been taught the rudiments left-handed, although she was of course at a grave disadvantage even without the pain and shock of her injury. It ought to be fairly straightforward, provided he didn't underestimate her at the last. He forced himself to relax, to let his weight sink to his knees.

She attacked, swinging a sideways cut at his head. Easy

enough to duck under that and then lunge; easy enough for her to turn the lunge and back away, using her feet to get out of trouble, just as she'd been taught. Loredan stayed where he was; time was against her now, she'd know she had to finish it soon before loss of blood made her too weak. He felt something under his foot and decided he knew what it was.

She attacked again; a feinted thrust at eye level, but he knew she was going to convert that into a cut to his forearm, so he moved his head out of the way and parried the cut; turned it and replied with a ferocious short-arm slash at her neck. She'd been expecting the counterthrust (as she'd been taught) and only just managed to get her blade in the way. Even as Loredan followed through the slash, in his mind's eye he could visualise his recovery, the short, fast lunge into her heart that she would be completely unable to prevent—

Their blades clashed, and there was a crack. Loredan's sword had snapped, six inches below the hilt.

Oh, for crying out loud, he thought; and, without thinking, he pivoted on his right foot, bringing his left fist round and ramming it into her face. He felt her nose crunch as her head was turned sideways; then she dropped backwards like a sack full of rocks and sprawled on the ground, falling across her own sword and breaking the blade.

Pity, he said to himself. *It was only modern, but it looked like a late-series Mesteyn, worth the price of a drink*. He looked down at the hilt in his right hand, at the grey frosting of the fractures in cross-section, noticing that the core had given way, in exactly the same way all the others had. *Enough to make a man believe in witchcraft*, he thought bitterly, and let it fall onto the stone floor.

He rested the palm of his hand on the pommel of his dagger. Now he really ought to finish the job; but what the hell, nobody was paying him. It would mean a verdict of *not proven* rather than *not guilty*, but the practical effect was the same. Certainly the difference wasn't enough to justify the unpleasant effort of bending down and slicing through the side of her neck, getting blood all over his cuffs and hands. He was free to go, and he was on his own time. Stepping over the girl's body, he walked out of the courthouse in dead silence.

Alexius turned to the woman on his right.

'He didn't finish it,' she said. 'I think you'll find that means all bets are off.'

Alexius looked at her.

'Tell you what,' she said. 'Double or quits on the next case.'

'I'm not staying for the next case.'

She sighed and dug in her purse, producing ten small silver coins. He thanked her and turned to pay his debts on his left, but the seat was empty.

The ushers were dragging her out. They dumped her in a chair near the doorway; as an afterthought one of them twisted a tourniquet round her wrist. Then they picked her up, one under each arm, and walked her out of the door. The spectators started to mutter; a good fight ruined by a cop-out, highly unprofessional conduct on the part of someone who was supposed to be an instructor. What sort of example was that to give the advocates of tomorrow? People started grumbling about wanting their money back, until they remembered that it had been free admission. Somehow, this seemed to make them feel more cheated than ever.

Back in his usual seat, out of the way and beside the window, Loredan poured himself a cup of strong wine and drank it down in one. His knuckles were sore, he'd done something to his right wrist and he ached all over. *Damn waste of time*, he said to himself, *but at least it's over. It'll be good not to have that hanging over me any more.*

There was always the possibility that she'd come after him again; but with only a thumb left on her right hand she wasn't going to be fencing any more, and from what he'd gathered from Alexius of her twisted motivation, killing him illegally wasn't an option as far as she was concerned. As for the Prefect and the Lord Lieutenant, he sincerely

hoped that that was the end of it. He understood enough
about politics to know that a *not proven* verdict ought to be
an acceptable second best for both factions. It meant that
the Prefect was neither convicted nor exonerated; that the
Lord Lieutenant's people hadn't made their case, but hadn't
lost face either. Both sides would want to see the issue
quietly forgotten about, and him with it. Which suited him
perfectly. It'd be interesting to see what effect the result
would have on enrollments in his school. It could go either
way, or it could have no effect at all.

A pity Athli wasn't here; it had always helped to have her
to talk to after a case, someone to drink with who could be
relied on not to say the wrong thing. As it was, he suspected,
he'd stay here drinking until he felt ill enough to want to go
home. He considered going to see Alexius – he'd certainly
be interested in the outcome of this particular fight, and the
Patriarch would probably quietly regulate the booze supply
so that he had enough to get himself straight without
getting sordidly drunk. But it didn't seem appropriate
somehow, to go making social calls so soon after cutting
someone's fingers off. For the rest of the day at least, he
wasn't really a fit person for the head of the Order to
associate with, and the news of his continued existence
would surely keep till tomorrow.

*So much for the clan and their much-vaunted silver
solder.* He poured some more wine – half a cup this time, for
there was no need for him to get drunk if he didn't want to.
Finish the jug, then get something to eat and go home,
spend the rest of the day lying on his bed staring at the
ceiling feeling bored and depressed. The perfect ending to
a perfect day.

He was three-quarters of the way down the jug and
making up his mind to have another when a shadow fell
across him. He looked up, and recognised one of the clerks
from the Prefect's Office, a short, fat young man whose
name began with a B.

'There you are,' said the clerk. 'I've been looking for you
everywhere.'

'Sit down,' Loredan grunted. 'Or get yourself a cup and join me.'

The clerk frowned. 'I haven't got time for that,' he said, 'and neither have you. You're to report to the Prefect at his office immediately.'

'Really?' Loredan leant back against the arm of the settle. 'Why would I want to do a thing like that?'

'Because I'm telling you to,' the clerk replied. 'And because you're still on the reserve duty list, which means you're obliged to obey the orders of your commanding officer.'

Loredan scowled. 'So sue me,' he said. 'I'm sorry, but I'm really not in the mood. And besides, why the hell would he want to see me? I'd have thought he'd have wanted me to disappear from sight.'

The clerk sighed and sat down, having first wiped spilt wine off the bench with his sleeve. 'On the contrary,' he said. 'I'll be frank with you, the Prefect's hoping to make good some of the political damage you've caused to this administration by treating today's result as a vindication. He feels that by reinstating you as Deputy Lord Lieutenant, he'll be making it clear to the city that his original assessment of you was correct, and—'

Loredan stood up. 'Tell the Prefect from me,' he said, 'thanks but no thanks. It's extremely kind of him, but I've already got a job and I don't want another one. Goodbye.'

'You seem to think you have a choice,' the clerk said. 'If you fail to report to the Prefect's Office forthwith, I shall have no alternative but to authorise your arrest as a deserter.' He grinned. 'Desertion's an offence for which you can be executed without trial in time of war. If, as you seem to believe, the Prefect wants to get rid of you, it'd be the most efficient way.'

Loredan sighed, and sat down again. 'At least can't it wait till tomorrow?' he groaned. 'I'm in no fit state to be respectful to my betters. Who knows, by this time tomorrow I might just be sufficiently bored and depressed to go along with this ludicrous charade.'

'You have your orders, Colonel,' the clerk said. 'Finish your drink if you must, and then I'll walk with you just in case you can't remember the way.'

Oh, well, Loredan said to himself. It's not as if I had anything else to do.

'After you,' he said politely.

By the time he reached home, Alexius was exhausted. The last flight of steps leading up from the great hall to the door of his chambers, represented an effort he nearly couldn't bring himself to face. The pains in his chest and arm had subsided completely and his head wasn't hurting, but he felt as if he'd just spent the last forty-eight hours down at the docks shifting sacks of grain. Something to eat, something to drink, followed by sleep.

He had kicked off his boots and was just about to lie down when the pageboy came in.

'Someone to see you,' he said. 'Another foreigner.'

Alexius swore under his breath. 'Name?' he sighed.

The pageboy looked perplexed. 'Well,' he said, 'he said his name was Loredan, but it isn't the Colonel. And, like I said, he's foreign.'

'Ah. In that case, you'd better show him up.'

And, shortly afterwards, Gorgas Loredan entered the room.

'It's all right,' he said, as Alexius waved him to a chair. 'I haven't come for my winnings. Actually, if I've understood the rules correctly, a *not proven* verdict makes all bets void, so we're square.'

Alexius thought of the fat woman who'd sat on his right, but didn't say anything. Gorgas stretched out in the chair, feet crossed, hands behind his head. There was, undoubtedly, a resemblance. Mostly it was in the eyes and the jaw; but fundamentally it was more a similar way of taking up space in the room rather than any markedly shared physical characteristic.

'What can I do for you?' Alexius asked mildly.

Gorgas smiled. 'How are you feeling, by the way?' he

asked. 'I was afraid you were having a heart attack, back there in the courthouse.'

'Much better, thank you,' Alexius replied. 'A little tired, but that's about all. Now then, how can I help?'

'I'd like to see my brother,' Gorgas said, 'but I don't know where he lives. Since you're the nearest he's got to a friend in the city, I thought I'd come and ask you. I'm not putting you out, am I?' he added. 'If it's terribly inconvenient, I can come back later.'

Alexius shook his head. 'Not at all,' he said. 'No time like the present, and I've nothing particularly urgent to be getting on with. You'll excuse me if I don't get up, though.'

Gorgas inclined his head. 'Of course,' he said. 'But if you could let me have his address ...'

Alexius wondered what to do for the best. To refuse would be embarrassing, possibly worse if Gorgas had a short temper. On the other hand, from what little he'd been able to gather, the two brothers hadn't been on speaking terms for a long time. If this was an attempt to restore diplomatic relations, he'd quite possibly be doing Loredan no good at all if he prevented Gorgas from seeing him.

Admit it, you're just curious. Curious was putting it mildly; he'd already been certain before the healing miracle in the lawcourts that Gorgas Loredan was somehow deeply involved in some aspect of the mystery he'd found himself in that night he'd tried to lay the curse. So far, he'd apparently managed to keep the disastrous consequences from hurting anybody but himself and the girl. For all he knew, Gorgas wanted his brother's address so that he could go there and kill him.

'Actually,' he said, 'I don't know where he is at the moment. For a while he was lodging at the second-city gatehouse, but he's moved out again.' *There; managed that without telling an outright lie. Will that do, I wonder?*

'Oh,' Gorgas replied, 'you surprise me. I was sure you'd know.'

Alexius could see his almost-lie reflected in Gorgas' eyes. *Damn, he doesn't believe me.* Nevertheless; he knew he'd reached his decision, and now he'd stick to it. 'I'm terribly sorry,' he said. 'If it's any help to you, I could always try and pass a message to him. I met him when we were both on the Security Council, you see; I can see if any of the other members are still in touch with him, though I must say I think it's fairly unlikely.'

'I see. Well, that's a nuisance. I'd have liked to talk to him before I leave, you see. It's been a long time – the truth is, we haven't spoken to each other for a good few years.' Gorgas Loredan yawned, covered his mouth with the back of his large, flat hand. 'I did something he's never forgiven me for, you see. I've wanted to try and put things right ever since, but I haven't had the chance till now.' His eyes were bright and steady, watching the Patriarch as if they were two advocates in a court of law. 'Perhaps if I told you about it, you'd understand why I'm so keen to see him, and that might just jog your memory.'

Alexius nodded, embarrassed that his lie had been so transparent. 'If you think it would help,' he said.

'It's not a very pleasant story,' Gorgas went on, 'and I'm afraid I'm very much the villain of the piece. I shall have to take the risk of you not wanting to help me after you've heard it.'

Alexius could feel his fingernails digging into his left palm, and wondered what was making him feel so tense. As if he didn't know. 'Your brother is indeed my friend,' he said slowly. 'In fact, I value his friendship a great deal. I would very much like to help him. If, as you say, your intention is to put right something that's been troubling him for many years, then I'll help you. If I decide it would be better if you stayed out of his life, I won't.'

'Fair enough,' said Gorgas equably. He leant forward, straightening his back and resting his fists on his knees. Alexius noticed the breadth of his shoulders and the thickness of his wrists. Bardas' big brother, in every sense of the word. But although there was undoubtedly a strong sense of menace about Gorgas Loredan – almost, at the risk of being melodramatic about it, a fierce vitality that smacked of evil – Alexius couldn't detect any malice at all directed towards Bardas, or himself. If he'd had to make a judgement then and there, he'd have to conclude that this strange, unpleasantly fascinating big man was sincerely fond of the brother he hadn't seen for so long; certainly genuinely concerned for and interested in his wellbeing. Well, why not? Even evil men sometimes love their brothers.

And whatever it was he could feel in the displacement – no, the gash – that this man made in the even flow of the principle, it wasn't evil in the sense of a purely negative, destructive force. Gorgas Loredan wasn't a nice man, he felt sure; but there was more to it than that. There was an ambivalence about him that made Alexius think of a weapon; an instrument solely intended for doing harm and damage, but equally capable of fulfilling its function for good or for evil, depending on who happened to pick it up. And then he realised, quite intuitively: *this man isn't entirely his own master, although maybe he doesn't know that.*

'Has Bardas told you anything about his family?' Gorgas asked.

'A little,' Alexius replied. 'I know your father was a tenant farmer.'

Gorgas nodded. 'In the Mesoge,' he said. 'Strictly speaking our farm counted as a manor because of its size, but in reality it was mostly mountain and forest; only a quarter of it was fit for anything. There were four of us, three brothers and a sister. Our mother died when I was eight; some sort of kidney infection, I think. Our sister's the eldest; she's a year older than me, and I'm two years older than Bardas; Clefas came next, a year after Bardas, and finally Zonaras.' He paused and smiled. 'Have you got that, or shall I go through it again? It isn't actually all that important.'

'Go on, please.'

Gorgas inclined his head. 'Like most of the farms in the Mesoge, it was owned by one of the old city houses; our landlords were the Ferian family. I expect you know of them. I believe they've declined rather a lot over the last few years, but back when we were children they were still a force to be reckoned with.'

'I've heard of them,' Alexius said.

'Well,' Gorgas took a deep breath, as if preparing for an effort. 'About eighteen years ago, when we were all still living on the farm, the landlord's son and a cousin of his came out for a holiday in the country. The story was that they were interested in buying racehorses, but I think it was more the case that they'd made the city a bit too warm for their own good and had to get away for a while, the way the sons of the nobility do from time to time. They soon got through their money, so they were reducing to billeting themselves on the tenants; not much fun for them, and even less for us. They were bored stiff inside a week; nothing to do all day but mope around the farmhouse with the goats, or go for long walks. They drank a lot and chivvied a few of the local girls, but they found them all a bit unappetising and stopped bothering after a bit.

'Except,' Gorgas said, frowning a little, 'for my sister. They liked her all right; she wasn't a great beauty or anything like that, but she was lively and had a sharp sense of humour, which made her a bit more like what they were used to at home. It didn't help that she thoroughly loathed and despised her husband – he was a pleasant enough man, but a peasant from his boots upwards, and they couldn't have children, which upset her. Anyway, these city boys took to hanging around her all the time. Gallas, her husband, didn't seem to mind too much; it was obvious nothing much was happening and anyway, you'd have to have run off Gallas' pigs or set fire to his beard before he'd lose his temper, or even notice. Our father and Bardas didn't like it at all, though. And I–' Gorgas turned his head away a little. 'I wanted more than anything else to get out of the Mesoge and go to the city. When those two young fools showed up, I suddenly saw a chance.'

He sat silently for a while, not moving; then, abruptly, he resumed his story. 'It was quite obvious our sister had the same idea,' he said, 'because as soon as she realised the two boys were interested in her, she started stringing them along, but without ever actually coming across; the message being, she was only too happy to play any games they liked, but only if they took her back to the city with them. Unfortunately, the two lads were too thick to see what she was doing; as far as they were concerned, she was leading them on and then mucking them about. They didn't like that; too complicated for their simple minds, and not really worth the effort. They made it clear that unless she did the right thing by them, they'd move on to the next farm up the valley. Our sister wasn't going to give in unless she got what she wanted; adultery for its own sake was never one of her vices. And all I could see was my chance of getting out of agriculture slipping away from me, unless I could sort something out quickly.

'It was the day when they announced they were leaving. Father made it perfectly obvious that he'd be delighted to see them go; likewise Bardas and Clefas, and our brother-in-law Gallas, who for once displayed a vestigial trace of backbone. Our sister flounced off looking enigmatic, and the two lads were sitting out on the porch waiting for their horses to be saddled up. As far as I was concerned, it was then or never. So I went up to them and started commiserating – obliquely, of course – about my sister's treatment of them.

'They said, plenty more where that came from, or words to that effect. I said they were quitting too easily; they'd got the signals all wrong, I told them, it was no good waiting for her to surrender gracefully like a good little pleasant girl, they had to go out and take what they wanted. I gave them the impression that that was how she always did business, and she'd been waiting for them to make their move and was just as puzzled as they were.

'They believed me, of course, and said that was a different kettle of fish entirely, and why hadn't I said anything before? Then they asked if I had any idea where she might have gone off to. Now, I knew she'd gone down to the river to do her washing, so I tried telling them how to find the place. They said they couldn't make sense of my directions, so why didn't I show them the way? That was fine by me, so off we went; me thinking that this was it, that I'd finally earned my passage out.

'There she was, just as I'd guessed. At first they tried to be nice; but when my sister realised that there was nothing in it for her she started getting stroppy, calling them names, and then when the Ferian boy tried to grab hold of her, she slugged him quite hard across the face with a stone and drew blood. That made them both lose their temper, and they stopped being nice after that.

'Well, I reckoned they could do without me, and I was making myself scarce when to my horror I saw people coming; Father and Bardas and Gallas, who'd heard screaming, and were running up with mattocks in their hands. That didn't suit me at all; the last thing I wanted was for my prospective patrons to get beaten up, or to explain exactly where they'd got their false information from. Maybe I panicked; but no, I'm being too soft on myself. I knew exactly what I was doing. I always have, all my life.

'The lads had left their horses tied up near where I was standing, and one of them had a bow and a quiver on his saddle. I grabbed these and ducked behind some rocks, and when Father and the others came running past I shot Gallas, killed him outright.

'The idea was to make them think it was an ambush by bandits and scare them off; might have worked, too – that sort of thing did happen occasionally – except that Bardas saw me and called out my name. I knew I was for it then, and there was nothing else I could do. I'd have to deal with all of them and then try and sort out a story later. So I shot Father and Bardas – I thought I'd killed them both, but I was careless – and then I went down to the river and picked off the Ferian lad. The other one – did I tell you his name? Cleras Hedin – ran for it and I was well and truly stuck then. I had to get him, but there was my sister to deal with as well. My idea was to make it look like we'd surprised the rapists at their work and there'd been a general battle, with me the only survivor. That wouldn't wash unless I polished off the lot, and now there was one halfway down the valley, and my sister standing in the river all bloody, screaming her head off at me.

'I did panic a bit then; I shot Sis, assumed I'd done the job, and then dashed off after young Hedin. There were only two arrows left by then and I missed with both of them, so in the end I had to run him down and sort him out with a lump of wood. By the time I got back, I was less than thrilled to discover that I was two corpses short; Bardas and my sister. I followed the blood back towards the house; but as soon as I came round the side of the hill I saw Clefas and Zonaras running out towards me with their own bows in their hands, and I decided to cut my losses and get out. I made it to the lads' horses, jumped up and didn't stop till I was well clear. And that's the last I ever saw of home, or any of my brothers.'

He looked up, grinning bleakly. 'I warned you, it's not a terribly nice story,' he said. 'I'm the villain of the piece, obviously enough, but none of the survivors come out of it exactly smelling of roses. Do you want me to go on?'

'You mean there's more?' Alexius said.

'Oh, yes. You're sure? Well, then. The next bit, by the way, is obviously hearsay, based on what my sister's told me since. I'm inclined to believe she's telling the truth. She's not very nice either, but I've never known her tell a deliberate lie.

'Apparently, once the dust had settled and all the bodies had been buried – actually, the Ferians were rather good about it all; they accepted the blame for the rape and set that off against the two killings, where most noble families would've had the survivors strung up without a second thought; so fair play to them – as I was saying, once everybody was buried or recovered from their wounds, Bardas started getting at our sister, saying it was all her fault for being a whore in the first place. He was upset, obviously; and since I wasn't there and the two city boys were both dead, she was the next likely candidate for a scapegoat.

'And then when it turned out she was pregnant, he really lost his cool and tried to throw her out on her ear. Well, the other two weren't having that, so Bardas flung out in a temper and went storming off to join the army. The others expected he'd be back inside a month, but apparently he was spotted by our mother's brother, Uncle Maxen, who'd been in the service all his life and had worked his way up to being General. So Bardas didn't come back after all; and *that* really annoyed Clefas and Zonaras, who were now having to do the work of six men just to keep the farm ticking over and pay the rent.

'They started taking it out on our sister; and Clefas always tended to make his point with the back of his hand rather than reasoned argument. She stuck it out till she was nearly due with the baby; then Clefas had a bit too much to drink one night and went for her with a knife. She didn't hang about after that; and the only place she could go was the city, where she hoped she could get something out of the dead father's people, the Hedins.' Gorgas lifted his head and looked Alexius in the eye. 'She's always been adamant that it was the Hedin lad, not young Ferian, who was the kid's father. I'm perfectly happy to take her word for it; she ought to know, after all, and, like I said, she doesn't tell lies.

'Well, the Hedin family wasn't anything like as grand as the Ferians. Nothas Hedin started off as a goldsmith, branched out into banking, and about this time was making a comfortable living. His boys knew the Ferians through racing, I think; Nothas Hedin was a miserable old devil but when it came to horses he used to spend like there was no tomorrow, and the Ferians were the same. They weren't happy about the situation but they took my sister in and told her she could stay there till the baby was born, and then they'd ship her off somewhere overseas where she'd be looked after and nobody'd have to look at her and be reminded of all the trouble she'd caused.

'I'd reached the city myself by that time, and was making a sort of living hanging around with a bunch of other lowlifes who did naughty things for money. You couldn't really call them assassins, they weren't as grand as that. We used to beat people up in dark alleys, set fire to shops, things like that. Anyway; quite by chance I found out that my sister was in town, and my first thought was that it was time for me to move on. I hadn't worried too much about the Ferians or the Hedins catching up with me for what I'd done, because of course I wasn't calling myself Gorgas Loredan, and until Sis came to town there wasn't anybody in the city who could recognise me. By that stage, though, I'd had enough of travel and adventure to last me for a while, so I hung about and waited to see what happened. I started snooping around one of the maids from the Hedin household so as to find out the news, and what I heard was that although Sis wasn't exactly pleased with me, quite reasonably enough, she was absolutely livid with Bardas, Clefas and Zonaras, and Bardas most of all. So I plucked up my courage and went to see her.

'I think she was so taken aback at seeing me that she forgot to yell bloody murder until after I'd had a chance to be reasonable; and so, after a few mutual recriminations for form's sake, we came to a sort of state of armed truce. After all, we were the only family either of us had still got, and the fact is that we'd always had a sort of special relationship back from when we were kids. I won't say it was forgive and forget exactly; but she had the baby to think of and I was feeling pretty sick about the whole business and badly wanted someone not to hate me to death, so we agreed I'd try and make it up to her as best I could, and we'd see if we couldn't find some way to make the future a degree less crappy for both of us.

'To cut a long story short; I managed to scrape a little money together – you don't want to know how – and we set off for the Island. After a bit of soul-searching Sis left the kid with the Hedin family; they were happy to bring it up as one of theirs provided Mummy promised to go away and never come back. Sis was fairly upset about it at the time, but we agreed a baby'd really get in our way, considering the line of business we planned on going into. I'll say this for my sister, once she's decided what has to be done, she doesn't let sentiment stand in her way.

So we went to the Island and set up in the moneylending racket; did very well at it, too, after a very shaky start. As to what made us turn the corner, that's another story; one that might interest you, Patriarch, some other time, because it sort of impinges on your line of work. Anyway, after a while we found we were making a go of things, our lives were settling down and somehow or other we'd managed to show all the fuck-ups a clean pair of heels; not bad going, considering. It was then that we both decided that our – what shall we call it: our mutual non-aggression pact in the face of a common enemy, namely Life? Something like that – our understanding, if you like, had more or less outlived its usefulness and it'd be in both our interests if we divvied up and went our separate ways while we were still on speaking terms. It was a good idea, I think. When you can feel a major bust-up looming ahead of you, it's not a bad idea to get out of each other's way before the stones start to fly.

'We moved all the way out to Scona and set up a proper bank, all respectable and above board. I have to admit, she's the one with the brains in our family. I'm not doing badly myself, but she's made a real success of the business, and as far as I can see she owns virtually everything and everybody on that side of the bay. Big fish and small pond, maybe; still not too dusty for a peasant's daughter from the Mesoge. And, as I remind her from time to time, if it wasn't for me she might well still be back on Gallas' farm hoeing turnips and mucking out goats. She won't admit it, but at least she doesn't throw things at me when I say it any more.'

Alexius sat very still, like a rabbit facing a snake. The sheer presence of the man was appalling and fascinating. 'And what about the child?' he said at last. 'Your sister's son, the one she left behind?'

'Daughter, actually. In fact, it's her I wanted to see Bardas about, thought I have a nasty feeling I've left it a little bit too late.' He sighed. 'I'm surprised you need to ask, actually. I'd have thought as soon as you heard the name—'

Alexius' throat became terribly dry. 'Hedin,' he said.

'They called the girl Iseutz,' Gorgas continued. 'Not the name her mother gave her, but they wanted something a bit higher class. Anyway, they brought her up with the dead boy's young brother. His name was Teofil.'

'Teofil Hedin. *Iseutz* Hedin.' Alexius' face crumpled in horror. 'Oh, gods, that *girl*—'

Gorgas nodded grimly. 'The irony is,' he said, 'she doesn't even know about Bardas and me and all the rest of it. As far as she's concerned, Bardas is the man who killed her darling uncle Teofil, the only one who ever cared for her. Grisly, isn't it? When it comes to luck, good and bad, our family strikes me as having had rather more than its fair share.'

'Oh, gods,' Alexius repeated. 'She's his niece.'

'Fortunately,' Gorgas said, 'she still is. More by luck than judgement,' he continued, shaking his head. 'It's my fault it's got this far; as soon as we found out what was going on, I raced over here, but the first I knew of this confounded fight was when I saw it posted on the courtroom door.'

Alexius wasn't quite sure what to make of any of that. He wanted to know how they'd found out, for one thing. He wanted to mention the dream he'd had during the reading of the depositions, the pains in his head, chest and arms that had come and gone away again; all manner of small points that seemed to be leading in a certain direction. He wanted to ask Gorgas if he knew two Islanders called Venart and Vetriz. He wanted to find out exactly what it was about his unnamed sister's way of doing business that might interest him because it sort of impinged on his line of work. He did none of these things.

'You said you wanted me to give Bardas a message,' he said, as neutrally as he could manage. 'What do you want me to tell him?'

'I'm not sure, really,' Gorgas confessed, scratching the side of his head. 'I suppose he ought to be told about Iseutz; who she really is, and all that. It'd have been better perhaps if he'd been told *before* he cut off all the fingers on her right hand; or maybe not, I don't know. Maybe if he'd known, it'd have cost him his life.' He leant forward and went on very earnestly, 'I love my brother, Patriarch. I always did. We were close; not as close as I was to my sister, but we grew up together, played together as kids. You can't help loving someone under those circumstances even if you end up hating them at the same time. If you've got a brother or a sister, maybe you understand. And I recognise that making it up to Bardas is going to be very difficult, since this whole mess is nearly all my fault; I made no bones about that from the very start, remember. I've got no illusions about myself. But I'm not an evil man, Alexius, just a man who once did some evil things. Maybe I still do, from time to time. But if there's anything I can do for my brother, I want to do it. Ideally, I'd like him to leave this city while there's still time; come back with me if he likes, or go wherever he wants. I'd gladly make sure he never wanted for money or things. I'd even try and make peace between him and my sister, though I doubt that'd ever be possible. Whatever; you've got to believe me, I certainly don't mean him any harm.'

Abruptly, he stood up. Alexius wanted to stop him leaving, but made no effort to do so. 'So what do you want me to tell him?' he repeated. 'Always supposing I can get in touch with him, which I can't guarantee.'

Gorgas licked his lips before answering. 'Tell him about the girl,' he said at last. 'He may not believe it, of course. If he does, he'll probably think I'm telling him now just to make him suffer, but there's nothing I can do about that.' He hesitated, then continued, 'Tell him I'd like there to be peace between us, if for no other reason than because he's my brother and I miss him. Tell him I love him, Patriarch Alexius. I think that more or less covers everything.'

Gorgas moved swiftly to the door, opened it and closed it behind him. When he'd gone, there was a large empty space in the room, a displacement that put Alexius in mind of the operation of the Principle and the uses it could on occasion be put to, for good or ill. He sat for a long time thinking over what he'd been told, trying to tease out of it something that would help him make sense of many things that had happened, to him and to others, over the last few months; coincidentally, since more or less the time when Temrai was known to have come to the city. He thought about Bardas Loredan lying half-dead among the bodies of his family, and remembered a dream he'd had during the emergency, in which he'd seemed to see Loredan riding through a burning camp with a torch in his hand, apparently looking for someone among the bodies of women and children; and a boy he'd somehow recognised as the young Temrai, hiding under a wagon and watching him. Behind it all there was one simple thing; he could visualise it in general terms, he could almost taste it, but it continued to elude him. He even got up and looked on a map to see where Scona was, but that didn't help particularly.

At times like this, he realised, he missed Gannadius, and he spared a thought for his absent friend, even now on the Island—

On the Island, thanks to the intercession of a virtual stranger, who had seen to it that he was taken out of harm's way, along with Loredan's clerk, who had been a sort of friend and companion to him. He wondered about that, too.

All these problems, all these questions; they should have given him a headache, but they didn't. *Tell him I love him, Patriarch Alexius...* What an extraordinary thing for him to say, a man who'd killed his father and brother-in-law, tried to kill his brother and sister, in furtherance of procuring his sister's rape. He believed what Gorgas had said; no reason to assume that such a man was incapable of love, or incapable of anything. In fact, he had a shrewd idea that Gorgas was capable of pretty well anything he chose to do, one way or another. An interesting man, and no mistake.

Eventually he thought himself to sleep and had no bad dreams.

CHAPTER NINETEEN

The clan was still working hard, every man, woman and child, but more to stave off boredom than because there was much need of what they made. Bozachai, the chief smith, had undertaken to replace the traditional leather armour with coats of mail, and the metalworkers spent the day drawing thick steel wire, coiling it round mandrels and slitting the coils with a chisel to make the rings. Women and children were given the tedious job of linking the rings together; one twist of the pliers opened the split rings, which were then threaded together, each ring interlocking with two from the previous row, and twisted shut. At first Bozachai had insisted that each link be sealed by welding or brazing, but after a while it was generally agreed that it wasn't worth the effort, and they stopped bothering.

Tilchai, the chief bowyer, tried to copy the city crossbows, taking as his models a handful captured during the original cavalry raid. Where the clan's version of the weapon used a bow made of horn, wood and sinew laminated together, the city version used a steel bow, as thick as a man's thumb in the middle and tapering to fingertip-width at the ends. The experiment proved to be futile; either the steel bows snapped, or else they turned out feeble and soft, taking a set after the first few shots and failing to carry more than forty or fifty yards. Temrai tried to remember how they'd tempered the bow-steel in the arsenal, but his recollections weren't precise enough. The venture was futile anyway; the city bows were so stiff that a special wooden lever was needed to force the string back over the twin hooks of the lock, and in the time it took to do that, an archer with an ordinary bow could have loosed ten arrows and sent them straighter and further.

New problems were cropping up every day. Pasture for the herd was getting thin within safe grazing distance of the camp. A freak cold snap killed off three-quarters of the clan's bees, which meant mead was suddenly scarce, smoked meat couldn't be glazed, milk and yoghurt had to be drunk unsweetened. Saltpetre for curing meat and oak bark for tanning leather were both getting harder to find. The hunting parties had to go further afield to find deer and wildfowl, which meant more men away from the camp and more culling of the herd than was usual for the time of year. There were several minor but virulent epidemics, mostly stomach complaints; only a few died, but morale in the camp sank and didn't really recover once the outbreaks were over. The ropemakers had shaved the clan's horses until they were the next best thing to bald; but still the bowyers made bows and the carpenters made engines that were doomed to be useless for want of strings and ropes. The causeway opposite the bridgehouse had been rebuilt, in spite of naggingly accurate archery from the bridgehouse tower that had claimed the lives of over fifty men, but nobody had any idea of what to do with it.

Yet no one suggested giving up and going away; not even in whispers or ambiguous hints. The enterprise of the city had long since stopped being an exciting adventure, but the clan had settled down into a siege routine that could easily last for ever if that was how long it took. Already some families were building stone walls for their tents and pens. A few had even taken their first tentative steps towards breaking up the earth and growing food instead of chasing or herding it. And nobody objected that planting was a waste of time since they wouldn't be there to harvest the result. It was automatically assumed that the camp would still be in the same place six months hence.

We might as well build ourselves a city here and have done with it, Temrai reflected, as he walked through the camp on his way to an undoubtedly pointless staff meeting. It would, after all, be the final irony if, in a few years' time, there were two mirror cities on either side of the river, their inhabitants distinguishable only by their accents and the colour of their hair. Then it would be impossible, and futile as well, to ask who was besieging who, or who had got the better of the war.

There was no point in hurrying – the meeting was due to start at noon – so Temrai took a detour down by the river to see how the water-wheel project was coming along. That, too, was a symptom of insidious permanence, but Temrai couldn't bring himself to dislike it on those grounds. He couldn't help remembering the bonemeal grinder which had been one of the first things he'd noticed when he arrived in the city. The thought that his people were now capable of making such a remarkable thing for themselves pleased him. Torsion engines, trebuchets and the arrow-makers' lathes were ambivalent at best, but a water wheel couldn't be anything else but a good thing. In his mind's eye he could already picture permanent mills built beside the clan's traditional fords and bridges back on the plains, standing ready for use when the annual migration brought them there – assuming, of course, that they could get this prototype to work. But it wasn't a difficult thing to build, compared to some of the items they'd managed to make, with nothing more than a few simple tools, plenty of timber and an unwillingness to believe that anything was impossible.

He arrived at the project site at a crucial moment: the point where the water wheel and the flywheel were mounted on either end of the main driveshaft. The design was his own; based, of course, on a standard city model, but adapted by himself to make use of the materials available. The frame was little more than four A-frames salvaged from smashed trebuchets; these supported the shaft, which had been cut from the trunk of a particularly tall and straight fir tree, planed and shaved *in situ* until it was as near to a perfect cylinder as made no appreciable odds. The timbers that they'd used for the spokes of the wheels were salvage, too; all that was left of the first generation of rafts, the few that had survived the fire. They were using better rafts now, rigidly held together by cross-members morticed and dowelled into place, copied from a standard city pattern. The paddles of the water wheel were heavily modified frame components from scrap torsion engines, and the nails that secured them to the wooden rim had been forged out of city-made bodkin-pattern arrowheads.

Mentakai, the carpenter in charge of the project, had rigged up simple pole cranes made out of further salvaged A-frames to lift the hub-sockets of the wheels level with the shaft. He'd had two options; to mount the hubs only and then assemble the rest of the wheels onto them, or to pre-fabricate the complete wheels and fit them fully assembled. He'd chosen the latter option despite considerable opposition from his fellow workers on the project, and a small crowd had gathered to see the outcome. There was even a group of apparently interested observers on the city wall, and Temrai wondered if there was anything they could learn from what he firmly believed was an improved design. When he realised the implications of that train of thought, he suppressed it at once; it'd be nice for generations of city people to call water wheels of his design Temrai-wheels in perpetuity, but it'd still be admitting failure. As far as the city was concerned, there would be no perpetuity. He thought about *that*, and found it strangely depressing.

'Of course it's possible,' Mentakai said to him in a low voice, as the water wheel was manhandled into position under the crane. 'My problem is that because of all this childish rivalry in the team, I'm only likely to get one shot at doing it my way. If it doesn't work, they'll say it's impossible and start pulling the wheel to bits, even if it's just a matter of a frayed rope breaking or a damaged frame giving way.' He shook his head sadly. 'Why people have to be so damned competitive all the time, I just don't know.'

'Human nature,' Temrai replied absently, his attention on

the work in progress before them. 'People like things to be a contest, they can understand better if there's winners and losers. It's just the way they are.'

The mule-train was harnessed up and set in motion, and for once the mules did as they were told. After an alarming creak and twitch on the ropes, the wheel lifted off the ground and slowly rose into the air, until an engineer standing up to his knees in the riverbank mud shouted to the mule-drovers and the train stopped. First snag: the hub socket was nine inches too high, which meant the team had to be backed up a tiny amount. That sort of precision is, however, hard to obtain with mules walking backwards; after a great deal of effort, cajoling and bad language the drovers managed to get the recalcitrant brutes to go back, but instead of dropping the hub nine inches, they lowered it by two feet. That was obviously no good; so the mules were driven forwards again, resulting this time in an overshoot of eighteen inches.

'You see?' Mentakai complained dramatically. 'Much more of this and they'll be saying it can't be done. It's not an easy job, for gods' sakes, you can't *expect* it to go right first time. You've got to stick at it until it comes out right, or else forget about the whole idea and go back to two men turning a handle all day long.'

Temrai made a noise like someone being sympathetic and carried on watching the show. The drovers backed up again (someone had figured out that the best way to get the mules to back up slowly was to cover their heads with a cloth; this meant finding cloths of the right size and shape and, harder still, persuading their owner to part with them.

Eventually, though, the man stuck in the mud yelled out, 'That's it!' with the same degree of exhilaration and relief that you'd expect from a man who's just watched his son being born. Immediately, teams of men standing between the A-frames pulled hard on ropes tied to the spokes of the wheel and guided the socket onto the shaft as if it was the easiest thing in the world. All that needed to be done after that was for the smiths to drive in the cotter pin that would keep the wheel fixed in place; no problems there – hardly surprising, since pinning was a standard part of making torsion engines, and they all knew a lot about that by now. They were just about to drive the mules round to be harnessed up to the flywheel crane when a problem they hadn't allowed for became disturbingly obvious.

They'd put the wrong wheel on first. As soon as the paddles of the wheel touched the water, the wheel began to turn, and the shaft with it. That, of course, made life even more difficult for the crews standing by to raise and guide the flywheel. Piloting a giant wheel into place wasn't exactly easy when the shaft was motionless. Trying to fit it to a beam which rotated ninety-odd times every minute was asking a bit much. There was a basic clutch system to disengage the flywheel, but nothing comparable at the other end. Mentakai swore under his breath.

'Just my luck,' he said. 'Now you watch; they'll have a couple more goes to confirm their verdict, just in order to show willing, and then they'll dismantle the machine. They haven't even *tried* to follow it through.'

Temrai frowned. 'What if taking it to bits really is the best way?' Temrai asked aloud. 'No way of knowing, I suppose, without having tried it first.'

'Not you as well,' Mentakai muttered. 'It's just a simple mistake, caused by rushing into things and not thinking them through first. Doesn't prove a thing about whether my way's the right one.'

There were ideas in all this that could be applied to other human activities, Temrai realised, sacking cities included. 'I suppose we'd better do it right,' he said. 'Tell them to take the water wheel off again and fit the flywheel, and *then* we can put the water wheel back.'

Getting the water wheel off proved far harder than getting it on; for one thing, it was going round and round in a strenuous and dangerous manner. Eventually they managed – well past noon by now, Temrai realised, but so what? They can have the meeting without me, it's not as if we have anything to say to each other – and the flywheel went on comparatively easily, thanks to all the practice they were getting. The second fitting of the water wheel was a mess; several ropes broke and one of the frames in the crane sprang a joint, the crews were all thoroughly soaked from splashing about up to their waists in the river, tempers were beginning to fray and the onlookers were making amusing comments from the sidelines. In the end there was a feeling of exhausted relief rather than jubilation when the water wheel began to turn and the flywheel reciprocated its movement. Still, it had been a success – more than that, an achievement, which surely made it all worthwhile—

Someone shouted, 'Look out!' but by the time the crews had realised what was happening it was too late. Three hundredweight stones, launched from the trebuchets on the bridgehouse tower, whistled through the air and landed; one in the river, throwing up a curtain of spray that seemed to touch the sky; one directly on top of the water wheel, crushing and cracking it, smashing the A-frames, snapping the driveshaft in two and smearing Mentakai's body over what was left of his project; and one on the edge of the crowd of spectators, killing a man and a woman and shearing both legs off a young boy.

The initial shock seemed to last for ever. Then someone screamed, men ran forward and put their shoulders to the stone under which the boy was pinned, the rest of the crowd wavered, not knowing whether to help the rescuers or run for cover in case there were any more stones on the way. Temrai shoved his way through the engineering crew, who were rooted to the spot staring at the mess where the water wheel had been, and started shouting orders, sending for healers, a stretcher, engineers to bring up five trebuchets for a return volley; the activity helped soak up the shambles in his mind, where images of the burning camp and the rafts burning on the water were blurring into a picture of the bonemeal mill, just the other side of the wall from here if he remembered it right, similarly shattered and destroyed, and in its hoppers the bones of hundreds and thousands of men and women, city and clan, being fed mechanically through onto the still-turning millstones.

They managed to lift the rock enough to drag out the boy; he was still alive and opening his mouth to scream, although nothing was coming out. Someone mentioned that the man and the woman who were still under there had been the boy's parents; Temrai took note of that and put it safely away in his mind for future reference. The first of the five trebuchets was dragged into position and the mules were detached from the hitching points on the frame and linked up to the counterweight; and then they decided to be obstinate and not budge, so there was cursing and the cracking of whips to add to the overall effect; and then someone realised they hadn't brought up a stone to shoot from it, and someone suggested using one of the two that were here already, and someone else thought that suggestion was in pretty poor taste; and Temrai looked up at the bridgehouse tower and told the engineers to belay his order to return fire, since there were no signs that the enemy engines were reloading and they had enough on their hands as it was without picking a fight.

'For me?' Colonel Loredan asked, puzzled.

The guardsman nodded. 'Bloke left it about an hour ago,' he said. 'Wouldn't give his name. There's a letter with it.'

'Oh. Oh, well. Thank you, dismissed.' The guardsman saluted and left, closing the door behind him.

Back in his miserable cell in the second-city gatehouse; same bleak stone walls, same stone shelf for a bed. Loredan looked at the bundle of cloth in his hand, shrugged and tossed it onto the bed-shelf. Something metal rattled against the stone. He'd open it later, after he'd got out of these hateful boots.

Why should anybody leave me a present? he wondered, as he dragged the left boot off his hot, sweaty foot. Although he was already late for a meeting he allowed himself the luxury of sitting and wiggling his newly liberated toes before putting on his sandals. *And why couldn't it be something useful, like a nice pair of felt slippers?*

Next he pulled off his coat, sopping wet from the afternoon's sudden downpour, and reached for his second best; an old friend, shabby and frayed but nicely moulded to his body by years of close association. Not the most appropriate attire for an audience with the Prefect, but he didn't exactly care too much if he got fired. His shirt and trousers were wet too, but he couldn't be bothered to change them. The heat of the fire in the reception room of the Prefect's palace would dry them off soon enough.

A quick drag of a comb through his hair; that would have to do. Now then; he'd open his present, and then he'd have to go.

It didn't take a genius to work out what was inside the cloth wrappings; a narrow, heavy bundle roughly two and a half feet long containing something metal. Someone had sent him a sword. He could do with one, sure enough. It was embarrassing for the Deputy Lord Lieutenant, the officer commanding the defences of Perimadeia, to be the only man on the wall with an empty scabbard swinging from his belt. He slit the string with his knife and peeled away the cloth; then sat quite still for a moment, staring.

A genuine Guelan. More than that; a genuine Guelan *broadsword* – there were only about five of them still in existence – rather than the more common but still murderously valuable law-swords that the great smith had made his reputation with. Yet a Guelan it undoubtedly was, he knew that before he drew the short, heavy blade from the scabbard and found the distinctive and uncopiable marks on the ricasso. No one had ever made military swords like the great Liras Guelan. Other makers' imitations were dull abortions, fit only for chopping wood or opening barrels. Nobody before or since had hit on that precise harmony of weight and balance that made it the next best thing to perfect, for single- or double-handed use, cutting or thrusting.

There was a special skill to using them, so the legend went (and for the first time, as he held the sword in his hands, he realised it was no fairy tale); if you tried to use it like an ordinary sword, the weight of the blade and the proportions – long handle and short blade – would defeat you. The harder you tried, the more effort you put into it, the more sluggishly the weapon would handle. But if you used the weight rather than fighting to overcome it, then the sword would seem to guide itself, adding its own force to the blow in apparent defiance of all the laws of physics. A Guelan broadsword, they said, should be allowed to fight for you; it knew exactly what it was doing, and all the wielder had to or should do was hang onto the blunt end and watch the fun.

Bardas Loredan had his doubts about people who waxed lyrical over lethal weapons; even so, he felt he could make allowances in this one rather exceptional case. All his working life, it went without saying, he'd wanted one (though it wouldn't have done for work, being outside the prescribed dimensions for legal use), and now here one was, its weight firm but not oppressive against the muscles of his upper arm, like a pedigree falcon deigning to sit for a time on his wrist.

This must have cost a fortune. He remembered the letter. Not wanting to put his marvellous new possession down, even for a moment, he fumbled awkwardly to break the seal and open the folded paper.

> *Bardas—*
> *I assume you got my message and the letter that followed it, so obviously you don't want to see me. I can't say I'm surprised. I'll understand if you don't want to accept this from me (though you'd be a damn fool not to; you wouldn't believe the trouble I had tracking one down, and when I found it the owner didn't want to sell). Take it, though; it can't be blamed for the sins of the giver, and you'll find a use for it, I'm sure. I've told it to keep you safe; that's why it had to be a Guelan – aren't*

*they supposed to have minds of their own? Try not to
break this one.
With my love,
Gorgas Loredan.*

Bardas Loredan looked at the letter, then at the sword, then
back at the letter, then back at the sword. Weapons, he
knew, are ambivalent, capable of doing good or evil, or both,
or both together, incapable of knowing or caring about the
use to which they're put. The same, Loredan reflected, is
true of the lawyer, the man who fights and kills for a cause
not his own in the name of justice. The weapon in his hand
and the skill that hand imparts to the weapon decide right
and wrong, good and evil; but the stronger and quicker on
the day prevail over the slower and weaker, and if a moment
before the fight the defendant had taken over the plaintiff's
brief and vice versa, it's hard to believe that the outcome
would be different. Maybe that's what I've become, Loredan
thought, or maybe that's what I've been all along; a weapon
in someone else's hand, created to kill and do damage,
either for good or for evil depending on whose hand I
happen to be in. And the Guelan – *aren't they supposed to
have minds of their own?* – perhaps it means something,
arriving precisely now, when I'm the advocate instructed on
behalf of the city of Perimadeia, entrusted with its defence
and the righteousness of its cause.

It must have cost him a fortune ... Yes, and over the years
he's cost me; maybe somehow he's been using me, along
with all the others, though I can't imagine what for. It's been
his actions that have governed everything I've ever done,
since that day beside the river when he left me for dead and
took away the life I should have had. If he thinks he can buy
me with this—

But a Guelan broadsword; it wasn't answerable for the
sins of the giver, just as the lawyer isn't responsible for the
acts of his client. *Above all*, they'd told him when he took his
oath at the enrollment ceremony, *an advocate fights for
justice, and justice is his only client.* And a sword cuts skin

and flesh for the man who swings it; and a man is a sword in the hand of his own circumstances, the things that have happened in the past that have made him what he is and their consequences in the present that he must address and deal with. Taking this from his brother wasn't all that different from taking the sword of the man he'd just killed on the floor of the courthouse. He'd earned it, in that sense; and once it was his, its past no longer mattered.

Gods, I'd make myself believe anything just to be able to keep this thing. It's worth more than I ever earned in ten years in the racket. And what the devil does he mean 'all my love'?

Loredan suddenly remembered the meeting he was late for. It was by a conscious act, no mere instinct of haste, that he unbuckled his belt, threaded it through the double loops of the scabbard-frog and drew it tight again; and in that instant he rejected the comfort that lay implicit in the excuse, *I was only ever following instructions; they made me do it; it wasn't me.* Bardas Loredan, a Guelan broadsword; weapons of such quality and antecedents with minds of their own ...

Well, well, he said to himself as he slammed out of the small, cold room and ran down the cloister towards the chapter house, if in the end I had to sell my soul, better keep it in the family than flog it off cheap to the charcoal people. But that thought didn't resolve the matter; a final decision would have to be deferred until he had more time to consider it, and if possible more data.

CHAPTER TWENTY

'I'd feel happier if I had the faintest idea what's going on,' Ceuscai muttered. The dim moonlight made the cloud of his chilled breath glow, as if his words had somehow frozen in the cold of the night. 'The first one was bad enough. And I didn't like this one at all.'

Beside him, crouched under the cover of a wagon, Temrai watched the torches burning on the bridgehouse tower, and shivered a little. 'Probably some family thing,' he replied, 'about which we neither need to know nor particularly care. My only worry is that it's some kind of trap.'

'Bound to be,' said the man on Temrai's left. 'Honestly, it smells like last year's cheese. Enemy General's brother comes and tells you he's going to open the gates and lower the drawbridge at midnight – Gods, Temrai, what else do you believe in? The old woman with the basket of winds? The tooth fairy?'

Temrai scowled, though nobody could see him. 'If it looks at all dodgy we won't go,' he said. 'But if this trap of yours involves opening the gates and lowering the drawbridge, then it's my kind of trap.'

'They could have all sorts waiting for us; boiling oil, pitfalls, engines, a whole company of archers loosing off point-blank—'

At the very least, Temrai said to himself. If the first hundred men through the gate get more than ten yards in, I'll be highly astonished. But that's all budgeted for under Acceptable Losses. We could lose a thousand in the first ninety seconds and still be doing better than anticipated...

'Hello,' Ceuscai whispered. 'Look.'

'I'll be damned,' said somebody else further down the line. 'The gate's opening.'

There was indeed a slight change in the texture of the shadows under the bridgehouse tower. Temrai caught his breath. In a small fraction of a second, he would have to give the order to move forwards if he wasn't to miss the opportunity. Once the order was given, there was a strong possibility that his forces might actually enter the city and begin to do the job. Once they were in, just suppose it all started to go according to plan; a detachment to storm the tower and seize the engines, stopping them from bombarding the causeway; two more to force the towers on either side, cutting communications on the wall and preventing the defenders from shooting down into his people as they came through the gate; a strong force to establish a bridgehead just inside the gate; then, assuming the city's main relief force hadn't arrived yet (three minutes into the operation, four if there was any resistance on the wall), a push outwards following the foot of the walls, with the aim of encircling the relief force when it appeared and cutting it off from retreat into the maze of streets and squares. If the plan worked, the city would be carved like an animal's carcass fresh from the spit, divided into manageable portions that the various detachments could easily digest.

Temrai had envisaged the attack as being something like netting rabbits at night on the plains. First, get between the grazing rabbits and their burrows before they see or hear you, and set up the nets. Then show the lights and make the noise, sending the quarry darting back towards safety, right into the instrument of their destruction. Then, methodically and at one's leisure, pull them struggling from the nets and stretch their necks. It had all seemed straightforward enough, put like that.

Once the order was given, he'd no longer be in control. Always assuming he'd ever been in control to begin with.

'Here we go,' he said, edging forward with his elbows until

his head was clear of the wagon. 'Best of luck, everyone. See you in Perimadeia.'

Gorgas Loredan stepped over the body of one of the guards and put his weight on the capstan handle. The drawbridge was massive; made deliberately so, in order that one man on his own wouldn't be able to lower it. He felt the strain wrenching the muscles of his chest and back; fairly soon the weight would take over, and he'd need to let go and jump clear to avoid being knocked flying by the spinning handles of the windlass. At that point, it'd be beyond his capacity to undo what he was now doing; a few inches more, and Perimadeia would inevitably fall.

He stopped and took off the quiver that hung across his back; the baldric was galling his shoulders, and was one more thing for the windlass poles to catch in once the point of no return had been reached.

Arguably, that point had come and gone many years ago.

He'd shot down all the guards he could see; there had been four, which agreed with the observations he'd made over the last few nights of careful watching. If the plainsmen played their part, and were ready and waiting on the other side, there ought to be men inside the city within the next six minutes; their irruption would be his opportunity to slip away, head for the harbour and the ship he had standing by. If things worked out, he'd be well out to sea by the time the city knew it was dying.

Suddenly he felt the handle pulling away from him, its downward surge greater than his own strength. He let go and stepped back hurriedly, and the windlass began to turn of its own accord. The sound it made, a sort of chattering whir, seemed horribly loud in the still night – *They'll be able to hear that in the second city*, he thought, *you'd have to be dead not to hear it and guess what was going on*. He let the moment linger in his mind; the last chance gone, the instant when the suicide feels the stool slip out from under him, or knows he can't regain his balance on the parapet. In a way it was a comfort; *oh, well, too late to do anything about it now, so what's the point of worrying?* The windlass spun like the wheel of a ship out of control; quite literally out of his hands now.

Job done; successful; no spear in my ribs or arrow in my back. Time I wasn't here.

Just for once, I got it right.

A scoop of shadow grew dense in front of him and became a man; a guardsman, on his way to relieve one of the watch. He was running, staring, not even interested in Gorgas Loredan. Let him go by; no point in picking a fight at this stage of the proceedings.

The guardsman noticed him, hesitated, stopped running just long enough to yell to him. 'Somebody's opened the gate! Get help, quick!' Then he disappeared into the shadows, just as the drawbridge reached the end of its chains, bounced and found its level. There were torches approaching in the distance, where the shadows of eaves overhanging an alley darkened the night. On the wall, someone called out. Suddenly there were men under the arch of the gate, running in, spreading out. An arrow hit the guardsman and he dropped dead to the ground.

Time I wasn't here.

More arrows flying now; Gorgas could hear them hiss as they flew past. Behind him somewhere a window smashed. A brief burst of shouted speech, quickly drowned out by the hollow drumming of feet on the planks of the drawbridge. More shouts overhead, sword blades clashing four, five times. *This is the first trickle of water appearing on the wrong side of the dam. Running out of time to get away. Time to move. Time I wasn't here.*

'What's happening?' someone shouted. Gorgas saw whoever it was; a guardsman with a lantern who ran towards the shapes of men gathered around the gate. 'What's happening?' he demanded of the first person he met, who drew a short sword and stuck it in him. More arrows hissing; they must be loosing blind, no light to see by. *Just for once, I got it right. Out of my hands now.*

There are ever so many orthodox reasons for bringing about the annihilation of a great city; revenge for some intolerable wrong; straightforward advantage, for example where a powerful and ambitious commercial interest decides that it would rather not repay the capital of the huge loan that threatens to strangle it; an overwhelming abhorrence for everything the city stands for; or simply because the grey of its walls clashes with the green of the grass and the blue of the sea. Some cities have been betrayed for the price of twenty acres of rocky pasture, or for love, or because they were there. Wise men in Alexius' Order often debated the proposal that cities are by their very nature an abomination, a wart or growth that the body of the earth sooner or later heals of its own accord. Cities have been burnt to the ground by madmen, children playing with flint and tinder, and the hem of a curtain being blown into the open door of a bread oven by a gust of wind. Some cities have been destroyed and rebuilt so many times that workmen digging a ditch for a latrine will slice through a dozen crusts of masonry and ash, like the layers of a cake.

Gorgas Loredan had his own reasons, revenge and hatred and level-headed commercial acumen among them. More to the point, he was doing as he'd been told. All fair enough, for someone analysing the pathology of his actions. But Gorgas knew; he knew he was doing it for the best and most wholesome of reasons, for the same reason as everything he'd ever done since he'd left the Mesoge. For family.

Guardsmen were coming up, bringing torches and lanterns. One stopped and fell forwards. Others pulled up, stopped dead, swore under their breath and turned back. One of them will run to the second-city gatehouse to summon the Deputy Lord Lieutenant. He'll grab his sword and his helmet and come running, shouting orders that nobody'll be awake to catch. He'll come running, straight into the oncoming enemy.

Gorgas Loredan drew a deep breath and started to run, not towards the harbour but up the hill. If he ran fast he might get there first, be in time to intercept his brother; *it's all over, I've got a ship waiting.* A moment for the message to sink in; another moment, and, *How did you know? Why've you got a ship waiting?* Well, he'd deal with that when the moment came.

Behind him as he ran, more shouting on the walls; not city voices, not bewildered requests for information but signals and confirmations, anxiously waited for. An arrow hit the flagstones beside him and skipped, its movement like that of an eager dog at his heels. Irrelevant; no arrow was going to hit Gorgas Loredan tonight, because Gorgas Loredan has important things to do, he can't be spared to make up the quota of first casualties. As he ran, his temples throbbed; *what a time to have a headache,* he said to himself, and tried to ignore it.

Someone grabbed Loredan by the shoulder and he woke up.

'Come *on!*' hissed the voice from behind the lantern. 'They're here. Some bastard opened the gate.'

Loredan blinked. His head was still full of sleep, and it hurt. 'What the hell are you talking about?' he mumbled. 'Who…?'

'The *savages,*' the voice replied. 'Come on, will you?' They're swarming all over the wall.'

Loredan stumbled off his bed and groped for his boots. 'How did they get in?' he asked. 'Did you say—?'

'Someone opened the gate. A *traitor.* There's half a company of guards holding them at the pottery market, and that's it.'

His feet didn't want to go in the boots; his left heel was stuck about halfway down, and he couldn't remember what you were supposed to do when that happened. He pulled the boot off and started again.

'Has anyone called out the reserve?' he asked. 'And what about the district garrisons? Surely—'

'I don't know, do I? I've just come from the gate – I was about to go on duty.' Whoever it was handed him his helmet.

'No, mailshirt first,' Loredan snapped.

'Where is it?'

'There, in the corner.' Someone had opened the gate; someone from the city had deliberately opened the gate.

There must be some mistake...

Fumbling for the straps of his mailshirt, he tried to think clearly about what had to be done. Alert the reserve and the district garrisons; each unit had an area of deployment assigned to it for this sort of emergency, he'd seen to it that everybody would know where to go and what to do. He'd need messengers—

'Leave that,' he said, 'and go and find the Couriers' Office. There should be at least ten runners there, standing by. I want them in the courtyard here in the next two minutes. Go on, run. And leave the lantern—'

The last part came too late; whoever it was had run off, taking the light with him. Loredan swore and located his helmet and sword by feel. The sword was, of course, the Guelan broadsword—'

Sure, I believe in coincidences. But this isn't one.

What else would he need? Wax tablets and a stylus; but he didn't have any here. Maps and plans, and they were all in the departmental chief clerk's office, being copied. The chiefs of staff, then; had anybody told them what was happening? He couldn't assume that, but they'd have to wait until he'd found more runners; raising the reserve and the garrison were the first priority. And still more runners, to bring him an accurate report of what was actually happening. Damn it, when he'd set up the Couriers' Office he'd assumed for some reason that ten would be enough. *That's your trouble, Bardas, you never think.*

What next? He racked his brains as he stumbled into the courtyard. When the runners showed up, he gave them their destinations and watched them dashing away into the darkness. Fortunately, the sound of voices and running attracted a few passers-by, clerks from the Department of Supply for the most part. He co-opted them as messengers and sent them running for the chiefs of staff, too fazed to question the messages they were carrying.

If they're on the wall already, what's to stop them forcing a way through all the way round? It depended on how many of them there were, and whether they were coming up on two fronts or only one. If they met no resistance at ground level, they could get across to the next staircase along and take on any defenders from both directions. *I should have made specific plans for something like this; but then, who'd ever imagine someone would actually open the gates?*

The various chiefs of staff staggered and bumped their way into the courtyard; the Chief Engineer first, accompanied by his first officer, both with their helmets and mailcoats on over long, old-fashioned nightgowns; the Chief of Archers, properly equipped and armed, with his four deputies; the four captains of infantry – guards, garrison, reserves and auxiliaries – in and out of armour, with and without staff; the Chief Clerk from Works and the Quartermaster. Supply was vacant at the moment, because the previous Chief Clerk had been promoted to customs, and it was a political appointment ... Second from last the Prefect. Last of all the Lord Lieutenant, his magnificent parade armour still tacky with storage grease, so that dust and fallen leaves stuck to his shins and ankles.

Quickly, Loredan explained, gave his orders. Nobody argued, most of them seemed to know what to do. He put the Prefect in charge of the wall, left the Lord Lieutenant to organise the defence of the second city, and at last was free to go. As he reached the long, broad downhill sweep of the Grand Avenue, he broke into a run. As it happened, he left the gatehouse at more or less the same time as Gorgas reached it. In the darkness and confusion, neither recognised the other.

Metrias Corodin was a maker of scientific instruments, and a good one too. By day he worked in a small but adequate shop on the second level of the western balcony of the instrument-makers' courtyard, torturing his eyes as he marked out the tiny calibrations on the scales and barrels of the instruments and scorching his fingers over the soldering lamp. In the evenings, he was the sergeant of his watch district; it was a social function as much as anything else, an honour bestowed on him by his neighbours in recognition of a useful and industrious life. He enjoyed the duty; a few hours a week of drill, a little paperwork, a good excuse to hold meetings that people could linger after to talk shop and share news and a jug or two of cider. The drill wasn't particularly irksome; as a young man he'd been something of an athlete, and he wasn't so much out of condition that half an hour's square-bashing or a morning at the butts was a problem for him, even if the straps had had to be let out a few times since the shirt was new.

Now he was standing in front of a line of bleary-eyed nervous men drawn up across the entrance to the coopers' square. His small company was wedged in between the coopers and the nailmakers, two substantial detachments, each with several sergeants. By a quirk of seniority and guild etiquette, however, he found himself in overall command of the defence of the lower city.

Until the real soldiers get here, he reassured himself, *which must be soon, surely.* Somewhere ahead, an indeterminate distance away, there were unnerving noises, shouts and yells and sporadic clashes of metal on metal. Something was coming this way, and he had a nasty feeling it was the war.

He tried to remember his basic theory; Ninas Elius' *Art of Urban Defence*, required reading for watch officials for the last hundred and twenty years. *Defensive actions in a confined space against an oncoming enemy* – he could remember swotting up on the section for his lance-corporal's examination twenty years ago – *are to be conducted in two phases, comprising the disruptive use of archery and the obstructive effect of an infantry line.* He'd learnt it, yes, but never stopped to think what it might mean. Shoot the buggers first and then hit them, he guessed. It seemed to be the sensible thing to do.

As he peered into the darkness ahead he cursed his poor

eyesight, and the years of crouching over his bench that had bowed his legs and cramped his back. His helmet felt loose on his head, despite his wife's last-minute packing with a woollen scarf, and with the sideflaps tied down he was sure he could only hear about half as well as usual.

The disruptive effect of archery ... Well, time to get ready to do something about that. Nervously, his voice higher and squeakier than it should have been, he gave the order to string bows, and set about bending his own; the end of the bottom limb trapped against the outside of the right foot, then the left leg steps over the bow until the underside of the knee is brought to bear on the inside of the bow, just below the handle; grip the upper limb firmly in the left hand and flex it inwards (and every time he did it, he felt sure the bow would snap, though it hadn't done so yet), while the right hand brings the loop of the bowstring over the nock, thus completing the manoeuvre. Standard bow drill, he'd done it many thousands of times; but tonight he had to try three times before he got it right.

The noise was nearer, close enough that he could make a good estimate of where they were; just inside the plumbers' quarter, where the tank-makers had their shops. He tried to imagine the scene, but couldn't; bloodthirsty savages swarming past shops he'd known since he was a boy, the idea was so incongruous as to be laughable. He gave the order to nock arrows.

A fairly new bow, this. Last spring, when the tournament season started, he'd finally been forced to admit that his old bow, twenty-five years old and still as sound as the day it was made, was getting too heavy for him to draw, and so he'd treated himself to a brand new one, a hickory and lemonwood ninety-five pounder instead of the hundred and twenty pound draw of the old self yew. Ninety-five was still too stiff, if the truth be told, but a man has his pride. The string felt dry against his fingers – shame on him for neglecting to wax it, he'd have nobody to blame but himself if it broke on him now. As for the arrow, he'd instinctively chosen the worst of the set, slightly bowed and a bit shabby in the fletchings; it always flew left and a little high; he knew the degree of variance well enough. This would almost certainly be the last time he drew it; other things more important in a battle than retrieving spent arrows, after all. The thought of aiming it deliberately at someone was quite bizarre; hadn't he spent the last fifteen years as range officer telling the archers never under any circumstances to point a bow at anyone?

Movement under the archway opposite—

Too dark to make anything out except a general impression of moving bodies, a wave of men advancing steadily, cautious on unfamiliar ground. Not our men, anyway. Without looking round, he stepped back into the line, heard his own voice giving the order to mark and draw...

(The strain of the bow against his left wrist; a sharp twinge in his back as he brought his shoulder blades together. He looked for a single target to aim at but there wasn't one, just a featureless line seventy-five yards away across the square)

... Hold and loose; his fingers relaxed and the string pulled away, slapping the inside of his left arm where the bracer protected it. He tried to follow the course of his arrow, but it was lost among so many, and now his voice was calling, *Nock, mark, draw, hold, loose!* and he was doing the drill in time to his own commands, as if he was once more a young boy under the sergeant's eye. He felt a muscle protesting in his left forearm, easy to pull something if you don't take care, but there wasn't time to worry about that, he had to keep up with the commands (*nock, mark, draw, hold, loose*) or else get hopelessly out of step, be the laughing-stock of the quarter—

A shape loomed up at him in the darkness and turned into a man; short, thickset, in early middle age, a spear in both hands and his eyes full of terror, plunging towards him not twenty yards away. *So that's what the enemy looks like*, he realised as he lowered his aim, picking a spot a hand and two finger's breadth above the handle and letting his fingers relax. He saw the arrow strike, the shaft vanish into the man's chest until only the fletchings and the nock were left; he saw the man run on two, three paces until his legs folded under him so that he pitched forward on his face; and behind him another – enough time to nock another arrow, he wondered dispassionately, as one second expanded into a substantial part of a lifetime. Perhaps, but if he was wrong he'd never have time to draw his sword. He let the bow fall (*my beautiful new bow, and someone's bound to tread on it*) and dropped his hand to his belt, feeling for the pommel of the old standard-issue sword that had been his father's—

Horrible, heavy great thing, cruel to the hands of a man who made his living by fine work; sword drill was compulsory but he'd never made an effort at it; enough that he should cut his fingers to the bone with a bowstring without rubbing the skin off his palms with a wire-bound sword-hilt ...)

—Which slid out of its scabbard with a rasping, grating noise and felt hopelessly heavy, lumpish in his hand, as the enemy came forward, running straight towards him—

He's got his eyes shut, Corodin noticed with amazement. *Bugger's charging with his eyes shut. Poor bastard must be scared stiff.*

—In his hand a short-bladed, long-handled sword with a single cutting edge, which he held above his head like a winnowing-flail—

Metrias Corodin the instrument-maker let him come, let him come; and when he was close enough to reach, he held out his sword and let the poor frightened savage run straight onto it; at which point he was close enough to hear the air escaping from the punctured lung, before the man dropped to the ground, pulling Corodin's arm down and yanking the sword from his grasp. Empty-handed, then, he looked up at the next one, coming straight towards him as the other one had done, a lance in his hands, the same terror reflected in his face. Too late to work the sword free, but he tried it anyway, felt it budge and start to move just as the other man's spearhead came into sharp focus, so close that even his dim eyes could make it out, down to the fresh marks of the stone on its broad, leaf-shaped blade. He waited for the lance to pierce him, in that long last second thinking, *I wonder if it'll hurt much*, and was still waiting when the man next to him in the line leant across him and fended the lance away before following up with a thrust that ripped into the other man's stomach and made him howl. Corodin was grateful to his neighbour – gods, if it wasn't Gidas Mascaleon under that big, rusty helmet, a cheapskate and a disgrace to our profession – but before he could say thank you, another one of the enemy slashed Gidas Mascaleon across the face, cutting right through his nose just above the bridge; and while he was still stunned with the shock and the pain, drove the sword into his chest and killed him.

Corodin had his sword free by now and looked round for the man who'd killed his neighbour, but somehow wasn't there any more. No time to look more carefully; another one of them straight ahead, running in, but slowing down to climb over the drift of dead and dying men that was starting to build up around the feet of the defenders. As Corodin watched, the man seemed to lose his sense of purpose; there was fear in his eyes too, but the man was thinking, weighing up whether the attempt was feasible. He stood there for a moment astride a dying man; a tall, thin boy with a straggle of beard and slim, muscular arms showing under the baggy sleeves of a mailshirt, a sensible lad who realised the attack was over, and turned his back and ran off the way he'd come.

'We've tried three charges,' the man said, a junior captain of the line. 'It's hopeless, we just can't budge them.'

'Why the hell are you bothering with that?' Temrai panted. 'Get your men out of my way so I can clear this lot out with my archers.'

Four volleys was all it took (*nock, mark, draw, hold, loose*) and then the few that were left standing broke and ran, leaving the way clear for another hundred yards or so. As his line advanced Temrai felt a cold rage inside him towards the young captain, the man whose mistake had cost the lives of many of his men; but he ignored it, concentrating on the way ahead, desperately trying to remember the geography, whether there was any point ahead that was likely to harbour an ambush, how the streets were laid out, whether there was another lane alongside this one that the enemy could come down and take them in flank and rear. Each time one of his men fell he wanted to run to him, protect him, get his body away from the danger just in case there was a little drop of life still left in him. But it was out of his hands now, he couldn't afford the luxury of indulging his finer sentiments and his noble nature, not when everything that happened here was his responsibility. He couldn't have run forward into the thick of the fighting even if he'd wanted to.

Sounds like an excuse to me, he told himself, but he knew that wasn't true.

Where in hell were the enemy? Three squares they'd crossed and not an arrow loosed at them, nothing in their path except a few parked wagons and the occasional trader's booth. A trap? Or were they struggling to bring their men up in time, or letting this district go so as to form a defence in strength at some more advantageous point? There was a map somewhere, but he couldn't remember who'd had it last; besides, he ought to know these things. He looked round and shouted, furious that in spite of everything he'd said the line wasn't keeping level. The right wing was trailing behind, the centre was too far forward. Gods, if they were to attack us now …

Down this one, Loredan muttered to himself, past the livery stable and the tavern that does cheap mutton pies, should bring us out opposite the beltmakers' guildhall, and that'll be right. Assuming they've advanced as fast as I think they have, and I haven't missed a turning in the dark.

Here we are; but we're too early, got to give them time to run up against the force blocking the chandlers' arch. Then we'll have them front and back, without room to turn or use their bows. At least, that's the theory.

Wonderful thing, theory.

He stopped and raised his hand, and behind him the column bustled to a halt. Slowly he counted to fifty – why fifty? Well, as good a number as any – before dropping his hand and turning the corner back into the Grand Avenue, which was full of people.

It was like a Navy Day parade, seen from behind. In front, in the distance, a solid wedge of people squeezed down the street, followed by the stragglers, the people who couldn't be bothered to walk fast and keep up. *We'll have them at any rate*, he muttered to himself as he ran forward, quickly selecting a man at random.

Whoever he was, he can't have known very much about it; and then he was down, with Loredan stepping over him and a scrum of soldiers close behind, surging forward and across to fill the width of the street. Only a few of the enemy had turned round to face them by the time they were close enough to make contact, and after that it was sheer hard work, swinging the arms and taxing the shoulders, like digging peat or cutting back an overgrown stream. It was possible to feel the ripples of panic spreading out, from the back of the crush where Loredan's men were cutting out their path, on into the middle where men were packed so closely that their main concern was avoiding the sharp butt-spikes on the ends of the spears of the men in front. It was a little bit like watching something melt, seeing the solid turn to liquid under the heat.

Gods, it was a trap after all, and I fell for it. Temrai tried to look back and see the extent of the disaster, but there were too many heads in the way; all he could see was heads and shoulders and a forest of spears. But he could feel the shock running through his army as the men behind shoved forward to get as far away as they could from the shambles they couldn't see. There didn't seem to be a way out of it; not unless by some miracle another part of his army happened along and took the ambush in rear. For an instant, Temrai's mind was full of a ludicrous vision of the Grand Avenue, crammed as full of men as a sausage skin, alternating strata of them and us, each layer stabbing the backs of the men in front, being stabbed by the men behind, until only the very front and rear detachments were left to fight it out on top of a mattress of corpses.

Someone was tugging at his arm. He turned his head.

'... Through the houses,' the man was saying. 'Break through the walls of the houses; they're only wood and brick.'

At first it sounded like gibberish, until Temrai realised what the man was trying to say. More or less opposite where they were standing, on the left-hand side of the avenue, there was a row of dilapidated cottages. He remembered them, recalled hearing that they'd been allowed to go to ruin by the owner, who'd bought them as an investment in anticipation of some development or other along this part of the avenue. On the other side of the cottages, if he'd got it right, there was a long alley that curved round the avenue like a strung bow curling back to its string. More than enough men to push in the walls of the cottages and then they'd be through, and the battle would effectively be rotated through ninety degrees. There might even be scope for an outflanking manoeuvre of his own.

'Do it,' he shouted over the noise. 'Take as many men as you can get. And hurry, for gods' sakes.'

Without tools or equipment, or any real idea of what they were meant to be doing, they threw themselves at the walls of the cottages, kicking in doors and shutters and scrambling through, burying axe-heads in the soft plaster. When the wall began to give the mass pressed forwards like a stampede of horses frightened by thunder on the plains. A few, maybe a dozen, were buried under chunks of masonry; the rest squashed and crushed their way through, like grass forcing its way up through a pavement. As soon as men started spilling out on the other side, Temrai could feel the tension relax, now that the men trapped inside the box had somewhere to go. He had no choice but to follow the flow towards the breach, wondering as he went how many of his people would be left behind, to be massacred as they tried in vain to get past and into the hole in the wall. Too many, he decided, and left it at that. It was a simple form of arithmetic, because no matter what the figures said, the result would always be too many.

Patriarch Alexius woke up to the sound of yells and people running. At first he assumed the building was on fire – it wouldn't have been the first time – but somehow the noise was different. He strained to make out some words among the shouting.

Whatever it was that was happening, it sounded important. Common sense suggested that it would be a good time to get out of bed and put some clothes on, but for some reason Alexius stayed where he was. The confused shouting still wasn't making any sense, and he'd woken up with a migraine. He closed his eyes, just for a moment—

—And saw a bench in a long, roomy workshop. He appeared to be at the dark end of the shop, but there was plenty of light near the open door, where two men were hanging what looked like a half-finished bow on a peg fixed to the wall. The younger man, who was little more than a boy, held the bow firmly on the peg with both hands while the older man (who was Bardas Loredan) slipped a hook over the bowstring and attached a cord to it. He fed the cord through a pulley, then looped it over one of the crossbeams of the roof; then he fished about under the bench and came up with a lead weight, marked on the side with tallies representing numbers. It was a heavy weight, because Loredan strained as he lifted it off the floor and held it under the end of the cord, cradled on his forearms, while he tied the cord to it.

'Hold it steady,' he said, and gently took his arms away, leaving the weight hanging from the cord. The bow on the peg bent as the weight drew down through the pulley, and Alexius noticed a number of marks scribed on the wall under the peg; the apex of the cone formed by the bent bowstring was touching one of them.

'Sixty pounds at twenty-four,' the boy said, having examined the mark. Loredan nodded, untied the weight and laid it gently down.

'More to come off the belly,' he said. 'Take it down and put it up in the vice, and get me the small drawknife.'

The boy did as he was told, asking, 'Why the belly? The wood's thicker on the back, shouldn't we thin it there instead?'

Loredan shook his head as the boy handed him an eight-inch blade with a handle at right angles on each end. 'You're forgetting your basic theory,' he said, 'about the back and the belly. You'd better tell me again, and remind yourself.'

The boy sighed; then, as Loredan spat on a flat brown stone and started whetting the blade slowly along it, the boy began to recite, 'The back of the bow stretches,' he said, 'and the belly is compressed. It's the stretching and the compression, balanced and in proper proportion, that gives a bow its strength. I *know* that,' he added in a wounded voice. 'I was just saying, there's an awful lot of wood in the back, so shouldn't you even it up?'

Without looking up, Loredan shook his head. 'You're forgetting what I told you about the heartwood and the sapwood,' he said.

'No, I'm not,' the boy replied, fidgeting with a beechwood mallet. 'Sapwood for the back, because it's young and can be stretched, heartwood for the belly because it's old and remembers its shape, even when it's been crushed up tight.'

'And the sapwood should be thin and the heartwood thick,' Loredan added, 'because what is compressed has more power when it expands again than that which has been stretched when it contracts. And *that's* the important bit,' he concluded, testing the edge of the blade against his thumb. 'The bit you always seem to forget.'

'Only because it's full of long words,' the boy replied. 'I'm not very good with long words. I'd remember it much easier if I actually knew what it meant.'

Loredan smiled. 'It does help,' he conceded. 'All right, then, think of it this way. Lord Temrai—'

Alexius saw the boy's face change, ever so slightly.

'—is the sapwood, because he was young and he stretched the clan to make them do something they weren't supposed to be able to do. By stretching them he gave them power.'

'I don't like this explaining,' the boy said.

'If you don't like it, it must be doing you good. Now then, the Patriarch Alexius is the heartwood, because he was old and he was crushed up and bent back when the city fell, and all the strength of the Order was squeezed into him; and that's how he got his power, which is much greater than the clan's.'

'Ah,' said the boy. 'Now I think I understand.'

'There's more,' Loredan warned. 'There's the reason why you don't make a bow out of just sapwood or just heart-wood; because the same power that stretches the sapwood also compresses the heartwood, and the stretching of the one compresses the other.'

'Now I'm not understanding again.'

'Never mind. Learn now and understand later. Without the heartwood to support it, the sapwood stretches too much and breaks. Without the sapwood to contain it, the heartwood compresses too much and breaks. That's why the sapwood's on the outside, facing away from you as you draw the bow, and the heartwood's inside.'

'I see,' said the boy. 'Or I think I do. We're in the belly of the bow, and they're outside, in the back.'

Loredan nodded. 'Sort of,' he said. 'Right, that'll have to do for an edge. Now, let's let the dog see the rabbit.'

—and opened them again, because someone had opened the door and was shouting something at him.

'What?' he mumbled. 'Speak up, I can't—'

'The *enemy*,' the boy in the doorway repeated, 'are inside the city. Somebody's opened the gates. The savages are taking the city.'

'Oh,' Alexius replied. 'That would explain it, then.' He

frowned, wondering why he'd said that. 'Do we know what we're supposed to do?'

The boy shrugged. 'The precentors and the librarians want to see you as soon as possible,' he said, 'about trying to hide the library or bury it or something.' He shuffled his feet nervously. 'Do you need me any more, Patriarch, or can I go?'

Alexius shook his head. 'No, you run along,' he said. 'I'd get home, if I were you, before your mother worries herself to death.'

The boy nodded gratefully and shut the door behind him, leaving Alexius in the dark once more. He sat up and felt for his slippers with his toes. Next, he should get dressed and go and see the precentors and the librarians; but was there any point, now that the city was about to fall? There was no earthly hope of saving the library, over a hundred thousand books ranged over a couple of miles of shelves. As for saving himself, that would be a sublimely futile effort; the strain of hurrying down to the harbour and trying to jostle his way onto a ship would kill him just as effectively as an arrow or a lungful of smoke. If he thought he'd be able to help organise an efficient evacuation, he'd go to it with a will. But the truth was that he'd only get in the way. If only there was some light, he could spend his last hours, or minutes maybe, admiring the justly famous mosaics on the ceiling and using them as a focus for some final act of meditation. But there wasn't; and he couldn't be bothered to grope around in the dark for his tinderbox. Ah, the hell with it; he'd never particularly liked the things to begin with.

His eyelids were beginning to droop as he slipped back into a doze when the door flew open again, and light flooded in from the stairway behind. But it wasn't the pageboy, or even a plains warrior with a dripping knife in each hand; it was someone he knew, if he could only fit a name to …

'Patriarch Alexius? Patriarch? Excuse me, are you there?'

His eyes snapped open. 'Hello?' he called out. 'Who's that?'

The glow of the lantern fell across the man's face. 'It's me, Venart. You remember, we met a while ago when you were...'

'Yes, yes, of course.' Alexius peered at him, wondering if this was another of those dreams. 'Please, come in,' he added. 'What can I do for you?' An incongruous conversation to be having in the middle of the sack of one's city, he reflected, but any interruption to his own death vigil was welcome enough.

'My sister,' Venart said. 'She - well, she sent me to fetch you.'

'Oh.' It would have made much better sense if it had been a dream, but it patently wasn't. He could smell the oil burning in the lantern, and Venart, pale-faced with embarrassment overlaid on terror, was quite obviously both here and now. 'That was - very thoughtful.'

'She insisted,' Venart replied. 'It's really quite unnerving, as if she somehow *knew*.' He stared at Alexius for a moment. 'Patriarch,' he said, 'I'm sorry if this is a rude question or against your ethics or whatever, but I'm worried. *Is* she a witch? It'd never have occurred to me in a million years; but all those things you said the first time we came here, and now this—'

She isn't; but perhaps I know who is. 'Please,' Alexius replied, 'don't ask me. The one thing I've learned in my recent studies into the subject is that I still know next to nothing about it.' He rubbed his eyes with his knuckles and added, 'Actually, if we're going to escape from the city, shouldn't we be making a start? I imagine it isn't going to be easy.'

'What? Oh, gods, yes, we must leave at once.' Venart half-turned, then stopped. 'You, um, don't want to take much stuff with you, I suppose? Only I don't think we ought to load ourselves down with heavy bags and parcels.'

Alexius considered for a moment. 'I don't think there's anything I actually need,' he said. 'If you'd be kind enough to hand me my coat; it's just there, on the stool.'

'No books or anything like that?'

Books of spells, grimoires, magical instruments, a brass jar or pottery lamp containing my familiar demon. 'No,' Alexius confirmed. 'There's all sorts of things I'd like to take, but nothing I can't do without. It's rather wonderful to be able to say that at my age, don't you think?'

As they set out, Alexius confidently expected he wouldn't survive as far as the second-city gate, let alone beyond it. But the streets were remarkably quiet; in the distance there were vaguely disquieting noises, but no recognisable shrieks of agony, no red glow over the lower city. He led the way from the gate, hoping his twenty-year-old recollections of back ways to the harbour were still reasonably accurate and valid.

'How did you manage to get here? To my lodgings, I mean. Did you arrive before it all started, or ...?'

'Yes,' Venart said (he was actually puffing, having to make an effort to keep up), 'I was having a late meal at my inn when I heard the first rumours, so I came over straight away. Actually,' he added, 'I'm going to have to leave you at the docks – there'll be a boat to carry you to the ship, assuming they haven't both been stolen yet – because I've got to go back and pick up someone else. Or try to, at any rate.' Venart was close to tears, Alexius noticed as they passed under a lamp. He wore the expression of a man who's in desperate trouble not of his own making, trouble he knew was coming and could so easily have avoided, that *it's-not-fair* kind of despairing rage that feels so much worse than ordinary fear or anger.

'Loredan?' Alexius prompted him.

He nodded. 'Though how I'm supposed to find the General in the middle of a battle, let alone persuade him to drop everything and come with me ...'

'I'm sure you'll do your best,' Alexius said with a trace of firmness, as if encouraging a child to do something he didn't want to, but which would be good for him. 'I expect you'll manage,' he added, truthfully.

They were no more than a quarter of a mile from the harbour; but now they had no choice but to leave the back alleys and join the surge of people in a main thoroughfare. It wasn't a pleasant walk, by any means; Alexius was reminded of excessively boisterous festivals, a student riot from his youth, the panic that had attended a fire, other similar precedents. But there were far more people here; women and children as well as men, all shoving and jostling, while on either side of the street the inevitable opportunists were indulging in some last-chance-to-steal looting of the better class of shops, and a few overturned carts and collapsed loads didn't help the flow of traffic. Witchcraft, he muttered to himself as the crowd crushed and compressed all around them without ever actually impeding them, without anybody so much as treading on their feet. There wasn't anything he could point to and legitimately call a supernatural effect; it was just that there were gaps and air pockets in the crush precisely where they wanted to go.

'The boat's not actually down by the docks,' Venart said in a loud, hoarse whisper. 'That'd be inviting people to come and grab it. So I told the boatmen to hide up under the arches of the long jetty, where I reckoned nobody'd see them. Mind you, I wasn't expecting a wholesale panic like this.'

Fortuitously the current of the stampede swept them directly towards the long jetty. Some fool had started a fire, accidentally or deliberately, in one of the warehouses, and its light reflected off the water was good enough to see by for some way. 'There,' Venart hissed. 'Oh, gods, there's people trying to get on it, just as I feared. Come on.'

Alexius saw a small longboat, six oars each side, standing off about fifteen yards from the jetty. Around it in the water men and women were swimming; some of them were trying to scramble over the side of the boat, and the oarsmen were hitting them with boathooks, the butt-ends of oars, even the wooden clogs from their feet. Venart shouted and waved; by chance one of the oarsmen looked up and saw him, and shouted to his fellows. They dislodged the remaining swimmers with difficulty and quite a lot of force, and rowed towards the point where Venart and Alexius stood.

'This'll be the tricky part,' Venart muttered. 'I don't suppose you're up to swimming.'

'Not really, no.'

'Pity.' Quite a few people were watching the boat coming in, others were scrambling to get to the front. It was the pushing and shoving behind them, in fact, that launched Venart and Alexius unexpectedly into the water, solving one problem but creating another.

Alexius felt the water close above his head. *Ah, well*, he thought, *it was worth trying, I suppose. But I knew it wasn't going to do any good.* Then he became aware of something pinching hard on his arm, and he was moving, being towed (still under the water) in the direction that he seemed to remember the boat being in. Since he was effectively dead already, of course, he could afford to be relaxed about the whole thing—

—Until he felt the first mouthful of water enter his lungs, and the panic, which happened at almost precisely the moment when his head broke through the water back into the air, and many hands grabbed him and hauled him upwards; then a bump as he hit the planks of the boat, and someone pushing down on his chest – trying to kill him? No, this was something to do with getting water out of his lungs. It was all rather unpleasant, and he wasn't entirely sorry when his eyes blacked over and he lost consciousness.

CHAPTER TWENTY-ONE

The Prefect wiped the blood out of his eyes and looked down the wall, towards the bridgehouse, and then up, to where Loredan's bastion used to be. On both sides, he could see large contingents of the enemy, each party outnumbering the force he'd managed to rally around watchtower sixteen.

Under different circumstances, he could justifiably claim to have done enough. Four simultaneous assaults from both directions by superior forces had been repelled, at minimal loss to the defenders. Enemy casualties had been heavy, not that that signified particularly; what did it matter how many were killed when they still kept coming?

Having assessed the situation and made what preparations he could, the Prefect took stock of his own condition, which wasn't good. He'd taken a blow from an axe just above the rim of his helmet; the axe hadn't penetrated, but the jagged edge of a crumpled piece of helmet trim had sliced deeply into his forehead, and the blood from the cut was making it hard for him to see. A short-range arrow had hit him in the ribs; again, the mailcoat had turned it, but the baffled impact had cracked at least one rib, possibly two, which made breathing a painful matter. He'd turned his ankle, which didn't help, and pulled a muscle in his shoulder parrying a sword-cut from a much stronger man. As far as he was aware, none of the handful of offensive strokes he'd managed to make had done anybody any harm, but at least he was still alive.

He'd known for the last half-hour that he was going to die. Defeat is a gradual thing; it begins with the apprehension that things could be going better, develops into the perception that the situation is not favourable and that action must be taken to redress the balance; then, gradually, the emphasis shifts from *they would appear to have an advantage* to *we might still win this if we pull something special out of the hat.* Then, one by one, the possibilities for salvation are cancelled, until a point is reached where the brain acknowledges that realistically there can only be one outcome. After that, it scarcely matters whether the vanquished party fights bravely to the last or stands still and allows itself to be slaughtered. If they fight on, it's for revenge (or spite, at any rate), or the instinctive feeling that falling in battle is somehow preferable, in some strange way *better for you* than being made to kneel in rows until someone yanks your head back by the hair and cuts your throat. And, even at the end, there's a misguided glimmer of hope. The beating of the heart and the action of the lungs are a comforting prevarication, giving an impression of options being kept open.

The enemy came on for the fifth time; and as the Prefect shouted the order to form lines, his voice was weary. Before this night, he wouldn't have believed it was possible to feel tired during a battle; there would always be the rush of excitement and terror that would damp down the pain in the arms and knees, compensate for the shortness of breath and the pain of wounds and injuries. Well; the first four times, possibly. The fifth and last time, no. Perhaps when the outcome is so patently obvious, the body can no longer make the effort.

Why haven't they used archers to clear us off? he wondered. True, it was dark, not enough light to make out individual targets; but a line of men jammed close together on the walkway presented a target any archer could hit with his eyes shut. There were various possible explanations; archers more urgently needed elsewhere, run out of arrows, an unimaginative captain or an intimate-combat fetishist. Made no odds, really.

As the enemy came in – walking, not running, which gave the whole thing an unnaturally calm, almost serene feeling – the Prefect tightened his grip on his sword-hilt and promised himself he'd do his best, this being his last opportunity. All his adult life he'd dealt in honour and service, the way a furrier deals in furs or a vintner in wine. On his lips the terms had had specialised political meanings, and he'd long since stopped thinking about what the words stood for in the world at large. Now, unfortunately a little bit too late, he'd been granted a little gleam of insight; service is what makes you stand in the line when nobody would try and stop you if you ran away, and honour is what's left when every other conceivable reason for staying there has long since evaporated.

Oh, well, here we go. A man loomed up out of the darkness, a shape under a leather cap, an arm thrusting with a halberd. The Prefect parried, realised the thrust was a feint, found it was too late to do anything about it. Now he was slumped against the parapet, still alive but suddenly too weak to move. The man had moved on, stepping over him and preparing to engage the next man who got in his way; he was no longer concerned with the Prefect, who was as good as dead and therefore no longer a factor needing to be taken into account.

I don't think I'm going to be all right this time.
I wonder if …
I …

It's going to be all right—
It had been close. Another ten minutes or so and the enemy would have rounded them up like sheep in a pen; but the counterattack by Ceuscai's men (who must have finally cleared the wall, or else they wouldn't be here) had come, not perhaps at the last moment, but fairly close to it. Now the enemy had fallen back; they'd lost fewer men and inflicted an alarming amount of damage, but the important

part of it was that they'd been forced to retreat. In effect, it was an admission that they could no longer defend the landward side of the lower city. Which meant, in turn, that if Ceuscai's people now controlled the wall, all exits from the city apart from the docks were cut off. The number who could escape through the docks was strictly limited by the number of ships and the space available on them, and the rest had nowhere to go but uphill. It's going to be all right.

Temrai wrapped a strip of cloth around the cut on his arm, using his teeth to draw the knot tight. It was a scratch, nothing more; the jagged edge of a damaged shield, dragged across him in the squash as they bundled through the hole in the wall. So far, he hadn't come within arm's length of the enemy, and for that he was extremely grateful.

'All right,' he said, raising his voice to make himself heard. 'Heads of companies to me, now. Captains, you've got five minutes to sort yourselves out and then we're moving on. Anybody seen Bosadai? No? Oh, right. In that case, you two are in charge of arrow supplies; get some squads organised to pick up what you can find and pass them around.'

The heads-of-companies meeting was short and to the point. Now that the hard work had been done, it was almost time to wrap it up; in fact, by the time the carters had returned to camp, loaded up the stuff and come back, it ought to be time. And then it would be finished.

Loredan stepped forward, putting his weight on his front foot and lunging. The other man was off balance and couldn't have made an effective parry even if he'd known how to. The first seven inches of the blade went in just below his throat, in the gap where the collarbones meet. He slid off the blade and dropped, making way for the next one.

It's all very well killing people, but we're losing this. They weren't just coming in twos and threes; the flow was continuous, and as soon as one went down there was another behind him and two squashing through on either side. Loredan stopped using the thrust and switched to slashes only; less risk of getting the blade stuck, and what he wanted was wounded men still on their feet and impeding the scrum rather than more corpses getting in his way and upsetting his balance. No place for finesse or precision in a ruck; hard swipes off the back foot, keep the blade moving fast, as close to the body as possible to make it harder to parry effectively, and, if possible, hit them around the face and neck, where it hurts and frightens most.

Dimly he was aware that the man next to him in the line had gone down, which meant his right side was exposed. He stepped back three paces, covering his retreat with a powerful slash that connected with something soft. He realised that he was resigned to the fact that the counter-attack, which was more or less their last realistic chance, wasn't going to happen now; the wall had definitely fallen, so even if they did somehow push the enemy back down the hill, all that'd happen would be that ultimately they'd be enfiladed by archers on the wall, pinned down and surrounded. The plain truth was that there were too many of the enemy now inside the city for his forces to push out again.

Without knowing why, he ducked. As he did so, a poleaxe flashed over the top of his bent neck, slicing the air just where his chin would have been. He estimated where the poleaxe-user must be and lunged at that extrapolated spot, dropping on one knee as he did so just in case the other man had a friend. The blade went into something; he twisted it sharply to the left and freed it, then moved smartly right out of the way of a lance-thrust. He was getting left behind again, which wouldn't do at all. From his kneeling position he sprang backwards, taking a chance on landing cleanly, and made it. As he landed he swung his sword again, feeling a jarring shock as it rang on a helmet.

Up the hill, then; and once they started on that road they might as well call it a day. Even if they were able to get the second-city gate closed and manned the wall, it'd only be a matter of time. They'd be penned up in a smaller, less advantageous siege, with no prospect of supply or eventual relief. The best they could hope to achieve by holding the second city would be slightly more favourable terms of surrender.

Then to hell with this, Loredan said to himself; *nothing more I can do, so let's just see if there's a hope in hell of getting through to the docks and out of here.*

Easier said than done. It wasn't just a matter of deciding he didn't want to play any more; he still had to find a way through the attack and round the hill. Quite possibly he'd left it too late, in which case he might as well lower his sword and get it over with. But that went against the grain, somehow; it was offensive to all the instincts he'd acquired over a decade in the legal profession. It would be tantamount to throwing the fight.

There was only one way he could think of, and if it didn't work he was finished. On the other hand, he wasn't exactly spoilt for choice. First he let fly with a broad sweep, very hard and slightly wild; it connected, sure enough, and while the other man was plunging about in panic with half his face carved off, Loredan dropped to his knees, his face only a few inches above the mat of corpses and nearly corpses. He found himself looking into the eyes of a man – one he'd just seen to? Quite possibly, no way of knowing, and did it matter? – who was still just about alive, his eyes wide in a horrified stare, his lips moving without sound, as if he was trying to pass on some tremendous revelation about death. Loredan crawled over him, first a hand on his face, then a knee, and then onwards, scrabbling and slithering over the dead and dying—

—*This is adding insult to injury, Bardas. Bad enough to be facing the greatest of all horrors, alone, frightened and in pain, without having some uncaring stranger kneeling on your face while you're at it*—

—For what seemed like hours, with shuffling feet and knees kicking and banging into him, stepping over his head, treading on his outstretched fingers. Still, it had to be done, and so long as nobody looked down, so long as they assumed he was just another nearly dead man wriggling about underfoot, there was a chance he might even get away with it.

He reached a point where there were feet but no more dead bodies, and decided it was time to stand up. He did so, and found himself face to face with a clan warrior, a kid of about sixteen who stared at him in horror as if he'd just shaken hands with the occupant of a freshly made grave. Loredan treated him to a knee in the groin and moved on, slipping sideways between two others and then—

—Out of the battle, as far as he could tell. Nobody was looking round at him, let alone following. He stood still to catch his breath, then hurried at a fast trot for the cover of an archway.

Maybe it's going to be all right. Perhaps; too early to tell, though. Anyway, the next bit's the easy part.

He peered into the darkness behind the archway. Now then; this leads to an alley which runs up behind the old fruit warehouse and comes out opposite the pin-makers' court-yard; turn right there past the chisel-grinders' row, carry on as far as the tavern with the barmaid with the unfortunate squint, then left down the plane-makers' arcade as far as the junction with the westernmost ropewalk, alleyway to the left, straight down that, should come out just behind the customs sheds.

He hadn't gone more than twenty yards into the darkness when his foot caught on something and he went sprawling. He landed on his side, jerked his knees up, pushed against the alley wall and was on his feet again in just over a second, with his sword in a classic two-handed guard. Whatever he'd just tripped over groaned.

Options: kill it in case it follows, leave it or investigate. While he was deciding, it groaned again. *Ah, the hell with it*, Loredan muttered under his breath.

'Who's that?' he said.

No reply except another low moan. Wondering what in gods' name he thought he was doing, he sheathed his sword, stooped and put out a hand. He felt a face; smooth, soft, a girl or a young boy.

'What's the matter?' he whispered.

'Arrow,' the voice replied.

'Can you get up?'

Groan. Loredan sighed. This was a complication he really could do without.

'I'll take that as a yes,' he said. 'Come on.'

Somehow he got its arm round his shoulder, then straightened his back and knees and lifted. It wasn't very heavy; almost certainly a girl by the feel, which maybe explained a little why he was doing this extremely rash thing.

'Now walk,' he said. 'Please. If you don't, I'm going to have to dump you.'

'I'll try,' she said. 'Difficult.'

'Sure,' he said. 'If it was easy, everyone'd be able to do it, and where'd be the point in that? All right, I've got you. Try and hold on if you can.'

'Can't.'

'All right, then, be difficult. But I'm warning you—'

'Can't,' the girl repeated. 'No fingers.'

'What?'

'No *fingers*—'

No fingers, no fingers. Who did he know in this city, young girl, skinny, no fingers?

Oh, for crying out loud—

Gorgas Loredan knelt behind the stairs that led up to a gallery of shops, waiting for the men to go by. There were about twelve of them – in other words, too many – and they had a wagon. He considered jumping on, hoping they wouldn't notice in the dark. No, forget it, not feeling lucky. The wagon, he noticed, was piled high with barrels.

To his intense annoyance, the procession halted about ten yards away from where he was hiding. The escort – they were close enough for him to confirm that they were plainsmen – lit torches from the lantern that swung from the side of the wagon and set about investigating the surrounding area. Gorgas began to feel decidedly nervous, and he had made up his mind to run for it and hope they were too busy to follow him when they stopped poking about and, splitting up into pairs, began to unload the barrels.

The idea of a quick sprint was still appealing. True, there was an archer sitting on the driver's bench with an arrow nocked and ready, but it seemed a reasonable assumption that his function was primarily defensive. No advantage to be gained by wasting valuable arrows taking pot shots at fleeing civilians in bad light. He made up his mind to start running on the count of five.

He'd reached four when two of the plainsmen rolled their barrel into a shop doorway and flushed out a pair of children, a boy and a girl, approximately six and ten respectively. They had the native common sense to run in different directions; but the archer swivelled round on his bench, followed the girl and shot her through the kidneys at about twenty yards, then drew and nocked an arrow in a single flowing movement and hit the boy square in the middle of his neck at close on forty yards, just as he was about to reach the safety of the alleyway Gorgas had been planning to use himself. By the time he'd looked back at the wagon, the archer had nocked another arrow and was looking round for something to loose it at. One of his companions muttered, 'Shot!' under his breath; the rest seemed to take it all in their stride and carried on with their work.

Running for it wasn't such an inviting prospect any more. Gorgas swore under his breath. Time was getting on and he had things to do and a long way to go. He also had a rough idea of what was in the barrels; if he was right, there would soon be yet another unwelcome complication.

The men nearest to him deposited a barrel no more than ten yards from where he was hiding, which made deciding what he was going to do that bit easier. The prospect was still galling in the extreme; he disliked doing the sort of thing he was now resolved to do even more than the type of people who tended to do it. Nevertheless; in extreme situations there comes a point when heroism is the safest and most logical course of action. As quietly as he could he wriggled up onto his haunches, pulled an arrow from his quiver (only three left; damn), held his bow out at a slant because of the confined space, with his head canted over to compensate; nocked, drew, held and loosed.

Even in bad light it was a routine enough shot, and Gorgas was a perfectly competent archer. Even so, it was a great relief to him when the arrow went home, making that *tchock!* noise unique to a bodkin-head arrow in manflesh, and the plainsman toppled sideways off the box and onto the ground.

Gorgas nocked another arrow as he stood up, fumbling a little and staggering as his cramped legs protested at the short notice. Only one of the other men had seen what was going on; and in the time between his seeing the shot and calling out to his mates, Gorgas was on his feet and moving well, to the point where he was nearer to the wagon than any of the plainsmen.

He heard several shouts and a grinding noise (sword leaving scabbard) as he vaulted up onto the bench, dropped his bow and grabbed the long-handled whip from its rest. The wagon team were mules, of course; better than one-in-three odds that they weren't going to budge, and that would be embarrassing. His luck was in, however, which made a pleasant change; even so, there was a man in the act of hauling himself up onto the tailgate by the time the mules moved off at a sharp trot. Without moving from his seat, Gorgas pivoted and lashed out behind him with the whip. He missed, but a couple of barrels chose that moment to fall over and roll against the tailgate, dislodging the one-man boarding party. Another plainsman grabbed one of the canopy stays and ran alongside holding it. Gorgas waited until he'd managed to hop up onto the running-board, his head nicely level with Gorgas' toecap, before booting him off. By the sound and feel of it, he went under the nearside wheels, which served him right for trying too hard.

He expected further efforts, but they didn't happen, and before he knew it he was round the corner of the street and going well. From the lack of pursuit he gathered that the remaining carters had written the wagon off to experience and were getting on with their work; a hypothesis that was largely confirmed by a *whoosh-boom* behind him, a disturbance in the air and a red glow visible out of the corner of his eye. The effect was repeated a number of times before he was out of earshot.

He's got the recipe right, then, Gorgas said to himself. Not bad going for someone who'd been brought up to regard the wheel as the high-water mark of his people's technological achievement.

As he drove (north-west and downhill, as far as the streets would let him), he heard and saw a lot more of the same, and blessed his luck for putting him in the way of a clan wagon. One of the first things he'd done was stick the deceased archer's cap on his head, and the parties of carters and soldiers he passed as he drove took no notice of him. They were all, needless to say, plainsmen; panic, fire and enemy soldiers had cleared this district of everyone who was capable of moving. The logic of it was probably what made him complacent, so that he stopped bothering to keep an eye out; with the result that he didn't see a man slip out of an alleyway as he drove past and run up on the outside. The first he knew was when someone vaulted up onto the box, pushed him off the bench and grabbed the reins.

He landed painfully, jarring his shoulder and snapping his two remaining arrows. If he'd had time he'd have been in pain; as it was, he only managed to hop on to the tailgate and drop down out of sight because his attacker reined up and brought the wagon to a stop.

This is all Bardas' fault, he couldn't help thinking; *I try to look after him, and this is what happens*. But he knew the accusation was unjust. Properly speaking, it was all of his own making, and one thing he'd always taken pride in was accepting the responsibility for his actions.

Even so; all this scrapping with strangers and running about ... And me a respected member of the international banking community.

The cart-thief, whoever he was, had jumped down and gone back to the alleyway he'd first appeared from. Gorgas grinned; a fine athlete, his assailant, but an idiot. He crept forward, sat himself down on the bench and took up the reins.

Just a minute—

There had been something familiar about the way the man had got down off the wagon. It had reminded him of another wagon, a creaky old haywain with a warped front axle; Clefas, Zonaras, Sis and himself underneath pitching up the stooks, Father and Bardas up on the wagon catching them and packing them down, cramming in more than the wain was ever built to carry to save having to make another trip—

'Bardas?' he called out. 'Is that you?'

The man had been on the point of hurling himself at the wagon, all set for an energetic free-for-all on the moving box. He stopped as if he'd run into a wall.

'Gorgas?'

He grinned, so widely that the glow of the fire on the opposite side of the street shone on his bared teeth. 'Now that's lucky,' he said. 'I've been looking for you.'

'*Gorgas?*'

'Well, don't just stand there, get on the damn wagon.'

Bardas Loredan seemed to collapse, like a punctured grain sack as its contents flow out onto the ground. Everything else he'd managed to cope with, even the bizarre shock of tripping over his ex-pupil sworn-enemy in a pitch-dark alley. But this wasn't something he could take in his stride; not on top of everything else. The headache was a fairly obvious clue, of course; similarly the suspicious ease with which he'd managed to get this far.

He was beginning to wish he hadn't. Likewise, the fish who suddenly comes across a fat lugworm floating motionless in the water changes its mind about the quality of its luck once it feels the hook draw through its lip.

'Bardas,' said the man on the wagon, 'we haven't got time. Get your bum on this seat and let's be going, while there's still a chance of getting through.'

Bardas had almost made up his mind as to the right thing to do when he suddenly remembered the girl, lying bleeding in the alleyway behind him. He closed his eyes and mouthed a curse. Gorgas' letter had mentioned a ship; the ship could carry the girl out, if she lived and Gorgas really could get through and he did have a ship waiting, and about a dozen other provisos. Once again, he had no choice in the matter. Once, just once, it'd be nice to be able to decide for himself. One day, maybe.

'You've really got a ship waiting?' he said. 'No lies?'

'If it's still there, which is getting less certain by the minute.'

'Right,' he said. 'There's a badly wounded girl in the alley back there. You help me get her up on the wagon, and you see to it that she gets away. Understood?'

'Do we have to? No offence, Bardas, but is this really the time or the place?'

Anything, anything to be able to make him pay, for the sheer satisfaction of ramming my fist into his face and hearing something crack. But I can't. 'Shut up,' he said. 'Over here.'

Fortunately it was too dark in the shadow of the tall buildings behind him to see Gorgas' face clearly. He was sure he couldn't have taken that. As it was, there was an indistinct male shape who took the girl's feet while he scooped her up under the shoulders. They staggered as far as the tailgate and slid her onto the bed of the wagon. Then her face came under the light of the lantern, and Gorgas said, 'Gods, Bardas, this is unreal.'

'What?'

'I was looking for her, too.' He lifted his head, and the light revealed him. 'Of course, you don't know who she is, do you? Bardas, this is your niece.'

No. What did he say? Isn't it ever going to stop?

'I'm not kidding, you know,' Gorgas said. 'This is your niece, Iseutz. Niessa's daughter.'

Bardas started to back away, trod in a pothole, staggered and fell over, landing on his backside and jarring his spine. 'Sorry to have to break it to you like this,' Gorgas was saying. 'Obviously, what with one thing and another, it must be a bit of a shock. But we haven't got *time*, Bardas. If you want to have a fit, do it when we're on the goddamn ship.'

Bardas Loredan shook his head, about the only part of him he could still move. 'I'm not coming on any ship with you, Gorgas. I'm going to stay here and get killed, just to spite you. Now get out of my sight, you and your...'

'Niece,' Gorgas said. 'And you're getting on this wagon, if I have to pick you up and carry you.'

Bardas smiled; at least, he opened his lips and showed his teeth. 'You've got to catch me first,' he said; then he turned and started to run.

He'd gone about fifteen yards when the stone hit him.

From the second-city gatehouse, the Lord Lieutenant had a splendid view of the fire; probably the best in the city. It was the sort of spectacle that had to be admired, regardless of the circumstances. The sheer impersonal beauty of the flickering red light was breathtaking. One thing was certain: there wasn't another man alive who'd ever seen the like.

Fire in the lower city was a nightmare that haunted everybody who held office in Perimadeia. Quite simply, there was nothing anybody could do about it. The place was and always had been a hell of a good bonfire poised and ready to happen. Once a fire managed to get established, it moved faster than a man could run, jumping from roof to roof across the thatched eaves that overhung the narrow streets, surging and swelling as it lit upon oil stores, pitch refineries, distilleries, sulphur bins, grain bins, cloth warehouses, timberyards; it was as if the people of the city had deliberately gone out of their way to provide a relay of inflammable materials, like a string of signal beacons spanning a country.

The critical point was past now; nothing to do but let it burn itself out. Tradition had it that the risk of fire in the lower city was the reason the second city had been founded; a high wall to keep the flames away from the important buildings, the houses of substantial citizens, the libraries of the Order, the offices where vital records were kept. The wall would do its job again, even with the fire-oil lashing up an inferno beyond all precedent. Whether that made him feel better or worse, the Lord Lieutenant wasn't sure. It meant that in spite of the fire they'd started, the enemy would inherit the second city – and the upper city too, of course, with all its empty wealth of decoration and embellishment – completely intact. The best part of Perimadeia, its beauty and opulence, would survive. Its people wouldn't.

Two hours ago, the enemy had forced the second-city gate. They'd improvised a highly efficient battering ram out of the driveshaft of the glorious new publicly funded municipal water mill. Three years of diligent searching it had taken to find a single tree trunk long and thick enough to make the driveshaft; then they'd had to pay an exorbitant price for it to the loathsome merchant cartel of Scona, and then a special ship had had to be built up to transport it, the Grand Avenue had been widened (at ruinous expense) to bring it up; special wagons, special cranes – the trouble and expense had been enough to chill the blood. In fact, the administrative part of the Lord Lieutenant's mind had marvelled at the ease and efficiency with which the enemy had torn the thing out and dragged it, by unassisted manpower, up the hill and against the gate, which had given way like a paper window.

A shout from below told him that the enemy were attacking again. The first attack had pushed them back onto a stretch of wall four towers in each direction on either side of the gate. The second attempt had failed; what remained of the city forces had thrown them back with substantial losses, had even recaptured a further five towers. The third – well, they'd lost fewer than a hundred men at a cost to the enemy of at least a thousand; but here they were, cooped up in the gatehouse and fifty yards of wall on either side, all of the city that remained under the control of the Perimadeian government. It was a realm you could cross in fifteen paces, and the Lord Lieutenant was in sole charge of it. For now, anyway.

On the wall to both the right and the left, the enemy line shuffled forward. The Lord Lieutenant noticed something different, and realised that they'd somehow managed to dig out the old archers' shields, big wickerwork screens behind which two bowmen could shelter, which had been mothballed at least twenty years ago. They seemed to work just fine; the few arrows left to the city archers were chunking into the wicker as if they were targets in the butts, and the line was advancing steadily. And below—

Below, they appeared to be setting up a couple of torsion engines – ah, yes, the two additional mangonels he'd ordered to fill gaps on the wall, which they'd been due to crane into position tomorrow afternoon. Now the enemy had them, and they appeared to be loading them with medium-sized barrels … The Lord Lieutenant nodded as he resolved the problem. The barrels were obviously full of fire-oil. A bit risky (drop one short and you'd risk causing damage to the buildings immediately above the wall) but a quick and thoroughly economical way of solving the tactical problem.

The Lord Lieutenant indulged himself with a last view of the city. From this high point he could see the docks – even at this distance he could clearly make out the crowds milling round the docks area, wedged solid in all the streets and roads that led to the harbour district. Everybody must have decided to head for the docks and take their chances; and now the fire was spreading that way, helped slightly by a gentle breeze. It was already licking around the edges of the crowd, and the mere thought of what it must be like down there, trapped between fire and water, crowding in tighter still as the flames advanced, was enough to reconcile him somewhat to the prospect of dying up here in relative peace and quiet.

In the event, the first barrel was a failure. As it flew upward the fuse blew out, and the barrel smashed harmlessly against the top battlements. Well, relatively harmlessly. A fair number of people, including the Lord Lieutenant, were soaked in the fire-oil, which was going to make life interesting as soon as one firebomb did what it was supposed to do.

The second barrel worked just fine, and the engineers watched with dumb fascination as the defenders, their hair and beards suddenly full of fire, streamed out of the choking smoke and melting heat inside the tower, straight into massed volleys of arrows from the archery contingents behind their shields on the wall.

'All done,' a captain reported, when it was over. 'What now?'

Uncle Anakai, who had never seen the like before in all his many years, had regret in his voice when he gave him Temrai's order. 'Burn the lot,' he said, 'everything that'll take. But not till we're through that gate up there – what's it called? Upper city? Whatever. Shouldn't take you long to get through there; apparently it isn't even garrisoned. So, torch the upper city first, then this. And then,' he added quietly, 'get yourselves up on this wall before it catches up with you, unless you want to play candles too.'

When he came round, Loredan was lying on his back on the bed of a moving wagon. For a moment he thought he was somewhere else entirely (maybe he'd been dreaming); then he remembered, all too clearly.

He turned his head and saw the outline of Gorgas' back, silhouetted against an alarmingly red sky. The thing he could feel lying under his left leg was the body of a girl, apparently his niece or what was left of her. He knew without having to check that she was still alive. That's one of the infuriating things about natural-born pests, the really tiresome and pernicious variety. Knock them about, cut their fingers off, stick them with arrows, hurl them about like stooks of hay; no chance at all of killing them. They're the ones that always survive, somehow or other. Probably, Loredan realised, why there's so many of them and so few of us.

Gorgas wasn't looking at him; his eyes were on the road ahead, a burning house that was starting to slide into the street, a platoon of the clan being herded onto a similar wagon for transport out of danger now that the job was over and the mopping-up could be left to the fire. And that's what Gorgas is going to do, damn his hatefully intelligent soul; he's going to creep out of the city in a convoy of enemy wagons. Then all he's got to do is slip away, find a boat or a small raft, and paddle out to meet this ship of his. The part that really burns me is, I'd never have had the wit to think of that.

The hell with it. Taking care to keep his head down, Loredan edged his way backwards along the bed of the wagon until his feet were hanging over the edge of the open tailgate. Then he pushed away with the palms of his hands until he slid off and landed, face down, on the hard ground.

You may be clever but you don't catch me, he said to himself as he scraped himself up and somehow found the strength to scramble to his feet. As he ducked down behind the pillar of an archway, he caught sight of his brother's head, outlined against a backdrop of fire, as if he was wearing the flames. If only that could be the last he ever saw of Gorgas Loredan, he'd be a happy man.

And the rest of your life's your own. The city was beyond saving, so his obligations in that direction had obviously lapsed. His chances of getting out alive were negligible, which released him from his obligations to his family. Athli was safe. Alexius – well, it would have been nice to have made an effort, but the old man was surely dead by now. He could choose what to do with his last half-hour or so with nobody to please but himself. If he wanted to, he could rush up to the first enemy unit he came across and die fighting. Or he could kick down a tavern door and get as drunk as time permitted. Or he could sit cross-legged in the street and meditate on the infinite. Wouldn't matter a toss what he did.

Or he could try and escape.

Futile, of course. He had no chance, none whatsoever. On the other hand he was starting from a point of accepting his own death (and taking it pretty damn well, at that). The intellectual challenge would be stimulating, if nothing else. He decided to have a go.

Putting aside what he thought of brother Gorgas as a man, his idea wasn't a bad one. By now, the docks were out of the question; burning people jumping into the sea and drowning, not the sort of thing you want to have going on around you during your final moments. But if he could get back along the Drovers' Bridge, possibly even find a horse, once he was safely over the river he could go anywhere, west, east or south by land, north if he could hitch a ride on a ship—

(No money; damn. If I see any it'd be worth picking it up, for food and clothes and fares).

—Anywhere but here, in fact. Maybe he wouldn't exactly be popular, but nobody would bother to chase him, surely. And he'd still be free, able to do what the hell he liked. It was an intriguing prospect, almost worth staying alive for.

Assuming, of course, that he could make it as far as the bridge and then across the river somehow. Instinct suggested that he should hurry, and he rationalised the urge by arguing that Temrai's next logical move would be to pull out his remaining men, take up the drawbridge and let the people left inside the city fry. In which case, it'd make sense to get to the bridge before closing time.

It'd be quicker by the backstreets, but that might prove to be a false economy. The fire would make the high-walled alleyways impassable, so he'd do best to stick to the wide streets. The best way, in fact, would be along the ropewalks, which were the nearest thing the city had to natural firebreaks. True, the warehouses on either side would be full of inflammable material, under ordinary circumstances. But ever since the now-discredited Colonel Loredan had bought up all the rope, the stock level in the warehouses had been well below normal. Loredan thought for a moment of the merchant Venart and his rope; now there was a man who had no cares and no worries beyond the trivial aggravations of the commercial life. It would be nice to be someone like that.

To reach the ropewalks from here without using the back lanes meant following this highway down as far as the potters' district, doubling back up the hill along the bowyers' avenue as far as the pipemakers' quarter, then taking the downhill fork through the sack-weavers' district. Nice wide roads all the way, but quite a lot of distance to cover. Running might be a good idea, except that a running man is never inconspicuous. He'd have to do it by walking fast.

It was all clear until he reached the pipemakers' arch. Then, as he came round a bend into the main square, he found he'd walked into some kind of last-minute battle; the pipemakers' company defending their homes and families to the last, that sort of thing. But he didn't have the *time*...

Walked into it, quite literally; as he rounded the corner he collided with a man clutching a pike backing away from another man wielding a poleaxe, albeit with more enthusiasm than science. Loredan tried to get out from under the warriors' feet; but the jolt had broken the pikeman's concentration, giving the poleaxe man his chance. It wasn't neglected. The pikeman had been city. Embarrassing.

Loredan stepped back and drew his sword as the clansman cleared the spike of his poleaxe from the wound. The fool made the mistake of attacking; Loredan sidestepped to his right, fending the lunge away from his body to the left, hands reversed, left elbow high; that put him in perfect position for a counterthrust the clansman had neither time nor space to parry. He went down like a coat dropped on the floor; but before Loredan could make himself scarce, another one appeared out of the shadows and came at him with a big Zweyhender sword. Crass mistake; the sword, which was loot, plainly wasn't the man's usual weapon, because he was swinging it like a woodcutter's axe instead of fencing with it, the way the maker had intended. He was completely open as Loredan stepped in under his raised arms and punched the blade of the Guelan through his ribcage. A quick and crafty twist freed the blade before the body hit the ground, which was just as well since it allowed him to bring the sword up in more or less the same movement to block an axe-cut from his left while shuffling right to get out of the way of a lance-thrust from directly in front. From that position it was no real trouble to work himself over to the right-hand side of the axe-wielder, using him to block the man with the lance. Then it was just a matter of disabling the axeman with a jerk of the knee, lunge behind him into the lancer, twist to disengage and bring the sword back across and sharply down to finish off the axeman with a cut across the back of his neck. *Easy as shelling peas,* Loredan thought with a slight surge of disgust. *But then, poor devils, they never had the advantages I've had.*

Not five yards away, a clansman was holding a city man by the arms while another two clansmen stuck pikes in him. Against his better judgement, Loredan came smartly up behind them and sorted out the two pikemen with successive cuts. The remaining clansman tried to use the dying Perimadeian as a shield, but he was a head taller than his victim, at least to begin with. When he'd finished, Loredan stooped down to look at the city man but he was past help; so that had been a waste of time.

Nobody else got in his way between the arch and the colonnade that connected the pipemakers' district with the ropewalks. The colonnade itself was a problem; the thatched roof was starting to burn, and Loredan just made it through before it collapsed. But that was all right; he was in the wide open spaces now, with no threat from the fire and room to run instead of having to fight. The ropemakers had rigged up a futile but ingenious barrier of cables, which he had to cut through. Some enthusiast in an upper window loosed a crossbow off at him while he was doing it, not doubt assuming he was the enemy. He missed. Someone else yelled, *hold, he's one of us*, and Loredan kept going. Dangerous as well as pointless to rectify the man's mistake, which was in any event a perfectly natural one. *How was he to know I'm no longer one of us, just one of me?*

As far as adventures in the ropewalk went, that was about all. The fun started again when he left the wide street and went under the perfumiers' arch into the square beyond. The perfume quarter wasn't a healthy place to be, what with all the distilled spirits and aromatic oils that were kept there, and Loredan arrived in it at more or less the same time as the fire. On all four sides of the square buildings were going up in fireballs and the air hummed with flying shrapnel from exploding storage jars. He managed to get out of there with no more than a few scratches and a small shard of jar embedded in his left thigh, but as he ducked under the remains of the arch he found he'd walked straight into a platoon of plainsmen indulging in a little last-minute looting in the pearl-drillers' courtyard.

I really don't have time for this, he mused, swinging hard from the left and feeling the blade carve a deep slice into someone's shoulder. The worst part was that even while he was fighting, part of his mind was on the time and the way ahead. He tried not to allow himself to get distracted, but it wasn't easy. One man nearly got past his guard while he was daydreaming; he had to take the thrust on the chainmail of his left shoulder, and his riposte was clumsy, though entirely efficient. Nevertheless, in spite of his haste he took ninety seconds or so out to retrieve a dead clansman's substantial collection of strung pearls. That ought at least to resolve the money problem, though it left his pockets uncomfortably stuffed.

Getting closer now, and that was a mixed blessing; not so much fire here but plenty more clansmen. Fortunately, these weren't aimless looting parties; most of them were too busy trying to sort out the horrendous traffic jam of wagons full of wounded or evacuated soldiers. He looked for Gorgas in the queue but couldn't see him. Grabbing a wagon for himself was out of the question with so many enemy soldiers around, while strolling along up the side of the jam wouldn't be too smart, either.

All right, then, we'll go *under* the wretched things. It meant crawling on his hands and knees, but time was no longer a problem. The gate wouldn't be shut until all the wagons were safely through. He could keep on wriggling until he was actually on the bridge itself; then all he'd have to do was slip out from under, drop unobtrusively into the river and swim to the shore.

I suppose sappers and people who work in mines must get used to this. Wouldn't suit me. More than the confined space and the pain in his elbows and knees, it was the general feeling of helplessness that troubled him. If anybody did happen to see him, he'd have no chance; they could flush him out like a rabbit into a purse-net, or come within five yards and shoot him, and he wouldn't be able to do a thing about it. After so many years in the racket, hand-to-hand fighting no longer frightened him particularly. He understood it, and though he was always one mistake away from death, at least he knew what he was doing and could estimate the odds. And besides, he was good at it, better than all but a few. Being in a position where he was surrounded by enemies but wouldn't be able to fight them was a new experience and a very unsavoury one. *Still, can't be much further now. Another two hundred yards, and we'll be . . .*

He stopped wriggling and held perfectly still.

The light wasn't marvellous, but the glow of torches and the fire in the background produced enough illumination to let him see a substantial contingent of the enemy straight ahead, working their way slowly down the line of wagons. From what he could see of what they were doing, he guessed that they were looking for someone or something – loot hidden under the box, a stowaway curled up in the back. They were even kneeling down and giving the undersides a cursory glance.

Bad news.

Praying that his hunch was right, Temrai paced along the line of wagons while his men continued with the search. He knew he was holding everything up, that the gate was still open when it should have been shut well over an hour ago; but it was his war, for which he would have to take the ultimate responsibility, so he was going to indulge himself by finding Colonel Bardas Loredan. Until he'd done that, nothing was decided.

He saw something curled up and wrapped in sacking in the back of a wagon and immediately stuck it with his sword. As it slit the coarse fibre, the blade clashed on silver, and a fine gilded chalice dropped out of the cut. More looting, in defiance of strict orders; but he couldn't be bothered about it now. He cut away the rest of the sack and swept the silver trash out onto the muddy ground, then called forward a detachment of his guards and ordered them to stamp the loot into the mud until there was nothing left visible.

Supposing he's dead already? Supposing he died and I wasn't there? Supposing he died early, when there was still a chance that the city might be saved, and he never got to see the fire, the women and children wearing fire in their hair? It'd be like organising the best surprise birthday banquet ever, and the guest of honour not showing up. Oh, gods, if anything's happened to him I'll never forgive myself...

Someone was talking to him, behind his left shoulder; Ceuscai's voice, reporting that his men had forced the gates of the upper city, that the whole of Perimadeia was theirs. The gold, he was saying, the silk and purple carpets, the onyx and sandalwood and silverware and tapestries, the amber and pearls and lapis lazuli and finely carved ivory, reliefs as delicate as fern fronds, the cushions and robes and curtains, the books – oh, gods, the books, how could there be so many words in all the world? – the porcelain and enamel and cloisonné and lacquerware, the flutes, lutes, guitars, trumpets, cymbals, bells, harps, lyres and tympana, the inlaid and damascened weapons, bows, bow-cases, quivers, armour, shields, caparisons and harnesses, the sandals, boots and slippers, the inkwells and writing tables and jewelled styluses, the water clocks and sundials, the plates, cups, jugs, platters, servers, finger-bowls, tureens, knives and napkin rings ...

'Burn it,' Temrai interrupted him. 'And no looting. Understood? I want *everything* burnt.'

For once, Ceuscai knew better than to argue. 'I've put in twelve wagon-loads of barrels,' he said, 'and the fuses are laid. When are we closing the gate?'

'When I've finished,' Temrai replied. 'Now get the fuses lit and pull your men out. I want everyone ready to go as soon as I've done here.' He turned and faced his old friend, his eyes full of fear. 'You haven't heard anything of Colonel Loredan, have you? Nobody's reported him killed, or taken?'

Ceuscai shook his head. 'I've had all the sergeants questioned,' he replied. 'Nobody's seen or heard anything. Is that why we're ...?'

'Are you still here?'

Ceuscai dipped his shoulders and walked away. A detachment of men came up, returning from fire-raising duty. Temrai called them over and set them to work searching the wagons. 'And look out for plunder,' he added. 'If you find any, I want the men's names. We're taking nothing out of here with us; I want that clearly understood.'

The men didn't look at all happy, but none of them said a word. The search continued, and the longer it went on, the tighter the knot grew in Temrai's stomach. Somehow he'd assumed it would be absolutely straightforward; that virtually the first thing he'd see when he entered the city would be Colonel Bardas Loredan, probably standing in the middle of the Grand Avenue with his sword in both hands, challenging him to single combat.

Maybe he's escaped ...

Temrai closed his eyes. If Loredan had escaped, then how in the gods' names would he ever justify all this, all these thousands of burnt people and all this meaningless, horrible destruction? It'd be enough to drive a man mad; to burn down a whole city and destroy an entire nation just to kill one single individual, and for that one individual to *escape* … He drove the thought out of his mind, repulsing the assault it had made on the citadel of his sanity. The gods who had given him Perimadeia wouldn't do that to him.

He bent down and peered under a wagon, and saw a pair of eyes fixed on his. It was a boy, eleven or twelve years old, his overgrown arms and legs folded awkwardly under the chassis, his face full of the sort of terror Temrai knew so much about. In his eyes, Temrai thought he could see an afterimage of fire and running, things he'd seen himself so long ago, as if he was staring into his own unpleasant memories. *Did you see your mother burn?* he wondered. *Your brothers and sisters wearing fire until all the flesh and skin was gone and there were only black bones, like the ruins of a city?* He felt pity clawing inside him, like a cat scrambling up a curtain, like the old white cat his mother had loved so much scrambling up the inside of their tent when it caught fire, and the cat had moved faster than the fire until he had nowhere left to go. He thought of a boy carrying that much fire inside him for the rest of his life, never being able to close his eyes without it being there. He thought about that, and took pity, and nocked an arrow onto his bowstring. *I've become a very cruel man*, he thought, *but not that cruel. I'll spare him that, at least.*

He bent the bow and looked across the belly, taking aim. He felt the string biting the joints of his fingers; then there was someone calling his name, *Temrai, look out!* and a terrible pain as something hit him across the back and side of the head. The arrow fell off the bow and he slumped forward, hitting the ground in a heap. It had been Ceuscai's voice; he looked up and saw Ceuscai, and between Ceuscai and himself the back of a man, familiar—

Colonel Bardas Loredan.

—Who was swinging a sword in both hands while Ceuscai was moving the shaft of his pike to parry the blow. Temrai could see Ceuscai had got it wrong, but there wasn't time; Loredan's sword hit him under the jaw on his right side and sliced, with a thick fleshy noise, the sound of butchers quartering carcasses or deer being dressed after the hunt, until it came out the other side; and Ceuscai's head toppled off his shoulders and hung by a strip of unsevered skin over his left shoulder; and then he wobbled and fell over, and Loredan had turned to stand over him.

—*Like a dream he sometimes had, in which the man he now knew to be Colonel Bardas Loredan had seen the boy cowering under the wagon, dismounted and walked over, stood over him, bent down and reached out a long arm, an arm that seemed to stretch for ever, following him wherever he scuttled and scrambled to, grabbing his arm or his wrist, pulling until he could feel the ball of the bone pull out of the socket and the arm come off, and when that happened the hand would grab his other arm or his leg or his neck, until he'd been pulled to pieces, the way children tear the petals slowly from a flower, and there was nothing left of him but whatever it was that was dreaming the dream; and then the hand grabbed that and he woke up ...*

Didn't they say that if you could break into a dream and catch the moment in your hand, you could twist it round the other way, make things happen differently? Was that what he'd done—?

'Get up,' Loredan said. Temrai tried to back away, get under the wagon; he could see men behind Loredan's shoulder, hurrying to rescue him, but just like in the dream they were too far away, there wasn't time. Loredan's hand was in his hair now, as terrifying as fire; Loredan pulled and suddenly he was on his feet, yanked round, one arm twisted agonisingly behind his back so he couldn't move for fear of it being torn out. He felt something cold and sharp under his chin.

'Get back or I'll cut his throat,' Loredan was shouting. 'Right, you, for once in your life do something useful and tell them to go away.'

Temrai tried to obey, but all he could do was squeak. He had never felt so terrified. It was the worst moment of his life.

'You,' Loredan was shouting, 'under the wagon, get out of there, you're coming with me. Anybody lays a finger on him and I'll kill the chief.'

Temrai saw movement out of the corner of his eye; the boy he'd been aiming at, wanting to spare him the pain, was scrambling out of the mud and standing up, scared out of his wits, not knowing what to do.

'Over here,' Loredan's voice boomed. 'Get the knife out of my belt and prod this bastard under the armpit – gently, for god's sakes, it's insurance, so if they try and pick me off their boss'll still die.' Gods, how calm he sounded, how terribly good he was at all this; how stupid, Temrai realised, even to try and measure himself against this man, who was clearly Death itself. All these years he'd been daydreaming of a grand battle, sword against sword like a Perimadeian lawsuit, with Justice guiding his thrust at the last and confirming the righteousness of his cause. How stupid—

'Easy,' Loredan breathed in his ear, 'do as you're told and everything's going to be fine. Now, we're going to take a walk, just as far as the bridge. You got that? Now move.'

A little twist on his arm, enough to have made him scream if he'd still had a voice; then Loredan's knee against his, nudging him forward, completely under the other man's control. He knew that Loredan could snap him in two like a twig, or slice off his head, or rip off his limbs one by one, and there'd be nothing he could do. He wanted so much not to die; or at least not this way, not killed by Colonel Bardas Loredan, as if death at his hands would be so much worse, more painful, more final than any other kind. Loredan could destroy him, break off his head, drink his blood and eat his soul; he was Death and the devil and all the horror in the universe, all the horror that he, Temrai the Sacker of Cities, Temrai the Slaughterer, had brought into the world—

'That's it,' Loredan's voice, intimate inside his ear, 'we're doing fine. Don't you just love it when stories have a happy ending?'

It seemed as if the whole clan was there, watching, backing away as they passed; because in spite of everything, the engines and the fire and the several million arrows he'd had made and caused to be loosed, there was no power on earth, let alone one puny nation, that could stand up against the horror of Colonel Loredan, the eater of souls, the bringer of Death and Justice, this terrible force his blind folly had let loose upon the world. As for what would happen when the monster had finished playing with him, he couldn't begin to imagine; the extremity of pain, or everlasting torment—

'Keep back,' Loredan snapped. 'Further off, you know better than that. Keep that knife steady, son, if you scrag him we're both dead. Right, you, we're going to turn around. When I say turn—'

It was an awkward, ludicrous, crab-scuttling-sideways manoeuvre, like a little child being taught to dance; and then Temrai was facing the clan, the line of wagons and a splendid view of the whole of the city, burning. *He's making me look at what I've done before he kills me*, Temrai said to himself, *because he's Justice and everything's my fault.* There was blood running down Temrai's face from the cut across his scalp; it was dripping into the corner of one eye, making him blink. They were under the arch of the gatehouse now, walking backwards onto the drawbridge. He could see the glow of fire reflected on the water; they were stepping awkwardly over dead bodies.

'This is as far as we go, Temrai,' Loredan whispered. 'Thanks for your help. You know, you remind me a bit of me when I was your age. You—' He was speaking to the boy, the one who'd been under the wagon. 'Can you swim?'

The boy said that he thought he could.

'That's good. Now put my knife back and jump.'

'Yes, sir.'

'Don't just stand there—' Temrai heard the splash; then

there was another horrible pain in his arm, and Loredan was whispering again, so close that the voice was inside his head. 'I ought to kill you, but I never could see any point in revenge. You might care to think about that.' Then a great force in the small of his back sent him sprawling on the planks of the drawbridge, and from the water below a great splash.

Then there were people round him, helping him up, shouting, holding up torches and lanterns, loosing off arrows into the water. Temrai shook himself free and stared at the water, but there was no sign of anything there; a few bodies floating, but not his. *He's swimming underwater,* Temrai thought; *or the weight of his armour's pulled him down and drowned him. No, don't be stupid, he can't die. He's vanished, or grown wings and flown away. He's gone, and I'm still alive—*

'Forget it,' he said. 'Leave it. Get everyone out of the city, close the gate and break up the causeway. I want this finished with now.'

His lungs were bursting and all his joints were full of pain. The mailshirt was a man grabbing hold of him and pulling him down; there was no escape this time, he was going to die – ironic, really, that he should die now, after the great escape—

'Wake up,' said a voice overhead. 'It's all right, it's just a dream.'

He opened his eyes, and saw the face of the boy, the kid he'd rescued from under the wagon. 'Wassis?' he mumbled through a mouthful of sleep. Behind the boy's head was blue sky, a few seagulls circling.

'It's all right,' the boy laughed, 'you're safe. You're on a ship, remember?'

Loredan sat up and winced; he'd forgotten about all the wrenched muscles. 'Sorry,' he said, 'I must have been having a nightmare or something.'

The boy grinned.'Look,' he said, pointing at the horizon, 'we've arrived.'

On the skyline, Loredan could see the outline of a city; a high wall, towers and domes, sunlight flashing off the gilded roof of a great temple. It was a place he'd heard of, one of those once-upon-a-time places that are reputed to exist, but he'd never thought he'd ever go there. And now, here he was.

It was smaller than he'd imagined.

'How are you feeling?' the boy asked. 'I think the fever's well and truly broken by now, but the captain says he knows a good doctor, just in case. He's been really nice, hasn't he?'

Loredan nodded grimly. 'Yes,' he replied, 'he has.' He saw that his tone of voice was worrying the boy, and he smiled reassuringly. 'Don't worry,' he said, 'we'll be all right. I've got relatives here who'll look after us.'

He stood up, stretching his cramped legs, and studied the city in the distance. That big shiny thing with the gold roof and the bobble on top was presumably the Great Temple. Even he'd heard of the Great Temple. It was the one building in this city that everyone knew about.

Then he turned round and looked at the mainsail of the ship, with the distinctive symbol painted in the middle. It was familiar enough, though strange in this context, the logo of the company whose ship this was; a bow fully bent, and seven arrows.

'This is wonderful,' the boy said, shading his eyes with his hand as he gazed at the distant city. 'I've always wanted to go to Scona.'

THE BELLY OF THE BOW

The Fencer Trilogy Volume Two

K. J. Parker

After the brutal and unexpected destruction of the famed Triple City of Perimadeia, the man who led the defending forces, Bardas Loredan, finds himself on the lonely island of Scona where he quietly establishes himself as a craftsman, fashioning bows.

But Scona is also home to Bardas' brother and sister, who run a successful business on the island. Unfortunately, the Loredan siblings do not share happy childhood memories. They also take cut-throat competition literally.

Before long, Bardas is thrown once more into a world of ruthless scheming and bloody rivalries. And what he has learnt about the nature of bows is about to change his life – and the life of his family – for ever.

Rich in magic, intrigue and imagination, the extraordinary story of *The Belly of the Bow* continues one of the most exciting new fantasy series of recent years.

Praise for *Colours in the Steel*:

'One of the most entertaining fantasy debuts of recent years … refreshing, thoughtful, different, absorbing'
SFX

THE PROOF HOUSE

The Fencer Trilogy Volume Three

K. J. Parker

'From the first page, it has a style, humour and
pace all its own'
SFX

The Proof House is the final volume in K. J. Parker's
brilliant Fencer Trilogy.

After years spent in the saps under the defences of the
apparently impregnable city of Ap' Escatoy, Bardas
Loredan, sometime fencer-at-law and the betrayed
defender of the famed Triple City, is suddenly a hero of
the Empire. His reward is a boring administrative job in
a backwater, watching armour tested to destruction in
the Proof House.

But the fall of Ap' Escatoy has opened up unexpected
possibilities for the expansion of the Empire into the land
of the plainspeople, and Bardas Loredan is the one man
Temrai the Great, King of the plains tribes, fears
the most …

Orbit titles available by post:

☐	The Belly of the Bow	K. J. Parker	£6.99
☐	The Proof House	K. J. Parker	£6.99

The prices shown above are correct at time of going to press. However, the publishers reserve the right to increase prices on covers from those previously advertised without prior notice.

orbit

ORBIT BOOKS
Cash Sales Department, P.O. Box 11, Falmouth, Cornwall, TR10 9EN
Tel: +44 (0) 1326 569777, Fax: +44 (0) 1326 569555
Email: books@barni.avel.co.uk.

POST AND PACKING:
Payments can be made as follows: cheque, postal order (payable to Orbit Books)
or by credit cards. Do not send cash or currency.

U.K. Orders under £10	£1.50
U.K. Orders over £10	**FREE OF CHARGE**
E.E.C. & Overseas	25% of order value

Name (Block Letters) _____

Address_____

_____

Post/zip code:_____

☐ Please keep me in touch with future Orbit publications

☐ I enclose my remittance £_____

☐ I wish to pay by Visa/Access/Mastercard/Eurocard

Card Expiry Date

_____